ERACISM

GARY JAMES

PublishAmerica
Baltimore

ISBN: 1-4241-6109-6
PUBLISHED BY PUBLISHAMERICA, LLLP
www.publishamerica.com
Baltimore

Printed in the United States of America

This book is dedicated to my beloved parents, Cecelia DaCosta-James and Leander Alphonzo James, affectionately known as Ceil and Tiny, my family, and children.

The photograph of my children was taken in my Harlem office in 1989, and it shows, from left to right: (girls) Ysis, Nia, Ebuni, (boys) Gary, Micah, and Faro.

CHAPTER 1

I told Van that I would get back with him out after the funeral, but I was feeling drained, tired and weak. I thought I would just chill-out and catch up with him another day although I needed the therapy, that dialogue and fellowship of one of my first friends. Van and I lived in the same apartment building in the South Bronx one of the roughest neighborhoods at that time, many, many years ago. 826 East 167th Street was the "hood" as they say these days, but back in the day we affectionately referred to it as the "block." The block was in our blood and was our planetary Sun that everything revolved around. The block was a "play street" run by the Police Athletic League (PAL) during the summer months. Because of the high level of organized activity as a "play street," the block became a focal point for people in the neighboring vicinity. However, within itself the block contained scores of people from all generations.

My father and Van's father lived at 826 East 167 Street as teenagers and by the time Van and I were born, our fathers were the primary partners of a Pigeon Coop located on the roof of our building. My grandparents and Van's grandparents immigrated to the United States from St. Croix in the Virgin Islands, when our fathers were teenagers and moved to the block. Van and I were 2nd generation residents of the block and that longevity inspired a sense of comfort and ownership of the turf. The sense of turf extended a couple of miles beyond the block to the north, south, east and west. My father had four younger sisters and they lived next door to our apartment with my grand parents. My mother was the sixth child and had ten siblings that lived to the north of us near Cratona Park. (Memories of my childhood days are beautiful, resourceful and strengthening, particularly at difficult times such as these).

In spite of the poverty that is associated with the South Bronx, youth of my generation for the most part had great aspirations of being responsible citizens and they demonstrated self respect and respect for their elders. Unfortunately, poor education, lack of employment opportunities, the emerging drug culture and social-political complexities undermined the aspirations and best intentions of my generation, is the same phenomenon as today. Now, in the first decade of the twenty-first century, the trajectory of the popular culture, lack of quality education and employment opportunities and a plethora of political, economic and social pathologies portend a dubious future for the majority of black folk irrespective of neighborhood.

In reflection, my experience during the ages of single digits was sheltered, innocent, healthy and without complexity, apart from the fear and sometimes horror of parental authority. And parental authority could be exercised on my "butt" by several other adults outside of my parents, grandparents and family relations. I was one of the fortunate children on the block because my parents lived and stayed at home, they were not physically abusive or chemically dependent on drugs or alcohol. I can only recall getting a beating from my father once during my entire childhood. I was in 5th grade and was doing poor in my school conduct, which was reflected on my report card. My mother warned me that if I didn't improve by the next marking period she would tell my father. On the next marking period in the category of class conduct, I was given the grade "NR" which meant, "not responding," and sure enough my mother told my father. The occasion of confrontation was memorable and I promised myself that I would not knowingly ever expose myself to such pain and helplessness and fear again.

By anybody's standards my father was a big man, standing 6 foot, 5 inches, and weighing 240 pounds. Following the first corporal punishment encounter with my father, he was able to exercise and maintain a decisive psychological impact on me that could be communicated very successfully with his eyes. And on other more serious occasions he would communicate to me with his eyes and an intense round shape of his lips. It was my mother who exercised corporal punishment on me and my siblings and used my father as the ultimate threat or weapon as the case may be. My mother would give us a spanking whenever or wherever she thought it befitting. You either got spanked with her slipper on you outstretched hands, which you had to extend on command (right and left). She would say, "Give me your hand. now give me the other one." The other spanking option was with a belt on the bear butt while bent over her knee or as we ran through the house when we got too big for over the knee technique.

Unlike me, Van would get beatings from his father seemingly at will and just because. My family lived on the 3rd floor and Van's family lived on the 4th floor and I could hear when Van got a severe whipping from his father. Van's mother wasn't the disciplinarian that my mother was, but his dad Elroy was more than enough. Van had five siblings, one older brother and four younger sisters. Oddly enough it seemed to me that Van was the only child that was getting regular spanking by Mr. Walters. Van and his sisters would come to my house and play with my younger brother, two sisters and me. As we were not permitted to play in the street during our years of single digits, we played in either apartment, the hallway or on roof where our fathers flew birds.

My father worked for the city of New York, first for the Transit Authority and then for the Department of Sanitation. He tested well on the examination for the Police Department academically and physically, but decided not to go on the force when he was called. My mother had a serious problem with the fact that he decided not to be a police officer, but the decision was his and he made it. I didn't have a preference either way, but my father told me much later that he decided against the police department because he had issues with the police culture in relation to the black community. My mother was essentially a housewife for most of my childhood. But, when I became a teenager my mother began working in Midtown Manhattan starting as a file clerk and ending up as manager of the department. However, when plans got underway for buying a house my mothers entrepreneurial skills blossomed. She became quite a sales representative for Wonderware and then Tupperware, earning a substantial amount of money. My father bought a car, which was largely financed by her earnings, in order to facilitate her growing marketing and distribution volume.

Most of our play time was under serious supervision because my grandparents lived next door to us and four of my aunts on my father's side were our direct supervisors and teachers during this formative period. Van's grandparents lived in the basement apartment and were the superintendents of the building. Despite not being able to play in the street with our peers, we were happy and content to explore the building from the top to bottom literally and the various apartments in between. My favorite game was playing house with Van's sisters, which gave me the opportunity to explore my sexual curiosities with my equally curious playmates. We played house, mother and father, children and had memorable encounters in the closet and under the bed. Warm and fuzzy nostalgic feelings emerge when reflecting on this period of youthful innocence, simplicity of life, and the integrity and responsibility of authority. Thankfully these memories and reflections give me balance and focus in this increasingly complex society and world.

I needed balance, centering and perspective in the wake of the death of the young man, Bryon Lee in my house in Queens. Questions and speculation

7

abounded as I struggled to get a handle on what was occurring in my immediate environment. I didn't have the energy to drive to the Bronx for a therapeutic fellowship and commune with my first friend. Van and I knew first hand about the devastation that heroin and cocaine wrought on our peers and older cats during the years that we were growing up in the South Bronx, in the 1950s. Now many years latter the drug addition epidemic has proliferated to all areas of New York City's black communities. It was now impossible to escape the drug scourge because it has infected the suburbs and urban areas of Southeast Queens, in epidemic proportions. It was difficult for me to contain my emotions when trying to console the young mans father who was completely distraught and in severe physical and emotional pain. I knew that I never wanted to experience similar grief, pain, anguish, loss and bewilderment in my lifetime. I prayed for myself and my future children and I prayed for the grief stricken father at the loss of his only child. And the dubious circumstances and mystery that led up to his dying from an overdose of heroin on his nineteenth birthday only three days after arriving home from college on summer break made a difficult matter seem even worse.

I had no framework or model by which to provide a context for understanding this tragic event that occurred in my home. In addition to the downward spiral of the respective black communities that comprise New York City, due to the drug culture and popular culture there was no light perceivable at the end of the tunnel anywhere in the country. This untimely death happening in so-called "middle-class" black communities of Springfield Gardens, St. Albans, Hollis and Cambria Heights, was a wake up call on a couple of levels. It was a wake up call for me in terms of exposing what was going on in my house as well as in the larger community of Southeast Queens.

My parents bought a house and moved us from our four story walk up four room tenement apartment in the "ghetto" of the South Bronx, to a beautiful house in Springfield Gardens Queens, about eight or nine years prior to the death of Bryon Lee. I was about 19 years old when the move went down, but it was planned for a couple of years earlier. A great discussion preceded the plans to move to the suburbs and purchase a house as opposed to moving into the newly developed and developing housing popularly referred to as the "projects." The Forest Houses were under construction around the corner on 166th Street and Union Avenue, the Bronx River projects on 170th Street to the east and Eden Wald projects to the north were popular options. Since I was the first-born and perhaps because of my age as well, I was privy to the discussions between my parents about the planned move. Both parents preferred home ownership to the housing project environment although it ultimately meant the sacrifice of material stuff and other possessions because of the financial demands of home ownership.

The main reason that my parents decided to move was the deterioration of the neighborhood. Heroin swept through the South Bronx like a plague of Locus and decimated the budding crop of young black men two to fours years my senior. There were also a few in my generation that were beginning to experiment with heroin and the informal underground economy. The phenomenon of Heroin addiction caught me and my generation by surprise. It seemed like all of a sudden I woke up one day and the dudes that I looked up to began to look dirty and unkempt. It was shocking to see my idols in such filth and squalor when their reputation among my contemporaries was based on how well they dressed and represented themselves in public and with the young ladies. But the transition could not go unnoticed as scores of junkies began roaming the streets, and families were being ravaged by drug addicted children and relatives. Crime rates increased dramatically and virtually no apartment was immune from the burglar or sneak thief as the children of old friends and neighbors became heroin addicts and therefore suspects.

I was a senior in Morris High School and my parents were concerned that I should be exposed to the larger society and a broader range of people during this period in my life. My parents were not particularly concerned about me experimenting with heroin as they were confident that I had a sense of myself and what the drug culture was about. My mother would always admonish me as a child not to follow the crowd. She would always say, "Whenever you see the crowd go one way, you are sure to go the other way, my son. Never follow the crowd."

I was taught to listen to the voice within me and to undertake creative endeavor, as, "There is nothing in the street," as my father would say to me. The larger concern of my parents was for my younger siblings. My parents wanted to provide a life for us that offered options beyond the grim horizon that was the fate of neighborhoods like the South Bronx in the late 1950s. My brother Lewis was four years my junior and my two sisters Judy and Cheryl were eight and ten years younger than me. My father had theories on the future of the South Bronx and other poor "colored" neighborhoods in the city. My father's theory about the housing projects was that they were management and containment facilities for poor black folk. And heroin and other addictive drugs are the tools at the neighborhood level to facilitate the continued subjugation and containment of the black masses as perpetual consumers. Therefore, under no circumstances was my father willing to move to the housing projects.

The subject of moving from the neighborhood was a topic of great discussion among many parents on the block and the surrounding neighborhood. Those families that had a capacity to move to higher ground planned their exit strategy and most were able to work their plan to a level of success. Van's parents were also among the working class. Vans father Elroy worked for the Post Office and his mother Doris was employed in a local hospital. Van's family was planning to buy a house also, but they were looking in the North Bronx area. On the other hand the majority of my friend's parents were not planning to purchase houses, most settled on the "housing projects" while the others stayed on the block until its demise. Ultimately there was a major population decline due to drugs and flight causing the block to bottom out into virtual abandonment. Finally the four-story tenement apartment buildings were demolished and replaced with two story, low quality, and low-income apartments. The demographic of the neighborhood changed from predominantly black to Hispanic leaving the remnant of the block's residents to scatter, to various surrounding Bronx neighborhoods. In the process of transition, many of my peers and in some instances whole families were eviscerated or rendered mummified by the ravages of drug addiction and the malignancies associated with inner city culture.

The contrast between the Southeast Bronx and Southeast Queens was as extreme as night and day. Apart from the neighborhood, environment and quality of life differences from the block, the relationship with my parents particularly my father changed one hundred and eighty degrees. My father and I became best friends. Virtually every morning about 2 A.M., he would come home from work and his first stop was upstairs to my room. He would knock then enter my room and say, "Hey, Champ, so what happening? What are you going to do?" He'd have a huge smile on his face as he was referring to an ongoing conversation we were having concerning my plans for the future. Our conversation centered on the fact that I was not interested in going directly to college, therefore he recommended that I take the various civil service tests. "Champ, you know that I don't want you to have to throw cans like I do, and I know you're not interested in a civil service gig, per se, but take all of the civil service tests, for crying out loud, because you never know when you may need something to fall back on in the future. Champ, I'm just trying to make the point to you that there is nothing out here for you and other colored fellows but civil service." I explained that I thought he was giving me sound advice, but if I had something to fall back on, I may tend to fall back. Whereas if I didn't have anything to fall back on, I know that I better not fall back and it will keep me motivated. This was the theme of an ongoing conversation we held that kept our spirits and relationship on a high level.

On one weekend at about 2:30 A.M. I was enjoying some hot and heavy sex in my bedroom with Carmen Rodriquez a girlfriend from the Bronx and the knock of my father hit my bedroom door.

"Hey, Champ!" we heard, and as my father stepped in the room Carmen ducked under the covers. My father was able to see Carmen's bulk under the covers. He looked at me, and then said in a loud voice, "Oops" and like a flash, stepped backwards out of my room. He waited for several minutes then he knocked on the door again then came back in sat down on the usual chair and said, "So, Champ, what you gonna' do?"

It was an unbelievable and a priceless moment, as my father proceeded as though nothing unusual had just occurred. Finally, Carmen stuck her head from underneath the covers and joined in the conversation.

When we finished talking he said, "Okay, it was nice meeting you Ms. Rodriquez," then left my room. Carmen said that she was afraid and embarrassed when he bust in, but as she listened to his voice and our conversation, she felt self-assured enough to emerge and join in the conversation. My father for his part never mentioned the incident in jest or other wise. I had no idea if he mentioned the episode to my mother. But he and Carmen became good friends and she simply adored my father saying that he was the nicest man that she ever met.

My new neighborhood and neighbors were very interesting and represented a new frontier in my development. When I lived in the Bronx, although I was seventeen plus years old, I had very strict rules of engagement in the street. During the summer, I had to be in the house by 9 P.M. unless I had special approval to stay until ten P.M. If I was not in the house by 9 P.M. my mother would look out the window and call me. It was difficult enough for me to deal with the jokes etc. from my friends regarding my Cinderella type curfew, so I made sure that I was in by 9:00 so that I would not be called from the window: "Vincent, Vincent, Vincent, it's time to come upstairs." The usual refrain from my friends in response to my mother's call: "Hey, Vinnie, your mother is calling you, man; you better get on upstairs." Teasing from my friends on that level could degenerate into fighting words as far as I was concerned. Therefore, I avoided that scenario at all cost.

Among the first things that shocked me when we moved to Queens was the fact that I no longer had a curfew. I could now stay out until 2 A.M. or 3 A.M., come in the house and get a smile the next morning from my parents. So I took full advantage of the no curfew rule and got to know all of my peers in the neighborhood. I hung out in their basements, backyards and got to know their families. The transition and experience was absolutely awesome, then the next thing that I knew, my father was giving me driving lessons. My parents always wanted me to be grown up, and at this point they were enthusiastically facilitating if not hastening my development into manhood.

Pineville Lane was the name of the street we lived on in Springfield Gardens, Queens New York. Commonly referred to by my peers as the "Ville" it embodied about thirty-five to forty detached one and two family homes. Pineville Lane was an arched shaped street that intersected Springfield and Merrick Blvd.' which are perpendicular to each other. The population of the Ville was integrated but, predominantly black American. The children and youth ran the generational gamut therefore my siblings had peers and playmates as well. There were several of my contemporaries on the Ville, both male and female and I soon became an integral component of the coed group. My whole family was very happy with and benefitting from the transition.

My mother had a full time job in a midtown Manhattan lingerie firm called Moon Dust. She began her employment as a clerk and worked her way up to the position of office Manager. In the position of office manager she was able to influence the hiring process and thereby was able to secure jobs for a number of family members, friends and relatives. I discussed with my mother from time to time particular incidents that occurred on my various jobs, and the kind of things I was experiencing when applying for jobs. Therefore my mother was acutely aware of the details associated with my numerous job situations. My mother always advised me on how to handle myself with pride and dignity, in spite of bigotry and racial discrimination that I would invariably encounter. She was very supportive of my seeking employment within the private sector. However, she admonished me to take my fathers advice, and to take the various civil service examinations regardless of my ultimate objective. She parroted what my father said. "You never know what is going to happen, and therefore you may at some point need to fall back on something." My mother also advised me that a position as helper in the printing department was available on her job and if I was interested in applying for the job, she would set up an appointment for an interview. I expressed my interest in the job and was subsequently interviewed and hired. The printing department was up until this point a one-man shop, and I was the second employee. Jack Tropper, my supervisor operated two printing presses and my primary role was operating the paper-cutting machine, loading paper into the press and removing the printed paper. My mother advised me to learn everything in the whole shop operation with particular emphasis on the operation of the printing presses. I developed a very good working relationship with Jack, which enabled me to learn all aspects of the print shop operation. I remained employed at Moon Dust for several months, much longer than any other previous job. But two incidents occurred that caused me to resign and seek other employment.

The first incident happened about three or four months into the job, when I had a confrontation with one of the owner's sons, Joel Sief. The printing shop operation included printing a 3 x 8 inch flyer with a style number of the particular garment at the bottom of the flyer and a photo of a modeled garment in the middle. The flyers were printed on a 9 x 12 sheet of paper which enabled the flyer to be printed at the rate of three flyers per sheet. I was then responsible to separate the 3 flyers on the cutting machine and trimming around the edges to finish the product. Apparently the style number of a particular product was inadvertently cut off the bottom of the flyer, due to poor registration during the printing process. The style flyer is used as an insert that is included in each individual package. The incident happened while I was in the process of operating the cutting machine and talking with my supervisor.

Joel Sief entered the shop slammed the door behind him and rushed into the shop area and looked directly at me and said, "Who is the asshole that did this?" He then displayed the defective flyer.

I replied immediately and directly to him eye to eye and said, "I require an apology from you because you cursed me, and your general approach to me is out of order, plus the style number problem is not due to my error, for your information."

Joel was inflamed by my "insubordination." The incident was ultimately blown out of proportion and it reverberated up and down the five floors of the midtown office building the company occupied. When I returned home that evening my mother confronted me and told me how proud she was of me because of how I handled Joel Sief.

My mother mentioned the incident to my father and he commented to me, "Champ, your mother told me that you handled yourself in such a way that made her proud of you. She described the whole thing to me. Keep up the good work, Champ; I'm proud of you too."

The second incident happened a couple of months later. The company was growing, business was booming and the printing department needed to expand. A new larger two color printing press was being purchased. There was now an obvious need to hire another pressman to operate the 1250 Multilith offset printing press. I was looking forward to the prospect of a promotion and salary raise, since I learned how to operate the 1250. However, I was not considered for the promotion. Instead a new employee was hired and I remained on the cutting machine with no opportunity for advancement. The new employee, Maurice Mcbride was a white young man about the same age as I and was quite a friendly and personable character. Although Maurice and I got along well, I decided that this was the appropriate time to move on, and my parents agreed with me. Since I now knew how to operate the 1250 Multilith printing press, my mother said that she would set-up an appropriate reference through the personnel department to confirm that I operated the 1250 printing press for the company. Therefore I could apply for a job as an experienced pressman, which would put me in a higher salary category. I gave the company two weeks notice to my supervisor then I hit the pavement.

My siblings and I were fortunate to escape the imminent tidal wave of drug addiction and the resultant crime and violence that engulfed the Bronx, Brooklyn and Harlem. But the notion of having escaped was, in fact, a grand illusion. It was inevitable that the heroin plague would reach Southeast Queens. The malignancy of the illegal drug culture and underground economy had already infected the social fabric of poor and middle-class black neighborhoods in Queens as I observed during my brief high school experience in Andrew Jackson. Hence, it was only a brief matter of time before the drug cancer became critical in Southeast Queens and other unsuspecting areas of the borough. It soon became obvious to me that my younger brother's generation were experimenting with drugs. I began to observe the same patterns in various neighborhoods of Southeast Queens as I saw in the Southeast Bronx.

I wanted to discuss my observations about these similar patterns in the Bronx and Queens with my father but I decided to postpone it because he had gotten sick. He had been home sick with a cold for about two weeks when it occurred to me to have this discussion with him. It was the only time that I could recall him staying home from work due to illness, so I figured that I would take advantage of this rare opportunity. When I got home my mother told me that he had gone to work. She told me that he said that he was tired of staying home and that he was just suffering from a flu type of cold. Approximately 1 A.M. that next morning my mother woke me up and asked me drive to Francis Lewis and Linden Blvd. to pick up my father because he was in pain and couldn't drive the car the remaining two miles home. When I arrived my father was outside of the car walking around the vehicle as a result of the pain in his lower back. He got in the rear seat of my car and stretched out, then told me that his back began to hurt while working on the sanitation truck. He said that when he left the sanitation garage in the Bronx and began to drive home, the pain got worse and by the time he reached Francis Lewis and Linden Blvd.' the pain became unbearable and he couldn't remain seated. He stopped and exited the car then asked a pedestrian to make the phone call home because the pain was so severe that he couldn't stand still to dial the phone. He thought that he might have strained his back while working. He didn't think that the pain was connected with the terrible cold that kept him in bed for the past two weeks. On the following day my father fainted while at home and we took him to the Veterans Hospital at Fort Hamilton in Brooklyn, for testing and evaluation.

Needless to say, I had to postpone the discussion with my father regarding the proliferation of drugs and its destabilizing and devastating impact on the black families and neighborhoods, in particular. His insight on the subject was very important to me because of the growing admiration for his perspective and technique for handling difficult and provocative situations. I had many observations that I wanted to discuss but had to put them on the back burner until he got out of the hospital. The proliferation of addictive drugs was the most pressing, the growing civil rights movement, race relations in the South and the North and many other subjects that were beginning to engage my curiosity. I was beginning to realize my own growth to maturity as I increasingly began to appreciate my father's experience, insight and world view. When I was fifteen I believed that my father was completely outdated, unsophisticated, and irrelevant to my modern day world. Now at the age twenty I was amazed at how much my father had learned in the last five years. How reluctant I was to recognize the fact that I was the one that was learning, and my father was already heavy and wise all of the time. Now I was forced to wait for his good health in order to get his dynamic and coherent perspective regarding this world that I was precariously growing in to.

The vicissitudes of my Bronx experience was a microcosm of the larger world that I was in the process of encountering. Queens as well, was beginning to experience the drug culture, albeit to a lesser degree. The case in areas of Brooklyn was as critical as the South Bronx and likewise in Manhattan's Harlem. The black communities throughout New York City were being ravaged and devastated by the drug culture and underground economy. Some areas were virtual leper colonies, with legions of ghost like zombies mulling around in circles occasionally darting in and out of vacant and abandoned tenement apartment buildings like roaches and mice in frenzied sexual heat. The blocks and neighborhoods to the east, west, north and south detailing the insidious malignancy was spreading to new generations. Harlem in particular seemed to be the hub of the abounding drug sub-culture. This was the venue of Malcolm X the gifted minister and disciple of the Honorable Elijah Mohammed, author of a comprehensive anti-drug program in the framework of the Nation of Islam. The Nation of Islam provided a positive impact that countered the surge of the drug culture and other complexities that perpetuate inner city hopelessness and the like.

A month or so passed before test results for my father's illness were available. My mother visited the hospital every day after work and all day Saturday and Sunday. I visited every other day and between visits I came to the hospital to pick up my mother and drive her home. Finally the test was completed and my mother and I discussed them with my father's doctors. His doctors told us that my father had an acute case of Leukemia and that he was not likely to live beyond six months. We were advised further not to discuss it with him or make him aware of the diagnosis and prognosis as the knowledge of such might cause him to lose the will to live. There was no particular treatment for the type of Leukemia that he had, therefore the current treatment was essentially experimental. At this point my mother was absolutely devastated and the whole encounter was a surreal experience. I held her and helped her walk to my car, following the session with the doctors. The ride home was almost like an eternity. After the deafening silence I said, "Mommy, if anybody could beat this thing, it would be Pop." She was silent, and then crying and sobbing shattered the silence. My throat was parched dry, and I felt a severe pain in the bottom on my stomach. I tried to comfort my mother with my hand on hers; I didn't know what to say or what to do. I knew that I couldn't cry in front of her under the circumstances. I had to show strength but it hurt too deeply.

When we reached home my mother went to her room, closed the door and I didn't see her until the next morning. The next morning she asked me to call her job to tell them that she wouldn't be in because of illness. The following visits to the hospital were very difficult, painful and superficial. My mother handled the situation as best she could and I tried to be as supportive of her as possible. My mother and I decided not to discuss it with my siblings for the time being, while selectively sharing the truth with family and friends. My father remained a stoic tower of strength, although he began to lose weight rapidly. I often wondered what was running through his mind, and how he could show such strength in the face of such rapid deterioration. My father lived about eight months following the diagnosis before his life was hidden in the glory of God. Two days before he died my mother told me that my father wanted to see me alone on the following day.

When I reached his room and entered it, I said, "Hi, Pop."

"Hey, Champ," he said. "I'm glad to see you."

As I approached his bed I could see that he was very weak, and he continued, "Look, Champ, I got Luke."

"No! No! No, Pop!" I said in a panic.

He reached and grabbed my hand, then said, "Listen, Champ, be cool; I got Luke." He looked me straight in the eye and said, "Champ, I want you to take care of your mother and the kids."

I was overwhelmed, crocodile tears rolled down both of my checks. I grabbed and hugged his frail torso and leaned my head on his shoulders trying to wipe the flood of tears, to no avail. I said "Pop—Pop, I love you."

"I love you too, Champ; be careful." I was dazed and left the hospital shortly thereafter. The following day, January 10, 1964 was my father's 34th birthday, there was a snow storm and I was shoveling snow to clear a path in the driveway, when a taxicab stopped in front of the house and my mother exited.

She looked at me with tearful eyes and said, "Daddy is dead." I embraced her and virtually carried her inside. She concluded, "It's all over; oh, God, what am I going to do?"

The silence in the house spoke volumes about the impact that my father had on all of us, although he uttered few words. He lived in the house not yet five years but every corner of the house from the floor to the ceiling displayed his silent joy and spirit was reflected. His creative genius and woodworking innovation transformed the so-called "trap," as he would sometimes affectionately refer to it, to represent the magazine pages of *Better Homes and Gardens*, while teaching us the practicality of a handyman initiative. He made my mothers work in the kitchen an absolute joy with his saw, by creating a knotty-pine masterpiece of walls, shelves, and cabinets that became a showcase of pride to neighbors and friends, while exhibiting his carpentry expertise. The inside and outside of the now "mini mansion" reflected his love, dedication and vision of what he wanted for his family. Before he got sick, my father talked about getting rid of his "old load" and buying a new car. Although I believed that it was just talk and he would never buy a new car for himself, the fact that he never did buy a new car or anything for his self hurt me very deeply. How could this have happened to such a good and righteous person, who worked so long and so hard for his family and others. Not to even have had the opportunity of being sick and convalescing for a while was a constant heart wrenching thought that resounded in my mind. He was just ripped-off from life and from the people he loved and who loved him dearly. How unfair for my siblings, who were now to be fatherless without rhyme or reason. My mother who was so self-confident, strong, focused and aggressive was now psychologically frail and aimless. My younger brother and sisters, who were not yet old enough to appreciate their father's depth, wisdom, and insight, needed him now more than ever. And I had nowhere to turn and no one to turn to. What was the fate that remained for us?

By this time my brother was a high school senior and was beginning to feel his oats and to do his own thing. At seventeen, my brother Lewis was almost as tall as my father, six foot and four inches, and had an off and on flirtation with the high school basketball team. Most of his friends were virtual giants, towering over me at a mere six feet even. Most of my brother's friends were good basketball players and played organized ball in high school and other venues. Several were in fact high school basketball stars and went on to college and professional basketball. Meanwhile, the cancerous malignancy of drugs was rapidly spreading among the youth of the Queens, black middle-class community, trapping off my brother and most of his friends. This pervasive drug culture phenomenon had a trajectory that was on a collision coarse with the hard working, heretofore, stable families and homeowners who were unaware of the imminent devastation about to engulf their children, property and neighborhood. Eventually the plague, unforeseen by most, took its toll on my brother's generation, and other subsequent generations in dramatic fashion and in unprecedented proportions. Perhaps seventy percent of my brother's generation fell victim to the illegal drug culture and underground economy, in one form or another. Many would pay with their lives, their potential basketball careers or forfeit the best years of their lives in dubious recovery from heroin addiction, and associated ills. The generations that followed my brothers were hit even harder. Now junior high and primary school students are major actors in the crime and violence and underground economy generated by the illegal drug culture. Hard working people, parents and the elderly are often hostages in their own homes, and are afraid to leave the house unguarded, and children can no longer play in the streets without being at high risk of crime and violence, with the proliferation of drive by shootings not just limited to the Forty project of South Jamaica. The Ville was now in the throes of this dynamic and devastating fast curve transition that was beginning to over take Hollis, South Jamaica, South Ozone, St. Albans, Springfield Gardens, Laurelton and Queens Village.

Van Walters, my old friend from the block was a stabilizing factor for me and I sought him out at every opportunity during the first several months following my father's funeral. When I would see Vans father and other friends of my fathers at events of family members and friends, the hurt and bewilderment on the faces of my dad's peers particularly Van's father could not go unnoticed by me. On one level it gave me great pride to see and feel the high esteem that seemed ubiquitous among men and women that knew my father or in some cases knew of him. But, on another more visceral and emotional level I was confounded by the sudden personal tragedy, and was having difficulty reconciling his death with God as I understood Him. Because of the effect my father's death had on my immediate family as well as my aunts and uncles and the responsibilities that fell to me, I had to contain and control my confusion. My immediate responsibility was for my mother who was absolutely devastated by the lost, and my siblings who had no understanding of what had occurred, could never appreciate what they had lost.

Fortunately, for the immediate future my "good job" was a blessing because it gave me the flexibility that I needed to attend the needs of my mother and siblings and the house. On the other hand my job gave me the mobility and exposure that generated personal conflicts in terms of my role and function as an employee of Continental Mutual Insurance Company. My job title was Legal Investigator/Claims Adjuster in the liability department of the maverick insurance company. The company was growing in leaps and bounds by writing liability insurance policy's in high-risk neighborhoods around the county. It just so happened that the high-risk neighborhoods around the county were predominantly black American communities. The motto of the company when it came to insurance losses and lawsuits was "no pay." The company was able to live up to its motto of "no pay" based on the sharp talents and skills of a highly motivated staff of investigator/claims adjusters that pioneered the advent of legal para-professionals. On the surface it was an impressive gig for a 22 year old, as it facilitated a brand new Ford Mustang, a daily expense account for automobile costs and lunch meetings. The gig was a hit with my contemporaries in Queens, but in the Bronx on the block the reaction was mixed. Preston Smith (Smitty), a partner in a pickup and delivery dry cleaning company on Farmers Blvd in Queens, said to me one afternoon while visiting his establishment. "Damn, my man, you got the best gig in the world. Your job is even a good job for a white dude, my brother. Man, you've got the ability to tell a cat or a kitten that you will meet them on 42nd Street in midtown at high noon on any day of the week and be able to keep the appointment. They pay your gas, car insurance, and give you lunch money. Man, you got a sure-enough, white-collar, white-boy gig." Smitty was a partner in a dry cleaning company with Kenneth Johnson and their cleaning service featured a pick-up and delivery service. Their company, Jiffy Dry Cleaning was very popular in St. Albans, Springfield Gardens and Jamaica, but both Smitty and Kenny complained about the long hours that were required to grow the business. Externally, I relished in their vocal admiration of my "unusual" gig but, no one was aware of the personal contradictions that I was having with the job.

From 9 A.M. to 5 P.M. I was suited up with a shirt and tie driving throughout the boroughs of New York City in my brand new 1964 Mustang investigating and/or settling liability insurance cases. The liability cases ran the gamut, from slip and fall scenarios, on the sidewalks, supermarkets, apartment buildings, car accidents, movie houses and entertainment facilities, private homes and recreations centers. Whatever was insurable the company underwriters wrote, and the company revolutionized the liability claims industry by the innovation of highly trained and motivated black American para-professionals to minimize insurance losses in the slum apartment buildings in Harlem, the Bronx and Brooklyn. From time to time I would inadvertently run into friends, family and associates from the block in the course of my workday.

On one particular occasion I parked the car to buy a pack of cigarettes when I heard: "Yo, cool Vinnie B., how are you doing, dude? Long time no see."

I turned in the direction of the voice and said, "GP, man, how the hell are you? And Eddie, my boy. Great to see you guys." I continued, saying, "I knew that I was bound to see some chips off of the old block. How is everybody doing these days?"

GP said, "Look, at you, Vinnie B. My home boy, if I didn't see you I wouldn't have known it was you. Looks like you're doing the right thing, my brother; talk to me."

Then Eddie started with his rap.

I responded, "Yea, okay, Eddie, be cool. Your head is so clean that I can see you thinking." I continued, saying, "We haven't seen each other in a little while, but I still know your moves when I hear them; even if I hear them from somebody else, I can identify your moves, man."

GP said, "Come on, you guys; cut out that your-move, my-move stuff, and let's rap, man. It's been three or four years since I've seen you, Vinnie, man; later for that 'move stuff' fella's; let's kick it. there is a whole lot of stuff going on, man. But yea, you're looking good, Brother B., in spite of what's going on."

Clearing his throat Eddie joined in, "Yea, B., there is a lot of stuff going on. Some dudes are getting strung out on dope, some strung out on revolution, and some guys are strung out on the pussy. but nobody is making money; ain't no gigs, man, no jobs at all. I mean, unless you want to work for the government, but if you got a record that's out. It looks like you got a good job, Vinnie."

GP followed up and said, "Yea, B., your gig must be real cool, man. But you always had some shit with you, B.; I remember when you wrote some reports for me that enabled me to graduate high school. Yea, B., good old Morris High School."

Eddie said, "Yea, look at you, Vinnie B., all suited up and shit. You're not on drugs, you don't look like no revolutionary, and your Brooks Brothers suit ain't slick enough for the jet set; you must be playing the Uncle Tom role since you moved to suburbs."

"Damn, Eddie, baby," I said, "we only have been together for a few minutes and you haven't missed a beat. I can't engage you now because I am on the job, and I've got an appointment right up the street. But, I shall return, Eddie, baby, just to engage you, my brother." Looking at GP I said, "Yea, GP, I'm on a case right now, but I will check you because I know that we have a lot to talk about, and how is your brother and sister doing?"

GP answered, "My brother is cool; he took the civil service test for the transit, and my sister is looking for a gig, man."

I responded, "I'm going to follow up with you guys so we can cover some new ground and recover some old times. I'll come on the block. Give me your phone number, GP, and I'll touch base with you so you'll know when I am coming."

GP said, "Here, let me give you the name of the cab company that I work for; I just moved, and I don't have my phone hooked up, yet."

Eddie jumped in saying, "Yea, that's right, B., don't ask me for no phone number, 'cause I'm between situations, but I still be on the block; that's right, I'll hold down the Fort, and I got your back, regardless to whatever, you dig, my man?"

I concluded, "Okay, later guys; I'll check you. It's on me."

It was a pleasant surprise to see GP and Eddie. I hadn't seen them since high school when my family moved to Southeast Queens some four years ago. Time sure flies were my thoughts as I entered the Bronx from Harlem across the 145th Street Bridge, I saw flash backs of growing up in my stomping ground of the South Bronx. The changes that occurred in the few years that I have been gone were unbelievable. Well, maybe because I am driving through gave me a different perspective as compared to walking on the crowded narrow concrete sidewalks that border the ghetto tenement dwellings. I knew when I crossed the 145th Street bridge I would see some of my old buddy-buddy cats from my adolescent years but I could not have imagined the state of the neighborhood's devastation and extent of human tragedy. I recalled how emotional I was four years ago when we moved off the block, to home ownership in Southeast Queens. I couldn't imagine not living on the block after living there for the first 18 years of my life. The thought of not living on the block and being around all of my friends and relatives was almost too much to bear at that time. I had no family or friends in Queens that I knew of, therefore I thought that I would be isolated with some square people. If I had a choice in the matter, I would have stayed but by parents would never have permitted that. In fact my father made the point crystal clear that we were moving primarily in order to change the quality of life and environment for me and my brother and two sisters. My father grew up on the block and lived in the apartment next door where his parents and five sisters continued to live. My paternal grand parents migrated to the United States from St Croix, in the Virgin Island, when my father was thirteen years old. My father lived on the block all of his life and as he would say so often it was his job to make life better for us. He forecasted the demise of the whole neighborhood by forces invisible to my eyes and he didn't want us to be caught in its wake.

Mysteriously, I began to feel a warmth and tickle internally and I started to smile inadvertently as I drove passed the anonymous silhouettes dodging through moving and parked cars. Shadowy looking men and women moving in and out of the hallways of mostly uninhabitable tenement dwellings and up and down the narrow, dirty concrete sidewalks. It was a strange uncanny feeling of happiness and joy. As the joyfulness began to radiate in my body and animate my face I smiled broadly realizing that I was saved from this apparent abyss by our move to Queens. The appreciation for my fathers forecast, prediction and prescription for the family, radiated an internal joy in my soul. Reflecting on GP and Eddie, my personal joy transformed to concern and general alarm. Eddie dropped out of high school six years ago and has been on his own ever since, living here and there with no visible means of income. Now at the age of twenty-seven, Eddie was the father of four children with three different women. He is not presently living with any of the three women, as he pointed out he is between situations. Although I hadn't seen Eddie for the past four years, I heard many reports from a range of people about his activities and pursuits. Eddie was almost four years older than me, and I along with others in my generation admired and looked up to Eddie in many respects. Throughout junior high school and his tenure in high school Eddie was one of the best-dressed cats around. As such he had more than his share of girl friends in the fine category. Coupled with his athletic ability, Eddie was a formidable presence on any scene. His gift of gab helped to give him the self-confidence to take control of the prevailing conversation. Eddie had a whole lot going for him but after he quit high school in favor of his emerging career as a number runner, his prospects narrowed. After doing six months in jail he started to play tag with heroin and hanging out with a different crowd, and the number bankers refused to deal with him anymore. Now Eddie had a heroin habit and was hanging out with younger cats to take advantage of their general admiration and naiveté. Eddie talks a sweet game and after you invite him to your house or take him with you somewhere, valuables turn up missing and he is usually a prime suspect.

GP was in my class in junior high school, and a few classes in Morris High School. He and I were among a group of high school students from the block that used to buy a quart of Three Robins apple wine after school and drink. During the wine sessions we would take note of Eddie moving gracefully from building to building picking up number receipts looking sharp and getting the eye of the older women and young girls. It looked like Eddie had it made and we were almost the same age. The after school wine session's were pretty regular and ultimately became part of teenage lifestyle of the block. GP eventually acquired a habitual taste for wine. He began driving a cab after graduating high school and seemed to be working regularly and making enough money to take care of himself and responsibilities. GP's brother Butch was also a good friend of mine, and I was aware that he had taken the civil service test, and I was also aware that he had just volunteered for the United States Army Paratroops. Most of my peers from the Bronx did not pursue college. They wanted to make money and began to play the role of a man, as they perceived a man to be. They tried to enter the labor force that for the most part relegated them to marginal and menial dead end employment. Rarely were they exposed to an employment career opportunity beyond civil service. As my father put it, "There is nothing out here for a colored fella, Champ; you need to take the civil service test so you can have something to fall back on that offers job security." Civil Service was the best recommendation for us, and many took the various tests. Some got involved in the dubious careers associated with the under ground economy, while others gave up the idea of conventional work. I had about fifteen jobs in six months before I landed the plumb employment situation. I had the habit of quitting a job very quickly if I believed it was beneath my dignity and didn't provide upward mobility. However, I had a problem with taking the civil service test, which made for sparkling discussion between my father and me. My father would always resort to his favorite phrase, "Champ, I don't want you to throw cans, but you need to take the civil service just in case you need something to fall back on."

I would say, "Pop, I don't want to throw cans either, but I don't want to take the civil service test because it might hurt my personal psychology. If I don't take the test, I will stay motivated."

I enjoyed the engagement with my father and I knew that he enjoyed it as well. As I got older my father would never try to impose his will on me, but he would advocate his position in the strongest possible terms and consistently. However, he ultimately respected my decision but always reminded me of his position. My father was a Corporal in the US Army during World War II and had a strong opinion about the armed services in this time of the Viet Nam war. "Champ," he would say, under circumstances of peace, the armed services is a halfway decent option for a colored fella. But in the case of a war, like now this stuff in Viet Nam thing, it ain't worth it, so the only way that you go in the service is over my dead body." I gave him no disagreement on the war issue. The war issue and the armed services as a career goal loomed large in the black community because of the lack of employment opportunities. The armed forces offered an immediate exit strategy from the ghetto, and a resource for future opportunities. As a consequence of the unemployment reality political reality on the ground, the armed services became a viable option in spite of the war. After landing my plumb job, I was able to keep my father's opinion in check, because he was in fact amazed at the scope of the gig that I was able to get.

The training at continental Mutual Insurance Company was intense and thorough, preparing me as a vanguard legal para-professional. The work-week was primarily a field operation requiring one half day a week in the office reporting to a liability supervisor. The work required an automobile for which I received a daily car expense account and the company also paid for my comprehensive automobile insurance policy. Because I was under 25 years of age, it would have been prohibitive for me to afford car insurance as I was an "assigned risk" because of my age. It was essentially white-collar work, covering the respective boroughs of New York City. My work tools included a Polaroid camera, a pen and a legal size-writing pad, cunning and a vivid imagination. The job exposed me to a range of life styles and conditions of various peoples in the different communities that constitute New York City. The education and experiences associated with this work was in fact priceless and formative. My mother and father were extremely proud and tended to generously exaggerate the nature and scope of my job. My father in particular took pride in driving my new Mustang to visit friends and family. He would often point out my ability to buy a new car while he couldn't afford to get rid of his old load. "Hey, Champ, so what you going to do now?" He would say often, "You got a hell of a gig, Champ; I guess you won't be buying the *Chief Newspaper* for the civil service test schedule now you got all these professional friends coming by. Keep up the good work, Champ; you know that you're all right with me."

My work took me throughout the boroughs of New York City with the exception of Staten Island. The venues included the business district of Manhattan and the private homeowner neighborhoods of Brooklyn, Queens and the Bronx. Most of the liability claims investigations were in the poor ghetto neighborhoods. Bars, Restaurants, Public Housing, Mitchell-Lama housing developments, slum tenement apartment buildings, department stores, supermarkets, construction sites and automobile accident cases comprised the work menu. In that capacity, I became acquainted with the nooks, crannies and various echelons that constituted the full range of New York City life. In the framework of this employment mission, I observed the pattern of similarity that connected my Southeast Bronx growing up experience with particular neighborhoods that characterized the proliferating new inner city, urban and suburban reality.

Jamaica Queens was a stark contrast to my south Bronx environment. No tenement multi-dwellings bordered by garbage-strewn gutters and filthy, broken-glass-covered backyards. Quite the contrary, only one- and two-story private homes with grass-covered lawns and backyards embellished with hedges, rose bushes, and other picturesque shrubs that were manicured regularly in the context of weekend family household chores. Driveways leading to one and two car garages and households with two parents dominated. This was our transitional environment setting, and we all greatly appreciated this new perspective and contrast in our daily lives. No one was more receptive to this new world than I. During the second day in the new house as I was outside on the front lawn a delegation of neighborhood teenagers came up to the house as the official welcoming committee. I was invited at that point to the house of one of the neighbors and met his family. Larry was his name and his basement was the popular hang-out spot during the week and weekends.

As I recalled, my first day in school proved to be very interesting. I was already a senior in high school and I attended Andrew Jackson High School for the remaining six months of the final semester. The primary difference between Andrew Jackson and Morris High School in the Bronx, was the student body racial demographic. Morris was predominantly black American and Andrew Jackson had a predominantly white student population. A couple of my new friends accompanied me to school and pointed me to the direction of my home room. While making my way through the corridor I recognized a familiar figure from the past. As we got closer to each other we both began to recognize one another, and it was unbelievable I thought to myself. It was David Webster, a good friend of mind from the block. After the shock and hardy embrace, David informed me that we had the same home room and teacher. After school he came home with me to surprise my mother. When we reached the house my mother was in the kitchen and was thoroughly surprised to see David. After embracing him, my mother then went into her room and came back out with a blue textured handkerchief that used to be white. Both David and I remembered that about twelve or thirteen years earlier we were painting scudders in my backyard in the Bronx. David had on his good clothes at the time, as he was scheduled to go with his mother on business. After realizing that his clothes were soiled with blue paint, and we were unable to remove the paint with my handkerchief he began to cry.

Upon hearing the crying from the backyard my mother looked out of the kitchen window then called us upstairs and she proceeded to clean David up to the best of her ability. She then called David's mother on the telephone and attempted to try and take the sting out of the situation. My mother kept the handkerchief as memorabilia of the incident. It was a joyous recollection for all of us, and we appreciated those moments of nostalgia. David told us that he lived near the Sellers family. Roger Sellers was a friend of mine from the block, and one of Roger's brothers, Carlton used to date my aunt on my mother's side, Ethyl DaCosta. David agreed to bring the Sellers boys over to renew old friendships. David and his family moved from the block about the same time as the Sellers family moved, around 1953 or 1954. After renewing our old friendship David and Roger became associated with my new friends on the Ville. The Ville was a pretty cohesive group that engaged in a range of collective activities such as horseback riding, ski trips, picnics, beach parties etc. Some of the social cohesion developed into a number of intimate relationships and in some cases, marriages.

My brief high-school experience generated many new friendships and associations. The friendships and associations were cultivated and served to broaden my exposure to the broader Queens scene. Some of the new relationships included transplants like myself from other boroughs, particularly the Bronx and Harlem, while others were born and raised in Queens. Racial tensions were not a major problem in Andrew Jackson High School at the time, but I heard that three or four year's earlier racial tensions were a source of concern among black students. Yet, there were still some areas in Laurelton and Cambria Heights wherein racial incidents against blacks were not uncommon. There were also still some areas that were strictly off limits for black people as a practical matter. The black students for the most part kept to themselves and socialized with each other in Andrew Jackson. The social environment outside of school was generally pleasant and seemed void of the perils of the inner city experience of drugs and the underground culture and economy. There was isolated experimentation with marijuana, however, based on my experience in the Bronx what I saw was a benign manifestation requiring no cause for alarm. But just prior to graduation I began to notice a familiar pattern among a few friends that was reminiscent of my observations in the Bronx. Shortly there after the suspicious pattern crystallized into revelation. A few friends began to isolate themselves from the larger group and began experimentation with addictive drugs, such as heroin and cocaine. My frame of reference made me aware of the 'intra-group' transition of a few. Perhaps twenty-five percent of my high school peer group enrolled in college or junior college. In the Bronx maybe five percent went to college. The majority including me were more interested in entering the employment world and beginning a life independent from parental oversight, constraints and authority. My introduction into the job market acquainted me for the first time with subtle and overt racial discrimination. Friends were experiencing similar difficulties in the pursuit of jobs or during their employment situations. After about seven or eight different jobs in a couple months my father approached me. He said, "Hey, Champ; what's the situation with all of these different gigs?"

"Well, Pop," I said, "I'm just not satisfied with the jobs that I have been coming up with, so I quit them."

"Look, Champ," he replied, "you need to buy the *Chief Newspaper* and get the schedule for the various civil service tests." He continued, "Champ, look, there is nothing out there for a colored fella; if you don't take the job you can still stay on the civil service list so you will always have something to fall back on."

"Yea, Pop, you make an excellent point, and I appreciate that," I said, then changed the subject. Then I asked, "Pop, what do you think about the armed services, some of my friends are joining up because they can't get jobs."

"Well, Champ, if there is no war it's a pretty good deal. But right now, with this war going on it's a tremendously bad deal. I could not handle the fact of you being in this war, Champ. I did World War II, and by the Grace of God I came home. I don't want you to face that kind of situation, risking life and limb, and if you make it home by the Grace of God you still have to deal with this prejudice crap. America is a good country, Champ, but it could and should be much better. You can't get a decent gig now because you're a colored fella, despite the fact that we fought and died for this country in World War II. And that's why I'm telling you to take the civil service test because there is nothing else for you since you don't want to go to college."

CHAPTER 2

The rebellions around the country between 1964 and 1968 were a bonanza for the investigative staff of Continental Mutual Insurance Company. Opportunities to investigate liability insurance losses in various states abounded. While I resisted the interstate travel opportunities my colleagues took full advance of the exposure, travel and additional money. The lucrative nature of interstate work was so attractive that some investigators relocated to their state of choice. I resisted the interstate travel opportunities to broaden my professional career because I was experiencing a personal dilemma as a result of the work that I was doing. The emerging "black political revolution" was having a major impact on me, as I traveled around the city. I ultimately developed a fundamental moral conflict with my job. I came to realize that my importance with the company was based on how well I minimized the company's insurance liability losses in the ghetto areas. But more importantly, my success and upward mobility was based on deceiving black folk with potential insurance liability cases. In order to do well on the job, I had to take advantage of the ignorance of black folk, and minimize the company's financial losses. I needed the additional money because of my increasing family responsibilities, but the work became too much of a personal moral contradiction. I began wearing casual clothes during work hours and stopped taking my car to the car wash every other day. A couple of my co-workers suspected that I was going through some personal difficulties but they attributed my preoccupation to the sudden death of my father and family matters that I had to deal with as a result. Ed Barnes reported to the same supervisor as me made comments about my car needing to be washed and the wheel hubcaps needed to be restored.

Ed said, "Damn, double O, it looks like you are not just neglecting your ride, seems like you're letting it go."

Double O was a nick-name that Ed's longtime friend Dorothy gave to me, and Ed got a kick out of using it. Dorothy (Dot) and I had a hot and heavy sexual relationship and apparently prior to me she, Dot was a prize that no one was able to get to in recent history. Dot was a single mother with a boy and girl and was a school teacher of some renown in her district. Somehow the lady from Brooklyn, fell in love with me and was serious about our relationship which was a shock to Ed and her other friends. Dot gave me the nick name Double O, as in 007, because she ultimately found out that I was dealing with a couple of sisters that she knew. After the revelation of my escapades, I became in Dot's mind a mysterious double agent character and therefore earned the nick name. Ed loved it because it gave him the opportunity to get back at her in response to his various broken heart romantic scenarios. From that point on, Ed looked at me with great esteem and would mimic my stuff. In fact Ed bought a Mustang as well. My "Stang" was British racing green while Ed's ride was midnight blue.

Ed was very pleased with the interstate travel and he took full advantage of the opportunities. Trevor Williams affectionately referred to by the Investigative staff as the coach also was happy to take advantage of travel opportunities. The coach and I had a special relationship because he trained me as a Legal Investigator/Claims Adjustor when I joined the company. The coach got his nick-name because he was in fact the basketball coach for our company team. The coach was also an avid and knowledgeable basketball fan and confidant to the boss. In addition to basketball, he missed no opportunity to provide coaching in other areas. The boss was a brother that rose to the position of vice president and claims manager of the company.

The coach began to pull my coat, he said, "Hey, Vinnie, these interstate travel deals are hip, man; they got built in connections, and you can live off of your expense account. I don't have to spend my check. When I was in California for three months, I banked my whole paycheck every week. That's right, man; I made big money and got big honey, too. Yeah, man, you know, them sisters dig cats coming out of New York City. You need to get down, man."

I replied, "No, Coach, no, man, I'm just not interested in the travel deals at this time; I'm trying to work out some personal things."

Coach said, "Is it some more family stuff? You know that I'm there for you if you need me, man. I know that you're going through some rough stuff."

"No, Coach," I replied, "I'm cool. Everybody is cool. It's not a family thing again, thank God. No, man, I just have to work through some conflicts with the work we do, in relation to the stuff that I see going on around the city and the country."

"So, Vinnie," Coach said, "What are you saying? Are you a Black Power revolutionary? I trained you to be a top-notch investigator, not a revolutionary. Tell me something, man. What's going on?"

"Don't you see what is going on in the city?" I asked. "You've been all over the country, and don't you read the newspapers? You were in California for three months! You told that the brothers in Cali look grim. Black folk are moving forward and taking control of their situation. I think that what we're doing for the company is part of the problem, man, not part of the solution. How do you reconcile that contradiction, Coach?"

"Vinnie B., baby," he said, "It's very easy for me to reconcile what you perceive as a contradiction. It goes this way, Brother Neo-Robin Hood. Black Power equals green money, and green money equals Black Power. Now, let me hear you repeat that three times."

"Yeah, okay, Coach," I said, "but what is your green power going to do if some white racist cop pulls you over in your slick convertible, pulls you out of your ride, and busts your bald-head, black ass?"

"Well, V., baby," Coach answered, "at least with my green power I'll be able to bail me out of jail and hire a good attorney. And if I do the right thing on this job, the attorney might owe me one. What will your Black Power do? Storm the Bastille and free you and all political prisoners? Then what?"

"Yeah, okay, Coach, you're still the coach," I said. Coach smiled and said, "Yeah, okay, Vinnie, baby, you're a bright boy; that's why I dig you, and as a young man you're entitled to go through your growing pains."

I was getting more active in the welfare-rights movement activities in my borough of Queens and at the citywide level. As such I was a technical assistant volunteer and eventually I was invited to join the staff borough as organizer for the Queens contingent of National Welfare Rights Organizations, (NWRO). In the capacity of staff organizer for NWRO, my para-professional stills were directed towards organizing rent strikes, pickets and demonstrations around social service issues, voter education and registration, community organizing and leadership development training. I was intrigued by the exposure and education that I was receiving in the area of electoral and community based politics. The escalating civil rights movement and the black youth and student movement generated the impetus for the new level of political activism in urban centers and inner cities of America. These community activities for "social justice" were having an increasing impact on me and my work as a claims adjuster and legal investigator. Until the rebellions in the ghettos that culminated in 1967, and the utterance by SNCC Chairman, Stokely Carmichael, of "Black Power," the youth and student movements operated in conjunction with established "Negro" elected officials and civil rights leadership. There was a growing dissatisfaction among black youth particularly from the non-southern contingent with the tactics and objectives of the southern-based civil rights responsible black leadership.

The political dichotomy between the emerging black youth of the ghettos and the established black civil rights leadership may have its beginnings in 1963 with the advent of the March on Washington. At that time Minister Malcolm X was alive and he was juxtaposed to Rev. King, leader of the Southern Christian Leadership Conference, Urban League, CORE and black elected leadership. Malcolm X pointed out how the March on Washington was co-opted by the big six black civil rights organizations under orders from the president Lyndon Johnson. And it was Malcolm X who said, "They need to stop singing and start swinging," referring to the civil rights movement. The message of Malcolm X resounded among youth in the inner cities and urban centers around the country, particularly in the North. Following Malcolm's assassination rebellions occurred in inner cities all over the country. Now the black youth and student movements were deciding on its own agenda, vis-à-vis, "Black Power." I didn't go to the March on Washington in 1963, because I was impressed with Malcolm's assessment and argument and his view that the black civil rights leadership were "a bunch of uncle Toms" whose politics were compromised. In addition to the portrait of reality that Malcolm painted, that impressed black youth of the North, the message that the National Democratic Party sent to the Mississippi Freedom Party during the 1964 convention in Atlantic City New Jersey, laid the foundation for Black Power.

The courageous Fannie Lou Hammer may have been the first to proclaim Black Power as a political strategy when she said, "We are sick and tired of being sick and tired." With the Atlantic City political scenario, it was clear that the White Democratic party leaders would bend or break to the rules to ensure that black folk remained politically impotent. And many in the northern contingent of the youth and student movements held the view that the civil rights leadership was not adequately addressing the situation in the North. There was a growing dichotomy between the agenda's of Black Power and that of the responsible "Negro" leadership of the civil rights movement.

There was a range of community-based activities that I was inspired to get involved with. In particular, the community control of schools in New York City was a hot political issue. The issue of community control was heightened by the Ocean Hill Brownsville, and the I.S. 201 experimental school districts were helping to raise the level of political consciousness and sophistication in the black community. A boycott of the public school system was formulated on behalf of the concept of "community control." The school boycott generated unprecedented cooperation among divergent black groups around the city, who organized Freedom Schools in churches and community centers. The fight for "community control" was ultimately co-opted by the political powers, and was transformed into the concept, "decentralization" which ultimately undermined the intent of "community control." The community control controversy established as well as destroyed some reputations, in the process of containing and managing the community control controversy. In Queens, the Queens Borough Council for Welfare Rights organized the Freedom School for Welfare Rights and the Parent Youth Organization, located at the Afro-Disiac Cultural Center, on 205th Street and Hollis Avenue, housed a multi-faceted programmatic approach to providing needed community based services. The Afro-Disiac Cultural Center stood amid a growing thorough fare of heroin and cocaine addicts. The center facilitated a day care center, Martial Arts, African dance and drums, Jazz concerts, and the Queens Council for Welfare Rights. The daily menu also included a schedule of spontaneous political and social discourse and events.

The Insiders Inc. was a local social club consisting of five young black men of my generation, who established the Afro-Disiac Cultural Center. Once the facility opened, activities were immediately generated and the Center soon enjoyed the reputation of being a constructive youth development center. As my community based activities increased I became a popular figure at the Center and the venue became the primary location for activities associated with my position as staff organizer for NWRO. The Center ultimately became the meeting room and headquarters for the Queens borough Welfare Rights Council. My skills and connections on a community based level together with my general availability made me quite an asset to the growing welfare rights movement in New York in particular. Welfare roles were increasing nationally which fueled a major membership growth in the respective welfare rights groups. The growth of the National Welfare Rights Organization (NWRO), under the leadership of the president Dr. George Wiley, generated funds and I was offered the opportunity to formally join the NWRO, as a salaried staff member. This opportunity I accepted with great enthusiasm in particular because it modulated the moral conflict that I had with my regular gig with the insurance company.

Welfare reform was a significant national domestic policy issue during the mid 1960s and the U.S. Department of Labor introduced the national

"Work Incentive Program" (WIP). The Work Incentive Program essentially proposed to dramatically cut social service benefits and require welfare recipients to enter employment training programs to acquire employable skills. NWRO formulated a national membership recruitment initiative to fight against the imposition of the proposed Work Incentive Program, because of some draconian provisions. NWRO developed and implemented a successful national recruitment program by hyping the acronym of the Work Incentive Program and coined it the "WIP" of the federal government against welfare mothers. Around the country the membership rolls of various statewide NWRO chapters around the country experienced substantial growth rates. In the context of protests and demonstrations around the country the National Welfare Rights Organizations were making a political impact at the state and national levels. In New York City, the Harlem based City-Wide Council for Welfare Rights, under the leadership of Beulah Sanders, was aggressively recruiting new members and assigning them to the respective borough organizations. Organized welfare mothers were taking over social service centers and there were concerted efforts by local authorities to have the police department detain organizers of the demonstrations and demonstrators. In the process of attempting to disrupt the demonstrations around the city, welfare mothers were being manhandled and abused by police officers. The "WIP" acronym tag of the Work Incentive Program proved to be an appropriate characterization of the way welfare mothers were being treated.

Interestingly enough, Richard Nixon the former Vice President of President Dwight Eisenhower was initiating his exploratory campaign for the Republican Party's nomination for President of the United States and he was running on a welfare reform platform. As such Vice President Richard Nixon was an ardent supporter of the federal Work Incentive Program and the would-be President was concerned that further success of the NWRO, WIP and membership recruitment drive might generate negative fall out on his projected Presidential campaign. A planning group of NWRO organizers got together and formulated a plan to interface with Mr. Nixon's people with a presentation. The end result of the scenario was that NWRO was awarded a contract from the U.S. Department of Labor to evaluate the Work Incentive Program. NWRO's evaluation of the WIP would help to inform welfare policy reform in Nixon's anticipated campaign for the Presidency. The contract award was one million plus and it facilitated the budget for NWRO to bring other borough organizers on staff, including me. As a practical matter the evaluation of the Work Incentive Program took a back seat position to the real objective of the evaluation initiative which was to utilize the contract as a means to continue recruitment for the organization. The membership-recruitment drive essentially took the form of a national voter education and registration program. I was responsible for organizing the voter education and registration drive in Queens. Portable voting booths were set up in target areas of Southeast Queens to accommodate the voter education and registration drive. This was my maiden voyage as a registered voter and I registered as a Republican in the summer of 1967, in the context of the WIP evaluation initiative.

The esoteric political objective of the community activist wing of the "movement" that I was associated with was to overwhelm the social welfare system as a tactic to break it down. This general objective was tactical and worked in conjunction with a broader strategic political scenario that included Marxist and radical international democratic movements. These sophisticated political forces had a significant influence in NWRO, the civil rights movement, and derivative Democratic political parties, as well as the Black Power and student movements. The unique application of grassroots community organizing tactics with the Republican Party activism in the context of an emerging Richard Nixon Presidential campaign, were successful in achieving NWRO's objectives. Community organizing tactics were for the most part exclusive to the Democratic Party and its various splinter groups on the political left. Making demands, demonstrations, marches, rallies, and boycotts etc, was conventional political wisdom of the Democrats. Although grassroots organizing tactics in the context of the Republican Party was successful for the NWRO objective to generate financial resources, there was considerable descent among Democrat partisans (liberal and left of center) in the movement concerning staff organizers interfacing with the Republican Party, and the anti-poverty program. The white political gurus of the civil rights movement orthodoxy argued against black organizers interfacing with the Republican Party. "They are racist, right-wing reactionaries." Hence, the tactics of the civil rights movement, Democratic Party and left of center ideology became the orthodoxy for black political activism to the exclusion of grassroots Republican Party electoral counterpart.

The Harlem rebellions in July of 1964, was a catalyst for similar rebellions that manifested in black ghettos around the country, beginning a series of long hot summers. The respective boroughs expressed their own unique rebellions and disturbances that caused the New York City Administration to take emergency measures. The approach was announced by Mayor John V. Lindsay, Vice Chairman of the National Advisory Commission on Civil Disorders, on April 12, 1967, with the formation of Summer Task Force, headed by an assistant to the mayor with direct and immediate access to the mayor himself and composed of 29 high-ranking city officials: commissioners, deputy commissioners, assistants to the mayor, and representatives of the Borough presidents. Each of the members of the Task Force was empowered to make immediate decisions for his department.

For the first time in New York City, top Police and Fire Department officials sat on a policy-making board with top level officials from the Human Resources Administration, the Youth Board, the Council Against Poverty, the Board of Education, the Housing Authority, the Recreational and Cultural Affairs Administration, Sanitation and Personnel Departments, the Human Rights Commission, and representatives of the mayor's office. The Summer Task Force met every Monday morning to do the following:

Coordinate the programs of various city agencies to avoid duplication and waste that had been prevalent before when the agencies planned for the summer independently. This ranged from the placement of play streets and fire hydrant spray caps to citywide recreational and cultural programs. Though the chairman of the Summer Task Force lacked the authority to dictate policy for the Council Against Poverty, the local community controlled umbrella organization charged with the distribution of city and Federal poverty funds, or the Board of Education, which is independent of City Hall, both these agencies and the others on the Task Force were able to use the information they received through Task Force meetings to avoid duplication and get the most out of the program dollars.

Utilize detailed information compiled jointly by the Police Department and Youth Board, which had been reluctant to share confidential information in the past, to indicate 18 areas of concern where interracial or poverty tensions could lead to summer violence. This information was detailed and voluminous, listing specific streets and gangs, potential problems and the names of youths and adults who had to be reached and drawn into constructive summer activity. Thirteen areas (each the size of most cities in the United States) were listed as areas of primary concern (Bedford Stuyvesant, Central

Harlem, East Harlem, Bushwick, Brownsville, East New York, South Bronx, Williamsburg, Coney Island, the Rockaways, Corona, South Jamaica, Fordham, East Tremont) and others of secondary concern.

As early as May 1, 1967, the city administration had begun to set up a decentralized and coordinating apparatus in each of the 18 communities. Eighteen members of the Summer Task Force (no one lower in title than a deputy or assistant commissioner or assistant to the mayor) were given, in addition to their other municipal duties, a single area and were directed to establish as soon as possible a local Task Force in that community. Initially, groups of neighborhood people and city officials started to come together in the first summer of the Lindsay Administration, in 1966, and then again into the second year to develop short-run strategies to maintain community order and prevent incidents from turning into disturbances and disturbances from turning into riots. The communities, however, made it quite clear that they were tired of being asked to help fight fires, to keep the community cool. Unless the city administration was willing to come to grips with the roots of disorders, the causes of the growing unrest, and the socio-economic maladies provoking increasing racial hatreds and tensions in New York, community leaders were tired of working with the city in the short run.

The Task Force was a mechanism designed to make the local agencies of the city government more responsive on an immediate and direct basis to community needs and desires. Basically developed from previous summer experiences of city officials and arising out of the needs and community demands for such an approach, the Task Force quickly became a middle management tool of the mayor to implement his policy of making municipal officials at all levels of government accessible and responsive to community people. Just as Mayor Lindsay had gone to the streets, just as he had taken his commissioners with him to the streets of the city, he was attempting through the local Task Forces, to bring local agency chiefs, directors and administrators into direct and continuing contact with the people they were paid to serve. The Task Force provided the mayor with a direct and immediate link to the most troubled and deprived neighborhoods of the city and likewise provided the neighborhoods with a direct line to City Hall. In effect, the Task Force could become an effective "eyes and ears" of the mayor and a "political rabbi" for the community. The neighborhood now had a friend at City Hall accessible and concerned at all times.

Yet what made the local Task Forces different from other city and community bodies was its unique membership. For the first time, community people, from the churches and from the streets, participated in a weekly confrontation and dialogue with the municipal administrators from their areas. The local city officials were not the public relations or community relation's staff but, rather, the district supervisors for the departments of that area. To be effective, the local Task Forces had to have the participation of city officials who could make decisions, make changes and "make things happen." Lesser staff or other staff whose job it was to defend or "sell" the agency's policies could not be effective in a Task Force role since they could not provide the kind of confrontation and interaction with other city agencies and the community people. To bring these city officials together on a regular basis as a "community cabinet" would have been in itself a significant decentralization of the municipal bureaucracy. The Local Task Forces, carried this one step further by bringing community people into a face-to-face confrontation with city officials, provided a new level of community participation in municipal operations and decision-making. No longer could any agency official blame another agency. No longer could one agency official make commitments that could not be kept because the continuing nature of dialogue held, each agency was publicly accountable for its promises at least one night a week before the entire taskforce. And, when a problem bogged down between agencies, the head of the Task Force, the mayor's man, was there to make a decision and cut through red-tape to implement it.

Local city officials, City Councilmen, State Assemblymen, Senators and Congressmen or their representatives enhanced the prestige of the local Task Forces they participated in, assuring its non-partisan service approach while, at the same time, enabling elected officials to get good insight into neighborhood needs and desires. Though the Borough Presidents could not be expected to attend the meetings of the 8 local Task Forces, two of them assigned top-level assistants to sit in on them. Community people were recruited from among leaders of the poverty program, civil rights, community council, neighborhood council, veterans, business, church, PTA, Planning Board and other organized groups. Non-affiliated individuals, equally concerned about their community's present and future, also participated in the local Task Forces. In addition to devising strategies to keep neighborhood peace, the local Task Forces began to cope with the lack of certain city services, the delays in other city services and the need for over-all improved services in their neighborhoods. Relying on the power of the head of the Task Force, ghetto residents were able to cut through red tape and bypass the maze of bureaucratic walls that developed over the years. Suddenly, in the most depressed areas of the city, ghetto people were beginning to make things happen. Granted they were little things, the garbage on the street, an abandoned car on another, the lights in one park, the lack of a play street somewhere else, but for most of these people, these things were very significant and built up good will in these potentially explosive communities.

What did the local Task Forces do during the summer of 1967 in New York?

They provided the Summer Task Force and the city administration with reliable and up-to-date information about summer neighborhood problems and tensions

They provided community leaders and local officials with reliable and up-to-date information about the city administration's summer plans and programs and assisted the city administration in identifying areas that had been untouched by poverty funds.

They developed a continuing dialogue and trust between the city administration and neighborhood leaders in the areas where they lived.

They provided community leaders and elected officials with direct access to the Summer Task Force and, through its chairman, to the mayor.

They provided and coordinated and significantly improved city services at the local level through the participation of local officials on a mandatory basis and through the direct route to City Hall.

They attempted to raise funds at the local level for special summer programs and to convince local Chambers of Commerce and businessmen to hire youths in the same way as the Summer Task Force did on a citywide level.

They provided recommendations to the Summer Task Force as to the placement of play streets and the distribution of bus trips and fire hydrant spray caps, all funded with corporate money. The local Task Forces were not funding or policy-making agencies for the distribution of poverty funds but they did serve as conduits for some of the money and most of the special programs financed with corporate funds.

They enabled the city administration to set up in each community where trouble might erupt, according to the Police Department and

Youth Board, a continuing community-city structure and a central community office with one man in charge to coordinate non-police and fire efforts should a disturbance occur.

On June 1, 1967, the mayor instructed all commissioners to stay out of troubled areas during the summer without first notifying the chairman of the Summer Task Force. For example, when trouble did occur in East Harlem and later in Bedford Stuyvesant, the chairman of the local Task Force coordinated the city operation, and played a major role, through the neighborhood contacts he had been building up since May, in working closely with the Police Department in restoring stability to these areas. By the end of June, the 18 local Task Forces were fully operational and meeting at least one night a week in a local community facility. On detailed street maps, hung in the office of the chairman of the Task Force, potential trouble spots, ongoing programs and community leaders were appointed for each of the 18 areas.

Set up with the Police Commissioner, who assigned four top-level officials to sit on the Summer Task Force, an around-the-clock early warning system in case of an emergency. Central police communications, which receives reports of all police activity, notified the chairman of the Summer Task Force at any time of the day or night with any report of a racial or poverty area incident or rumor. Upon receiving a call from police communications, the chairman of the Summer Task Force, who was reachable 24 hours a day through his office, an answering service and a car phone, would evaluate the information and then, if he felt the incident warranted it, he would call the chief inspector of the Police Department for details of the incident and the police action. Then, if the incident seemed serious enough, the chairman of the Summer Task Force would call the head of the local Task Force for the area where the incident had taken place.

Of more than 1,000 calls received from police communications during the four month summer period, the chairman notified the heads of the local Task Forces some 200 times. And in two dozen of these instances, the head of the local Task Force found it necessary to proceed immediately to the area. Thereafter, conferring with the precinct captain and community leaders and investigating the incident first hand, the head of the local Task Force would report back to the chairman who, if the situation warranted, would notify the mayor, discuss the situation and make recommendations.

What did the heads of the local Task Force do to assist police?

At first, police captains and inspectors may have been hesitant to share information and work closely with non-police officials. Within a short period of time, it became apparent to everyone concerned that there were areas in which non-police officials could greatly assist the police during times of tension. One of the most dramatic examples of this Task Force—Police association came late last summer in the hours immediately following the slaying of a black teenager by a black detective in Bedford-Stuyvesant section of Brooklyn. Within minutes after the shooting, a rumor that the youth had actually been gunned down by a white detective and that the police were trying to cover up began to spread throughout an already tense neighborhood. Within an hour, three white members of the Summer Task Force who had been working in the area since early June, convinced a group of militant black nationalist that the police version was true, and working together as they had all summer to improve their community, they walked the streets that night and the two nights following dispelling the rumor and helping to restore stability to Bedford-Stuyvesant.

In East New York, within two hours after the stabbing of a black teenager by a white teenager and the recurring report that a gang fight was scheduled for later that evening, the head of the East New York Task Force was able to convince two street leaders, who trusted him because he had been working with them in the past to set up a meeting with the two gangs of youth involved and head off further violence. The quick response was in direct contrast with a 1966 incident in East New York where a tense interracial situation was allowed to inflame and explode before anyone but the Police Department, which could do nothing to solve the problem.

In East Harlem, after a policeman shot and killed a Puerto Rican, the head of the local Task Force, working closely with the police and Catholic Church, was able to set up a series of religious processions at night which helped clear the streets and lessened the tension.

In the South Bronx one night, a neighborhood group angered by the apparent failure of the Sanitation Department to pick up garbage in their community, decided to block a main thoroughfare by placing garbage cans in the middle of the street. The police captain, fearing a mass arrest might cause a serious disturbance, telephoned the head of his local Task Force who was able to have a sanitation truck at the scene and the street cleaned within an hour after receiving the call. In the Morrisania area of the Bronx, a group of

40 black and Puerto Rican mothers started a sit-in in the middle of a busy street to protest the failure of the school district superintendent to tell them exactly when a new school would be opened. In the past, the Police Department would have been forced to make a mass arrest and chance that it might trigger a disturbance; this time the police inspector called the head of the Summer Task Force who, through his local man, was able to convince the women to leave the street by arranging a meeting with top Board of Education officials that afternoon.

In these examples, the Police Department was put in the position of having to consider making mass arrests of people whose grievances were aimed at other city agencies and who were breaking the law only to protest the failure of these agencies. Without the Task Force structure, the police could only enforce the law and chance the repercussions; with the Task Force, the arrests were not necessary. However, had the Task Force been unable to convince the citizens to end their protest, the arrest would have been made. The interaction between the Police Department and the Task Force did not limit itself to this one area. By July, the chairman of the Summer Task Force and the heads of the local Task Forces at times were able to turn up vital confidential information, through neighborhood contacts they had developed, that proved of value to the police. At the same time, they often were able to check out rumors and quickly dispel false and inflammatory ones.

Why did the Task-Force structure succeed in New York?

From the inception of the Task Forces, the mayor made it clear to all his commissioners and agency heads that he was placing the highest priority on the program and he instructed his entire administration to respond immediately to any requests from the chairman of the Summer Task Force. In practice, this meant that when the Task Force chairman asked the Sanitation Commissioner to clean up a certain street at 2 A.M. or the Parks Commissioner to clean a certain swimming pool at noon, the street and the pool were cleaned immediately regardless of the hour. This provided the instant response to abrasive every-day community problems that ghetto residents had never known before. Needless to say, they were impressed by the response and the administration's interest in their problems. Therefore, dozens of potentially explosive problems were eliminated before they became community causes.

The mayor himself, through his almost nightly walking tours in the most depressed areas of the city and through his willingness to meet with anyone, from ministers to militants, if it would help ease community tensions, convinced people that he really cared about them and that he was sincere in his statements about rebuilding the ghettos. The mayor's attitude, that "The streets are where the action is," and that he and his administrators had the responsibility to roll up their sleeves and get out into the streets where the people were, had a significant effect in those areas. Almost all of them highly explosive, where government officials and governmental concern were visible usually only at election time. The chairman and the heads of the local Task Force became well-known figures, the mayor's man, in each of the eighteen areas of concern, spending many hours searching out the adults and youths who could reach the unreachable adults and youths in bars and in churches, in youth centers and in cellars, in schools and in after- hour clubs. Not all groups and individuals fitted into the structured Task Force concept. Some, particularly the more militant groups, refused to involve themselves in established structures but they must still be contacted by the mayor himself and by his top troubleshooters and an attempt must be made to draw them into constructive, non violent activities one way or another. In New York, experience had proven that many groups or individuals who had been labeled anti-white, ready to riot and totally unreachable by members of their own community and the press turned out to be far more constructive and cooperative in face-to-face confrontations and relationships. The Five Per centers, a group of some 500 to 700 black youth who were supposed to be violently anti-white but proved to be quite different, was an excellent case in point. Yet if a group or individual did prove totally uncooperative, the dialogue must continue and the group must not be allowed to exploit summer tensions. Quick response to community problems and the rumors through the local Task Force structure helped considerably in under-cutting the activities of these isolated groups in New York. Improved community services and special citywide recreational, cultural and remedial programs sponsored by private citizens and corporations drew community people to the local Task Forces and, with the local support made them work.

The establishment of a citizen Summer Committee, headed by Thomas P. F. Hoving, head of the Metropolitan Museum, and Andrew Heikell, chairman of the Board of Time Inc., raised private funds and developed private sector jobs. Through the efforts of the Citizens Summer Committee and a movie premiere, more than $650,000 was raised for the mayor's Commission on

Youth, a tax-exempt organization which served as a conduit for the chairman of the Summer Task Force, to provide play Streets. In addition, more than 5,000 corporate jobs were developed. These flexible funds, some $200,000 of the total raised were to be used at the discretion of the chairman of the Summer Task Force, enabled the city administration to bus more than 18,000 youngsters out of the city to recreation areas each weekend and respond instantly to a neighborhood crisis that a bus trip or a play street frequently can diminish problems. For example, dozens of play streets and special programs were set up in Task Force areas in late July when it became apparent that the poverty program had bypassed them.

Using corporate and Federal funds a series of Youth Councils were set up in the 18 target areas of concern. Youth between the ages of 16 and 24 who had been singled out by the Police Department and the Youth Board as having street leadership ability regardless of previous police records were hired and put to work developing programming for other alienated youth in the potentially explosive areas. This was not a matter of paying off the toughest kid on each block to keep their communities cool. This had been tried before, in New York and in other cities and it just didn't work. These youth did help to keep their communities cool, particularly during several tense days and nights in Bedford-Stuyvesant, but they did a lot more, creating, organizing and running remedial libraries, neighborhood cleanup campaigns, police-community dialogues and sports competition in their own neighborhoods. At the end of the summer of 1967, two community representatives from each of the 18 local Task Forces asked to meet with the mayor in City Hall. Their unanimous demand: the local Task Forces created only to last out the summer, be put on a year round basis. A telegram from community leaders in the Bushwick section of Brooklyn to the mayor best summed up the feelings of the 18 target communities.

Dear Sir,

As members of the Bushwick Advisory Committee to the Emergency Summer Task Force, we strongly urge the continuance of this kind of liaison with the mayor's offices on a year round basis. As you well know, temporary cooling programs cannot alleviate the problems of the ghetto during the hot summer months. If the concern of the city administration is not demonstrated on a year-round basis by this kind of direct attention, it is doubtful whether community support can continue to be mustered for emergency situations. As community leaders, we urgently request that a reconstituted Advisory Committee continue meeting on a weekly basis after Labor Day until it becomes apparent that bi-monthly or similar kind of schedule is sufficient to handle problems in Bushwick.

In other words, if the city administration wanted community people to risk their lives during the summer, the city administration and the Task Force had better be there year round.

In late September, the mayor announced his decision: the Urban Action Task Force would supersede The Summer Task Force and the operation would now be year round. Since then, the over-all Task Force has been meeting once a month; the local Task Forces have meetings monthly or bi-weekly; and community representatives from each of the 18 areas would be brought together once a month starting in the spring. As a permanent structure, the Task Force provided a unique opportunity not only to bring government closer to the governed by cutting red tape and improving services but also to generate community participation in planning, policy and implementation dimensions of the municipal agencies. Through constant interaction, through constant exposition of neighborhood problems and needs, through constant and continuing efforts to simplify the delivery of city services and through the use of community pressure, the Task Force offered a unique and practical approach to community involvement at the neighborhood level. In addition, the non-crisis emphasis had been on providing improved municipal services, the Task Force had also played a major role in improving inter-group relations in interracial communities. By drawing blacks, Puerto Ricans and whites together in community oriented projects, in common effort and in common concern a common bond did develop. To simplify it, rather than fight each other, they joined together to fight the bureaucracy that has been defeating them all.

It was planned that the 18 local Task Forces would be expanded to as many as 25 by June 1968. Through city funds, community secretaries, who must live in their Task Force area and were selected by the community members of the local Task Force, had been hired and already set up offices in ten of the areas. By February 1, they were all at work full time expanding the participation in their local Task Forces, helping residents cut through red tape on a daily basis and bridging the communication gap on a permanent basis. Community secretaries for each of the other local Task Forces were expected to be hired in the next few months.

Through the use of corporate funds, raised by the New York Urban Coalition, private contributions and the fall premiere of the film, *Funny Girl,* a series of special Task Force programs were already in operation or planned. These included a winter-spring bus program taking ghetto youth to museums, the theater, and sports events. Other special events had been under way since December 1 for all 18 Task Force areas; a cooperative program of bi-weekly community newspapers to be put out experimentally by the community members of several of the local Task Forces was being developed with Columbia University's School of Journalism; a series of youth confrontations, taking youth leaders out of the city for a weekend of dialogue and exposure to each other and top-level city officials in an informal setting, was scheduled to start in the spring, and a bowling program bringing police officers and ghetto youth from their own precincts together in team competition to build up better relations at the street level started in February. By March 1, the Urban Action Task Force represented a pack of special city-wide cultural, recreational and remedial programs, totaling between $1 million and $1.2 million to the New York Urban Coalition which replaced the Citizens Committee in raising corporate funds for the summer of 1968. The Urban Coalition worked with the city's Manpower Agency and the chairman of the Urban Action Task Force, who served as the president's Council on Youth Opportunity coordinator in New York.

What did the Task Force structure mean to New York?

In the short run, during the summer of 1967, it played a small but effective role in easing neighborhood tensions and helping maintain the stability of the city. Yet it was in the long run that the Task Force was significant to New York and most other cities. For the Task Force concept was a step forward in the decentralization of municipal government. From here on in, city government no longer remained isolated behind the walls of City Hall and hoped to survive; City Hall today was where the people were, in their neighborhoods both rich and poor, and it must be responsive 24 hours a day, 52 weeks a year. There was little doubt that the success of the Summer Task Force, born out of crisis and uncertainty, and the community demand for its year-round continuation were indicative of the need and demand for the permanent decentralization of municipal government.

These steps taken to improve the coordination at the top levels of municipal government and to build up communication and bridges of understanding between the city and its citizens did not by themselves prevent riots in New York in 1967. And, no matter how successful they were, they would not by themselves prevent riots in 1968. What is important to remember, however, is that they did improve, though slightly, the operation of municipal government and they did improve the dialogue between the government and the governed. Today, as we head into another long hot summer, neither of these is a small achievement for New York or any other cities.

All of the ghetto communities around the country and in fact the whole nation were stunned, shocked and bewildered by the dramatic and tragic chain of events that would record 1968 as a year of infamy in the history of the United States of America. The rebellions and disturbances in the ghettos of America were indeed paled by the assassinations of Rev. Dr. Martin Luther King Jr. and Senator Robert Kennedy, respectively. These two dreadful events coupled with the brutal spectacle of the Democrat National Convention in Chicago, marked a critical credibility turning point between the government and the governed.

The Kerner Commission Report was published on March 1, 1968, after taking fifty volumes of testimony, visiting the riot cities, interviewing over 1500 city officials, ghetto resident, police and military personnel, conducting exhaustive studies and investigations on every aspect of the problem, consulting with experts across the country, and meeting together for 24 days to review and revise drafts, it issued its report. For weeks the report blanketed the news media of the nation and sold over a million copies in paperback within the first month, it had become the most widely discussed public document of our time. It was not simply a report about the condition of the "urban Negro" or control of the "ghetto riots" of 1964, 65, 67. It was a report on the convergence of three tidal forces in American life, the "Negro revolt," "urban poverty," and the "decay of the inner city." It was not, therefore, a report about a Negro problem. It was a report about an American problem, which it summarized in these words:

> This is our basic conclusion: Our Nation is moving toward two societies, one black, one white, separate and unequal.

Violence was part of the problem. The Commission condemned violence as fundamentally inconsistent with progress in a free society. The report stated at the beginning:

What white Americans have never fully understood, but what the Negro can never forget, is that white society is deeply implicated in the ghetto. White institutions created it, white institutions maintain it, and white society condones it.

The commission saw the problem of public safety and public order as fundamentally related to the issue of social justice and the condition of the inner city. It saw men without jobs and families without men. It saw schools where children are processed instead of educated, until they returned to the street, to crime, to narcotics, to dependency on welfare. It saw institutions breeding chaos, and injustice breeding violence. It called, therefore not only for strengthening police forces and improving their ability to control civil disorder, but also for a massive and sustained commitment to national action in the fields of employment, education, housing and welfare reform, and for immediate local action to improve police-community relations, to stimulate better coverage of the problems of minority communities by the news media, and to revitalize relationships between city government and the urban poor. The relationship between city government and the urban poor was part of a broader question, whether the inner city could ever become an effective political community. This was the crux of the urban problem in America. Unless we can learn to deal intelligently and compassionately with the tensions and frustrations of the black and Hispanic poor that underlie the problem of civil disorder, we will inevitably become a garrison state, a society in which the police and the army have become the dominant institutions of urban life, a society permanently polarized along lines of race and class. Already, military considerations, the mobilization, deployment and logistical support of large-scale control forces, are affecting the planning and decision-making process of civil government in our major cities. One wonders whether the citizen, or even the city official or professional administrator, understands how quickly the pressures of public fear and the call of demagogues for repressive strategies can weaken the most fundamental democratic values. One wonders also whether those who lead the call for repression, for strategies of control based primarily on counter violence, can possibly have lived through the last decade and still believe that such strategies offer a viable solution to the problem of public order.

The issue is not whether we should support the police. The issue is whether the central city and urban society of which it forms the core, can survive. The forces of change have all converged on the city but nothing has had more drastic consequences than the population trade-off that has occurred since World War II. On the one hand the rising affluence of the white middle class has steadily accelerated the historic tendency of Americans who are moving up, to move out, to the suburbs, to better homes, better schools and a better life. On the other hand, the mechanization of agriculture and the continuing deprivation of the rural south has brought a massive influx of black and Hispanic migrants to the city, victims of the poverty culture and the educational waste land of the rural south and critically dependent on public assistance and public resources. In 1961 blacks accounted for almost half of the families on welfare in the United States. In that year over half of all the children in the country who were in families assisted by welfare programs were black and lived in the central cities. In 1968 the proportion was approaching 80% in Chicago, New York and Detroit. At that time in Los Angeles County, the welfare budget was almost half a billion dollars. But central city resources, jobs, industry, retailing and the tax revenues that go with them, had eroded just as steadily as the level of human needs has mounted. The public plant of the city, schools, hospitals, prisons and juvenile correction centers, are obsolete and deteriorating along with the housing stock.

Unit costs for public services are sky rocketing as productivity in private industry pushes up pay scales throughout the economy and local government employees begin to organize and bargain collectively. Who are the people who are affected by these forces? They are two groups: one is the poor and the other is the middle class both white and black. The difference between these two groups is not only income, it is power. One group can make itself heard in city hall, without marches or protest or sit-ins. The latter has access, and it knows the political ropes and it makes campaign contributions.

Change has also had drastic consequences for the urban poor. Once they had their own channels of influence and appeal and political structures that made it possible to bargain effectively over allocation of resources in the city. These were called political machines and they were "corrupt" and so eventually they were wiped out in a wave of local government reform. They saw the end of partisan primaries, the replacement of the ward system with at-large elections, the establishment of independent commissions, and the coming-of age of the professional city manager system. These reforms effectively sanitized city hall, at least in a relative sense. But in converting the politician from a power broker to an administrator, they stripped away an elaborate structure which the urban poor particularly the ethnic minorities of an earlier era had found essentially to their long climb up the political power ladder of American society. The Kerner Commission concluded that sustained economic and political impotence in the face of rising white affluence and the powerful hopes that arose due to the great judicial and legislative victories of the civil rights movement were chief catalysts of urban violence.

The report states:

No democratic society can long endure the existence within its major urban centers of a substantial number of citizens who feel deeply aggrieved as a group, yet lack confidence in the government to rectify perceived injustice and bring about needed change.

The challenge of the Kerner Commission Report to American society was the challenge of change. Can we bring about urgent needed change in the city through democratic processes in the midst of virtual financial bankruptcy, carefully protected political paralysis, and growing polarization between major segments of the community? Unfortunately, this can't be answered simply by looking to city hall. The problems of urban America are generated in rural Mississippi and Washington, D.C. as well as the black ghettos of the inner city. The solutions lie in corporation and labor-union boardrooms as well in the chambers of the city councils in the black community itself. John Gardener put the problem in the form of an allegory. He looked at the society in the perspective of an observer from the twenty-third century. He saw that industrial technology and communications science had cause human expectations to rise sharply in the twentieth century, men came to demand more and more of their institutions. But while aspirations swept ahead, human institutions remained sluggish, which was not surprising because, he observed, they were designed to obstruct change rather than facilitate it. He continued the allegory in these words:

Because of failure to design institutions capable of continuous renewal, twentieth-century societies showed astonishing sclerotic streaks. Even in the United State, which was then the most adaptable of all societies, the departments of the Federal government were in grave need of renewal; state government was in most places an old attic full of worn-out relics; municipal government was a waxworks of stiffly preserved anachronisms; the system of taxation was a tangle of dysfunctional measures; the courts were crippled by archaic organizational arrangements; the unions, the professions, the universities, the corporations, each had spun its own impenetrable web of vested interests. Such a society could not respond to challenge. And it did not.

The key question for those of us who are stuck to the twentieth century is what is to be done? There would seem to be three possibilities. The first is to do nothing; accept more of the same. This is the accepted mode of American liberal tradition, (as distinguished from the mode of the American conservative tradition, which is to do nothing as near nothing is possible). This is the most likely response, and it seems that we will continue to pursue urban development strategies on the basis of Federal programs which are conceived and administered to achieve different and often conflicting purposes and which are almost impossible to manage because of their complexity and because of the erratic and inadequate funding. The second possible course is to cut back on national policy objectives in the field of the social development and to buy more sophisticated military equipment for the police. This seems to be the thrust of the "law and order" exponents, who appear to feel that the time to change institutions (if there is such a time) is when people have learned to behave themselves. History suggests that this point of view is not only illogical, it is suicidal.

The third possible strategy, and the least probable one, is to formulate programs for reshaping and renewing the key institutions of the society at every level of our national life. At the federal level, apart from the obvious questions surrounding the office of the president and the functioning of the Congress, there is a critical need to reexamine the assumptions underlying Federal agency involvement in the implementation of urban programs. Should Washington, D.C. continue as an operation command post with line authority over every aspect of this program, or should it function as a staff city? Or, to put the issue more bluntly, should the national government continue to generate massive operational entanglements in local communities on the premise that federal incompetence is preferable to local and especially southern incompetence? The need is to design a system through which federal resources can be translated into services and benefits to people without local dependence on administrative mechanisms. This means essentially a system based on incentives and rules designed to induce people and institutions at the local level to move together at the same time in the direction of national policy goals. Under this type of system, the responsibility for program operations would rest with local communities and private organizations, while policy guidance and the setting of appropriate conditions remain in the hands of the national government. This is not an academic or theoretical problem. As the Kerner Report states;

> The spectacle of Detroit and New Haven engulfed in civil turmoil despite a multitude of federally-aided programs raised basic questions as to whether the existing "delivery system" is adequate to the bold new purposes of national policy.

At the state level, the key question continues to be: What is the role of state government in an urban society? Does it have one? Aside, that is, from passing resolutions expressing moral outrage with the antics of university students and faculties? The Kerner Commission said this:

> State government has a vital role to play. It must equip city leadership with the jurisdictional tools to deal with its problems. It must provide a fuller measure of financial and human resources to urban areas. Most importantly, state leadership is in a unique position to focus the interests and growing resources, political as well as financial, of the suburbs on the physical, social and cultural environment of the central cities.

If this is true, then why is California helpless to bring about desperately needed comprehensive tax reform programs? What ever became of the State Development Plan and the bold dream of creating policy guidelines for resource allocation and regional development in a state that will have a population of 30,000,000 people by 1985, with 95% of them living in urban areas? The answer is that the state government as an institution is still keyed to the needs of a bygone era. And those who thought that the Supreme Court's epochal decisions on urban-rural reapportionment would materially change the system in our lifetime are bound to be disappointed. But it is at the local level, in the central cities of our metropolitan areas, that the dilemma of institutional obsolescence directly intersects the two burning issues of our time, race and poverty.

The heat generated by these issues has turned city hall into a giant pressure cooker, with all the cooks, politicians and bureaucrats alike, waiting around nervously for the lid to blow off. The problem lies not only in the archaic and rigid structures of municipal government that John Gardner calls a "waxworks of stiffly preserved anachronisms." It lies just as much in our out molded image of the city and its role in a changing urban society. Our local communities are still organized around the principle that the good city is a good garbage collector. Years ago, at a time when this country was paralyzed by the "Great Depression" we looked to the national government for new policies and new initiatives and new institutions to meet the pressing social needs. It is time now, when the problems of race and poverty and the decay of the inner city threatens us with urban chaos, to develop local initiatives and local institutions as the energy channels for the national resources which are dedicated to social needs. There is nothing in the Constitution, which requires that all our hopes and all our possibilities for social innovation and progress be consigned for federal instrumentalities. Indeed, there is a powerful new thrust toward a system based on community initiatives contained in Model Cities Legislation, including what amounts to a block grant feature under which the city can aggregate federal funds under a variety of programs and deploy them in accordance with its own priorities. Unfortunately, and typically, Congress has determined that this relatively powerful and important program should have relatively little money.

There are cities, which are creating a new role for African Americans in the life of the community, and cities, which are creating new bonds among all the institutions of the metropolitan region. In New York City, Mayor Lindsay's involvement of major corporations and labor unions in city initiated programs led directly to the formation of the National Urban Coalition. In Atlanta and Louisville, in St. Louis and Detroit, there are dynamic new relationships between city government and employers, union's financial institutions and groups within the minority communities. The city of Compton has recently entered into an agreement with the University of California at Los Angeles whereby the University will provide graduate student interns as resources to the city on a full time basis along with faculty-student taskforces to work out solutions to the city's most pressing problems. The city of Fresno is experimenting with a program for insuring home loans, which do not qualify for conventional, or F.H.A. financing. But we have not begun to think systematically about the new linkages and the new institutions, which are necessary to create the effective political community. And we will not begin until we recognize that our traditional concepts have lost their validity and their usefulness for all the parties involved, until we

ɔrt, that the priority task of city government today is to
⁄s and generate community energies aimed at nothing less
⁄asic democratic values to all citizens. This means building a
ne city and its role, an image that is relevant to the needs and
vɪ⊔. ɪs of the citizen who cannot opt for suburbia.

It means developing new institutional devices to assist in solving basic community problems, community corporations to generate economic development and the ownership of business enterprises, quasi-public management firms which can bring the systems management approach to urban problem solving, credit agencies to stimulate capital formation in the ghetto, non-profit housing corporations which can draw on the construction capabilities of private enterprise. It means finding ways in which the citizen can seek redress for his grievances against public instrumentalities, and ways in which he can make his voice heard on the decisions that affect his own neighborhood and his own life. Above all, it means developing a program oriented to results rather than means, a program based on the needs of the people, a program to overcome the petty bickering, the drift that we have come to characterize the governance of the city. There are so many possibilities in a society as rich in human and material resources as ours. All our urban institutions, private enterprise, labor unions, the churches, the foundations, the universities stand ready and poised to deepen their involvement in the life of the city. To realize these possibilities will require many things, including of course, more federal money for the cities, but more than anything else, it will require the qualities of strong democratic leadership on which a free society must always rely. The Kerner Commission Report is a plea from that leadership.

President Johnson wanted to be President of all of the people, yet, it was clear that within the coalition that elected him in 1964, an important part was the black vote, now there were major conflicts within it. The Mississippi Freedom Democratic Party not only gained recognition at Atlantic City during the Democratic National Convention, but its rejection of compromise gave the Johnson Administration a stinging indication of how real and overt his conflict was with the civil rights movement. Unlike the war on poverty, the civil rights movement began outside of the government, and had, in the beginning, been beyond the control of the government. However, after having reacted to the movement's demands for a decade, the government had learnt that it was impossible to satisfy the broadening black political movement. Therefore something else had to be done by the administration, not only to ensure the equality of the black American, but also so that the government wouldn't continue to be merely a reacting force to the "movement's" perpetual demands. It was thought by some that the president's Howard University speech, June 4, 1965 ("To Fulfill These Rights") was designed to "leap frog the movement." The speech was drafted by Richard N. Goodwin and Daniel P. Moynihan. The speech was prepared following the internal discussion of the Moynihan document at the highest level of government, and before the report was leaked to the public. There seemed to be realization of the limitations of the legal apparatus as an effective force to adequately address the final solution of the civil rights problem. There was also a realization of the weakness of the bureaucracy to deal effectively with civil rights matters. As within the movement, the administration was beginning to realize that civil rights laws and the Supreme Court would not produce racial equality or consensus. A new administration policy had to be developed. It was in this atmosphere that the Moynihan first introduced the White House staff to the ideas that were later to be written down in the "Moynihan report." Long before the report was in final form, Moynihan discussed his views with people in the Administration and found listeners anxious for new ideas. The Report itself fit an existing need within the administration. It gave the administration a specific target and a specific means to measure the effectiveness of existing new programs aimed at the pathologies of the urban slums. It was little wonder that after distributing the paper, Moynihan received very positive feedback from high administration people.

The liaison between the government and the civil rights groups had come a long way. But, the easy and frequent interaction at high levels that existed between business, or labor or other pressure groups and the White House was still not in existence. For their part the Administration was reluctant to develop close relations for fear of stimulating demands that could not be met. The civil rights groups had a comparable reluctance; too much camaraderie might be taken for "Uncle Thomism," particularly since it was not likely to lead to significant changes in the law or more vigorous government enforcement of existing law. The Johnson Administration had settled on a kind of symbolic liaison. From time to time, the president would telephone and talk with the top civil rights leaders or call them and tell them how much he needed their support. But beneath this elaborate structure of staff linkages between pressure groups and the White House that existed in other areas just simply did not exist for the black community. If the president succeeded in persuading the public, including the black American public, that he was now in charge of the civil rights movement it could only weaken their already small influence, particularly because they had no complementary power base in Congress, hence no independent political leverage. This was the civil rights manifestation of the "benign Machiavellians" of the Johnson Administration. By embracing the movement figuratively (and its leaders physically) the president maximized his own option in action and minimized theirs. The Moynihan report and the controversy it created were eventually pressed into the service of this strategy.

Needless to say, the Johnson Administration marks the high water point of the relationship between the Office of the president of the United States and the black community. Contemporary political history has not yet seen a comparable interface at the presidential level on behalf of the black community on par with other interest pressure groups. And given the optimal interface situation to what extent will real-time obstacles of racism and bureaucracy undermine its practical application. While the government should play an appropriate role in the rehabilitation of the black community, the black political leadership would be misguided to continue to promote government remediation of the black community crisis. The conventional political wisdom and strategy for political empowerment as articulated by the black political leadership, official and unofficial must be challenged from within the black community. With all due respect to the importance of direct-action tactics that have proven to be so successful during the civil rights era. It should be pointed out that the institution of Jim Crow in the South was much different from the institutions of discrimination and segregation in the urban centers, both north and south. In many ways the South could be viewed as an under developed country which, has been moving away from single crop farming to an industrial economy. The need for labor in the industrial centers of the South as well as the North has encouraged migration from the rural to the urban centers. In an industrial economy it is most efficient to hire on the basis of skills. Arbitrary hiring, or hiring or not hiring on the basis of skin color, is not congruent with the requirements of an emerging industrial society. Therefore, the removal of Jim Crow can also be seen as required for the South's industrial development.

Similarly, segregation of public accommodations only impedes on the flow of commerce. To a large extent by the 1960s segregated lunch counters were a manifestation of the previous society. The movement attacked these forms of racism at their weakest point for tactical reasons. Because they were only symbolic and furthermore a barrier to industrial progress, small numbers of civil rights workers could, by placing their bodies on the line, attack segregation in the South with success. Also, supporters of white supremacy in the South had proved themselves to be considerably less skillful than the northern functionaries and power figures that supported de facto segregation and discrimination. The southern racists strengthened the civil rights movement by accommodatingly playing their roles in open, often brutal, public confrontations; northerners avoided or minimized open confrontations. Notwithstanding the benefits achieved during the civil rights era, a new strategy and tactic is required to move the black community into the century, as the industrial society gives way to the age of technology and new global power relationships. The transition will not be a simple maneuver, and therefore the conventional political and economic and social paradigm must be challenged.

In the wake of the publication of the Kerner Commission report, March 1, 1968, and the release of the Moynihan report, further confusion and controversy was generated and hyped by the mass media. In addition, as a result of the growing and aggressive anti-war movement and the emergence of a broad grassroots direct action coalition President Johnson reluctantly decided not to seek re-election in November 1968. A broad nationwide coalition was being formulated to stop the business as usual attitude of the nation in the form of a "poor people's" campaign, designed to bring Washington DC to a halt, on behalf of the poor and peace and anti war issue. Dr. Martin Luther King Jr., the author of the "poor people's" campaign had forged a coalition with a range of political forces that included Marxist groups as well as "radical" students and "Black Power militants." The pending Washington campaign and the broad coalition of direct action proponents presented a new and dangerous dynamic for the domestic intelligence apparatus. As the poor people's campaign was being planned and local as well as international political forces were converging on Washington, and other targets, Dr. King was assassinated April 4, 1968. Simultaneously, there were rebellions in black communities around the country. For almost a week many ghettos of America burned. "Burn, baby, burn!" was a popular cry from the ghetto quarters. The rebellions of 1968, eclipsed the previous rebellions of 1964, '65, '66, and '67, and solidified the credibility gap between the government and the governed in general and the black community in particular. On June 6, 1968, as Senator Robert Kennedy was at a campaign stop following his landslide victory in the California

Democratic Primary election, he was assassinated. The spectacle of the 1968 Democratic Convention in Chicago will live in infamy as the intolerant forces of law and order and repression demonstrate the lack of control and discipline on national television. Following the assassination of Dr. King, the 500-member Black Panther Party grew to 4,000. Following these brutal, clandestine and unconventional warfare tactics, and all out covert assault against various elements of the black community and continues in the face ineffectual black responsible elite political leadership.

CHAPTER 3

Charles Dickens had it right with his best-of-times, worst-of-times paradoxical scenario. Surely, this was the worst of times; witness the proliferation of drugs, police brutality, and covert assaults, against black youth and their organizations. Assassinations of local and National "responsible" and "militant" black leadership were not simply shots across the bow, these were in fact acts of political warfare, lethal in nature. There was political warfare on two fronts, from the perspective of the black youth movement. On one level I was engaged in a conventional and unconventional war with the "man" and his institutionalized "racist system." On another level we were engaged in an internal struggle with the "responsible" black leadership, particularly in the context of the civil rights orthodoxy. The organic internal dynamic between the "ruling black bulls" and the "emerging black bucks" and its outcome, would ultimately determine the leadership and political direction of the black community. However, at this point the civil rights movement and the black youth movement was being neutralized by, infiltration, co-option, and/or assassination. Yet, there was great optimism and high expectations across the broad cross section of the black community, largely due to legislative and statutory victories relative to segregation and voting rights. These apparent social and political victories were compelling to say the least and had a positive impact. President Lyndon Johnson's Great Society-concept in the framework of the war against poverty, and manpower development programs were generating hope on the grassroots level. Likewise the black youth and student movement through various "Black Power" conferences were beginning to focus on electoral politics, and an empowerment agenda, as well as focus on community control of local institutions.

My work at the Afro-Disiac Community Cultural Center in Queens was at the epicenter of this dynamic social and political process. I was on the payroll as a staff organizer for the National Welfare Rights Organization (NWRO), for more than a year and the Afro-Disiac, was my operational base for the

59

Queens Borough Council for Welfare Rights, and the Parent Youth Organization (PYO). PYO, was comprised of welfare and neighborhood mothers and neighborhood youth, some of the youth were members of the "Nation of the Five Percent." I was getting a wealth of training, exposure and experience as a result of my status as a staff organizer for the "movement" however, I was getting the sense that there were matters of international political intrigue as well as some basic local-yokel racism that was causing me discomfort and inspiring heavy thought and contemplation. The assassinations of President Kennedy, Malcolm X, Martin Luther King and Robert Kennedy, weighed heavy on my mind in the context of my developing political sophistication. Each assassination was in my view a high level political hit, by clandestine forces that operate outside of the conventional realm of government operations. The "rogue force" operates in the context of "unconventional" warfare and moves by its own inertia, and with an absolutely free and unaccountable hand. The same anonymous esoteric rogue force was devastating the youth and student movement, through sophisticated infiltration, subversion tactics and assassination. It also became apparent to some in the civil rights leadership and me that domestic sophisticated white racist political interests on one hand, and sophisticated international geo-political interests on the other hand were manipulating and marginalizing black political development. In both instances, a white paternal political agenda was imposed on the legitimate political aspirations and efforts of the black community. Developments in NWRO, helped to fuel my growing concern that outside forces were manipulating black political and civil rights leadership. This overriding concern was the basis for me to begin focusing on local politics, and an exit strategy from NWRO.

Beyond the "ruling black bulls" that constituted the civil rights leadership, black movement politics were becoming radicalized and revolutionary, in the framework of derivative Marxist ideology. NWRO was in the Marxist and Socialist orbit. In addition racial tensions were beginning to surface in the ranks of the organization. The NWRO membership was broad and reached into all states that had a social welfare system. As such, during national conferences virtually all states were represented. In a national forum it was abundantly clear that white welfare recipients far outnumber black welfare recipients. Accordingly, at national conferences black folk resembled a fly in a bucket of milk. An incident occurred during a national staff advance conference held on a college campus venue. NWRO staff generally traveled the country by bus and the trips were always a joyous "integrated" fellowship. Although black organizers were like a fly in a pail of milk I was impressed initially that blacks and whites in the movement were politically astute enough to transcend the popular racial dilemma. On the occasion of this particular national staff advance there seemed to be an under current of racial tension from the outset. First there was an unsubstantiated rumor regarding public nudity and group sexual activity. The rumors generated quite a bit of curiosity, however there was a quiet resolution of the matter without any hard determination as to whether it did or did not occur, and who may or may not have participated. Then, on the heals of the nudity and sex question an alleged racial incident occurred. According to the allegations a black staff member from upstate New York, was harassed and explicit racial epitaphs were used against his person. A New York caucus meeting was called regarding the incident and it was resolved that a representative from the New York caucus would raise the matter directly to the Executive Director of NWRO, Dr. George Wiley. The report came back to the caucus that he (George) promised that he would address the matter during his remarks at the close of the staff advance session. There was much speculation amongst the New York Caucus as to what George would say or do, and we awaited his remarks with great anticipation. When George finally addressed the gathering, we were shocked and disillusioned because he did not mention one word about the incident. His silence on the matter spoke volumes to me, and others.

The matter did not sit well with Bob Mahea, the NWRO organizer for the Bronx. Bob wanted to confront George about it; he ultimately relented after considering the perspective of others. The consensus was to be cool, as opposed to confrontation, and being cool meant that each of us had to make a personal and independent decision as to their respective response. I decided, and voiced my view that this was most likely my last staff advance, as I intended to resign as an NWRO organizer. I felt that my local situation was more important and it had strong potential to compensate for the $200.00 per week that I was being paid from National. Bob was more concerned about his financial situation than I was, because he was not rooted in the Bronx. Bob was a Native American from somewhere in the mid-west, and moved to the Bronx as a condition of employment as organizer. However, he resolved to pull out of NWRO and began drafting a resume before the staff advance concluded. Another matter helped to tip the scale in favor of my leaving the organizing staff.

Professor Francis Piven of Columbia University and political guru of NWRO delivered a provocative presentation at the general session of the staff advance. My assessment of her presentation was that welfare recipients, in the framework of NWRO were to be a component of the shock troops, and vanguard cadre for all out radical revolution in the streets of America. There was apparently a policy decision to change the NWRO objective of a "guaranteed adequate income" to a "guaranteed annual income, without a rational explanation." I was beginning to feel and appreciate an international political dynamic of increasing Marxist influence and undercurrent of clandestine agenda's competing with conflicting agenda's, within the movement. I came to believe that people like me, and the welfare mothers that were the backbone of the organization were expendable troops, on behalf of a perpetual revolutionary process. The revolutionary process predated the civil rights movement, student and black youth social and political movements. In fact, it was clear to me that domestic political forces and clandestine international political forces were exploiting, if not subverting the whole black socio-political movement. The recent assassination of Rev. Dr. Martin Luther King Jr. set off bells in my head. It was my assessment that the radical anti-war movements sophisticated domestic and international political forces infiltrated the black social, political movement at large, and influenced the policy decisions to achieve their domestic and geopolitical objectives. These sophisticated political forces in the framework of the "peace movement" and the "democratic movement" influenced Dr. King in particular to take a public position against the Viet Nam war and "military-industrial complex," and for a "guaranteed annual income." The anti-war and guaranteed annual income movements were essentially vehicles to inspire a general strike, and mass demonstrations of poor and "minority group" people in the streets of America. America was at war with Marxism and the Soviet Union in a contest for world control and domination and planetary hegemony. The East (Soviet Union) vs. West (United States) political paradigm was a conventional war and an unconventional cool war, carried out by surrogate countries. The black political movement was a mutable force that was used by both east and west as fodder and tactical political deceptions. In the balance, the legitimate social, political and economic aspirations of black folk were compromised or derailed.

I suspected that these same sophisticated political forces were at work in the domestic and community based Black Power organizations. The Marxist based international (democratic) revolutionary movements had trained and radicalized many black organizations (agencies of revolution) and charismatic individuals. The same pervasive elements began exercising increasing influence on the social policy of the Democratic Party, social and political science curriculum in colleges and universities, and compromised the social and political objectives of the civil rights movement. With these profound conclusions in the forefront of my mind, the unfolding developments within NWRO had a chilling and sobering effect on me. I was convinced that I should pull out now, before I had crossed the Rubicon. If I was not careful, I could be trapped-off as fodder in the sophisticated geopolitical machinations, of the rogue force. The workshop during the staff advance included, tactics and strategies for the 1968 Democratic Convention in Chicago, the Poor Peoples Campaign in Washington, and a mass national demonstration of welfare recipients in support of a "guaranteed annual income," and clandestine operations by the radical cadres, to instigate the authorities and rebellion. Paradoxically, some members of the radical left formulated the "Keep America Hump Free" movement then dispatched for the Democratic National Convention in Chicago. The "Keep America Hump Free" was also a curious development to me, because the movement people were for the most part members of the Democratic Party. I asked my self, "Why would they deliberately sabotage Senator Humphrey?"

The local situation in the black community of Queens had its own intrigues, dynamic and factions amongst "official" black leadership and organic community based youth leadership. Apart from the black political and civil rights leadership, there were a number of informal groups: the Brothers Art Shop, the Green Lantern House, Egbey Ife, the Nation of the Five Percent, the Democratic Liberation Party, the Black Panthers, Insiders Inc. and Afro-Disiac Community Cultural Center, among others. These community-based groups embodied a diversity and political spectrum among the black youth and young adult community. Juxtaposed to this informal constellation of community-based groups were the "official" if not "responsible" black leadership. The responsible leadership included: politicians, prominent clergy, the Southeast Queens Community Corporation (anti-poverty program), the Jamaica NAACP, Queens Urban League, the South Jamaica Steering Committee (urban renewal program) and a host of community boards and committee's that impacted the delivery of community services. The Southeast Queens Community Corporation and the South Jamaica Steering Committee were the most dynamic of the conventional community agencies and they had the greatest and most immediate and significant impact on the community. The Southeast Queens Community Corporation, was an anti-poverty program under the guidelines of the Federal

Office of Economic Opportunity (OEO), managed and administered on the New York City level by, the Council Against Poverty (CAP), the Human Resources Administration (HRA), and the Community Development Agency (CDA).

There were similar anti-poverty agencies in each of the boroughs (poverty area), that managed and coordinated neighborhood programs (delegate agencies) in education, manpower development, youth development, economic development, day care services among others. The Southeast Queens Community Corporation had about 22 delegate agencies providing services. There were counterpart agencies in other "poverty-stricken" areas in Queens, such as Rockaway, Corona, and East Elmhurst. The Southeast Queens Community Corporation had an annual budget of about 1.2 million dollars. The annual budget was dispersed among the respective community based "delegate agencies" located throughout the target area of Southeast Queens. The Board of Directors of the Southeast Queens Community Corporation was composed of 51 members elected from their respective districts in a community wide general election to a two-year term of office. All elements of the "responsible black leadership" had representation on the "community corporations" board of directors. But, the agencies were controlled by local Democratic Party politicians and political operatives.

A board of directors likewise governed the South Jamaica Steering Committee Inc., with 51 members that represented organizations in the "urban renewal" area and were elected in a community wide contest for a one-year term. The South Steering Committee was an umbrella organization, representing organizations, and funded by the New York State Housing Development Agency (HDA) as a mechanism to generate support for the planned "urban renewal" among the residents in the "redevelopment area" and to coordinate community support for the "urban renewal development" process. The redevelopment of South Jamaica (Jamaica Center) was a multi-million dollar community economic development undertaking. The comprehensive economic development included the removal of the Jamaica El train, and the construction of new subway stations, the construction of York College, commercial and housing development and the relocation of residents displaced by "urban renewal." The "responsible black leadership" with virtually no external challenges from any community based insurgent political force managed these community based quasi-governmental agencies. The "ruling black bulls" can be characterized as the black elite, of the broadening Southeast Queens middle class. Cronyism, nepotism, and paternalism were the means by which things happened and/or didn't happen as the rule.

In the case of the Southeast Queens Community Corporation, only the well connected were able to get their program funded or were able to manage an on going delegate agency of the corporation. In my capacity as a professional organizer for NWRO, I was well aware of government Community Action Agencies, but organizers were strictly admonished by the national leadership, not to interface or interact with anti-poverty and urban renewal programs specifically. Although I was always curious about that admonition, I never pursued it particularly because most of the welfare rights mothers participated on the board of director's level of both organizations. As such I was kept up to date with developments in the organizations as they occurred, and I therefore knew who the players were. Now that I was officially divorced from the foreign political intrigue and stealth perils associated with the "national black movement," I was obliged and comforted to organize locally with a new perspective and sense of urgency. I prepared an outline of a local cooperation initiative to present to black groups in the neighborhood and the groups operating out of the Afro-Disiac Community Cultural Center.

A Black Power Caucus of Queens (BPCQ) was convened at the Afro-Disiac, in order to make a general presentation. Represented was the Nation of the Five Percent, Brothers Art Shop, Egbey Ife, the Green Lantern House, Parent Youth Organization, Insiders Inc., We The People, and a number of other organizations and individuals. I made a presentation to about 35 people, complemented with a flow-chart diagram and some written material photo copied for distribution. The presentation consisted of a general summary of the state of the national Black Power movement and an emphasis on a new formalized local organization and coordination system, dubbed the "concept." The "concept" embodied political organization, black culture, day care services, martial arts, creative arts and theater development. Also included was an economic development component, focused on creating a manufacturing capability to produce dashikis, and other African garments, art and artifacts and Afro hair piks. The establishment of a factory to facilitate the project and a research-and-development committee was initiated to follow up the process. The overriding theme of the "concept" was the need for economic development and independence within the black community. The organizations that were operating programs based in the community cultural center were asked to contribute one quarter of their weekly proceeds to the maintenance and development of the "concept." The 2 ½ hour meeting proceeded, much smoother than expected, yielding success in some areas and not too much success in other areas. After the session I felt a general satisfaction and relief because I was able to communicate the whole concept and action plan, in an uninterrupted and coherent fashion. The most glaring failure was the lack of a budget and the inconsistency among some people to follow up. Nevertheless, I was confident that the few people that were responsible for the work ahead would continue to be steadfast and responsible for the work left to be done. The maintenance of the community center was increasingly becoming a challenge due to the $200.00 per week, that I was no longer receiving as an organizer in the "movement." In addition, the factory and manufacturing project needed funds for a site, equipment, materials etc., before it would be able to generate income. Therefore, generating a budget became a major priority because of the self-reliant feature of the concept. But it soon became clear that the "concept" needed financing for basic survival. Since I was no longer restricted from interfacing with the anti-poverty and urban renewal programs, they were my first stop, in the pursuit of project development funds.

The Southeast Queens Community Corporation became a focal point for the concept because youth development programming became a priority area for grant funding from the Federal Office of Economic Opportunity (OEO). We were attracted by this funding prospect, therefore we began to research the guidelines and explore the feasibility of securing a grant and administering the budget. The opportunity for successfully getting the grant award, according to well-informed sources was remote at best, given the history and pattern of anti-poverty grantee awards. The first obstacle was the Southeast Queens Community Corporation's Board of Directors, because all proposals were required to be submitted throughout the local community corporation, and the corporation had to sign-off on all grantee awards. Technically, all funded programs were classified as a delegate agency of the local community corporation. As such the Southeast Queens Community Corporation was the oversight and administering agency. Another obstacle was the fact that the Afro-Disiac was already politically juxtaposed to the "responsible leadership," and therefore had no political leverage in the relevant political quarters. While we had the expertise to prepare and submit a quality-funding document, and to successfully manage and administer the program and budget, we did not have the political connection with the various leadership elite to secure the funding. A major factor that was in our favor was the recent criticism of the anti-poverty program's shortcomings and political corruption regarding funding awards. Throughout the anti-poverty program citywide, there were revelations of financial malfeasance and political corruption, therefore Federal guidelines got more rigorous to mitigate against political business as usual. In Harlem it was the political corruption scandal associated with the HARYOU ACT anti-poverty program and in Queens it was the Jamaica Community Corporation and Brooklyn and the Bronx had similar scenarios with their anti-poverty programs. The Jamaica Community Corporation restructured and morphed into the Southeast Queens Community Corporation. Mandates and stricter oversight and the prospect of the Southeast Queens Community Corporation being taken into receivership because of internal problems loosened the grip that local politicos had on the funding process. In addition, the recent rebellions around the country, caused youth development programs to be a priority and the Fed's wanted to develop direct lines to youth development.

A significant development in our favor occurred as the Federal Government mandated an open submission in the wake of political corruption revelations. Such was the background environment that surrounded our attempt to get funding for the youth development project that we envisaged. As I began to acquaint myself with the various systems, agencies, guidelines and protocols of the anti-poverty super structure and infrastructure, it became clear to me that the expertise and skills that I had acquired as a legal para-professional and as a staff organizer for NWRO were formidable assets. My skills in proposal writing, project development management, leadership training and community organizing made me competitive with the "responsible black leadership." The ruling black bulls were in control of the community-based organizations that managed the resources targeted to the black community. In response to youth rebellions that characterized the late 1960s, the Federal Office of Economic Opportunity (OEO) designed specific guidelines to attract inner city youth to participate in the design, development and implementation and evaluation of "Youth Development Programs" called project 59. Project 59 according to OEO funding guidelines provided for the direct access of youth and young adults for funding opportunities within the framework of the anti-poverty programs. The black political elite and anti-poverty professionals were unsuccessful in the Herculean attempt to thwart direct access to funding resources by local youth organizations. Consequently against all odds and political prognostication we were awarded the grant to operate a Youth

Development program in the area of economic enterprise development training, under the sponsorship of Parent Youth Organization (PYO). From the out set a controversy developed because it was clear that we managed to thwart the ruling black bulls' crony and patronage system.

The Parent Youth Organization, Youth Development Economic Enterprise Training Center was funded with an annual budget of $88,000.00. The budget was earmarked and line-itemed with practically no flexibility. To complicate the problem the budget modification procedures were a logistical impossibility in real time. Seventy five percent of the budget was for hiring staff. Twenty percent for administrative costs and five percent for supplies and equipment with no wiggle room in between. The anti-poverty program was clearly structured only as a political patronage mechanism that was inimical to the eradication of poverty in the targeted areas. I had previously heard about the built in failures of the anti-poverty program but now I was dealing with them first hand. In order to achieve the goals and objectives of the concept and Parent Youth Organization (PYO), a major deception had to be organized and implemented to accomplish the programmatic aims. In fact, according to our research and development plans, we needed to invest from $7,000.00 to $10,000.00 in cash in order to set up a complete wood working shop with a range of tools for medal work as well. The plan was developed and implemented to maneuver and manipulate the program budget and put the project on line. The process was successfully completed, and PYO opened and started up full throttle to put a real time economic development and entrepreneurial training center in operation. The short-range objective was to get the whole "concept" up and running before our cover was blown, which would inevitably occur.

Our youthful idealism and naiveté was the primary motivating factor that generated a false perception of the ultimate outcome. I believed that at the end of the day, when the facts of the matter were revealed PYO would be commended for creating a self-reliant youth economic development pilot project, feasible for replication in the ghettos around the country. For some reason, I was convinced that once the money checked out, and it was clear that the enterprise was an altruistic demonstration project with no individuals gaining financial advantage, we would be commended. My expectation was that the project and the people that sacrificed to make it happen would receive appropriate recognition. Within a couple of months the program was up and running full blast, operating from two sites. The PYO Community Center and its myriad activities was complimented by a factory located three blocks away that manufactured Afro-piks, African cultural artifacts, and Dashikis. The Afro-piks were made in six different styles and mounted on a framed display board. The display boards were offered to any vendor or retail store interested in carrying the products. Each of the six product styles where packaged in a transparent plastic bag and sealed. One dozen piks were given on consignment along with the display board; this comprised the introductory-offer package. Citywide distribution caught on quickly, and soon we were delivering products in Brooklyn, Manhattan, the Bronx, and Queens. The first phase of our operation plan was completed and the system was operating well. The project developed jobs in manufacturing and distribution for local youth.

The Ville was under going rapid transformation as a result of the spreading drug culture. My brother's generation was hit very hard by the drug culture, but the succeeding generations were virtually annihilated. Virtually all of the generations that lived in the Ville area were impacted. Because of the project grant I was able to hire a few youth from the Ville, and interface them with the youth development process. I tried to interest them in the Afro-pik manufacturing process on a piecework basis, but with little success. They showed up a couple of times, but were not really interested in serious work, only fun, or fast money. From time to time they would show up on Friday or Saturday evening during the disco-dance program. The parities and the social events were the extent to which they were interested in interacting with the community development program. They were already mesmerized by the drug culture and under ground economy. Sometimes my brother Lewis and his peers would show up at the center for social reasons. I would on occasion have to take issue with my brother and his best friend, Pres, because they were obviously high from heroin. Pres and my brother were the tallest people in the disco; therefore it was easy to see when they were going down into a heavy nod. One Friday night, a few of my brother's friends showed up during a disco dance at the center. It was Calvin, a former schoolmate and a basketball teammate of my brothers on Andrew Jackson High School's team.

Calvin came in with a full two-car entourage that included three young men and five young ladies. Calvin and his main man had just bought two brand-new Oldsmobile Tornados. Calvin and crew had become fascinated with robbing banks. At this point they were on their way down south to North Carolina to visit some friends, basketball stars on their college campus. I led my brother and his friends to my basement office so they could talk, and I could get rid of the spectacle of six giants leaning nodding over as if in a contest to see who can go the lowest without falling. The young ladies decided to stay upstairs and enjoy the disco dancing. *What a drag,* I said to myself, *to see all of these potential college basketball stars wasting their lives on drugs, crime and the underground economy.* I resolved not to be too heavy with the political pressure on this night as it was useless. I'll just observe tonight. My resolution did not hold too long, however, because Calvin and one of his boys got into a controversy. Calvin's boy wanted to let the ladies ride with them all the way to North Carolina. Calvin wanted only to drive the ladies as far as Washington, DC where they had intended to stop anyway, and once there, give the ladies some money to fly back to New York. Calvin said, "I got some other hammers in North Carolina; we got to take advantage of the southern hospitality, man;" then they all started laughing without end. The substance of the controversy was too much for me to handle so I broke the scene up and required them to leave the premises because they were defiling the environment.

Without question, PYO's youth development program was the brightest star in the sky of the Southeast Queens Community Corporations delegate agencies. The program made a unique mark on all levels of the anti-poverty structure, during the many activities and meetings that were conducted. All systems were going, as we approached our fifth month of funding. Then the grant funds came to an abrupt halt due to the "Judas principle." It seems as though the PYO program Director Ronny, made a complaint to the management agency, the Community Development Agency (CDA). Ronnie complained that his paycheck was always late because of the way that the PYO Board of 'Directors were dispersing the funds. As Ronny told me later, he was promised a better job by a manager at CDA if he (Ronny) could provide damaging information about the PYO program. In the wake of Ronny's complaint the program funds were suspended immediately, and information was provided to the city Department of Investigation (DOI) to determine if laws were broken and if criminal prosecution was in order. PYO was caught totally by surprise by Ronny's action. I knew that Ronny drank too much alcohol sometimes, but neither I nor anyone else was aware of any grievance he had. Ronny was the son-in-law of Mrs. Archery, as he was married to her eldest daughter Loraine. I hired Ronny as a personal favor for Mrs. Archery, although she never requested that I find a position for him. I was aware that Ronny had recently lost a job and needed employment. I did it because I had a lot of respect and admiration for Mrs. Archery, and I appreciated the fact that she introduced me to the welfare rights movement.

I knew that she was just as surprised, hurt and disappointed at this development as I was. Nevertheless, at this point the imperative was survival and we focused intently in that area. We were preparing for the eventual lost of funding but we were not prepared for the city investigation and political process. Ultimately the process did much to mature my youthful idealism and political sophistication. On the local political level, the "ruling bulls" were rejoicing, as they envisaged a worst case scenario and some people would be going to jail. There was great speculation relative to our fiscal malfeasance and criminal activity, since we were so young impressionable and inexperienced. Likewise the city agency officials and black responsible leadership expected a major expose involving stolen money and black radical and revolutionary activity. There was even speculation that guns would be found on the premises when the program was finally taken into receivership. However, a core group within PYO new that the records would reveal no financial malfeasance or individual enrichment. We knew that time and the truth were on our side.

For the first six months, the Department of Investigation took sworn statements and utterly intimidated everyone that knew me in my residential neighborhood, as well as the community center neighborhood. They tried to shake down what they believed was hidden in the eaves of the organization's records, vis-à-vis, financial malfeasants. After six months of intense scrutiny and investigation it was clear that there was no fiscal malfeasance, however the investigation was kept open at the request of the local black "responsible leadership." The objective in keeping the investigation open was to maintain some political leverage on me as well as to keep my organization destabilized. In the interim, the program continued to operate with self-reliant success. The factory generated survival subtenants. The day care center that was operating under the direction of my mother was healthy, and other activities that the Afro-Disiac facilitated continued with relative success. In spite of the programmatic success of the PYO project, it was clear that the "responsible black leadership" wanted us to disappear. In fact they were rigorously trying to bring about our demise in a cowardly and clandestine manner. Accordingly, the Board of Directors of the Southeast Queens Community Corporation was preparing to seize our equipment and take the program into "receivership." Correspondence between the Executive Director of the community corporation, Dr. Griffith, and the Commissioner of the Community Development Agency (CDA), Major Owens, and David Billings, the Chairman of the Council Against Poverty

(CAP), was brought to my attention verifying their intention. A dynamic plan had to be hatched and implemented quickly. I talked the situation over with some associates and a plan was developed to take direct militant action against the Southeast Queens Community Corporation, forthwith. A letter was drafted to the staff of the community corporation that there was going to be direct action taken against the Corporation and requested that they go home on a specific day. Sufficient copies were made and the following morning the plan was put in motion. Two youth entered the Corporation premises and distributed the notices throughout the building. Ten minutes after the messengers exited the building, about fifty youth entered the Corporation then proceeded to turn over the desks and chairs on all three floors of the building. Staff people were politely asked to remove themselves from the danger and to please pardon the necessary interruption. The tactic was effective but it was only a part of a more ambitious strategy to impact the Southeast Queens Community Corporation, and "responsible black leadership."

While the strategy was in place to address our difficulties with the Southeast Queens Community Corporation, and the broader citywide anti-poverty program, we began to engage the South Jamaica Steering Committee Inc. PYO was approached to work in coalition with another group, the Alliance of Muslims and Christians headed by Hasan Hakim. Hasan introduced the situation involving the South Jamaica Steering Committee, to me. The short of the story was that the multi-million dollar redevelopment of South Jamaica (Jamaica Center) was in process under the umbrella of the South Jamaica Steering Committee. The "responsible black leadership" within the Committee united and defeated the insurgent community-based leadership that emerged and won the previous general election to the Board of Directors of the Steering Committee. Hasan Hakim and the Alliance of Muslims and Christians were members of the defeated group and they were at this point seeking our support (PYO), to help them defeat the "official political clique" at the next annual election. I met with Hasan and Fred Oliver, the former chairman of the South Jamaica Steering Committee after they were defeated by the previous leadership. The "responsible" black leadership was again in control of the South Jamaica Steering Committee, under the chairmanship of Dr. Canute Bernard. Now defeated, Hasan and other former leaders of the Steering Committee needed to engage the help of some young troops to help regain power.

We ultimately agreed to work in coalition with the group to regain control of the Steering Committee at the next election. I subsequently met with the core group, and from that point PYO participated in the ongoing strategic planning process to win a majority of the seats in the next election. Our basic strategy was to provide information to the target area population in order to demonstrate that current "responsible black leadership" had already cut deals with the politicians and powers that be, and was withholding important and beneficial information from the impacted community residents, in the so-called pit area. The other component of the strategy was to convince the present Steering Committee, minority opposition that we had the manpower, expertise and operational base from which to launch a successful campaign. PYO had an operational base as well as a successful activist reputation. We had the physical facility, manpower, typewriters, copiers, mimeograph machines, telephones and all of the nuances associated with organizing. Hasan Hakim, published a monthly magazine, (Community Broadcast) therefore we had what it would take for a successful insurgent community empowerment campaign. Although this was PYO's maiden voyage into electoral community politics, we were uniquely prepared as a result of my professional experience as an organizer in the national movement, in addition to my training as a legal para-professional. I was confident of my political skills and well aware that many of the political hacks in Jamaica Queens, had few skills, little ambition and motivation, and generally did a poor job. Their positioning, and claim to prominence was largely due to political cronyism.

Following the success of the direct militant action against the Southeast Queens Community Corporation, we evaluated the feasibility of taking direct action against the Community Development Agency (CDA) and the Council Against Poverty (CAP). According to what I learned from Frank O'Rourke, a Director at the Human Resources Administration (HRA) PYO's problems were the local black political leadership, "If Councilman Spigner went to David Billings (CAP) and advocated on your behalf, your problems with the city would be over." What Frank said to me confirmed my suspicions regarding the intent of the "responsible black leadership" towards PYO. After my meeting with Frank, I considered that there might be a technical possibility that PYO and the staff had a contractual right to the balance of the contract grant award. Since there was a finding by the Department of Investigation of no fiscal malfeasance on the part of the PYO Board of Directors. We decided to go forward with plans to move against CDA and CAP and attempt to receive the balance of the contractual award, which amounted to about $35,000.00. We could not get the local politicians to work with us therefore we had no other choice but to take matters into our own hands. This was the general consensus, and we had nothing to lose under the circumstances. A plan was devised to take control of the offices of CDA and CAP, and demand the balance of the grant. The plan was to enter the building located at 349 Broadway and take over the offices of the Council Against Poverty located on the ground floor. This was achieved by marching in 50 children from the PYO day care center, and conduct games with the children in the premises. This first phase was executed without a hitch with my mother directing the operation with about seven or eight assistants. I executed the next phase with about twenty brothers upstairs to the offices of the commissioner of CDA, Major Owens. We entered the commissioner's office and pealed off flanking two walls in the office. Our entrance interrupted the business at hand, and the commissioner's guests left the office immediately. The commissioner stood up and grabbed the telephone all in one motion. The commissioner was on the phone with officials at HRA, and shortly there after we received a check for $35,000.00, which represented the balance of the grant award. While we were elated with the victory, thoughts relative to the battle that lay ahead of us were sobering. Ultimately, a battle for control of the Southeast Queens Community Corporation would have to take place if the grassroots community and at-risk youth community were to get access to services and resources that were targeted to their community.

The election campaign to the board of directors of the South Jamaica Steering Committee progressed very well. When the Honest Ballot Association certified the election, our team had won two thirds of the seats thereby giving us a decisive victory and margin of control. Melvin King was installed as Chairman of the Board of Directors, Hasan Hakim was appointed the Public Relations Chairman, and I was appointed chairman of the Multi-Service Committee, and so on. The work of the new Steering Committee leadership was underway, with the greatest of dispatch. The Multi-Service Committee had a broad scope of responsibility in terms of the redevelopment of South Jamaica. The construction of a multi-service center on Linden Blvd. was a component of the committee's mandate. But more immediately some new health service district lines were in the process of being gerrymandered, that would minimize the access to health services in the poorest areas. The previous chairman of the South Jamaica Steering Committee, Dr. Canute Bernard was at the time also the Commissioner of the Comprehensive Health Planning Agency. The health-planning agency, gerrymandered the health service district lines in such a way that compromised and minimized the health service delivery and resources directed to the "urban renewal" area.

After a close examination and the convening of public hearings on the matter. The Multi-service Committee, made a formal recommendation to the Steering Committee, Board of Directors to take corrective action. The Multi-service Committee recommended that the Steering Committee Board of Directors formally enjoin the New York State Comprehensive Health Planning Agency from imposing the gerrymandered health district lines on the target community. The Board voted to confirm the recommendation and filed a law suit to enforce the resolution against the state agency. The Steering Committee argued that insufficient information was disseminated to the impacted community in the process of coming to a final determination on the district lines. In the course of the ensuing controversy other events were occurring, particularly the National black Political Convention, scheduled for Gary Indiana in the Spring of 1972. This Black Power conference became a focus as Delegates to attend the convention had to be nominated and elected in an open community-wide election.

The Jamaica NAACP to a large extent controlled the nomination and election process for delegates to the Black Power Conference, as the meetings were conducted at their venue on Linden Blvd, near the intersection of Farmers Blvd. The process was not opened to the community at large until the eleventh hour, so we had to prepare on an emergency basis to get enough people there to insure that we were represented as Queens delegates. Within days of the election we prepared ourselves to win some seats to attend the Gary Convention, in the context of the official Queens delegation. Jim Heylinger, a member of the NAACP, and operative of the "responsible black leadership" was elected and voted Chairman of the Queens Delegation. We managed to win seven seats; therefore we had a significant presence at the convention and our youth representative, Shaka Zulu, became a Vice Chair of the Delegation. The convention was indeed momentous and had far reaching political implications and impact, in positive, negative and revolutionary terms. The work of the Black Power convention was intense, noteworthy, healthy, educational, and was a political milestone. Although the romance and drama of the occasion tended to overshadow some of the substantive achievements. Some of the fundamental achievements that continue to be over shadowed are:

1. The interface that developed between some responsible black leadership and various elements of the Black Power movement.

2. A redefinition of Black Power in terms of political and economic empowerment.
3. The focus on local electoral politics and the control of community-based service institutions.

These were among some of the positive developments that resulted from the National black Political Convention. The Gary convention closed on a note of community empowerment and charged the delegates with political task of seizing control of local, community-based institutions. This was in sharp contrast to the integrationist and nationalist ideological dichotomy that was articulated by Roy Innis of the Congress of Racial Equality (CORE), and people like Jetu Weiusi of the East Cultural Center and Abu Badeka from Brooklyn. Parent Youth Organization had already begun its campaign to control local institutions and were looking forward to bigger and better acquisitions, in the context of the objectives of the Gary Convention.

The Parent Youth Organization's, day care center and the Afro-pik manufacturing factory were financing these political objectives and maneuvers. This caused some strain on the organization therefore we needed to devise a financing plan to relieve some of the organizational strain and provide a budget for the ultimate goal. We pursued a way to facilitate the community election campaign to take control of the board of directors of the Southeast Queens Community Corporation. The Youth Service Agency, (YSA) a program of the Youth Board of New York City became the object of our attention, as recommended by an agency professional Mr. James Bland a PYO board member. YSA and the agencies of the anti-poverty program were individual and autonomous entities of each other. While there existed no direct adversarial relationship between the two New York City agencies, the similarities of the two missions overlapped in some areas sometime, causing organizational friction. As a result of being both burned and spurned by the anti-poverty program in the face of a successful community based multi-faceted program, we felt that we had the necessary and appropriate credentials to engage the Commissioner of YSA. Ted Gross was the Commissioner of YSA, and our intelligence indicated that there were open YBRI employment slots available in the YSA budget. We prepared a presentation and program outline and identified a cadre of eight people to pull off the plan. A sit-in was staged at the office of Ted Gross, for the purpose of arranging a meeting with him. The operation took all day and it was not until about 4 P.M. that it was confirmed that he would be in the office and we could get an audience. At 4:45 P.M., Ted Gross walked into YSA dressed as provocative as ever, wearing emerald high heel platform shoes with a bronze Suede mini-knapsack slung over his left shoulder. The presentation team included Jabar, Barbara, Smitty Billy and me. After being seated in a semi-circle around his desk and exchanging barbs, I opened my presentation. About thirty seconds into the presentation Ted Gross interrupted.

He (Ted) said, "Okay, guys, I don't want you to get too heavy," then he told his Secretary to send Jim Nolan into the office. When Jim Nolan entered the office, Ted continued, "Jim, take these honorable people into your office and help them with their program."

We moved the meeting to Jim Nolan's office, and after a brief meeting we negotiated a deal for $10,000.00 in cash and five YBRI job slots at 100.00 per week and a part time Secretary slot.

The deal was a major shot in the arm and it provided the basic budget for the up coming campaign to run for the board of directors of the Southeast Queens Community Corporation. There was a difference of opinion between my group and the members of the coalition that now controlled the Steering Committee. The Steering Committee group did not see the utility of getting bogged down in the wrestling match for control of the anti-poverty program. The inside scoop was that our Steering Committee coalition partners were not confident that we could pull off the coup, plus they were essentially satisfied with the fact that they controlled the Steering Committee and had a role in the redevelopment of South Jamaica. I understood their reluctance to get involved in the infamous anti-poverty dynamic. One of the differences between my group and the Steering Committee group was the generation gap. I was the only young adult in their inner circle and planning process. In addition they had no vested interest in the anti-poverty program, as we did. Parent Youth Organization had a vested interest in the Southeast Queen Community Corporation. We viewed ourselves in the context of the "black youth political vanguard," and it was our responsibility to challenge the black political ruling middle class for the control of the community resources and we were prepared to meet that challenge.

The time had come for the area wide election to the board of Directors of the Southeast Queens Community Corporation. We undertook to engage the community election process on our own, with only our internal resources, and newly acquired budget. There were many issues that put this objective out of the realm of practicality. Not the least of which was the vast geographical area, and the associated logistical challenges. The target area was about five times the target of the South Jamaica Steering Committee. Nevertheless we initiated the process and fielded thirty-five candidates, five people in each of the seven election areas. We realized when we went into the process that we were long shots and under dogs at best. Yet, the spirit was high and we got substantial voluntary support at a high volume level. The whole of Southeast Queens community did a double take when the news broke that a majority of our candidates won seats to the community corporation's board of directors. We were in fact shocked at the scope of the victory. The responsible black leadership initially thought our victory was a rumor. They were stunned to a drunken stupor, when the results of the election were certified. We had done the impossible, but little did we know about the nature of the battle ahead. The size of our victory made the idea of me running for Chairman of the Board a practical consideration. Political maneuvering and membership polling staked out the final contestants for the Board Chairman. I was a finalist along with Jim Heylinger. When the final vote was counted I was announced as the new Chairman of the Southeast Queens Community Corporation having won with a margin of one vote. I immediately pulled my hands out of the pockets of my blue velvet dashiki with my gavel in my right hand and said, "I now call the meeting of the Board of Director to order."

Within the next ninety days, the South Jamaica Steering Committee held its bi-annual election and our coalition won a second term to office. Now both elections were over and the people had spoken. We were willing to share power with our adversaries for the purpose of developing a broad based comprehensive community development approach on behalf of all of the people in the target areas. As new leadership, and confirmed leadership respectively, we made it a point to reach out to our election opponents as well as the black responsible leadership, to demonstrate our intent to build a broad base leadership coalition. Unfortunately, our political overtures were more politically naive than astute, and our leadership was about to be undermined in viscous and malicious ways. The "responsible black leadership" became obsessed with destabilizing and removing our leadership from the Southeast Queens Community Corporation and the South Jamaica Steering Committee. Since our leadership was legitimate, by way of a community wide election the "responsible black leadership" therefore had to use other than legitimate means to remove us. Dirty tricks, political and legal maneuvers, false rumor and innuendo became their tactics.

The assault was relentless and operatives were enlisted and volunteered from all quarters. The opposing forces on the Southeast Queens Community

Corporation board of directors were in a feeding frenzy, and other opponents to my leadership came from out of the woodwork. Malik Kimani a board member and publisher of a local newspaper lead the charge with a scathing two-page column entitled the "Queens Gate." The "Queens Gate" had a special marketing feature because it was generally known that I was registered a Republican, perhaps the only one on the community corporation and Steering Committee board of directors. Following the escalating controversy associated with President Nixon and the break in at the Watergate Hotel, I was fair game for the allegations of political intrigue. I was twenty-nine years old and Malik was around my age, give or take a couple of years. Malik was a dubious character in my view. I met him about four years earlier, when he was a member of the leadership of the Democratic Liberation Party (DLP). The DLP rented the Afro-Disiac, for political rallies from time to time. On one particular occasion an incident occurred during a DPL rally that brought the Police Department to the Afro-Disiac. As one of the proprietors of the center I confronted the police officers and outlined the nature of the Center and the activity currently underway. The police officers left the premises and the rally resumed without incident. Malik climbed on the stage, and interrupted the proceedings as the police officers left and delivered a lengthy monologue. Malik extolled and complemented me and the way in which I handled the potentially volatile situation, and impressed on the audience that the incident was an example of how inter-organizational coordination and support among Black Power groups was essential for black liberation. There was little doubt that Malik fancied himself as a leader of his people. Not too long after this event The DLP experienced some political and legal problems, and many of the members were arrested and some went to jail. There was quite a bit of intrigue around his (Malik's) disappearance and now he was back as a newspaper publisher, leading the political charge on the community corporation board of directors. I could not help myself, so I confronted him privately and challenged him to a physical duel, for which he declined with a cowardly disposition.

The "Queens Gate" was a fabulous political fiction story and it was compounded by the activities of the Vice Chairman of the Board, Mrs. Ruth Giles, who was initially a confidant elder, and associate on the Steering Committee. Ruth Giles was a sharp minded and devious senior citizen of sixty-five years plus and new the anti-poverty program inside out. About six years earlier, at a Board meeting of the Southeast Queens Community Corporation Ruth Giles who was vying for control of the agency had a heart attack, following a vociferous debate with other board members including Mrs. Cynthia Jenkins and Ms. Thelma Miller and others. After the heart attack she retired from active community political life, having lost her seat on the community corporation. However, during our first attempt to win control of the South Jamaica Steering Committee we effectively pulled her out of mothballs. Ruth Giles had a wealth of experience and knowledge about the community organizations and the personalities involved; therefore she was initially a valuable asset. I appealed to Mrs. Giles to join with the Parent Youth Organization, in our quest to seize political power since she was savvy and new all of the players. In fact Ruth was the only member of the Steering Committee coalition that supported our political move on the Southeast Queens Community Corporation, and she joined the effort. Therefore, from the out set we were allies and confidants. However, when I emerged as the strongest candidate for the chairmanship, a breach developed in our relationship. The problem developed as I realized Ruth wanted to be the Chairman of the Corporation. Her argument was that I was too young and inexperienced; she wanted me to defer my candidacy to her and be the Vice Chairman. During this process with Ruth and me, I became convinced that her ambition to be the Chairman was based on her idea of reconciling her history at the Corporation in the context of passed events. When I agreed only to support her for the Vice Chairman only, her loyalty began to shift and she in fact supported my opponent Jim Heylinger for the Chairmanship. Ruth made a deal to support Jim and she turned pale when I was victorious by one vote.

Immediately following my victory, Ruth Giles started to work. As the Vice Chairman she had access to my desk and files. Ruth made photocopies of everything that was in my desk, whether it was pertaining to the business of the community corporation or of a personal or private nature. In particular she copied checks totaling four thousand dollars, that were paid to the order of the Queens Council for Economic Development, Inc. The Economic Development group was formulated by Hasan Hakim, and me and had no connection to the South Jamaica Steering Committee, or the Southeast Queens Community Corporation. Nevertheless, the photocopies of the checks in conjunction with the abounding "Queens Gate" rumor and innuendo sparked a barn fire of speculation and legitimate curiosity. Ruth Giles went on a spectacular offensive. She challenged every action and expenditure being made during my leadership, and told me in no uncertain terms that she was going to replace me if it was the last thing that she did. She accused me of taking "unilateral actions," making money as a result of my position as Chairman, while deceiving the Board of Directors. The "Queens Gate" story fueled the blistering false rumor and innuendo assault, which was under scored by the photocopies of four checks for $1,000.00 each. Due to the rumor and innuendo, the Queens Council for Economic Development was seen as a phantom organization designed to veil a financial deception. I appealed to the Secretary of the Board of Directors, Viola Plummer to impose her dominant personality into the fray to neutralize Ruth and to perhaps mediate the controversy in an orderly fashion. The situation only escalated when rumors began to circulate that I was about to be indicted, for activities associated with PYO.

Sure enough, on the following week I received the notice to appear before the Grand Jury in Queens County. The indictment was based on my activities three years earlier as the Chairman of the Parent Youth Organization. The City Department of Investigation issued a final report, suggesting the possibility of fiscal malfeasance. The report was given to the Grand Jury, and I subsequently gave testimony to the Grand Jury and an indictment followed. I convened a special meeting of the Southeast Queens Board of Directors and submitted my resignation in order to concentrate on defending myself in court. The assault from South Jamaica Steering Committee angle was just as relentless, vociferous and covert. Finally, a minority report emanated from the multi-service committee, which I chaired that called into question the procedure that resulted in the law suit against the Comprehensive Health Planning Agency. The minority report was some how miraculously transformed by a sophisticated parliamentary procedural maneuver that resulted in the formation of a "Committee of the Whole." The "Committee of the Whole" maneuver had the effect of suspending the initial action against the health agency. Finally the Honorable Judge William Booth was interfaced into the situation to mediate between the aggrieved factions in an informal and unofficial capacity. The end result was the destabilization and discrediting of the community-based leadership of the Southeast Queens Community Corporation and the South Jamaica Steering Committee. Hence, all future community based insurgent political activism was nipped in the bud. This scenario was, in fact, a microcosm of the broader citywide and national assault on the black youth and student movement.

The indictment put my personal freedom and family situation in a critical position to say the least. The paradox however was indeed perplexing, as my adversaries were the ruling black political elite. On one hand we were engaged in a process attempting to realize legitimate aspirations within the black community as a result of systematic white personal and institutional racism. Within the framework of this struggle, overt and covert operations in the context of conventional and unconventional warfare was conducted to thwart the black youth movement and keep the black community destabilized. Concomitantly, the most insidious adversary in the process is the ruling black political elite. As I reflected on my current predicament, vis-à-vis, a youthful "political outsider." Hence a target for political destruction. I wept for those youthful idealists who had already been taken out for the count, and pondered the dubious outcome of my fate. The energy of the black youth and young adults in the urban centers and inner cities of America, continued to be obscured and undermined by machinations authored by the black political ruling elite, as well as the "system." The assault was a double whammy, from within and without, each factor as lethal as the other. There existed no mentoring process to cultivate and discipline the enthusiastic youth and young adults of the 1960s and 70s, therefore their vitality and commitment to change the conditions of political and economic dependency was methodically short-circuited.

There continues to be an unspoken political fratricide that pervades the black community's landscape. The prospect of inter-generational cooperation is undermined by the ongoing adversarial relationship between the ruling black elite and the grassroots youth. The subtle fratricide is complicated by the economic class distinction in the black community. The dichotomy between the black "middle class" and the poor sustains and perpetuates the conditions that plague the black community at large, as we have become our worst enemy. In fact improving the inter-generational communication across economic and educational lines, outside of the conventional political lines may be a good beginning in reordering the extended family infrastructure. However, the responsible black leadership has relegated the issues to external causes and remedies, while in clinical political denial about the malignant internal dilemma. Studies continue to abound relative to social pathologies of the disappearing black man and family, and the black ruling elite continues to undermine youthful insurgent political leadership and community based electoral activism, dynastic fashion. As a consequence there is no process of apprenticeship or "rights of passage" available to the overwhelming masses of poor black youth who are at risk.

Notwithstanding the myriad factors that conspire to undermine the upward mobility of the black community, black males in particular are the primary solution. Changing the spots on a leopard, vis-à-vis, changing the hearts and spirit of the racist bigots and institutionalized racism, is an exercise in futility and politically diversionary. The fundamental solution to the crisis in black America is an internal cathartic process in the context of the black community. Although there are many political risks associated with criticizing the black political ruling elite, no earthly entity is beyond creative and constructive criticism. The basic facts are clear; the black political leadership in America does not have a practical strategy for political, economic and social development of the ravaged broad masses of poor black people. Beyond the rhetoric of moving the poor to the "middle class" there is not a solvent plan or expectation. Too often the political dialogue and rhetoric is superficial and partisan, ignoring the fact that electoral politics is a tool to be utilized with skill, tact and sophistication in order to achieve a defined result. The black political leadership is directly responsible for the low level of voter registration, participation, and application. The short span of popularity that many black politicians and leaders enjoy with their black constituents is due largely to the bankruptcy of the partisan political dialogue. The African American herd of voters is perennially led to the slaughter by the political Judas goats, which maintain relative control by deception and sleight of hand.

CHAPTER 4

Parent Youth Organization et al., took a devastating political hit, and the recovery seemed questionable at best. The direct impact of the political blow to my organization and family as a result of this situation was enormous and profound. We were already experiencing financial problems because I did not sufficiently distinguish my family responsibility from my professional and organizational responsibility. In fact the two entities tended to merge in my own mind. The psychological and emotional impact was just as devastating as the financial prognosis was grim. I had to relocate my mother and sisters to St. Croix, in the United States Virgin Islands to escape the imposing economic and political pressures and to reconstitute their lives at least temporarily. My mother was able to land a position in her new incarnation as an elementary school teacher, in St. Croix V.I. I was now facing virtual homelessness, due to the financing demands for my legal defense. The fact that my mother, sisters, and brother were in the Virgin Islands was a great psychological relief. I did not want them to take any direct political hits, or see me absorb any more punishment. The organizational operations and the "concept" were devastated as well. Other than several confidants, everyone scurried, scattered or took advantage of what was salvageable in the ruins of the "concept." Internal deterioration of the concept had started about a year prior to my indictment. Some of the groups that were renting the Afro-Disiac facility for their program began to renege on their financial commitment. There was wide spread theft of products from the factory, and accounts receivable began missing money. There were rivalries and attempted political coups, of organizational components. At one point I was shot at by Billy Heath a tenant who lived in the apartment of the factory premises, as a result of a peripheral rivalry, with Elly Brown, proprietor of the Brother's Art Shop on Linden Blvd.

By the time that I was indicted and I needed financial support for my legal defense, the financial capacity of the organization had been totally undermined. There was a copycat factory set up in the basement of the house of a local resident, manufacturing the same six Afro-pik style as the concept. One of our key people was responsible for providing the technical assistance to help establish the copycat factory. Therefore, I had to borrow funds in order to be bailed out of jail, following the indictment. Many of the "responsible black leadership" were generally about in the same generation of my father, but there were no father figures or images among them. I was perplexed. I asked myself, why couldn't they see that I am a young man trying to make a contribution to the greater good? Why do they see me as their enemy? Why doesn't one of them pull me aside and give me some wise elderly advice? I was in deed perplexed by their passion and the lengths taken to insure that I was out for the count in the political game. After working through the personal hurt and the rejection of my elders, the "responsible black leadership," I began to appreciate the magnitude of the leadership deficit in the black community. Apart from their dynastic and partisan objectives and obligations, there was no interface with the neighborhood and community youth. No mentorship mechanisms, apprenticeship opportunities, or open lines of communications between the generations. The so-called "generation gap" in the context of the black community was more accurately termed generational isolation.

The lack of a structured interface between the generations in the black community accounted for the estrangement between the generic civil rights movement, and the Black Power movement respectively. During the 1950s when I was growing up, there was a family and neighborhood extended-family infrastructure that interfaced the generations and fostered inter-generational activity. The informal extended family infrastructure as well as the nuclei family structure that was the backbone of black survival up to the 1950s, was devastated by drugs and social welfare policy, unemployment and underemployment. Except for the children of the ruling black elite and well placed black middle class, the broad masses of black poor are locked out of the process and are kept out by the ruling black bull elites. This "black responsible leadership" with their organizations: religious, social, educational, and civic etc. embody the only remaining opportunity to constructively engage the youth, but they continue to estrange youthful energy, without providing a channel to maturation. My disillusionment with the responsible black leadership and their level of political sophistication was balanced by my disillusionment with the political sophistication among many of my peers and generation. Although I was profoundly disillusioned, it was clear to me that the major question was how I was going to survive and generate income.

Getting back on line financially was a necessary exercise that was made a little easier with the help of some friends. Bob Handman, the 1199 union representative, who was on the South Jamaica Steering Committee and a member of the Communist Party, Mr. Philip Price, the brother in-law of Hasan Hakim, and Dr Earl Johnson a personal friend were among several people that went beyond lip service. Earl Johnson introduced me to a colleague of his that had a potential employment opportunity. Apparently there was a position of Project Director for the Sickle Cell Disease Education and Screening Clinic, located at Queens Hospital Center, Affiliation of Long Island Jewish, and Hillside Medical Center. Dr. Earl Johnson was a colleague and neighbor of Dora McBarnett, the Coordinator, of the Hematology Department at the Hospital Center, and she was a key player in the hiring process. I applied for the position and a couple of interviews later I was hired. After reviewing whether the sickle-cell program was meeting its contractual obligation, and meeting with the contract-compliance people at the US Department of Health Education and Welfare, the funding agency, I outlined a process to improve the program operation. I was in fact inspired and invigorated by the significance and scope of the project. The Sickle Cell Disease Education and Screening Clinic was a demonstration project with twenty-four similar projects in at risk communities around the country. The project seemed tailor-made for my skills and expertise, and it was an excellent transitional opportunity with a therapeutic benefit. The inside scoop on the politics of the project was that the sponsors of the program, Long Island Jewish Hospital-Hillside Medical Center, wanted to keep the program out of the political patronage system of the ruling black elite, and maximize the opportunity for programmatic success. The political scenario that I was in the process of recovery from, positioned me opposite to the local political clubhouse gang, and with the expertise and skills to manage the project. Accordingly, the sponsors did not want to compromise the effectiveness of the program by surrendering the employment positions to the black political elite. Hence, someone black was needed who knew their way around the political court, and someone who could handle the type of political intrigue that would be designed to challenge the control of the program. Obviously, I was a proven candidate.

The program focused on improving the health education and health care delivery system in the black community therefore it provided me with the sense of fulfillment as I was making a contribution to the greater good. The program also enabled me to de-emphasize my heretofore primarily political imperative and focus on my personal and economic situation. The stability of the employment situation enabled me to appreciate the education my recent experience with political hardball had provided me. My bumps and bruises were still in the process of healing and I was not sure how to refocus my political activism, if at all. During the four years that I was the Manager of the clinic, it expanded one hundred and fifty percent. When I began employment, the annual budget was $100,000.00 and when I left the program was funded at a level of $250,000.00. Concomitantly, the target area increased from the borough of Queens to include the whole of New York City. The project developed health education and genetic counseling protocols, and I was published in a major health periodical, *JAMA*. My political activism was null and void at this point, although I maintained some essential contacts. In practical political terms I was able to thwart the wrath of the responsible black political leadership, by landing a plumb employment situation beyond the pail of their control. Consequently, the general perception was that I had a political support infrastructure that came to my rescue.

The employment provided me with a constructive professional environment in which to reflect, rebound and regroup. My mother, and siblings were getting along pretty well in the Virgin Islands. My mother was a schoolteacher and now taught the second grade. My frequent visits had a special significance because my family was doing fine, and the international travel that I was exposed to was providing me with a holistic world view. However this particular visit to St. Croix had a special meaning because I was there at the specific request of my mother. I hesitated to speculate as to why she wanted me to make a special trip, as it could be virtually anything. I knew that she was very happy there. What could it be? Maybe she wanted to get remarried or something. She made arrangements for me to come to her school to see her class and meet some people etc. After a beautiful afternoon, we started to her house, and she was driving. It was a typical bright and pleasant Virgin Island day and I could look into her eyes and see how happy she was, as I could not get a word in edgewise. It made me so happy to see her like this and she was describing every little nuance of everything. It was wonderful; I hadn't seen her like this since the death of my father. She smiled broadly as tears of joy rushed down her plump high checks. Then the expression on her face began to change and I realized in the gut of my stomach that something else was happening. After she got it all together she made me aware that she had been diagnosed twice and it was confirmed that she had stomach cancer and surgery was required. They did not have adequate medical facilities there in St. Croix; therefore she had to come back to New York City for the Surgery. My mind was completely washed out and hung to dry. Without thinking I said, "Well, Mommy, fortunately I am working in a hospital, and I can insure that you get the best medical care. As soon as I get back to New York, I will make arrangements and get you to back as soon as possible." The rest of my visit was over shadowed by the specter of more family grief.

The most pressing challenge was to get suitable living quarters for my mother and sisters. As a stopgap measure, I rented a two-bedroom apartment in a newly developed complex, on Union Turnpike in Forest Hills Queens, New York. After about six months we moved into a three bedroom cooperative apartment in Rockaway Beach, NY, a pleasant environment with a significant senior citizens population. My position as Project Manager at a health care facility was a significant asset. The initial diagnosis was confirmed and all professional opinions recommended immediate surgery to remove the malignant stomach tumors. My mother and I discussed the situation thoroughly. The prognosis for a full recovery was grim. She understood, albeit painful, that she was not likely to return to St. Croix, and teach school again, although we remained prayerful. She said, "I will accept my fate as it comes, Vincent, but you know that I still believe in miracles and the power of prayer." The completed surgery did not yield any new information to alter our general expectation. She was now under going monthly injections of chemotherapy. The chemo treatments were devastating to her physically, emotionally, and psychologically. She experienced extreme loss of hair, the nausea associated with that treatment required a two-week recovery period. For the first two weeks after the treatment she was not able to eat anything, as nothing would stay in her stomach. Her lack of eating had an immediate effect on her weight. She was losing weight fast. The two weeks following the two weeks of nausea was traumatic as she prepared to repeat the cycle. After a few months, she was able to get some relief from the nausea because of a remedy suggested by a family friend. It was suggested to her to smoke a marijuana cigarette during her bouts with nausea. Initially she had a major problem accepting the suggestion. Finally she relented and the treatment apparently had some impact. My mother and I got even closer under the circumstances and we talked about many things including the planning of her funeral.

At one point when we were planning her funeral, she looked in the mirror at her face and began laughing hysterically, she said, "Look at my face; it's disgusting. You better make sure my casket remains closed." Continuing to laugh she concluded, "I prefer that people remember me as I used to look. I look terrible now."

Finally, my mother decided that she wanted to stop with the chemo treatment and said, "Let God's will be done." About two years after my mother returned to New York City she died as a result of the stomach cancer. She was fifty-three years old. May God bless and rest her soul.

My mother suffered a great deal physically due to her illness, and died in a frail and grotesque physical condition. But her strength of character, mind, personality and spirit eclipsed her obvious physical condition. She was just like my father, who at the tender age of 33 years, looked his mortality straight in the eye and walked right through death's door without a blink. My mother's death was followed by an overwhelming sense of loss, relief, then release. I have always admired my parents in life, and I likewise have great admiration for the dignity they maintained and demonstrated in death. During the traumatic and dramatic ordeal with my mother's health situation, my professional relationship with the Director of Hematology had deteriorated significantly. In addition the program was about to be phased out as the US Department of Health Education and Welfare was itself in the process of change. Generally, the program had run its course; efforts were being undertaken to include the test for Sickle Cell Disease within the scope of the third-party insurance reimbursement process, thereby eliminating the need for a special Federal appropriation for the sickle-cell-disease test. All signs pointed to my gig being over at the Queens Hospital Center, and my personal and professional life had reached another juncture. With the little time that I had available and my meager financial resources I decided to take a coarse in basic etymology at Brooklyn Technical college to qualify for a Pest Control Operators license administered by the Environmental Protection Agency (EPA). After I received my Pest Control Operators license, I identified some approachable markets and developed and implemented a relatively successful marketing plan. Soon I had a few modest contracts and an office to operate from. However things were financially difficult, as I was recovering from the loss of five of years of steady employment and the expenses associated with my mother's health and funeral expenses, as she had no insurance. In hindsight it could have only been the Grace of God that made the way possible.

A financial boost came when I prepared a successful public relations and promotion campaign for a religious organization, the Christian Revelation Crusade (CRC). In the course of discharging my responsibility to CRC, as the managing consultant, I had to conduct regular seminars and workshops in leadership development and research-grants development. This professional situation enabled me to lease some office space on Jamaica Avenue and 168th Street. The new office space was more than adequate enough to accommodate the expansion to my newly formed entrepreneurial and public relations consulting company. After about one of year operating at that location, I developed a substantial client base, in conjunction with the Christian Revelation Crusade. The pest control operation was also moving towards the black. As a result of the new religious interface, I developed a relationship with the Rev. Dr. Robert Moses Kinlock, who engaged my consultancy. Dr. Kinlock was a well-known civil rights activist and worked along with the Rev. Dr. Martin Luther King and others. Rev. Dr. Kinlock was the Commissioner of the Commission for the Elimination of Racism of the Council of Churches of the city of New York. One of my responsibilities included organizing the annual Dr. Martin Luther King Jr. Memorial Concert held every January, following his assassination at the United Nations, Dag Hammarskjold Auditorium. The concert was an annual support effort directed toward generating support for a national Dr. King holiday. My other responsibility was to coordinate the black and Arab Dialogue group in conjunction with Dr. Mohammed T. Mehdi of the Arab-American Relations Committee.

Dr. Kinlock was also embroiled in a controversy that ultimately resulted in him being evicted from the Commissions offices located at the Riverside Church building. Dr. Kinlock was very active however he was in his late eighties, and was a picture of health in the view of his age. Dr. Kinlock took sick one day and was admitted to St. Luke's Hospital in Harlem. His health deteriorated rapidly and in a matter of a few days expired. Dr. Kinlock's swift and shocking demise impacted many of my associates, in particular Bishop Valmore Holt, who himself was in his late sixties and not in his best health. Bishop Holt was an ex-Navy man and a computer expert. He was a certified genius and at the age of sixteen graduated from New York University as a physics major, and held ninety-four patents in computer technology. I met Bishop Holt about a year earlier when a friend Butch Addison introduced him. Butchie, who was an attorney, had come to my office and introduced two of his business, associates David and Barry Laws. David and Barry were computer whiz kids and nephews of Bishop Holt. The whiz kids asked Butchie to join their new company Hard Stats, as the General Counsel. Hard Stats had a patent on a computer gadget that cut the cost of international telephonic communications in half. According to Butchie they had some potential investors as well as major clients and they were about to take off. In addition, he said the company had the technology to transmit an image as well as audio combined, that would be introduced shortly. Butchie brought them to my office for the purpose of exploring a possible public relations agreement. The PR deal never materialized but, in the course of negotiations, I had the opportunity to meet Bishop Valmore Holt the teacher and mentor of the whiz kids. Ultimately Bishop and I developed a professional relationship and we were in the process of establishing a computer lab in order to develop projects.

Bishop Valmore Holt took the sudden death of Rev. Kinlock very hard. The Bishop was in the process of completing a computer-based design to interface hi-technology with social and economic community development needs in the black community. This project was a spiritual imperative for Holt and the sudden death of Dr. Kinlock dashed the impetus for the project and he soon became despondent. When I first met Bishop Holt he told me that he was sick, but at the time I had no idea that his situation was as severe as it turned out to be. I was in the process of pulling off my first political event, sponsored by the Voters Anonymous, political education organization, which I had recently founded. The program featured a debate between Ambassador Levin of the State of Israel, and Dr. Mohammed T. Mehdi, of the Arab-American Relations Committee, at York College in Jamaica. During the debate I was able to interface with some local political officials for the first time in several years. About two or three months or so later as I was in the process of entering my office and I was met by a City Marshall who proceeded to lock me out of my office. To say that I was shocked would be a gross understatement, and I proceeded directly to my Attorney's office, John Lewis. John said that he would get an Order to Show Cause and get the case restored to the calendar. After a couple of weeks of being locked out of my offices without positive results, I decided to get a second legal opinion regarding my situation. Following the review of my documentation the second legal opinion Attorney Mitchell Alter, advised me that the original lawyer lost a judgment for possession of the office by default, and was unsuccessful in having the case restored to the court calendar. Mr. Alter recommended a legal malpractice attorney, as he felt that I had substantial grounds for legal malpractice. I met with the malpractice lawyer, and began considering the events that may have led to this situation.

A few months earlier, a little strain developed in my relationship with the landlord, following a rumor that I had someone in the offices for residential purposes. The problem came to a head when a leak developed in my second floor space that caused damage to the tenant below. There was a subsequent landlord and tenant case in process as a result of this situation, and apparently my attorney for some reason did not appear in court at the appointed time. A default judgment was entered against me for possession. The possibility of a successful malpractice suite did not reconcile the massive disruption and dislocation of my business activities. Also, everything that I had managed to recoup from my previous dislocation in addition to my recent acquisitions were locked up. It was now December; two months after the marshal locked my doors, when I received the news that Bishop Valmore Holt had died, as a result of lung cancer. I now understood why he was so distraught about the death of Rev. Dr. Kinlock. He most likely envisaged his own demise, without having completed the project. Holt told me on a few occasions that he was sick and did not have too long to go. But, because of his strong looking physical condition, I had no idea that his time remaining was so short. If I had known that he had lung cancer, I would have no doubt commented to him about the fact that he smoked so many cigarettes that he looked like a chimney. After his funeral I was bewildered and felt for the first time as sense of failure. The next time I went to see attorney Alter, he told me that while reading the *Law Journal*, he noted that John Lewis had been disbarred. This news amounted to nails in my coffin, as the malpractice suite was useless to pursue now since he was disbarred.

I speculated wildly as to the scenario that resulted in the loss of my office space and property. It was obvious that there was a default judgment entered against me in the landlord and tenant court. However, the personal circumstances that caused my attorney not to appear left many interesting and unanswerable questions. Although the ultimate responsibility is mine, I was concerned that he did not give me any prior notice so that I could have appeared personally. Also, the disbarment and indictment suggested that he was in a situation that may have compromised his as well as my position. Unfortunately, whatever the facts were my interest swung in the balance and I lost heavy. I wondered whether there were still some odious political machinations at work in a covert destabilization scenario. I ruled no abstract or remote possibility out of the realm of possibilities. I had not been involved in political organizing or direct action tactics for several years. In fact I thought that I was being particularly careful not to give the impression that I was interested or involved in challenging any ones political position or power relationships. All I was trying to do was to build my business in order to take care of my family and responsibilities, and help to incubate others enterprises and entrepreneurs. While I perceived that my activities as pro-economic and Apolitical, a few friends like Chris Banks, Hasan Hakim among many others pulled my coat about the perception of my political organizing.

Hasan Hakim brought to my attention that a distinct political perception was generated because of the level of activity that was being generated from my office on a daily basis.

Hasan said, "Ruth Giles was right about how fearful, treacherous, and low-down the black ruling elite are; they are insecure, man, and paranoid, and they will continue to go for your jugular vein." He said, "You can't rule out nothing, man; they could have compromised your attorney, and then thrown him to the wolves when they were finished. That's what they do, man. I am talking from experience, I know what they did and tried to do to others, and the black ruling elite is our problem, not the white man."

I did not rule out any of the possibilities he articulated, however I was clear that what ever had occurred it wouldn't bring the office or property back and I had to get my recovery process on. It seemed as though my political history always preceded me, and I conceded to myself that as a result of my political history there would be no mediocrity in my life. I was coming to the conclusion that I had to maintain an on going political component in order to safe guard my business interest and discharge my family obligations. I had to remain politically solvent; therefore I had to keep my political expertise engaged as a matter of survival.

Political activism necessarily had to become an operational component of my overall public activity. I had deluded myself into believing that I could successfully pursue my business, cultural, community and other interests without an active political component. The recent experience with the Southeast Queens Community Corporation and the South Jamaica Steering Committee, made me a little politically gun shy, but that had to change. My political disillusionment was corrected as a result of my present circumstances. The testimonies of my friends and associates reminded me of the nature of black community politics and my own political history and legacy. The observations of Hasan, Chris and a few others lubricated my rusted political senses. Although some of the points that they raised were broad and sweeping, the political truth associated with the points were instructive in helping to formulate the new political application. Hasan reminded me that political perception is sometimes more dynamic than political reality.

He said, "The reality of your current political activism is insignificant and benign, but the perception of your political activism is significant and malignant. This perception is fed by your history and background as an effective community organizer. You are viewed as the proverbial leopard which, of course, cannot change his spots."

Hasan continued, "Let me break it down for you, okay? You are the only black business on Jamaica Avenue. You have 2,500 square foot executive office complex, with wall- to-wall carpeting and central air conditioning on the corner of 168th Street and Jamaica Avenue, the hub of the Jamaica commercial district. You have people coming in and out all day for copies, word processing services, and every other week you got 30 to 40 people coming for workshops, responsible-looking people with jobs. You sponsored a great debate with the Ambassador Levin of the State of Israel and Dr. Mehdi, and both of them showed up.

"The political perception of what is going on here is scarring the political hell out of the black political power structure. As far as they are concerned, man, they took you out years ago, and not only are you alive, but you're alive and kicking with a growing constituency on Jamaica Avenue. You can think that you are being an apolitical nice guy if you want to, but I think that you better take a deeper look. You can talk that benign stuff if you want to, but you better keep your political ducks in a row if you want to safeguard your family and business interest."

CHAPTER 5

New York City black electoral politics is generally based in two distinct camps. The Harlem (Manhattan) political "old guard," holds the historically senior position and the Brooklyn, political "vanguard," an out growth of the local black political empowerment movement of the 1970s. Harlem is without question the most popular black community in the world. It is distinguished by historical political leaders like J. Ramon Jones (the Harlem Fox) and Congressman Adam Clayton Powell Jr. Harlem as a community was the archetype of black American politics growing out of the Harlem renaissance period because of the arts, culture and literary activity, as well as politics. On the other hand Brooklyn politics is an outgrowth of Harlem politics that developed during the modern civil rights era in the 1950s. As civil rights politics gave birth to the "Black Power," student and youth movements of the Brooklyn contingent spun-off and became independent in the late 1960s and 1970s. Among the dynamics that precipitated the Harlem and Brooklyn political dichotomy was a split in the leadership of CORE (Congress of Racial Equality) that may have crystallized the divergent political trajectories.

CORE was among the prominent civil rights organizations that are directly responsible for facilitating the sit-ins, boycotts, marches, voter education and registration and other non-violent political activities credited with desegregating the South. Following the success of civil rights and voting rights legislation there was great euphoria among the civil rights leadership and follow-ship that quickly morphed into political confusion as to where do we go from here?" In 1968 there was a bitter and controversial struggle for the leadership of CORE that resulted in the ascension of Roy Innis to the chairmanship of the renowned training ground for non-violence civil rights activities. Innis, during his inaugurating speech declared that CORE not only had a new chairman but, in fact had a LEADER! Then the new chairman promptly declared CORE to be a Garvey-ite organization and proceeded to unceremoniously remove white folk from the organization.

Although national in scope, CORE was a Harlem based organization. Following the ascension of Roy Innis to the chairmanship of CORE and his controversial declarations, the Brooklyn contingent of the organization seceded and became distinguished as "Brooklyn" CORE. Brooklyn CORE leadership consisted of names such as Sonny Carson, Les Cambell, and Al Vann, among many others. The Brooklyn and Harlem political juxtaposition also has origins in the fight for "community control" of local schools and "quality education" that was the basis of experimental school districts in Brooklyn's Ocean Hill, Brownville, and Harlem's IS 201, in 1967. The education controversy exposed the racial divide that characterized the New York City Public School system of the time and positioned Brooklyn black community as political militants, radicals and revolutionaries. There was a clear generational distinction that ultimately emerged as the Harlem based political leadership embodied the veteran political elite referred to by the larger community as "responsible" leadership, as compared to Brooklyn's political "militants" and "anti-Semites."

While on the surface at the present time there is a perception of unity of purpose and objectives between the two camps, at the end of the day there is an adversarial element. The "old guard" and "vanguard" political leadership has marginalized black political power, growth and sophistication. Fraternity and political diplomacy pervades the public discourse and interrelations, but the numerical political potential of the black community is squandered by political fratricide between the two political camps.

By the mid 1970s Brooklyn and the political vanguard had generated its own history as the leaders of grassroots and community political activism in the city. City-wide and national "Black Power" conferences were convened and hosted in Brooklyn and national "Black Power" advocates and organizations established links to the Brooklyn vanguard. During the National black Political Convention held in Gary Indiana in 1972, the Brooklyn delegation emerged as the dominant political force among the respective boroughs that comprise New York City. True to form, the Brooklyn delegation and the delegation from CORE flexed their political muscles which tended to overshadow the grassroots objectives of the Gary Conference with the political rhetoric as to whether the Convention would endorse a "nationalist" or "integrationist" political philosophy. Poet and political activist Leroy Jones a co-convener of the Gary Convention and a political adversary of CORE's Roy Inns, was associated with the Brooklyn delegation curtailed the "nationalist" vs. "integrationist" rhetorical exercise.

The political hegemony that Brooklyn was able to exercise in relation to grassroots and community organizing in comparison to the other boroughs was solidified as echelons of Harlem based political Guru's were feted by the Brooklyn vanguard. Prominent among the Harlem political guru's that held court with the Brooklyn political leadership was the Honorable Basil Paterson, the former Lieutenant of New York City and senior member of the Harlem political elite leadership. Others include community activist and former organizer of the social workers union, Lloyd Douglass, and "internationalist" Elombe Braithwaite.

Brooklyn became affectionately referred to as "the People's Republic" of Brooklyn because of the level of political diversity, ecumenism and inter-generational coordination. In the context of youth development Brooklyn possessed a quintessential mascot who doubled as a youth leader. Leader of the Grassroots Youth Movement (GYM), Rev. Al Sharpton, a charismatic boy preacher now in his late teens was being mentored by the Brooklyn based black political leadership. Hence, Rev. Sharpton, had a niche role to play in maintaining and asserting Brooklyn political hegemony around the city and beyond. Rev. Sharpton became a popular keynote speaker at functions organized, convened or co-hosted by members of the Brooklyn political vanguard. In the framework of GYM, Rev. Sharpton generated his own constituency among the youth in particular but some adults outside of the Brooklyn political-activist orthodoxy supported Rev. Sharpton activities among the youth. In the context of GYM, the youthful and glib Rev. Sharpton's popularity grew as his crisp and pointed political rhetoric eviscerated the prospect of competition for his coveted positioning with leaders of the "Peoples Republic of Brooklyn."

Ultimately Rev. Sharpton began to lose credibility with his Brooklyn-based mentors when he became implicated in a political sting that may have compromised key members of the Brooklyn political activist leadership. Rumors, accusations, allegations and speculation began to abound from the activist community that Rev. Sharpton was an informant for the Police, etc. It was alleged that Rev. Sharpton wore a wire at various meetings with members of the Brooklyn activist leadership inner circle. The allegations began to develop a life of their own when Rev. Sharpton admitted to wearing a police wire, but he asserted the purpose of the wire was to bust drug dealers, and clean up the community for the youth. The revelation by Rev. Sharpton that he wore a police wire generated a major political upheaval within the echelons of leadership in the Brooklyn political vanguard. The Rev. was publicly denounced by members of the vanguard leadership and became virtual political pariah, by many on the Brooklyn political leadership contingent. Rev. Sharpton retaliated politically by relocating his GYM organization base to Harlem.

The Brooklyn and Harlem political camps have their own community-based operatives and organizations that thwart local insurgent community based electoral candidates, and have relative support in the other boroughs. Both the Brooklyn and Harlem political camp have elected representatives in the city Council and State Legislature and constitute a lion's share of black elected officials in the city and state. However, the partisan internal adversarial process keeps the community politically marginalized by continually sacrificing serious voter education, registration and application activities, to the community at large. In the framework of city-wide electoral politics, the subliminal adversarial relationship between the two black (Democratic) camps is exploited by white political and economic power brokers, relegating each respective camp to its local base of a shrinking, apathetic and disillusioned voter pool.

Consequently, it is virtually impossible for any black electoral candidate to achieve a citywide position unless outside political interest groups cut a deal with one or the other of the black Democratic camps. In relation to statewide or national electoral politics, both camps are relegated to the partisan politic within the confines of the so-called "black vote." And the black vote is ultimately positioned as a partisan political monolithic, requiring no quid pro quo. On the positive side a few anointed "black political leaders" and orthodox black leadership elite receive largess for cameo comments and appearances that give a perception of political power. The historical voting pattern and electoral rhetoric is politically sophomoric and has rendered the black community politically impotent and without political leverage capacity. This process has also insulated the black political ruling elite. The victim of this odious political machination is the black community at large. Voter disillusionment, voter apathy and political ignorance are the product of the black political leadership's sins of omission and commission.

Likewise, black civil rights organizations perpetuate their own political self interests and patronage by smoke and mirrors and slight of hand. As early as the spring of 1965, following the success of the voting rights bill, the civil rights movement entered a new and un-chartered phase and did not know what this new undefined phase would be. Like other social movements of the past, they faced the threat of destruction because of their own victories. Not only was there a growing uncertainty and conflict at the intellectual level of the movement, but also the civil rights organizations began to experience a marked decline in public support in the form of financial contributions. From the NAACP to the newer and the more radical organizations, the high-water mark of contributions had been the year or more earlier. There was substantial concern and fear that legislative success was lowering motivation for contributors to dig in the pocketbook. Consequently, 1965 was a period in contemporary history when the civil rights movement discovered explicitly that abolishing legal racism would not provide black Americans with equality. It was at this same time that it became especially clear that defacto segregation and subtle racism were tied to America's most fundamental social, economic and political institutions. Moreover, leaders of the civil rights orthodoxy were increasingly becoming estranged from their rank and file, as inner city partisan political leadership divided among itself.

In spite of the growth in the number of black elected officials and the victories of the civil rights era the conditions in the black community have not improved appreciably. Crime, violence, illegal drugs, delinquency, teenage pregnancy, unemployment, under-employment, and psychological deficiency are epidemics that continue to plague black Americans in general and the inner city population in particular. There is no question that local, state and national government have a significant role to play in the amelioration of these problems. Additionally, the private sector, churches, educational institutions, social scientists and professionals of varying disciplines all have an appropriate role to play. However, the ultimate solution is the challenge to every black American in general and each black person in particular.

The nature and state of black electoral politics can be traced to the birth of the modern civil rights movement in the 1950s with a marriage of political convenience between blacks seeking to eliminate racism and achieve their legitimate aspirations as citizens of America and the liberal-progressive wing of the Democratic Party. In the southern states racism was blatant, overt and expressed in the segregation of schools and public facilities and accommodations. In the North the racism and segregation was sophisticated, sublime, and very well disguised. Nevertheless, the outcome of both northern and southern racism was the same on the respective black American communities. Poor education, poverty, discrimination, bigotry, unemployment and under employment, and lack of access to services, facilities and rights of citizenship was the black American reality in the North and South. The plight of black Americans in the North and South and their struggle to achieve racial equality was the ostensible motive for the political marriage of convenience.

The political marriage achieved an impressive array of social and political victories and gave birth to the modern civil rights era. The land marked Supreme Court decision, vis-à-vis, Brown v Board of Education (1954), perhaps consummated the marriage and the political concept of "integration" was established and marketed as the politically "progressive" paradigm, for "social justice." Social integration and social justice became the political objective and calling card of the emerging civil rights movement. The civil rights movement became a political component of the liberal-progressive wing of the Democratic Party. The liberal-progressive wing of the Democratic Party had a political conjunction with Marxist-oriented technical assistants that taught and trained volunteers in the growing "integration" movement that embodied civil rights. Liberal and progressive Democratic Party organizers and political operatives trained black Americans in the struggle relative to political organizing, protests, demonstration, marches, sit-ins, voter education, registration and other political tactics and techniques. The conditions of racism and poverty in the black community were on the front burner of the American agenda due to the effectiveness of the integration and civil rights organizing strategy. Victory was on the immediate horizon was the perception of many in the black community, and black youth in colleges and the community were responding to the Clarion Call. The victorious nuptial between the black movement in the South and North, and the liberal-progressive and Marxist oriented "democratic" movement had as much negative fall-out on the black community as positive developments. On the negative side, the legitimate political aspirations of the civil rights and Black Power movements got trapped off and compromised by the on going adversarial relationship between the rulers of America and advocates Marxist revolutionary ideology, in their geo-political rivalry.

Apart from the legitimate political aspirations of black Americans for justice and equity, and the elimination of racism and bigotry there were larger and more complex issues within which the black American experience existed. The planet was in fact divided and politically polarized along the lines of capitalism and Marxist based socialism, until the recent demise of the Soviet Union. The "East" vs. "West geo-political rivalry was an ongoing internal political dynamic between white people for virtual planetary control commonly referred to as the cold war. The East vs. West political divide in the context of the "cold war" was a conventional and unconventional battle of ideas, engaged on the ground by political surrogates and pawn states of the "third world."

Anti-Communism and Marxist "dialectical materialism" continues to be the subtext of America's geo-political world view, despite the demise of the Soviet Union. Since the infamous Committee on un-American Activities hearing an overt and covert preoccupation with "Communism" has constituted the political subtext of "official" political and intelligence action, domestic and international. Consequently, the political marriage of convenience from the outset had built in clandestine liabilities and indiscernible sophisticated political machinations, as it related to the black American political movement. On one hand the black American political movement unwittingly exposed themselves, as a political target for the permanent American government to infiltrate, control, manage and marginalize. When the black American leadership wedded the fair white political maiden, it was love at first sight and for better or worse. While the statutory and legislative victories satiated the immediate and cursory political appetite, the ravages to the black American political movement inflicted by the permanent American government anti Communism and Marxism operations mitigated the perceived civil rights victories.

On the other hand, the marriage itself was politically one sided in favor of the liberal-progressive wing of the Democratic Party. As trainees in the electoral political process black leaders were in no position to question or challenge the good will, political strategy and tactics of the liberal-progressive community organizers and technical assistance, especially in the light of increasing local and national political victories. The goal of "racial" integration and social justice as a means to achieve equity for black Americans with the larger white community was questioned in some quarters of the black community. The debate of "integration" versus "desegregation" continues to be a conversation in the black community outside of the civil rights leadership orthodoxy. But the goal of infiltrating and integrating the racist southern Democratic Party and sophisticated northern counterpart had resonance among the black leaders and the vast majority of youth both black and white. Infiltration of the Democratic Party and mass participation in the electoral process generated tremendous fear among Democratic Party leadership particularly in the southern states and violent reaction was the political order of the day. Despite vicious violence in the form of lynching, bombings, horses, water hoses, police brutality, tactics of fear and intimidation, black Americans infiltrated the Democratic Party in the South and ultimately broke the back "racial" segregation vis-à-vis, their participation in the Democratic Party's elective process.

The apparent success of the political marriage of blacks and whites in terms of the achievement of civil rights and voting rights legislation was complemented by the advent of an elected black political leadership in the North and South. But the proliferation of black elected officials has not positively impacted the condition of the black community generally. Moreover, the black community inherited a "civil rights" leadership locked into a partisan electoral political empowerment elusion. The vested political interests of the black elected and civil rights leadership in the partisan political enterprise has reached the point of diminishing returns. As a practical political matter the civil rights and elected black leadership never dealt with eradicating poverty and economic development in the black community. The financiers, political gurus and technicians of the black American civil rights and elected leadership were ambivalent at best about facilitating the independent political and economic development of the black American community. Advances and victories associated with and attributed to the civil rights and elected leadership focused on achieving "social justice" and "social integration" categorically. Real-time political power of any community is generated by the leverage approach to electoral politics and the benefactors of the civil rights and elected leadership had partisan self-interest in their agenda singularly.

Adherents to the social "integration" philosophy of the civil rights movement, and revolutionary philosophy of the Black Power movement were political pawns in the East vs. West geo-political exercise. The sophisticated and revolutionary partisan political nexus created a double whammy that continues to devastate the black American community, particularly young men. The current remnant of the black political ruling elite perpetuates the outdated partisan political rhetoric. The double whammy consisted of an imposition of a black political class to manage the black community and the codification of racism and discrimination, with "right wing" and "reactionary" opponents as the ultimate enemy. On the other hand, the political association with the "Marxist" revolutionary philosophy influenced civil rights and Black Power movements, and social-policy ideas of the black ruling elite.

Under the umbrella of a coalition with the liberal-progressive wing of the Democratic Party, the emerging organic leadership in the black community was destroyed by a conspiracy of domestic intelligence forces, self-defeating social policy and politically diversionary social justice activities. The Black Power and youth movements and the black community in general were all blindsided by the comprehensive unconventional war being conducted to undermine their legitimate political aspirations. The domestic unconventional war, overt and covert operations involved virtually all agencies of the American government. The domestic intelligence apparatus was in place and engaged against Marxist ideology prior to the contemporary civil rights era. The domestic intelligence apparatus was focused on the alleged Marxist infiltration of the Democratic party, civil rights and Black Power movements; therefore there was considerable "official" concern relative to the new "integration" political coalition.

The political strategy in the South to break the back of the Democratic segregationist was to infiltrate the Democratic party and become a factor in the political power equation. The Democratic party was in fact infiltrated in the North as well as the South, and segregation was positively impacted and blacks achieved some political visibility, but no real-time political power. The political visibility is now in the form numerous black political officials, civil and voting rights legislation and "progressive" social policy. Unfortunately, the black community at large, cumulatively has less now than during segregation. While the East vs. West political paradigm is irrelevant to the current challenges confronting the black community, it has bequeathed to us an entrenched black political ruling elite that continues to promote outdated political organizing tactics and strategies.

Overt and covert operations have undermined much of the black community based self-determination organizational activities. Recent official revelations resulting from the Freedom of Information Act provide irrefutable evidence of a concerted effort, if not conspiracy against the black male leadership around the country. Like hi-tech smart bombs, the subtle and not so subtle and pervasive social welfare policy has played a devastating role on the family by removing the black male from the household. Psycho-social policies have served to demoralize both men and women, providing no incentive or mechanism for upward mobility. Multi-dimensional are the factors and circumstances, which account for the present state of the black community. The political dynamic within the black community may have the most profound effect on the black community crisis. While a compelling argument can be made on behalf of the current level of political sophistication among the black community, just as compelling is the fact that a state of emergency exists within the black community in spite of the obvious political and economic advancement of a few. The prognosis for the many is exceedingly grim. There apparently is no political and economic strategy on the horizon, capable of moving the black community from point A to point B. Unfortunately, new achievements have not substantially impacted old problems. Therefore the question may very well be, is the present black leadership competent enough to master the logistical challenge of moving the black community to political and economic ascendancy in the twenty-first century?

Basic economic survival was my priority, and my pest control operator's license served me well as an immediate cash-generating vehicle. Although the exterminating business did not enable me to adequately underwrite my familial economic responsibilities, I was able to maintain my dignity and individual self-reliance. I was fortunate enough to develop a working relationship with a couple of Real Estate companies on Hillside Avenue, that provided a weekly cash flow, but circumstances caused me to pursue new markets in Manhattan. I was familiar with Harlem from my days growing up in the South Bronx, and my work with Continental Mutual Insurance Company and staff organizer for the "movement." Although my new residence was Harlem, my base of operation was still in Jamaica Queens however precarious. In order to reassert my political activism on a firm foundation it was essential that I begin in Queens in spite of my dubious base. Although I was registered as a Republican since I first registered to vote in 1967, my political activism experience was founded and focused on the Democratic Party politics in the context of infiltration, agitation, education and manipulation on behalf of the civil rights, black youth and student movements. While the target was the "white power structure," racism and discrimination perpetrated against the black community, the "black responsible leadership" became the most formidable opposition to grassroots, community-based activism and community empowerment. On a practical level, the "responsible black political leadership" was an effective buffer protecting the status quo against aggressive black youth militancy, thereby insulating their relative position of political influence. I earned my political stripes during this dynamic process, and in so doing I became astutely aware of the internal politics within the black community among competing views, generations and economic classes in the various boroughs of New York City. Hopefully, during that process I learned enough about politics, the system and black folk to prepare me adequately for the politics of the 1980s and beyond. Nevertheless, my current predicament required that

I pull out all stops to achieve the objectives for my family and community. My resolve to at least leave a legacy of Herculean effort was firm. I could not conceive of compromise to mediocrity given the breath of life in me.

My visceral impulses were to compromise the vision and dream that I had for family, community, and myself: then resign myself to the fate of a basic survival lifestyle in the company of the legions of black men whose spirit had been broken. But the spirit drive within me could not reconcile the notion of resignation to observer status, as vicissitudes of life imposed its will on those that acquiesced. My will to be an active participant and contributor to increasing the practical options that constitute the current verisimilitude in the black community. I am in complete control of my legacy, save the Lord, and I am determined to leave a legacy of Nobel effort for my children. Although I was absolutely convinced that my legacy of Nobel effort would be an important corner stone for my children's foundation for eventually breaking through the "tangle of pathology" cycle. My motive for persistent struggle was for personal reasons as well. I was my worse critic, and I knew that if I would compromise my vision and dream to mediocrity, I would eventually live in a personal hell as a consequence of my own wrath, lamenting my lack of affirmative action, first person singular. In addition, I realized that I would be plagued by self-consciousness and psychological deficiency, having relegated my life to marginal black male survival. Therefore, my constitution was firm and irreversible. The greatest obstacle to the black community achieving a stable orbit is the political, economic and social inertia maintained by the black conventional leadership, vis-à-vis, the gate keepers. A cathartic process is required in order to attain the required escape velocity for a stable economic, political and social orbit. An internal combustion challenging the conventional leadership and approaches to problem solving in the black community is in order. This cathartic process is a prerequisite to the black American community moving from point A to point B. I was already positioned on the cutting edge of this cathartic process and in my conviction it was pointless to retreat or to concede defeat in the middle of nowhere. I began to press forward with renewed determination and greater political wisdom.

Black political activism was never a part of the Republican Party politics. For various reasons, the Democratic Party maintains a virtual monopoly on grassroots political activism particularly in the area of "minority rights." Contemporary political organizing technology had its genesis in the Marxist movements that proliferated around the world and in the United States, in the 1950s, 60s, and 70s. The political organizing techniques were adapted as tactics of the "integration" and anti-racism movements in the South and North. The Democratic Party, primarily in the South, was the most notorious segregationist and racist, therefore they were deliberately targeted and infiltrated to establish a political front in the fight against American segregation and racism. The civil rights and Black Power movements based in the black community entered into coalitions with the white Liberal and progressive's elements of the Democratic Party, formal and informal in order to accomplish their mutual objectives. In the process of achieving the mutual objectives of abolishing segregation and racism, the political technology and rhetoric have created stereo-types, concepts, definitions, and perspectives. These civil rights political tactics are dated in some cases and must be challenged and modified, in order to achieve real time objectives in the twenty-first century. While these perspectives were strategic and relevant to a particular organizing objective, the organizing objectives have changed since the civil rights and Black Power era, however the black community is still locked into "movement's" organizing and application concepts and techniques. Protest politics, emotional marches and demonstrations as well as the vague movement for "social justice" amount to political diversions from the practical and legitimate aspirations of the masses of black folk. I was aware that I had to break through decades of political conditioning, conventional wisdom, and established power relationships in order to achieve any level of visibility and effectiveness.

I felt my self uniquely prepared for the task, however, I felt comforted in the belief that time was on my side of the aisle. Time was on my side because it was obvious to me that the level of political sophistication in the black community was at a crossroad, vis-à-vis, the limitations of partisan politics as a singular strategy to achieve political leverage and empowerment. My assessment was that the grassroots community understood the need for a multi-political party strategy for general election politics and a bi-partisan electoral strategy focused on the primary election process singularly. Unfortunately, the black political leadership must keep the old game alive for the purpose of self-preservation. The intellectual argument for a broader, more comprehensive and sophisticated political strategy in the black community is a compelling one, however, because politics is an emotional and a rhetorical exercise; the intellectual merit as a motivational impetus had no chance of success. For the purpose of the greater good I developed a plan to promote grassroots Republican Party activism in the black community, to operate in conjunction with grassroots Democrat activism to develop political leverage and accountability in the black community.

CHAPTER 6

The police investigation of the death of young Lee Morris from an overdose of heroin in the basement apartment of my house in Queens was cursory and it developed no worthwhile leads. Pancho, a friend of Lee Morris and tenant in the basement apartment was in jail as a result of getting busted for possession of stolen property and conspiracy to sell stolen goods. Pancho finally got caught stealing clothes from his employer Larry Morrell, owner of the Fly Shop in midtown Manhattan. This time Pancho wasn't coming right back into the world, according to his friend Rameen. Rameen gave me the full scoop on Pancho's situation, which he had intimate knowledge of. I suspected that Rameen may have been down with his boy Pancho on the deal at some level and was informing me of some details at the instructions of Pancho. Rameen approached at the center and said,

"Peace, Brother Vinnie, how is the revolution going?"

"Peace, Rameen," I answered, "how are you doing? I haven't seen you for quite a little while. How are your brothers doing?"

Rameen didn't answer my question but said, "I was with your star boarder, Pancho, a little while ago, and he asked me to stop by and talk to you about the apartment."

I responded in a strong and determined tone. "If you just left him, why didn't he come here himself to talk to me about his apartment? He seems to speak well for himself as I recall. And if I remember correctly he believes that he has a gift of gab. So what is the deal? Pancho promised three months ago that he was going to give me some rent and as usual, it never happened." I said, then asked him, "So what is it now, Rameen? What is the new message that you came to deliver?"

Rameen said, "Well, Mr. B., I'm here to deliver a new message from Pie 'cause he can't deliver it personally. And it's a new message." He continued, "See, Mr. B., Pie got arrested last month, and now he's on Riker's Island facing a year up north. The bust is a meatball, Mr. B., and he's going to have to do a bullet on this meatball. Anyway, Mr. B., Pie wanted me to ask you to look after his things until he gets out."

"Well, Rameen," I said, "the next time that you see Pancho, tell him that you told me. Okay. And give him the mailing address of the house."

I was already aware of Pancho being busted and was currently on Riker's Island. I first learned about it from Jabar one of the young leaders of the 5 percent Nation and who worked as a coordinator of production in the Afro Pik factory on Hollis Avenue. It seems as though Jabar's older brother was on a visit at the Rock and saw Pancho get a visit. The news was not surprising because Pancho was in and out of the Tombs like a revolving door. It was only a matter of time before he would have to serve some time, because the volume of arrests was escalating due to his increasing dependence on heroin. On the other hand, I was particularly disturbed and confused by the information that I got first hand from Karen Snell, a good friend of mine who was a nurse on Riker's Island. Karen advised me that she saw Pancho in the intake infirmary on Riker's Island. When she saw him she was convinced of who it was, but she wanted to be sure before confronting him. Then Karen searched the medical chart in order to confirm his name and identity but could not find his name Barry Smith. All of a sudden she felt sick as she noticed that Pancho was using the name Byron Lee, his dead friend. Karen immediately disappeared so that Pancho would not notice her, under the circumstances. I was absolutely floored by that news and I began to reflect on the incident itself and analyze the days and weeks before and subsequent to the tragedy.

Pancho's use of his dead friends name was troubling and raised many question that required hard and verifiable answers. I was certain that Pancho had a heroin habit but the fact that he would use his dead friend's name caused me to consider what Pancho knew and when he knew it. Pancho was like a young stepbrother to me. My blood brother Lewis, is 5 years my junior and Pancho is 10 years my junior. Pancho became my stepbrother several years ago when my mother informally adopted him into the family. Pancho came from a dysfunctional family that lived in Brooklyn. Pancho's parents lived together, but they were both notorious heroin addicts.

Consequently, Pancho was a "street kid." He began hanging out in Southeast Queens after meeting and befriending Rameen at a party in Brooklyn. Rameen lived on the Ville with his parents and had two older brothers and a sister. Pancho became a familiar sight in the neighborhood with Rameen and their peers, which included others, some four or five. Pancho stood out among his peers because he was the last of the youth to be seen in the night and the first one out in the Ville in the morning. At some point it became obvious that Pancho was sleeping anywhere that he could as his appearance sometime betrayed his situation. He apparently had a good relationship with employer Larry Morrel, who owned a men's clothing store in midtown Manhattan. Affable by nature Pancho was able to maneuver himself into a person's heart because of his personality and virtually homeless situation. Apparently Pancho was able to influence his employer to some how keep him on board despite tardiness and unpredictable behavior. My mother was among the people that thought he was a nice young man, and reached out to him with compassion and sympathy.

I reflected on the first conversation that I had with my mother about Pancho, she asked, "Vincent, where does that young man Pancho live? I saw him sitting on the steps of Junior High School 59, about 7 A.M. Do you know his parents?"

"His parents live in Brooklyn," I answered, "but he hangs out around here with his friends. Pancho and Rameen are tight."

She replied, "He was with your brother and his friends the other evening. Rameen's brother was a part of the group, but I didn't see Rameen there with them."

I said, "Well, Pancho and Rameen like to hang out with the older guys, such as my brother and your son Lewis, and Rameen's brother Edward. Frankly, I think they do too much hanging out and not enough hanging-in on more constructive pursuits."

Perceptively pursuing the issue she asked, "What do you mean, Vincent, when you say more constructive pursuits? What are they doing?" Then she continued, "Actually, when I see them at night on the Ville, they remind me of you when we first moved to the Ville, hanging out all hours of the night and coming in all times of the morning. I'm sure you could have been engaged in more constructive pursuits during those days."

"Yes, you're right, Mommy," I said.

She concluded, "Well, I got him some lunch the other day because he looked hungry. And I let him do a few things for me so he could make some change."

I had to be careful with what I said to my mother about Pancho and my brother. The fact was that they, along with Rameen's brother Ed, and Rameen, were playing tag with heroin. I learned from a buddy of mine that my brother and Ed were skin-popping heroin, while Pancho and Rameen were snorting it. I was certain about my brother playing tag with heroin, but I had to keep that fact from my mother in her delicate condition. We moved from the South Bronx in order to escape drugs but heroin was alive and well in

GARY JAMES

Southeast Queens if you knew what to look for. I was overjoyed that my
mother was now living in St. Croix VI, and not witness to the deterioration of
Southeast Queens in general and the Ville in particular due to the
proliferation of heroin and cocaine. Now the situation for Pancho was grave
in view of what I heard about him in the joint. But, in addition to the fact that
he may have to do a year in jail under the name of his dead friend; I had to
consider if Pancho was directly or indirectly involved in any way with his
friend's death. As a result of these new revelations I had to give some thought
and reflection to this situation and try to revisit the sequence of events leading
up to Lee's death and try to connect the dots going back a few years.

I remember meeting Byron Lee for the first time in the fall of his freshman
year when he visited Pancho prior to leaving for North Carolina State
College. Pancho had just started living in my basement apartment when he
brought Lee to the house. Lee was the only child of a single father that
obviously delighted in his progeny. Lee was a handsome young man that
dressed very well with quality clothes. After seeing him at the house several
times I suspected that his father had a direct hand in the style of clothes that
Lee wore. He wore classic the Peter Prep motif, what we called collegiate in
my day. He was a well *mannered* and respectful young man who gave an
excellent first impression. On the night that he died as Pancho told the
detectives and me, he was lying in the bed dosing off at about 2 A.M. when
he heard a knock on the side door leading to the basement. Pancho claims to
have walked up the stairs and seeing that it was Lee at the door he opened the
door. When he opened the door, Lee fell forward and down the steps to the
basement apartment and lay prostrate face down on the basement floor.
Pancho said he immediately ran down to Lee and knelt down to move him at
which time he noticed that Lee was foaming at the mouth. Pancho said that he
got scared and ran out side through the same side door into the driveway, but
he said that he didn't see anyone out there. Pancho then sat on the curb of the
driveway and Pineville Lane.

I remember it was a Saturday morning in August about 3 A.M. when I
arrived at home after having closed the Afro-Disiac following a rental for a
disco dance. Pancho was sitting on the curb crying when I arrived at which
point he wiped his eyes and told me to go inside the basement and look at Lee
who was lying on the floor just below the stairs. I sprinted to the basement
descending the steps two at a time. When I touched Lee, he was as cold as ice
and it was obvious to be that Lee was dead. At that point I told Pancho that his
friend was dead then I called the police department. At this point Pancho
became uncontrollably hysterical and began rolling on the floor.

110

At the time, I had no reason to question the scenario that Pancho laid out as to the sequence of events that resulted in Lee's death. Although at the time I was aware that Pancho was playing tag with heroin as well as my brother and Pancho's man, Rameen and his brother, Ed. Now a few years later events are unfolding that are causing me to revisit this incident as well as consider who else may have been implicated. Obviously I can't do anything about it now, but I need to know all of the objective facts surrounding this tragic event. In hindsight, Pancho, Edward, Rameen and my brother may know more than I was lead to believe. But apart from what I may have been lead to believe, it was my responsibility to be more probing and investigative in that situation. But the truth is better late than never. As I revisited and analyzed the death of Byron Lee, I re-examined potential roles others may have played in the tragedy.

My brother and Edward were turned out in heroin by two of my peers that I began to disassociate with following high school and entering the job market. Michael and Russell were involved in a pattern of behavior that reminded me of friends in the Bronx when they began playing tag with heroin. Apparently my brother and Edward got intrigued by the behavior of Michael and Russell and began mimicking their behavior and hanging out with them. Likewise Pancho Rameen and some of their peers got intrigued with the pattern of behavior of my brother and Edward and began to mimic their behavior. As a rule, the younger guys, get turned out by the older guys, who are the first means of getting the drugs and learning the ropes. And I recall observing that pattern with Pancho and my brother and Byron Lee seemed to have been turned out by Pancho through his association with my brother and his peers. Now things were beginning to connect and make sense.

I began to speculate on plausible scenarios leading up to the tragic end of Lee's truncated life. Pancho had given me a heads up that Lee was home for the summer vacation and was expected to come by the house. I speculated that Pancho may know about what went down prior to Lee's overdose, or Lee some how met Rameen, Lewis and Edward before he connected with Pancho. I could conceive of Lee somehow reaching Rameen without the knowledge of Pancho. Lee may very well have been interested for whatever reason, in establishing his own direct contacts for the purchase of drugs and reached out to Rameen to facilitate the drug buy and contact with Edward and Lewis. Lee's father made sure that Lee Jr. was well financed as well as well dressed. It is conceivable that Rameen facilitated the contact and drug buy with the others without the knowledge of Pancho. Lee may have knowingly or unknowingly financed the drugs for all of the participants, and they all shot the drugs. In the coarse of walking to visit Pancho, Lee may have had an overdose reaction and the others proceeded to walk him, which is the typical technique for dealing with the problem of heroin overdose. The objective is to keep the person moving to work through the intoxication. Perhaps Lee was not responding and when they reached the side door of my house, they apparently, stood Lee up against the door and knocked on it, then left. When Pancho opened the side door Lee fell forward down the steps to the basement, where he died.

Alternatively, Pancho played a role in the tragic events. In this scenario Pancho and Lee may have been in route to the house with others or just the two of them. If it were only the two of them, Pancho would have had a difficult time walking Lee to detoxify him on his own. Perhaps Pancho was able to get Lee as far as the house and decided to take Lee inside but could not negotiate the basement stairs with the dead weight of Lee, and Lee fell down the stairs and sprawled face down on the basement floor. Whatever the facts are, Lee died years ago and there is nothing now that can be done to determine who else was involved. I lamented the fact that I was not as responsive to the incident as I now believe I should have been. But the knowledge that Pancho was using Lee's name in order to disguise his own identity was haunting as it raised questions that I never considered before.

It was useless to revisit and reflect on Byron Lee or Pancho at this point, as nothing will be resolved and justice will not be served. Moreover, there were more pressing issues that I needed to confront, not the least of which was saving the house. In any case, I was concerned about the safety of Pancho in jail because of what Karen shared with me about observations that she made. Apart from the fact that Pancho was using a false identity, Pancho was in the prison infirmary suffering from wounds he received in a fight that he had with another inmate. When Karen inquired regarding the details of the fight she was informed that Pancho was assaulted by another inmate but he (Pancho) never fought back to defend himself.

Karen said, "Vincent, Pancho took a serious beating by his cell mate, a co-worker told me that Pancho just backed up into a corner and tried to cover himself with his arms, but never raised a hand to defend himself."

I responded, "What did Pancho say the fight was about? Did he report it to anyone in corrections? Did he give the infirmary staff any names of people involved?"

She said, "Vincent, this thing has been really bothering me. But the fact is Pancho was sexually assaulted and has the wounds to prove it. I did not want to confront him and blow his cover about the false identity and the sexual assault."

I asked, "Is there an investigation underway by the correction department?"

Karen replied, "Investigation? There is no investigation because Pancho won't give up names or provide information about the incident. He won't even say where the incident took place. And to make matters worse, he is referred to as dessert with the nick name of Pie."

"Keep me abreast of developments as you learn them." I concluded.

I was shocked but not surprised by Karen's revelation concerning Pancho and his behavior in the joint. On reflection, there were signs of his disposition not to fight back, but at the risk of losing his manhood I would think an organic response to defend and resist would automatically kick in. I recalled an incident when Pancho came busting through my door crying Vinnie, Vinnie, they are trying to take my shit. Pancho related the story.

Pancho came to me and said, "Vinnie, I rolled up on the Square (Farmers Blvd and 122nd Ave.) in a cab with two cartons of clothing that I got from Larry Morrel. I was going to sell the stuff at a bargain price, and the dudes started taking my shit. Then Jimmy pushed me in the chest and I fell backwards over somebody that was bending over behind me. So I got up and ran around here."

I said, "Pancho, you mean that your boys, the dudes that you hang out with on the Square and get high with, took your shit?"

"Yeh, man, ain't that fucked-up shit, man? I'm sorry, Vinnie. But why do you think they did that, Vinnie?" he said.

"So you ran here?" I said, "Now, okay, my brother, Pancho. What would you like me to do? Go to the Square and protect your interest?"

"No" he screamed, "No, Vinnie, I just want to bring the stuff here, if it's okay."

I barked, "So now you want to keep you stolen property in my house. Now, you know that the big intelligence boys keep a sharp eye on me because of my political and community organizing agenda. Some folks are just waiting, if not conspiring to make a criminal connection to my activities. Pancho, why would I expose myself in that way?"

"No, man, my shit ain't stolen," he replied."Larry let me have the stuff."

I was crisp, and said, "Yeh, sure, Pancho. And your boys let you have it also."

Pancho's boys were always taking advantage of him, but they remained his hang-out and get-high buddies. I was hard pressed to understand why he continued to subject himself to such constant abuse. Maybe Pancho has a little bit of machismo in him. I must be misguided to believe that most of these young black men would prefer to work on changing the circumstance as opposed to just hanging out day in and day out, just getting high, I thought. On the other hand, Pancho was quite successful with the young ladies. Pancho stood about 6 foot 1 inch, and weighted 190 to 195 pounds. He had a light, olive-brown skin complexion, and had black curly hair, a broad smile, and a well-trimmed mustache. The young ladies thought that he was cute and good looking, and in fact Pancho admitted to me that he believed that his greatest asset was his "good looks."

I knew that Pancho was mainlining heroin along with his buddy Rameen, and Rameen's older brother, Edward, and my brother, Lewis, were without doubt, their mentors in the culture. I was perplexed by the fact that I was so intently engaged in the community political empowerment process while many of my other peers were vicariously engaged in other than serious pursuits. I was impressed with many of the members of the 5 Percent Nation because of their focus on personal discipline, improving the condition of the black man in America, community affairs and education. Interestingly enough, I recall that it was members of the 5 Percent Nation that comprised the core group of factory workers and salesmen for the Concepts Afro Pik manufacturing enterprise. I considered that Pancho, Rameen and other members of their crew may be good additions to the core group of production and sales people. Although the nation of the Five Percent youth were a little younger than Pancho and Rameen et al., the Five Percenter's were not impressed with the knowledge, wisdom and understanding of the "slick" brothers. Prominent personalities among the Five Percent group was, Jabar, Natune, and Malik. Jabar, Natune, and Malik lived in Hollis, a neighborhood in Southeast Queens but spent most of the time in Harlem where they had become members of the Five Percent Nation. When the Afro-Disiac and Parent Youth Organization (PYO), set up operation on 205th Street and Hollis Avenue, Jabar, Natune, and Malik were the first youth that visited from the neighborhood. We had not yet been awarded the anti-poverty grant at the time but the day care center was in operation and the Afro-Disiac Community Cultural Center had begun the African dance, drum and language classes on Saturdays and the martial arts classes on Tuesday and Thursday evenings.

As soon as the programs began, Jabar, Natune, and Malik participated at various levels. All participated in the drum classes on Saturday and all three of them participated in the marshal arts classes. When the Afro-Pik factory got underway, they were the key personnel in the manufacturing and marketing process. Their counterparts, Pancho, Rameen, and his friend Mark were not interested in participating at any level. However, Pancho and his boys frequented the disco dance program that occurred on particular Friday and Saturday nights. When Pancho and crew showed up at the social event they invariably became a distraction if not public spectacle as they would ultimately begin their nodding gyrations caused by heroin addiction. Jabar, Natune, and Malik made note of the antics of Pancho and friends with both suspicion and instruction.

Jabar said, "You see, those brothers show and prove that they have fallen victim. They are supposed to understand that they have a responsibility to the youth in the community. But look at them; they are nodding and falling over everything, and then they go and try to talk to the young sisters. Those brothers need to have the knowledge of self, because they are lost. I talk to them to try and teach them civilization."

Natune injected, "That's right, Brother Jabar; we got to manifest the culture and teach the brothers the one to ten. I saw where the brothers were coming from when they didn't participate in anything. They are the 85 percent, Mr. B., and they are ruled by the values of the 10 percent. We are the Five percent, brother, and our job is to teach civilization to the 85 percent."

Malik took his turn. "That's right, brothers. We got to teach the what?"

Jabar and Natune said in unison, "Civilization." We got to teach civilization to the who?"

"Eighty-five percent."

" Teach civilization to the who?"

"Black man. Every time I see that dude, Pancho, he looks like he is stimulated on heroin and cocaine."

I closed the informal session by saying, "You young brothers got a real good idea of the stuff that is going on out here; maybe yours is the generation to flip the script. But, I essentially agree with what you said in terms of the need to teach civilization to the 85 percent."

Surveying the overall situation for black folk from my prospective was a morbid exercise at this stage of the game. I remembered that when I left the staff of NWRO and began to work on community based politics I was very optimistic about the ultimate outcome of the black political revolution. At the point that we got the $90,000.00 grand award under the auspices of the anti poverty program I held a sincere belief that black political revolution was going to be over and successful within the next year of so. Now that I have been sobered by the vicissitudes of time and experience, and some political maturation, I am dubious about the ultimate outcome. Yet I remain inspired to continue for no earthly reason that I can understand. Perhaps it is the visceral human instinct for survival that continues to motivate me. I have, without question, been in survival mode for years, but the current crisis is more serious as compared to others. Heretofore, I always had a facility from which to conduct business. Now my very domicile was in the process of being lost due to foreclosure.

CHAPTER 7

Whitmore's Restaurant was a popular eating spot located on Prospect Avenue between 167th and 166th Streets, just around the corner from the block. As I entered the modestly appointed restaurant memories of my junior high school days abounded with visions of me sitting at the counter with Wilfred and Jimmy-Lee, two friends that lived across the street from at 829 East 167th Street. My two friends and I frequented Whitmore's whenever we mustered up enough money to buy a malted milk and pie à la mode. We would sit in the restaurant for a couple of hours enjoying each other and spinning tall tales about our fabled sexual exploits, wants and desires. Jimmy-Lee had a lot of bully in him and tended to pick on anyone that he could beat up, or thought that he could. Wilfred was a favorite target for intimidation by Jimmy-Lee, and I would always come to Wilfred's defense. The three of us were the same age and in the same grade. Wilfred was the shortest among us and Jimmy-Lee who was just a little shorter than me always wanted to wrestle with guys smaller than him. I was tall for my age; by the time I entered junior high school, I was 5 feet 10 inches. The three of us attended Public School, 99 on Stebbins Avenue and Home Street and Wilfred and I attended Junior High School 40. Jimmy-Lee attended 120 Junior High School, as did most others on the block. Junior High School 40 on Prospect Avenue and Ritter Place had a reputation of being one of the toughest schools in the Bronx, but Wilfred and I had no alternative as 120 was overcrowded.

How things have changed, I thought. Wilfred had a younger brother and sister and his family moved off the block soon after we did to the newly developed Sound View Housing Development. Wilfred joined he United States Army and did a tour in Viet Nam came back unscathed. I heard that he got married and is about to be discharged. Jimmy-Lee's family bought a house in the North Bronx, but Jimmy's life took a tragic turn when he got hooked on heroin. He finally was able to kick the habit with the help of Methadone after the drug lifestyle took its toll on his body. Subsequent to kicking the heroin habit he became an alcoholic and ultimately died of a liver disease. Visiting the old neighborhood invariably generated a broad spectrum of thoughts and memories. Before entering Whitmore's I stopped into Mr. Morris' Candy Store and left a message for Van to meet me in Whitmore's. While considering the dinner menu, Van arrived.

Greeting me he said, "Yo, Vinnie B. What's up? How is the family and the movement?"

"The revolution continues, VW," I said. "What's up with you, my brother?"

Van replied, "Well, ain't nothing happening until you start something. I was just thinking about you the other day because we haven't talked in a while, and as usual a whole lot of stuff is going on. Ain't no telling what will happen next. But whatever it is, it's going to happen. Did you hear about Jake?"

"Yes, I heard," I answered, and stated, "Jakie got a manslaughter beef on him. I got the word, but what the hell happened? Jake wouldn't hurt a fly. So what the hell happened?"

Van began, "Jake had got strung-out on drugs, but you know Jake, man. He just did his thing and didn't bother anybody. You know. Anyway, one of the young gangster type kids from around the corner apparently figured that he could bully Jake because he was a junkie. At some point Jake was coming out of a nod when he caught the dude scooping out his radio and other stuff, and he ran off. The next day Jake confronted the dude when the dude was coming through the block with a couple of his boys. Jake confronted him about returning his property. The dude screamed at Jake, and called him a stupid junkie, then he told Jake that he took his shit and that is it. If Jake wanted to get the stuff back Jake would have to bring it in order it get it. He told the dude that he will give him a week to bring his property back. And if the dude didn't bring it within that time Jake said that he would come and get it by any means required. About a week latter I heard that Jake went up to the dude and stabbed him to death, then called the police and stood there until they came."

"Wow, man," I said, "I didn't know it was that kind of situation. These young dudes nowadays are 180 degrees from where we were. Looks like these young boys have taken over the neighborhood and show no respect for the older generation."

Van said, "What older generation, brother? You can't be thinking about our generation because there is just a remnant of us left, brother. Now when we were coming up, the older dudes turned us out. We emulated them, and they took us under their wing to some extent. Most of our generation has been taken out by drugs and the black revolution, so who is there in a position to put the young brothers on point or to provide an example of how things are supposed to work? Look at the dudes in your own family, man. You had one of the largest families around in terms of potential manpower."

VW was right, and he made a serious point in terms of my own family. The fact is that nine of my thirteen male first cousins were no longer living due to heroin addition, alcoholism, or violence. The names, thoughts, and memories echoed in the recesses of my soul. Juan, Billy, Robert, James, Wesley, Howie, Warren, Butch, and Carl.

I answered, "You are right, man; two-thirds of my cousins are gone. But not forgotten.

Van continued, "Brother, the black community is in a state of free fall. We are challenged from without, and we are challenged from within. Unfortunately, the black leadership, political, economic and social, is preoccupied with trying to get white folk to free us instead of developing our own emancipation budget and freeing ourselves."

I reacted, "Emancipation budget. Damn, VW, you're getting pretty heavy, brother. You need to walk me through this emancipation budget."

Van paused a moment, took a deep breath then said, "Well, Brother B., I been checking out your moves, and I know what you're trying to accomplish. In fact I've been meaning to share my own analysis with you about moving black folk from point A to point B. The key is focusing on our ultimate emancipation and coming up with a budget to finance our emancipation."

Van presented his analysis: "Various studies and some individuals have pointed out that black Americans spend 600 billion dollars annually, and the benefits thereof are essentially lost to the black community. The problem is compounded because apparently there are no plans in place to address the economic imperative of wealth creation in the black community. Interestingly enough, when one examines the civil rights movements in the nineteenth and twentieth centuries it is observed that black Americans were by and large participant beneficiaries along with the Republican (Abolitionists) movement in the nineteenth century and liberal Democrats (Progressives) in the twentieth century respectively. White organizers financed both civil rights movements primarily while black Americans provided the physical capital (numbers) that electoral politics is measured by. Black Americans were organized politically based on the philosophical and theoretical application of the political process. But the political and electoral process cannot operate or be sustained on philosophy and theory it requires an ongoing financial investment.

"Money is the mother's milk of politics, and he who pays the piper calls the tune. Accordingly, black political officials owe their re-election campaigns to interests other than the black community. The black community has been politically organized to focus on their numbers and not sufficiently on their cucumbers [money]. And investing financially in politics is generally not in the realm of possibilities for the black dollar. Black Americans for the most part only spend their money to buy something tangible and object oriented. Spending money on something without an instant gratification does not compute very will with most black folk.

"Black folk have yet to finance their political emancipation, and the internal financial potential lies dormant for the lack of a vision and plan for investing economically and politically. From a pure economic standpoint the potential ROI (Return on Investment) from a 600-billion-dollar annual market is an attractive investment. Therefore, political investment banking by black Americans in the advancement of the black community seems to be a no brainier. But the idea of financial investing and the building of economic wealth is a low agenda item among black Americans for any number of reasons.

"Once upon a time there was a place called the black Wall Street, located in Tulsa Oklahoma, prior to the modern civil rights movement. History records that black Americans in this town achieved unprecedented financial success and a formula for creating wealth in the black community. Their growing financial success as a community angered their white counterparts who began a campaign of terror among blacks, and ultimately and literally whites burned the town down, forcing most black Americans to flee from the area.

"Since the Tulsa black Wall Street phenomenon, finance and business culture has been a weak suit of the black community. There is an overriding 'good job' mentality that pervades the black community. And career objectives resulting from higher education is generally employment oriented. Other than the "individualists" and "elitists" who have access to capital and the kinds of financial instruments for wealth creation and community economic development, most other black Americans are preoccupied with the basic survival scenario. Hence, there are only a few that have the disposition, commitment and responsibility to make sacrifices for the many. Needless to say, 600 billion dollars annually is an attractive investment opportunity for the visionary black entrepreneur. Surely there is sufficient financial and economic potential to finance an emancipation budget for the twenty-first century."

"Damn, man," I said, "that is a profound assessment and analysis." I continued, "That's why I came to the Bronx to check you out and dialogue, to benefit from your vast worldly knowledge and analysis."

Smiling and with a bit of levity in his voice he said, "I know that you dig what I'm talking about Brother B. We are on the same page in terms of how to deal in this rough camp. The problem that me and you have is logistical; you're here, and I'm there. And no money. If we had some bank, we could seed the emancipation budget. We need to work on the emancipation budget, Brother B."

"As usual, VW, I'm glad that I came to check you out," I continued." It is always therapeutic and far-reaching. I love that emancipation-budget concept. But as you said we are on the same page in terms of the "how to" of black empowerment. I have termed the same idea as the need for numbers and cucumbers. Specifically, it is not enough that the black community has the numbers over other political minorities in America. But black folk don't use their cucumbers [money] to politically advance and apply our numerical advantage. And we don't deploy our numerical advance to leverage the political process."

Van said in conclusion, "Well, you know the story, B.; the civil rights leadership are the anointed leaders who are funded and supported by their partisan political benefactors to perpetuate race politics and hate. Their so-called political-empowerment strategy and tactics consist of protests, demonstrations, rallies, and boycotts only."

Van and I enjoyed dinner and an insightful and deep conversation that lasted for four hours, at which point Whitmore's was in the process of closing. We parted, and I made my way back to Queens to address the situation head on. I didn't say anything about the pending foreclosure situation because Van wouldn't have been able to do anything about it, apart from empathizing with my difficult situation. But the purpose for visiting with Van was served and I felt strengthened and centered by the experience.

CHAPTER 8

My transition to Harlem was miraculous in view of the practical situation that beset me. My house was foreclosed following a protracted legal battle that juxtaposed me with a real estate syndicate with enormous political clout and financial resources. The problem with the mortgage began during the time that funds were suspended from our youth development program and I was the subject of an open-ended investigation by the New York City Department of Investigation (DOI). At that time all efforts were directed to sustaining the program with the expectation that program funds would be forth coming following the conclusion of DOI's investigation. The legal battle ensued when I approached the mortgage company with a certified check for the outstanding mortgage payments and they refused to accept it. I retained an attorney to litigate the matter and I was hopeful about a favorable resolution. I remained hopeful of a favorable outcome but my optimism became tainted when my attorney advised me that the property had an added value because a new street and the construction of fifty or so one and two family homes were about to get underway. In the final analysis, a portion of the property was incorporated in the larger real estate development deal and my interests would not be included on the table.

On the heels of losing my office operation on Jamaica Avenue and 169th Street, the loss of my house and the impending dislocation had my back against the wall. This crisis seemed much more ominous than the PYO anti-poverty scenario because we had an Afro-Pik factory on 203rd Street and Hollis Avenue with a sales force distributing products throughout the city, and the Day Care Center on 205 Street and Hollis Avenue that was generating income. This time things were a whole lot different because there were no cash-generating operations in place and no discernable entrepreneurial opportunities available. The immediate prognosis was grim at best and I was drained of creative energy as I pondered my dubious fate. I was considering establishing a business presence in Harlem but had no financial resources to pursue any ideas or opportunities. Fortuitously, while pondering my fate in

Baisley Park, I bumped into Harold Williams a brother I met a few years earlier, who owned a house in the neighborhood of the park. Harold was a beautiful brother about 5 or 6 years my junior, but we connected when we first met at an ecumenical Christian service. At the time we met we struck up a heavy conversation that explored our similarities in terms of spiritual nature and personal values. In the course of that initial conversation I leaned that Harold was a master offset printer and worked for a major printing company in Manhattan. I related to him my brief experience in offset printing when I worked in the printing department where my mother worked, and how I enjoyed the work. Harold would visit me in my office on Jamaica Avenue from time to time and we would talk about spirituality, Christianity and the printing business. Visits to my office was therapy to Harold as he said because he was beginning to have problems on the job that he wanted to talk about and get off his chest. Also, Harold was impressed with my word processing and computer function as this capability was the first wave of computer technology.

Harold was also impressed with Bishop Valmore Holt, my mentor who gave me a crash course in computer technology and facilitated the purchase of desktop publishing equipment that gave my company a competitive advantage in the early 1980s. Harold often made the point that my desktop publishing capability facilitated the pre-press process for the offset printing operation. And Harold was impressed with my ability to turn out quality layout masters for flyers, posters, newsletters, letterheads, business cards, etc. Consequently, our conversations were very engaging and far reaching and we also discussed the potential and feasibility of a business partnership. We hadn't seen each other since the loss of my office function. As I sat on the park bench staring at the lake in deep thought I heard a familiar voice:

"Praise the Lord. Here is my brother; something told me to jog around the lake and release myself from some of this tension and praise the Lord. And I jog into my good brother. Peace, man. How are you doing?"

"Harold, my brother, praise Him. Praise the Lord back at you, brother," I retaliated and said, "I see that you're out there working hard."

"Yeah, man," he replied, "I'm working hard jogging around this lake, but I am hardly working as it relates to my job. The abuse is getting a little heavy for me, so I've taken the days off that I have earned and working enough hours to pay bills and keep hope alive. What's up with you? I'm surprised seeing you sitting down, chillin'."

"I must chill right now, my brother, just to keep my wits about me. I am experiencing some major setbacks that require deep contemplation."

With a cordial expression of shock on his face, he said, "Setbacks, I never heard you acknowledge setbacks. I only remember you talking about and sharing the lemonade that you made from the many lemons that you receive. You mean to tell me that you don't have a glass of lemonade for me, brother?"

Smilingly I replied, "No, brother. No lemonade today, only lemons and limes. No other ingredients, like honey or sugar, to make the drink palatable."

Harold launched into Spirit mode and pronounced, "Well, you know what He said, brother. You've got to stand. Regardless to whom or what, you've got to stand. You know the deal. You know the struggle, brother. But what is the deal, or rather, what is the latest?"

Feeling a sense of release and relief I began, "Well, my brother, that which I fear most has finally come up on me. I finally got a ruling on the matter with my house, and I have lost it. I was with my attorney the other day, and he advised me about the ruling, and he is preparing a check for me amounting to $3,000.00, which was escrowed for the mortgage payments. So I figured that I would come up to the lake and contemplate my fate, and try to come up with some options."

Harold responded with sincere concern. "Wow. That's pretty deep, brother. That's real deep. What's up with the prospects of relocating the business to Harlem? Any movement on that score?"

"I identified a storefront in Harlem on 5th Avenue between 125th and 126th Streets that had been vacant for a few years. I talked to the owner of the brownstone, and it is available for lease. It's a commercial space, and therefore it will not accommodate my residential needs; therefore I have to first concentrate on a place to lay my head that can be called home."

Harold said, "Well, brother, in the interest of full disclosure, I am exploring my options in terms of other employment. Business or professional options, because the environment at my job is overwhelming at this point. So, brother, to make a long story short you need to stand in spite of the challenge, and let's see what we can come up with. I'm going to put some ideas and thoughts before the Lord, and I will get back to you. I'm going to finish this jog around the lake, put some stuff up before our Lord, then get back to you. Keep standing now, brother. And praise the Lord."

After a couple more meetings, Harold and I decided to establish a partnership and lease the storefront. The sign went up proclaiming, "DESKTOP PUBLISHING AND OFFSET PRINTING." Harold brought some printing contracts with him and immediately we began to generate business from businesses and people in the neighborhood. Harold reacquainted me with the offset printing press, but I primarily took care of the pre press operation. I was able to take advantage of my political consulting experience that added to the notoriety of the new printing establishment. As a matter of fact, shortly after we opened shop Ed Lurie, the Executive Director of the New York Republican State Community contacted me and offered me the position of state-wide coordinator of the "Black Desk" in the up coming gubernatorial race. After a few overtures from Ed, and the assurance that there would be a credible campaign budget, I agreed to the position of State-wide Coordinator for People for O'Rourke. My own assessment of the opportunity as well as the assessment of most of my political confidants agreed that it was a win-win situation. Whether the GOP gubernatorial candidate Andy O'Rourke won the election or not, the fact that I was the HNIC, (Head Negro In Charge) could only benefit me and the grassroots movement in the future.

On May 24, 1986 The New York Voice published the following piece headlined, "**Republicans Plan Meeting in Harlem.**"

Anthony Colavita, chairman of the New York Republican state community will be the honored guest speaker on Saturday, June 7, at 55 West 125th Street, in Harlem.

The theme of the event is: "Dialogue with Washington and Albany" and is being sponsored by the New York City black Republican council as a fund-raiser to kick off their ongoing voter education-registration and electoral activity, said Vincent Burton, spokesperson for the black Republican council.

Accountable Government

Burton said, "The black Republican Council is developing a group of quality candidates that will begin to restore accountable government to New York City in particular." Other invited guests include U.S. Senator Al D'Amato, congressman Bill Green, and members of the federal and state government, members of Congress, and the State legislature. For further information contact Vincent Burton 212.316.0900

On September 2, 1986 the following press release was disseminated by the People For O'Rourke campaign:

O'Rourke to Inaugurate Harlem Office

Republican Gubernatorial candidate Andrew O'Rourke today announced the appointment of Vincent Burton as statewide black Community Coordinator of the People for O'Rourke. At the same time Mr. Burton, chairman of the New York City black Republican Council, announced that a gala ribbon-cutting ceremony in Harlem and a cocktail reception in the Bronx will highlight a full weekend of activities from Friday, September 5, through Sunday, September 7, as the black Republican community gears up its statewide effort on behalf of Mr. O'Rourke and other Republican candidates.

Mr. O'Rourke will be the featured guest at the opening of the campaign headquarters at 6 P.M. Friday evening at 175 West 126th Street. The ribbon-cutting ceremony will be attended by national as well as local Republican Party officials.

The evening will also highlight the official announcement of candidacy by Joan Dawson, seeking the 70th A.D. District State Assembly seat currently held by Geraldine Daniels. Also, in attendance will be Edward Nelson Rodriquez, 7th District Congressional candidate from Queens, and other Congressional and state candidates.

Another of the weekend's activities will be a cocktail reception in honor of Guy Velella, 34th District State Senator and Chairman of the Bronx County Republican Committee. The reception, featuring U.S. Senator Alfonse D'Amato and Mr. O'Rourke, will be held on Sunday, September 7, from 4 to 8 P.M. at Parkside Plaza Elegant in the Bronx. Hosting the affair will be State Senate candidate Alton Chase, Bronx Coordinator of the NYC black Republican Council.

In announcing the schedule, black Republican Council Chairman Burton charged Mario Coumo not only with betraying the trust of the black community but also with undermining the political process generally by his conduct toward former lieutenant Governor candidate Abraham Hirschfeld. Mr. Burton called on voters to join the effort "to replace the arrogant Cuomo regime with the constructive enlightenment of an Andy O'Rourke administration."

"We intend to encourage Democrats, Independents, and Liberals to vote for Republicans in November," said Burton. When Cuomo and

126

the Democratic Party find a dry well in this election, they will certainly miss the water. We intend to replace the one-party Democratic tyranny of this state—and especially New York City—with an accountable bi-partisan government." New York City activities will be part of statewide ceremonies being planned for a number of communities.

On Wednesday October 22, 1986 *The New York City Tribune* published this piece entitled, "**Black GOP Leader Issues Call for Radical Surgery to End Corruption**," by Vadim Kotler, *Tribune* staff.

Vincent Burton, chairman of the New York City black Republican Council and coordinator of People for O'Rourke, a group backing Andrew O'Rourke, the GOP's candidate for governor, said yesterday that radical political surgery is required to remove the cancer of corruption and bring political accountability to New York.

Burton spoke at a press conference held by black and Hispanic candidates and party leaders. He said that the bipartisan leadership was needed to end corruption in New York.

"It's a historic occasion," said Joseph Holland, the Manhattan coordinator of the city Republican Council. He said that the meeting aimed at creating a foundation for a united political movement among black and Hispanic Republicans.

"Expectations that blacks will continue voting for the Democrats are a myth," Joseph said, predicting victory for the city Republican minority candidates on November 4. "blacks have been voting Democratic for the past half century, but things will not necessarily continue that way," Joseph said.

The press conference, held at 55 West 125th Street and organized by the New York City black Republican council, was just the beginning of the high-visibility campaign for black and Hispanic grassroots leaders, said Burton. "The council was created 4 years ago to create voter awareness and participation in the black community," he said.

"The Democratic Party does not have concrete projects for empowering the black community, as many of the anti-poverty programs have not worked," Burton said. "The Republican Council carries the message of self-reliance to the black community by stressing the entrepreneurial spirit and commitment to responsibility," he said.

"The black community has to generate its own resources,"
Burton said. "To establish political ascendancy, we have to establish
self-reliance."

"When there is one-party domination, social and political
sewage goes to the party, and corruption becomes inevitable," said
Vincent Baker at the press conference. Baker is the author of
Republican Party and Black American: A Political History.

Burton also charged that Gov. Cuomo is undermining the
democratic process by refusing to debate the Republican
gubernatorial candidate, Andrew O'Rourke.

October 25, 1986, the *New York Amsterdam News* published the
following article entitled, **GOP Rally in Harlem:**

Lionel Hampton and his world-renowned band will lead a
Harlem rally on behalf of Andy O'Rourke, Joan Dawson, David
Kennedy, Rubin Estrada, Nathurlon Jones, and other Republican
candidates on Tuesday, October 21 at the James Varrick Community
Center, 151 West 136th Street, NYC. Senator Roy Goodman, chairman
of the New York Republican County committee, is sponsoring the gala
affair. Dubbed "Uptown Tuesday Night," the purpose of this event is
to begin to activate and build the local Republican Party. "We are
focusing on building a good district leadership," said Leroy Owens,
District leader in the 70th AD.

The 7 P.M. rally will follow a press conference convened at the
CAV building, 55 West 125th Street at 11 A.M. The theme of the press
conference is, "Sweeping New York Clean of Corruption." The
activities are being coordinated by Leroy Owens; Vincent Burton,
NYS Republican Committee/Black Republican Taskforce and Nelson
Rockefeller Jr. Ethnic Coordinator of People for Andrew O'Rourke.

Under the umbrella of the New York City black Republican Council were
assembled an impressive group of black and Hispanic community leaders and
candidates. A quote in the July 9, edition of *Big Red News*, a New York City
metropolitan weekly, read, "The distinguished group of new-breed,
insurgent Republicans plan to renegotiate the terms by which political
business is done in New York City and State." The group includes Joe
Holland, chief council to the State Senate Housing and Community

Development Committee; Alton Chase, community activist and Bronx district leader; Richard Thomas, political activist and architect, Staten Island; Duane Jackson community activist and entrepreneur, Brooklyn; Vernell Thompson, community activist and developer, Queens; Cecil Ellie, investment counselor, Nassau; and Rev. B. Leslie James social activist and ecumenical coordinator. Candidates for elective office include Joan Dawson, housing activist and educator, NYS Assembly 70th A.D.; David Kennedy, NYS Senate candidate 29th S.D. Harlem; Melanie Chase, U.S. Congress 18th C.D.; Alton Chase, NYS Senate 32nd S.D.; Ann Francis Potts, NYS Senate, 30th S.D.; Elvira M. Lebron, NYS Assembly 73rd A.D.; and Elizabeth Francis Cruz, NYS Assembly 77th A.D.

A groundswell of GOP activism and support was emerging sending political shock waves to virtually all quarters of New York City electoral politics in general and in the local and state Republican Party leadership, in particular. The dynamic visibility and application was unprecedented and directly threatened the clandestine political power relationship between the both political parties as well as the internal political machinations with the Republican Party. In short, political business as usual was being potentially threatened by the emerging dynamic force that was not under the control of the county leadership. There was from the outset an "upstate" vs. "downstate" political dichotomy that my official involvement at the state level animated, particularly at the New York Republican County Committee level that was the political order of the day. The upstate vs. downstate dichotomy was complex and composed of several components. From both points of view, (downstate and upstate) there was an ethnic dimension that juxtaposed downstate and its Jewish American power base and upstate that was politically dominated by WASP leadership. The ethnic dimension was the social construct and general political subtext of relations with all other communities. Another factor in the dichotomy was the manner in which political business was conducted in New York City at the GOP county level. The downstate problem from the standpoint of the state was the fact that there was no viable or credible district leader infrastructure in the respective counties that comprise the city. As it relates to the black community, particularly in Harlem where the black political elite resided, County GOP leaders appointed local district leaders that had no links to the community. On the other hand the electoral process specifies that district leaders are to determine, by the part election primary, not by appointment. By appointing the district leaders to the GOP county committee, the County leader is able to circumvent the party primary election and the "anointed" district leaders are accountable only to the county leadership that appointed them.

Both political parties deliberately de-emphasize participation in the party primary to keep the numbers small and manageable. Hence, sometimes less than 15 % of registered voters participate in the primary election. Generally, the small numbers of primary-election participants fall into two categories, cronies of the party leadership factions and astute and informed citizens. On the Republican Party side the general problem is compounded by the fact that in Harlem and the Bronx for example the appointed district leadership infrastructure is also comprised of Democratic Party operative. Therefore, whereas the polling sites are supposed to be manned equally by Republicans and Democrats in the context of polling inspectors, etc., the Republican participation is overshadowed by Democrat poll watchers. In this way, the New York County GOP maintains a system of "plantation" politics. The GOP closed-door policy relegates insurgent political aspirants to the Democratic Party, where there exists a minimal opportunity, vis-à-vis, the political party primary, to achieve ballot status to compete in the general election. Moreover, the GOP county leadership appoints district leaders that have no organic relationship with the district they represent. Thus, appointing people from outside of the district and thwarting the party primary election is the character of local plantation politics.

The motive for these insidious and odious political machinations is political self-interest, and racism. The self-interest component stems from the fact that the Republican Party County Chairman in Manhattan and the Bronx for example are elected officials of the New York State Senate, in an overwhelmingly Democratic constituency base, averaging 5 to 1 in the city. Therefore in order for the GOP county chairman in Manhattan and the Bronx to safeguard their interest as elected officials, they apparently made a political bi-partisan accommodation to scratch each other's back. In Manhattan for example Congressman Charles Rangel, the dean of the Democratic New York Congressional delegation, also runs on the Republican ballot, until very recently. And there is a substantial patronage arrangement between the New York Republican County Committee, and the Congressman's office. The outcome of this esoteric political arrangement is that the Republican Party county chairman in the Bronx and Manhattan are insulated from viable competition for their respective New York State Senate seats. Concomitantly, black Democratic elected officials are insulated from the emergence of viable black and "minority" Republican Party candidates to compete for the office. The process is racist because this contrived structure is intended to marginalize and control the politics of the black community. And the process thwarts the democratic process while undermining citizenship.

The intensity and success of our community and political activism was a grave threat to the political status quo in many ways unknown to us at the time. As we attempted to move the political empowerment process, the complexities became exposed bringing forth new revelations of real-time hardball politics. We found ourselves inextricably engaged in a dynamic political process with an open ended and dubious eventual outcome. Without doubt, the county leadership had the greatest impact on the political reality on the ground and I was learning about that first in the context of political baptism by fire. According to my contacts at the New York Republican State Committee, they were receiving considerable political flack from the chairman of the New York Republican County Committee for "imposing Vincent Burton" and "his leadership" on the county structure. None of the appointed black district leadership in Harlem participated on the gubernatorial campaign in any meaningful way. And while I deliberately made every effort to include county leadership I was rebuffed and efforts by the county chairman to have me replace on the campaign was ongoing. In some instances the Ethnic Coordinator of the campaign Nelson Rockefeller Jr. took the liberty of intervening and modulating the sentiments of the GOP County Committee chairman.

While the state GOP committee was being pressured by New York Republican County Committee Chairman for enabling me and disrupting the local political status quo, our activism attracted the White House and the Republican National Committee. On August 13, 1986, I received a letter from the White House over the signature of Haley Barbour, Deputy Assistant to the president and Director of the Office of Political Affairs, in my capacity of Chairman of the New York City black Republican Council:

Dear Mr. Burton:

Thank you for your letter of July 30, addressed to Mr. Regan, and the attached proposal for a black Republican Statewide Taskforce, which I read with great interest.

The concept itself is very good, and I would appreciate your keeping me informed of its progress. If successful, it is certainly a prototype that could be used in other states, and we would be happy to work with you and the Republican National committee to that end.

Please feel free to contact me or Barbara Hayward, who is the White House Liaison with the New York State Republican Party, any time you feel we may be of help.

Best wishes in your endeavors.

Sincerely,

Haley Barbour
Deputy Assistant to the President
Director Office of Political Affairs

The interest of the White House in New York City politics generated a sense of possibilities at the grassroots level and helped to solidify the emerging local black Republican leadership. On the contrary, the Republican Party County Committee particularly in Manhattan intensified its political pressure on the Executive Director of New York Republican State Committee, Ed Lurie to sever relations with me, and the insurgent New York City black Republican Council. Ultimately, within the context of the O'Rourke gubernatorial campaign changes began to take place reminiscent of political business as usual. While on the surface the idea of Republican Party candidates competing with their counterpart Democratic candidate appears to be the objective of the electoral process, in the real political world it is much more complicated than that. Inexplicably the manager of the O'Rourke campaign Frank Dean, was replaced with Mr. Barry Nelson, from out of the state. When I asked Ed Lurie the obvious questions concerning developments in the campaign, I was assured that it was a positive change and the campaign was still online. However, soon after the campaign staff change, budgetary provisions for a realistic campaign effort in the black community diminished significantly. Lines of communication began to break down too frequently and decisions were not made in a timely manner. A chief concern among the New York City black Republican Council was why the escalating municipal scandals were not issues on the state and local GOP platforms.

Governor Mario Cuomo refused to debate candidate O'Rourke during the campaign process. The O'Rourke strategists seized upon Cuomo's refusal to debate and featured in the daily newspaper a large photo of GOP candidate Andy O'Rourke standing with a life size replica of the governor proclaiming the dummy that won't debate. In fact the whole campaign strategy from that point centered around, the dummy that won't debate, and never focused on the topical issue of corruption in government. Despite the Herculean efforts on the part of the New York City black Republican Council and the grassroots community, at the end of the day it was political business as usual, and the governor Coumo won the election decisively. The perception in the black community is that the Republican Party does not intend to make a serious initiative in the black community. That perception has transformed into an emotion.

Following the results of the campaign Gibson approached me and said, "So what's new? Republicans ignore the black community. What's new this time, Vinnie? Isn't that, in the course of the Republican Party, business as usual, ignoring the black community? They may have played you out of position, V."

Darryl chimed in, "Yeah, Brother B., Gibson's got a point, because some people were beginning to believe GOP hype, but the party dropped the ball and you too."

Somewhat biting at the bit I responded, "Well, they did drop the ball. And maybe they dropped me too, but I think it's a little more complicated than that."

Darryl reacted, "Well, Brother B., It seems pretty simple to me. Maybe you are making it more complicated than it really is."

"Well," I said, "I got a call yesterday from Mrs. Barker, the Senator's right hand and the Executive Assistant of the county committee, as you know. Mrs. Barker offered me an employment opportunity in Congressman Rangel's office. She called me on the phone and said, "Vincent. I thought that I would give you a call to find out if you would be interested in a job opportunity in Congressman Rangel's office. You are the first one that I called."

Unusually quite up to this point Chase engaged the conversation, "That's real interesting, brother. So what did you say to her?"

I began, "I thanked her for the consideration and phone call, but I told her that I would have to regretfully decline the opportunity because I just recently opened my business, and I needed to grow it, before I took on an additional responsibility. The call and offer hit me by surprise, but on another level I thought it was bizarre. Here I am, in the wake of the gubernatorial campaign, a prominent Republican, employed by the dean of the black Democratic leadership. That job would play me out of position if I accepted it. The State Republican Party didn't play me out of position just because they dropped the ball."

Darryl got a little defensive. "Don't take it personal, Vinnie baby, I'm not suggesting that they played you for a political sucker when I said that dropped you and the ball!"

Chase contributed, "I agree with Vinnie when he says that it's more complicated than meets the eye. I have prior personal experience that informs my belief in terms of how complex and sophisticated this electoral political exercise is. I have some thoughts and reaction to that phone call you received, but first let me share this development."

Chase continued, "I got a phone call too the other day, but it wasn't from Mrs. Barker or my county leader in the Bronx, Senator Guy Velella. My call was from Ed Lurie, the Executive Director the Republican State Committee, which was out of the blue, because Ed. and I don't generally rap. I generally talk to him through Vinnie. But to get right to the point, Ed told me that now that the campaign was over I should deal directly with him at state, as opposed to dealing through Vinnie. I didn't respond directly to that instruction, and he concluded, saying that he just called to tell me that. I talked to the Queens and the Bronx coordinators and they told me that they got a similar call with the same message. The message is that state for some reason is clipping Vinnie's political wings."

Laughing, Darryl said, "Well, nobody called me, but that's what I'm talking about. That what I feel. They dropped the ball because things were getting too heavy for them to manage. And the political status quo was beginning to be threatened."

Chase took it a little further. "Now, Brother B., my thoughts about that gig in the Congressman's office. Wait a minute. First let me say that I agree with your decision to grow your business and not go to work for the congressman. That being said, dig this. Leroy Owens, the head district leader and the Senator's fair-haired boy didn't get the call. You got the call, brother. You were given a compliment, B. It's called patronage. They were extending patronage to you, far and above what they offer the anointed and appointed ones. Now that the campaign is over, the state had to concede to local pressure from the county and back off of you. On the other hand, the county reached out to you to play the political game their way, vis-à-vis, no electoral competition with black Democrats. I've been a district leader in the Bronx since the 1970s, and I know the moves; the county extended a political patronage olive branch to you, brother."

CHAPTER 9

Mr. Dolphin and John Wood were the only members of the New York Republican County Committee that stopped by the print shop from time to time and participated in the political roundtable conversations. The absence of the few other district leaders was conspicuous and set the tone for much speculation as to why they deliberately avoided the conversation, and engagement. I was disillusioned by this development because the beginnings of the Harlem grassroots Republican activism were auspicious, growing out of Joseph Holland's campaign for the New York State Senate in 1985. At that point, the heretofore, informal grassroots GOP movement was formally established and the foreseeable electoral and political future seemed bright and attractive. The idea of establishing a printing company crystallized following the campaign because it became apparent that a printing and documentation capability was central to prosecuting a campaign and sustaining a political movement. I had experience in pre press operations in terms of typesetting, layout and design, knowledge of how lucrative the printing business was and had the benefit of an associate who was a master off set printer. Moreover, I engaged the expectation that the local black Republicans in particular had a shared vision of providing a viable political and electoral alternative to the one party monopoly in the city. The high point of that vision culminated at the outset of the O'Rourke gubernatorial campaign and my position as statewide coordinator in the black community. The vision having now matured, has been demoralized and compromised by a level of complexity and sophistication that has engulfed me. I couldn't resist making comparisons between by experience working on political and community activism on the political left and now on the right.

Notwithstanding the local and state political resistance to new ideas and grassroots community and political activism, there was still a strong interest at the national level to support our efforts. All of my subsequent efforts to work in conjunction with local and state initiatives were ignored or undermined and my initiatives were boycotted by the "official" black

Republican leadership, at the state and local levels. Although the State Committee declined to enable the "Black Republican Taskforce," we were determined to finance and enable it ourselves as "grassroots" Republicans. During the gubernatorial campaign, I had the distinct honor of meeting and befriending the great Lionel Hampton, who was the Vice Chairman of the New York Republican County Committee. There was a mutual affection between Lionel Hampton and Nelson Rockefeller Jr., the Ethnic Coordinator of the People for Andy O'Rourke campaign. I was a recipient of good relations with Mr. Hampton because there was an obvious working synergy between me and Rocky. Accordingly, Lionel Hampton expressed interest in supporting the ongoing efforts of the GOP Taskforce. With that backdrop we began formulating plans for a fund-raiser in the context of a "Living Memorial Banquet" for Lionel Hampton. One year after the campaign we scheduled the "Lionel Hampton Living Memorial Banquet" at a midtown venue. The plans developed well and Mr. Hampton was enthusiastic about the living memorial idea coupled with the GOP grassroots initiative. We started the fund-raising process and began receiving financial contribution from far and wide. Notable among the prompt contributors, was honorable Ned Regan, the New York State comptroller and the Vince Albano Republican Club, among others. As a result of the immediate response we became optimistic relative to the potential for the success of the event and the launching of the Black Republican Taskforce '88.

Our enthusiasm and optimism began to turn sour when I received a phone call directly for Mr. Hampton who, by the tone of his voice and nature of his remarks was clearly unnerved.

He said, "Hello there, Gates [Gates was a term of endearment that Mr. Hampton used ubiquitously in addressing his friends], I'm sorry to call you so suddenly," he said, "but there is a problem developing about me attending the planned event. I don't know what the details of the problem are, but Gates, the Senator called me about it, and you know, I serve as the Vice-Chairman of the New York Republican County Committee at his pleasure. Like I said, Gates, I don't know what the problem is, but I won't be able to attend the event that you are planning in my honor. So, I would appreciate it if you canceled it, okay, Gates?"

"Okay, Mr. Hampton," I said. "I understand the problem, and I will get right to it. Thanks for giving me a heads up on it. God bless, good night."

Mr. Hampton concluded, "Okay, Gates. Keep on trucking."

The cancellation of the planned Lionel Hampton Living Memorial Banquet was an unexpected and dynamic development that could have a seriously negative fallout for me and future business and political relationships. It was common knowledge that we had solicited and collected funds for this event, now it had to be canceled, and the contributors needed to be contacted. Whether the cancellation of the event was a deliberate attempt to sand bag me and the movement was a moot point, I had to react quickly and directly before the word got out that Mr. Hampton will not be in attendance and that I was trying to pull off a scam event. I immediately contacted the people that authored the contribution letters from the State Comptroller and the Vince Albano Republican Club, and I also sent a report to President Reagan's people who were monitoring local events, since we worked on his reelection campaign in 1984. I got a prompt reply from the White House, which proved to be very helpful in modulating the situation and generating understanding of local and national political dispositions.

The White House—February 22, 1988
Mr. Vincent Burton
Chairman
Black Republican Taskforce '88

Dear Mr. Burton:

On behalf of President Reagan, thank you for your message and enclosures. We appreciate hearing about the Lionel Hampton Living Memorial Banquet and other activities planned by the Black Republican Taskforce '88.

The enthusiasm of loyal supporters like you and your colleagues help to preserve the mandate that will keep our nation on the right course throughout the next decade. Hard work, a legacy of eight years of success, and improved outreach into our minority communities will ensure that Republican Party reaps significant gains in state and local elections.

You have my appreciation and best wishes.

Sincerely,

Franklin L. Lavin
Deputy Assistant to the president
Director of the Office of Political Affairs.

The correspondence from the White House helped us to negotiate a smooth landing for our GOP grassroots enterprise after having survived the attempt to shoot us down. And as a follow up I was contacted by Congressman Jack Kemp's people and asked to be a delegate in the 16th congressional district in Harlem during the Congressman's bid for the Republican Party nomination in 1988. There was a definite and consistent interest on the part of the national party and White House in supporting GOP grassroots activism in New York City. On March 28, 1988 I received the following letter from Congressman Jack Kemp.

Dear Vincent:

It is not really possible in just a few words to adequately thank you for everything you have done to help with my campaign. We will always remember the days of commitment, effort, and to quote Churchill, the "blood, sweat and tears" involved in the triumph we all hoped lie ahead.

While the nomination is not ours, I think it's fair to say that we have made a difference in, and a significant impact on, consequences and that issues are important. Even more, we helped set the terms of debate for the future. Without your help this would not have been possible. Without your willingness to give of your time and talent "the cause" we believe in would not have been moved forward.

Long after the words are forgotten and the issues have undergone change, the spirit that sparked our efforts will remain and go forward. That spirit will go on as long as we are willing to continue the battle for the enduring principles of country, family and progress that transcend any one campaign or any moment in time.

Joanne and I and the whole Kemp family thank you for all of your help and your sacrifices. This was not the time for us to prevail. But that time will come, and I know we will be there together.

Sincerely,

Jack

With the election of George H.W. Bush to the presidency, good relations with the national party leaders continued uninterrupted. Likewise, the boycott of our activities by the "official" black Republican leadership was as intense as ever. The only change in the political environment was my appreciation and understanding of the political reality on the ground and that it would be fruitless and futile to coordinate activities with the county and the "official" black leadership. The challenge of the Black Republican Taskforce was to reach out to the unorganized, disaffected, disillusioned, and apathetic voters in the framework of a bi-partisan political empowerment initiative on the quest for new political paradigm.

Chase came in, and we began our usual political conversation. He began with a jocular question. He said, "Peace, Brother B. Is today the weekly, how-to-build-a-grassroots-political-movement day? Or do I need to come back on another day?"

"Chase, my brother," I replied, "every day that you come in here is how-to-build-a-grassroots political-empowerment-movement session. You're never at a loss for words and ideas. What's up?"

Chase stated, "Now that we realized that our agenda is divergent from the county and the "official" black Republican leadership, perhaps we should capitalize on our national assets and do a local bi-partisan local power move on our own."

"Come on with it directly, man," I said, "We might be on the same page, as I think I know where you are going."

He said, "You were Kemp's delegate in the 16th CD here in Harlem, Congressman Rangel's constituency. Now that honorable Congressman Jack Kemp is the current Secretary of the US Department of Housing and Urban Development (HUD) perhaps you should contact the Congressman in the context of a bi-partisan and cooperative effort to bring Secretary Kemp to Harlem and perhaps have a symposium."

I answered, "Looks like we're on the same page, brother. Here is a copy of a letter I sent to Congressman Rangel last week appropriate to your point, I think. I suspect that I will get a reply shortly, but I wouldn't be surprised if he doesn't touch base with the county chairman before he replies. You know that Mrs. Barker told me categorically that the county has a better patronage relationship with Democratic Congressman Rangel than Republican Congressman Bill Green.

On March 27, 1989, I received a return letter from the honorable Congressman Charles Rangel.

Dear Mr. Burton:

I appreciate receiving your letter of February 21, urging my involvement with you in a planning committee for housing and health.

I am pleased to see that the Black Republican Taskforce is going to be joining us in efforts to build the Harlem community and to provide housing for our citizens. The public officials in our community and others who have been involved in this process for some time, have been seeking to involve the Republican administration for the last eight years with very little success. We have renewed hope, however, because of the new president's commitment to social progress and the enthusiasm and energy of a new Secretary of Housing and Urban Development, Jack Kemp.

I have agreed with the new Secretary that it would be good for us to pursue enterprise- zone legislation so that communities like Harlem could mobilize and coordinate resources necessary to bring about meaningful change.

My bill, H.R. 6, will be scheduled soon for hearings, and I expect that we will have support of the leadership to pass legislation that will enhance the capacity of the Federal Government to bring resources to community such as ours.

Of course, with the Republican administration you can play a very large role in making certain that this mobilization occurs and that we have the attention and commitment of the administration towards securing the goals to which we mutually aspire. We face real budgetary problems, and I believe that at this stage it would be very difficult for us to accomplish what we want to unless we have the total commitment of the administration to tackle the major problems that we face in our community.

Thus, the partnership that I propose is that we in the community work very closely with the Republican Taskforce and that you assume the leadership for us in intervening with the Federal government in a manner that will secure the kind of support that we need in order to carry forth the programs of redevelopment that we envision.

I hope that you will work closely with the Harlem Urban Development Corporation and its president, Donald Cogsville. I find that this coordinating mechanism is one that is most useful to secure the kind of resources and unity that are necessary in order to further the development of our community.

I look forward to your help in getting Jack Kemp to visit our community and to having the attention of the Bush administration placed upon the priorities that we see for our people.

Sincerely,

Charles B. Rangel
Member of Congress

After several follow-up meetings with the Congressman's office people I concluded that my only option for a relationship with the Congressman and his colleagues would be vertical in nature with no possibility of a horizontal discourse or relationship. Also, it was clear that the pervasive political pressure to marginalize me and the "grassroots" GOP grassroots movement might have also been exerted on the Congressman's good offices. While we were virtually locked out of local politics, overtures from national political quarters continued. On November 28, 1989, I received a letter from Mr. Lee Atwater, Chairman of the Republican National Committee.

Dear Mr. Burton:

In September I convened the first Small Business Advisory Council (SBAC) meeting on behalf of the Republican National Committee.

SBAC is a 30-member advisory group of small business entrepreneurs from across America. This group will meet with the president and vice president, local legislators, department heads, and business leaders to identify issues crucial to the small business community.

The SBAC will address different ways to improve small business access to capital, resolve problems in rural small/economic development, develop minority businesses, and increase small business involvement in international trade.

The president has demonstrated his commitment to small business through his unwavering support for a capital-gains tax cut. This important legislation will spur economic activity, create jobs and encourage new small businesses, to be formed.

President Bush and you are committed to supporting the growth and expansion of America's small businesses.

I have appointed Jim Whitehead as director of SBAC, and he will be responsible for keeping you informed of our activities. Please feel free to contact him with your comments or suggestions. We welcome your active participation. Thank you for your continued support.

Sincerely,

Lee Atwater, chairman
Republican National Committee

The National Republican Committee and the White House were consistent in their interest in supporting local grassroots Republican activism. I was getting a better appreciation of the dichotomy between national, state and local Republican Party politics, in an expert witness capacity. Although racial politics was the subtext of their respective power relationships, in application it was the local county committee structure that maintained and manages the plantation political system. But in New York City the political plantation system was not only pervasive, it was also deceptive because of the strange bedfellow relationship between the two major political parties, vis-à-vis, Democrats and Republicans. Tragically, the plantation system relegated organic grassroots community leadership to the Democratic Party or their derivative splinter political organization. While at the state level, was displeasure in some quarters with the way some county committee leadership in New York City had compromised the district leader infrastructure, they couldn't override the county structure. While the national party also respected the county structure the feds reserved and exercised their right to support the work of local efforts. Hence there remained hope for developing meaningful links from the grassroots level to that national party.

Apart from the plantation politics that characterized that state of New York City electoral politics, there were some structural problems that facilitated this egregious racist political system. Specifically, the GOP county chairman should be restricted from competing for elective office in the general election. The fact that the Bronx and Manhattan GOP country chairmen were State Senators in an overwhelming Democratic city (5 to 1), was a political reality on the ground automatically defeating the prospect of a strong local Republican Party. In hindsight I could see the nature of the power relationships that we were up against. Understanding the nature of our opposition was a critical accomplishment, but developing a viable strategy with feasible applications was a difficult challenge in view of the complexity and sophistication of the political deception.

At this point it was time for me to take advantage of an opportunity that developed from the connection with Mr. Lee Atwater, Chairman of the Republican National Committee (RNC). For the past couple of years I was being encouraged by members of the South African Government to visit the country. I resisted taking them up on the invitation while Nelson Mandela was in prison, but when Mr. Mandela was released and visited Harlem, I decided to check with the South African Consulate to see if my invitation was still open. To my surprise and delight my invitation was still open so I took advantage of the unique opportunity.

On January 22, 1991 I received the following letter from the South African Consulate.

Dear Mr. Burton:

I am very pleased to confirm the invitation to you and Mrs. Burton to visit South African from February 24, 1991 to March 15, 1991 as guest of the Department of Foreign Affairs.

Your visit will entail a compact program, which should provide you with an opportunity to experience at first hand the broad scope of South Africa's dynamic socio-political environment. Details of your program will be finalized by our guest section in Pretoria, after we have had an opportunity to discuss your personal interests and specific requests regarding your future visit.

Should you accept this invitation, it would be appreciated if you could acquaint yourself with the contents of the attached list of conditions relating to all official guests.

Please direct any inquiries to Miss Yolanda Kemp of the Consulate-General. She will be responsible for all arrangements preceding your visit.

I trust that your visit will both enjoyable and fruitful.

Yours sincerely,

Consul General

CHAPTER 10

On Saturday afternoons the print shop became a venue for informal round table political discussions about local, national and international issues and events. As the owner of the print shop I enjoyed the exchange between friends and associates and looked forward to it following a week of hard work and diminishing economic returns. When I opened the printing shop in 1986, the general assessment was that the future was promising due to the projected redevelopment of Harlem's 125th Street commercial corridor. However, in view of the lack of a strong residential market base, due to pervasive building abandonment, drug addiction, crime and violence local businesses and entrepreneurs would have to be prepared for long range survival. Since the facts on the ground would doom new business development I concentrated on the commercial market, as opposed to residential. Now here in 1993, the many retail businesses that opened in the '80s are now closed. The highly touted business and economic renaissance of Harlem had not yet occurred and I needed to come up with a plan for survival or an exit strategy, to cut my losses. In addition to the slow economic improvement curve, the Harlem political leadership was embroiled in controversy as a result of the demise of Freedom National Bank, Harlem Third World Trade Center, the Harlem on the Hudson project among others.

Fifth Avenue, between 135th and 124th Streets was one of the notorious crack strips in Harlem, perhaps the most infamous. The print shop was located on 5th Avenue, between 126th and 125th Streets, in the belly of the beast. The advent of crack cocaine in the early 1980s exacerbated a growing epidemic of drug addiction, setting in motion legions of walking corpses that wreaked havoc with random violence on the community and enriched local drug lords. In the context of drug turf wars the various stakeholders and role players declaring war against each other that imperiled lives of the innocent, with drive by shooting raids, burglaries, and armed robberies. Now the neighborhood was grotesque due to business and residential abandonment and legions of crack addicts that seem to predominate the street. Murders, countless shootouts, robberies and assaults were part of the daily expectation. Virtually every day, the police (five-O) had to respond to a crime situation right in front of the print shop. Directly across the street was Mohammed's Mosque # 7 of the Nation of Islam, and the newly constructed National Black Theater facility. The National Alliance Political Party and the Hebrew Israelite community were located next door to the right and left of the print shop respectively. Although each respective entity operated their own programs with some degree of success, the activities associated with the crack cocaine and drug culture, got the lion share of the neighborhood market. The crack epidemic in particular not only took a major portion of the local economy, but, also destroyed the business environment and remaining residential quality of life.

Drug transactions were done without discretion on sidewalks, hallways, and stoops, in retail stores in front of children as well as old folks. When drug dealers were busted by plain-clothes police officers they and their workers were back on the street no later than the following day. If you didn't show deference to the drug dealer's transaction, you ran the risk of intimidation if not worst. Consequently, the drug sale activity in front of the print shop was very heavy as the result of its location on the infamous "crack" commercial strip. When I opened the shop, drug transaction activity was so heavy in the front of the premises, that it became a business management issue that had to be directly addressed. There was a drug dealer that lived in the apartment building over the print shop storefront. The second building to the left housed another drug dealing operation and on the corner of 126th Street and 5th Avenue another "crew" conducted their crack cocaine enterprise. The three dealerships competed with each other but maintained a non-aggression and non-violence agreement that virtually eliminated competition-based drug shoot-outs. Although 5th Avenue between 125th and 126th Street was a no gun fire zone, the level of competitive drug transactions were so intense that it was necessary for me to confront the stakeholders and role players. I outlined an area in chalk on the sidewalk in front of the print shop. The outlined area in front of the print shop was approximately 15ft X 25ft. The area stretched from the print shop door on the left to the stoop steps of the apartment building to the right side of the shop. Within the bolded chalked area was written and underlined "WAR ZONE."

I set the tone after outlining the "war zone" by meeting with the principle people associated with the three competitive dealer groups. I met with the drug dealers stakeholders of each group separately and presented the same deal. The deal essentially made the point that my printing business had a clientele that was intimidated by drug transactions and were fearful of being innocent victims of random violence between drug dealer groups. Therefore, drug transactions must not be conducted within the outlined area in front of the shop. The direct approach yielded a positive result from all quarters although from time to time I had to remind some of the new or hard-core salesman, to respect my business trade. The three groups competed for customers within a two-block radius. The crack was sold in clear tiny glass vials with plastic caps of various colors and each dealer maintained a particular colored cap to distinguish their brand. All during the day and evening you could hear the crack salesmen market their wares by broadcasting their product: "gold caps," "gold tops," "original gold."

"Orange is out," "orange out."

"Blue," "blue," "blue is out." The traffic was 24 hours a day and 7 days a week. Interestingly enough, one of the three groups was female controlled, and they made the lion's share of the money. As a practical matter, the group controlled by the sisters was the most violent and boastful and enjoyed the most business. Three or four times during the week the police would raid the various drug sites, make a bust or two and the person was back on the street dealing in 24 hours in most cases. During the summer months when my son James was in New York working with me in the shop, he would intently watch the drug sale activity in front of the shop. Apparently young James could not understand why the dealers were not arrested and punished, and why in most cases the police turned a blind eye to such blatant criminal activity. Moreover, I could not adequately explain enough to James, the obvious contradictions within the law enforcement and the daily life's reality in the inner cities and urban centers.

I was a relatively newcomer to Harlem from Jamaica Queens, following the demise of my office operation on 168th Street and Jamaica Avenue in 1981. I was able to establish a political consultancy in Harlem based on some introductions facilitated by Joseph Gibson, a recent graduate of Albany Law School who moved to Harlem from Westchester to help manage some family owned real estate. In his late 20s Gibson was associated with a network of his peers who were college graduates and/or young professionals eager to make a political, economic and social impact on Harlem in the context of their respective career objectives. In the wake of a foray into electoral politics as the campaign manager of the young Harlem based Attorney, Joseph Holland a candidate for the New York State Senate in a Special Election in 1985 to

replace Senator Leon Bogues who recently passed away, I generated so
attention concerning the potential of my political activities in Harlem.
Although Joseph Holland lost the election to the Democratic Party candidate
David Paterson, he was appointed to a prestigious position with a State
Senate Committee as the General Council of the New York State Housing
and Community Service Committee. For my part, I was introduced to
Chairman and Executive Directors of the New York Republican State
Committee, The Honorable Anthony Coliveta and Edward Lurie,
respectively, by members of the New York Senate Majority Leader the
Honorable Warren Anderson's staff, Thomas Slater and Steve Rice. The
objective of my introduction to the New York Republican State Committee
was to help the State Committee to formulate an outreach initiative to the
black Community.

While the outreach initiative that I formulated to the black American
community was met with significant opposition by the New York Republican
County leadership, the initiative was received well in some quarters upstate,
initially. In response to my inquiries as to why the State Committee was back
pedaling on the implementation of the "Black Republican Taskforce" I was
informed by Ed Lurie, the Executive Director of the Republican state
Committee that there was an "upstate/downstate dichotomy" that
undermined Taskforce implementation. The unauthorized interpretation of
the "upstate/downstate dichotomy" was that Chairman of Manhattan County
Republican Party State Senator Roy Goodman was opposed to the imposition
of the Black Republican Taskforce leadership on the Harlem black political
status quo. I was well acquainted with the political reality on the ground in the
context of black politics in general as well as the anointed and appointed
black Republican District leaders. I knew that Ed Lurie was articulating the
political truth because I had previous experience with local political
machinations of the Republican Party County organization as well as the
Democratic Party's political machinery. Interestingly enough the prospect of
a viable black Republican Party opposition to local black elected Democrats
presented an enormous political problem with respect to how political
business is done in Harlem and other black communities throughout the city.
The popular notion that politics makes for strange bedfellows was a case in
point as it relates to the politics of Harlem.

Despite the "upstate/downstate dichotomy" I was approached by Ed Lurie
in 1986 to coordinate the political campaign for the soon to be Republican
Party nominee for the governor of the State of New York, Honorable Andrew

nt Westchester County Executive. During a dinner
velt Hotel in midtown Manhattan, Ed Lurie advised me
State Committee was interested in outreach activities in
y in general but more importantly the State Committee
nning a serious well financed campaign to reclaim the
State House ... ember. I knew that Ed was a real-time political objective
of the Republican State Committee because the GOP lost the State House
following the governor Nelson Rockefeller years. As the result of the death
of the wealthy and popular Governor Rockefeller, the Republican Party State
organization lost a tremendous financial benefactor as well as a personality
rally point that generated party cohesion with a legacy of strong leadership.
With the demise of the Rockefeller wing of the Republican Party, which was
generally characterized as "moderate Republican," the "conservative" wing
of the party wrested control of the party apparatus. In 1980, Republican Party
stalwart, the Republican Party's U.S. Senator Jacob Javitz was defeated by
Republican Party insurgent candidate Al D'Amato, with the help of the New
York Conservative Party. With the election of Al D'Amato as the U.S.
Senator, the Conservative Party gained hegemony in the New York
Republican State Committee. The Manhattan County Republican
organization was regarded as a "liberal" wing of the GOP which
characterized New York State Senator Roy Goodman, chairman of the
Manhattan County Republican Committee and "conservative" Republicans
on the state and national levels.

In both instances, "liberal" and "conservative," the local party leadership
was opposed to cultivating an organic local Republican Party constituency
and developing a viable alternative to black Democratic elected leadership.
Therefore, as a practical political matter, grassroots political and community
activism was methodically and deliberately thwarted and under mined by the
local Republican Party leadership as well as from the quarters of the
Democratic Party opposition. Moreover, in order for an insurgent black
candidate to gain ballot status to run for elective office, he or she was
relegated to the Democratic Party primary election process, which was
wrought with sophisticated political obstacles that favored the incumbent
and party machine candidate. An alternative to the political mine fields
associated with getting ballot status a Democratic Party candidates subscribe
to the various "splinter" political parties that were essentially offspring of the
two major political parties in one form or another. The bottom political line
was that both the Democrat and Republican Parties conspired individually

and collectively to track and undermine potential independent community based political leadership. In terms of the general public there was an elusion of a political adversarial relationship between the Democrat and Republican Party in New York City electoral politics in generally and in the black community in particular. On the contrary, at the state and national levels there was a genuine interest in some quarters for a dynamic change at the local level on behalf of advancing the Republican Party and therefore there was a potential to generate the political support and resources from target state and national political officials.

Apart from the practicality of political investment banking in the black community by the Republican Party, key personalities in the current black Republican leadership were under a controversial cloud and political scandal. To what extend the emerging political crisis had on the advent of the State Committee's out reach to me and my activities was unclear, but I was convinced that the unfolding political scandal at the U.S. Department of Housing and Urban Development (HUD), and escalating controversy associated with the New York State Council of black Republicans and the National black Republican Council (NBRC), were consequential in the state party's out reach overtures to me. Ed Lurie and I had frank and candid conversations about the current controversies and prospects for the future and I was persuaded by Ed's sincerity and commitment to ensure that the Black GOP Taskforce and gubernatorial campaign effort would be financed and that there would be a follow up agenda for party building and political investment banking in the black community. In view of the current controversy and the perception of the history associated with the New York State Council of black Republicans and the National black Republican Council (NBRC), I advised Ed that I needed a letter on the letter head of the New York Republican Party State Committee, representing that the Black Republican Taskforce was working under the auspices of the State Committee and as such was responsible for recruiting in the black community.

The controversy and scandal threatened to taint the Reagan administration and expose prominent black Republicans in New York State to criminal indictments for fraud and political corruption. The central issue was the activities of the Secretary to the Department of Housing and Urban Development (HUD), the honorable Samuel Pierce in relation to the distribution of Urban Development Grants in various states around the country. Congressional Hearings were convened and some of the parties involved received subpoenas to testify before Congress. A potentially damaging expose' of Republican Party corruption was minimized in the wake of the unceremonious resignation of Samuel Pierce as the first black Secretary of HUD. Other black Republican Party leaders around the country were linked in some way to the HUD "UDAG" scandal, prominent among them was Fred Brown, a Republican Party District leader in the Bronx, New York, who also doubled as the president of the New York Council of black Republicans and the president of the National black Republican Council (NBRC). I knew Fred Brown and was very familiar with both organizations and was on speaking terms with the leadership of the New York based organization. Brown was well placed politically at the national level and heretofore was the exclusive Head Negro In Charge, (HNIC). And at the local level among the "liberal" and "conservative" components of the Republican Party, Brown was the go-to black guy to coordinate political cameos and to run down field political interference to mitigate the emergence of organic community based black Republican leadership.

The swirling political controversy and scandal at HUD was implicating Brown as a key player which resulted in him playing an uncharacteristically low key role in local politics for the immediate future. Concomitantly, the State Republican Party was aware of the potential political liability associated with Brown as the coordinator of the "black Desk" in the projected GOP Gubernatorial campaign. Under these extraordinary political circumstances the New York Republican State Committee was hard pressed to identify a credible black Republican alternative to the usual Fred Brown political scenario. I was aware of the unique political circumstances that may be central to inspiring the State Committee to reach out to me to fill the void for a black Republican go-to guy for the gubernatorial campaign. However, I was impressed that there may be a political paradigm shift in the state party leadership in favor of cultivating a genuine Republican Party community based leadership to help the party become competitive with the Democratic Party and black elected officials, particularly in Harlem. Alton Chase was a bit more cynical than me about the long-term commitment of the State Committee to meaningful political investment banking in the black American community.

Alton Chase was a longtime Republican Party district leader in the Bronx, and a former member of the New York State Council of black Republicans and the National black Republican Council (NBRC). I met Alton Chase in 1980 during a meeting at the Hyatt Hotel in 42nd Street and Lexington

Avenue. I had requested the meeting following a series of meetings with Fred Brown concerning convening a voter education symposium at the Bronx Community College under the auspices of NBRC and in conjunction with Voters Anonymous, a political education organization founded by me. Me and Fred agreed to pursue the prospect of a voter education symposium further and Fred agreed to introduce me to the New York City leadership of NBRC, and a follow up meeting was scheduled for me to meet the local leaders of NBRC. At the meeting Alton Chase was introduced as the NRBC Vice President of the Bronx organization. Other NBRC leaders were Cyril Brown, VP for Manhattan, Thomas Archer, VP for Queens, Hanks Williams, VP for Brooklyn and Tina Joseph, VP for Staten Island. I ultimately tabled the plans for the voter education symposium as I became convinced that Fred Brown and some of his leadership people were not interested in pursuing a political empowerment agenda. After extensive meetings with the NBRC local leadership I concluded that NBRC's agenda was social, such as pool and boat parties, social functions and political cameo appearances designed to portray "racial" diversity at targeted GOP events. My suspicion that Fred's intentions were to sand bag the symposium at the eleventh hour was conformed during a candid and blunt conversation between me and Alton.

"Brother Chase," I said, "I met a few times with your NBRC colleagues on the symposium agenda, and I'm getting a mixture of signals in my own mind based on the reaction that I am getting. Hank Williams, the vice president for Brooklyn, is a very weak leader, and he is seriously overshadowed by all viable local GOP leaders: District Leader Arthur Bramwell, District Leader BoBo Garfield, and Mrs. Lugena Gordon, president of the Freedom Republican Club. Hanks' reputation for non-action and political folly precedes him. Vice Presidents Cyril Brown (Manhattan) and Tom Archer (Queens) are preoccupied with phantom real estate and development deals touted by Fred in the context of his social agenda. Cyril and Tom have no interest in politically educating and organizing black folk. Tina Joseph has some interesting things going on in Staten Island, but she is preoccupied with Fred.

"In fact, you, Chase, are the only one that appears to be serious about the initiative. But in addition to their foot dragging, I just met with Professor James at Bronx Community College to confirm the venue, and I got some dubious vibes about their commitment to make their facility available for the symposium."

Chase said, "I'm glad that you raised that issue because I appreciate what you propose to do, and I am supportive of it and see a role for me to play in the project. I did not want to say anything to compromise the project or to unduly alarm you concerning my perspective on the symposium idea and its implementation. Therefore I decided to wait it out and see how the project developed. Now that you have made your own assessment and analyzed the feasibility of pulling the project off, I feel comfortable in being candid and blunt with my views. In short, I concur, that you understand that the project runs the risk of being undermined by internal forces that don't want to see projects like this succeed."

Chase continued, "Fred has a habit of putting viable projects in his back pocket and sitting on them." He recalled his campaign for the New York State Senate and shared with me the fact that he ran a serious campaign but his candidacy was both undermined and sand-bagged by Fred and the Bronx County Republican Party organization. He said, "They just wanted to generate the illusion of Republican Party opposition, and I was disillusioned in the process. They advised me that they were doing a major mailing and door-to-door campaigning, but as I ran my campaign I double-checked on what Fred and the County leadership said they were doing, and realized that it was all untrue. I was a serious candidate, but the county organization had something else in mind that had nothing to do with my campaign."

CHAPTER 11

The National black Republican Council (NBRC), an advisory group established by the Republican National Committee in 1972, was now the strategic focal point. Although NBRC had no political leverage or practical function in the context of local party policy, the Council had significant access, structure and financing. The centralized NBRC governing structure was located in Washington, D.C. at the headquarters of the National Republican Committee, with a staff and budget. NBRC sub-divided the country into regions, with a regional coordinator. New York State was under the jurisdiction of the northeastern regional office. NBRC essentially stayed out of local politics, thereby not causing friction between the national, state and local party structures. New York State had an interesting political set up; there was the New York State Council of black Republicans with Fred Brown as the president. Interestingly enough, Mr. Brown was also the regional coordinator, as well as the president of the National black Republican Council. Needless to say, Fred Brown required meeting if I was going to get involved in black Republican electoral politics. "You need to talk to Fred," was the virtual universal refrain among many black Republicans as well as the official Republican leadership. I managed to find this out directly, when I contacted the Republican National Committee leadership in Washington, to discuss my plan for increasing black participation in the Republican Party vis-à-vis a grassroots voter education and application.

After my ideas were entertained at the Republican National Committee headquarters, I was courteously directed to Ron McDuffie, the Executive Director of NBRC, who referred me to Fred Brown before abruptly leaving for lunch. Mr. McDuffy's Secretary was very cordial and gave me some insight as to the politics of NBRC, and the need for practical visibility on a local level particularly in New York. Fortuitously, a local group in the Queens area headed by political guru, Nat Singleton was hosting a political reception, and Fred Brown was the featured speaker. I first met Nat Singleton in 1966 during the time I was an organizer for NWRO. Nat Singleton had a political club located on Linden Blvd. in St. Albans, named Jamaica Political Action League. At that time Nat was a Republican and a major player in Mayor John Lindsay's political apparatus. Nat became a Democrat during Lindsay's transition to run for the Presidency, but maintained contact with the Republican Party leadership. He was perhaps the most politically astute background player in Queens and continued to be a significant player on both sides of the political aisle. When I was an organizer, I had occasion to meet with Nat in the context of some welfare rights issues. Present at the meeting was Carl Turnquist, an associate of Nat's. Carl was a Director in the mayors Neighborhood Action Program (NAP). During that meeting it was suggested that I should follow the example of one of my peers, Van DeVore, and things of interest may come my way. Van was the Executive Director of a youth program called Young Adults at Work, a delegate agency of the Jamaica Community Corporation, later to become the Southeast Queens Community Corporation.

I discussed with Nat my interest in local Republican politics and he indicted that he would be inclined to support me should I actively seek the Republican District Leadership in the 29th AD, in opposition to the incumbent Geraldine Jones. Also at the event was an old friend Morris Lee, now a Republican District leader and a Nat Singleton protégé. Morris introduced me to Fred, and I was able to express my interest in meeting with him in the near future. The objective of my meeting with Fred Brown was to work with his citywide leadership to develop a Republican constituency base, and to develop black Republican candidates to compete with local Democratic Party electoral candidates. I had developed a plan to achieve political empowerment in the black Community, vis-à-vis, a multi-party voter education program and a bi-partisan, primary election strategic plan. The plan was to be introduced in the context of a citywide political education symposium, and my plan was to seek a joint venture with the National black Republican Council to pull it off. The joint venture would include NBRC and the organization that I founded, Voters Anonymous, Political Education Organization. This was the message I communicated to the Republican National Committee, during my DC visit, which was trickled down to Fred Brown in various forms and aberrations. Fred scheduled the meeting at the Grand Hyatt Hotel on 42nd Street and Lexington Avenue, a favorite venue of his I found out later. The meeting finally came off after about three cancellations by Mr. Brown. We had a smooth initial meeting, and a second meeting was scheduled and I requested that his representatives from the various boroughs be present and he agreed. The follow up meeting included Alton Chase, VP Bronx; Tom Archer, VP Queens; Tina Josephs, VP Staten Island; William Hanks, VP Brooklyn; and Cyril Brown, VP Manhattan. After several meetings, I was convinced that the plan and strategy in hand was not feasible for a lot of reasons. The overriding factor that led to aborting the plan was the attitude and general interest in the business as usual approach to the political process on the part of Fred Brown. Plans were laid down and Bronx Community College was the venue but, Fred was foot dragging and I was sensing recalcitrance on the part of the venue contact and a couple of the local players. My seasoned political eye saw that there were some barriers being set up to thwart the initiative.

In hindsight my initial plan was grandiose and required substantial manpower, organization and budget. Moreover, without the full support of NBRC and the New York State Council of black Republicans the plan was not feasible. As a practical matter, I realized that a more traditional approach for penetrating the local Republican organization would be the ultimate solution. However, my macro-grandiose plan was useful as a hands-on intelligence function, and a research-and-development tool. The approach enabled me to directly interface with the top-level players, assess the strengths and weaknesses of the organizations structure, and provide me with a real-time overview of the political landscape. Obliged to make a graceful exit from the city-wide initiative, I resorted to joining the Queens branch of the National black Republican Council, under the leadership of Tom Archer, the VP for Queens. I became a member of the NBRC Executive Committee of the Queens organization that was comprised of Tom Archer, Vernell Thompson, and me. Tom and Vernell were not aware of my political organizing skills and expertise. As I reviewed my initial approach to NBRC, it was clearly too ambitious thereby raising suspicions and questions in Fred's mind that could not be answered. Fred seemed to be in virtual control of all black Republican politics locally and was a factor nationally. He was already at the top of his political game, therefore my unsolicited plan and pro-bono consultancy was likely to cause him concern in the context of a potential political power play. The rumor was that Fred had some reservations about me, and considered me an outsider. Now in my new capacity as member of the executive committee of the Queens organization, I had the opportunity to get to know the players first hand, and they will be able to get to know me.

The respective borough Vice Presidents were interesting people and all of them were well acquainted with their local areas. Alton Chase was a

Republican District Leader in the Bronx and the VP of NBRC. Chase was a strong grassroots organizer, tall and articulate, and the central person in control of the Fred Brown's ground troops in the Bronx. Indeed, the black Republicans in the Bronx under the Leadership of Fred Brown were formidable on the level of the Bronx Republican County Committee organization. Although Alton Chase continued to be a supporter of Fred Brown, he (Chase) was disillusioned because of what seemed to be legitimate personal reasons. I was impressed with the loyalty, strength and organizing skills of Chase. Generally speaking all of the borough representatives were loyal supporters of Fred, and each person demonstrated some degree of local strength and support.

Perhaps the most visible if not successful of the borough operations was the Independent Republican Club, located on 138th Street and Seventh Avenue, in Harlem's Strivers Row. The extent to which the Republican Party had a community-based infrastructure in place was in fact a revelation. Clearly, a substantial potential existed to generate electoral competition for the Democratic elected officials, develop leverage politics and advance the cause of the black community. Why the electoral competition was not taking place in the black community, was an open question. The GOP potential was in place, however the political will and perspective of the black political leadership was the reason why the black community remained politically impotent. Despite the fact that a, black Republican organization and structure was in place, there was no voter education and registration or any sort of interface with the community at the grassroots level.

Tina Josephs, vice president of the Staten Island NBRC was among Fred Brown's strongest supporters. Tina was a warm, enthusiastic and politically astute, middle-aged, attractive lady. A long time resident of Staten Island, Tina managed to develop a core group of male supporters that I met on several occasions. Her organization was a testimony to her skill and integrity as a political organizer and community leader. Tina and I cultivated a good working relationship. She respected my expertise and contacts and it was a pleasure for me to consult with her on local projects. Tina supported my efforts to stimulate local Republican Party grassroots activism and to build a cadre of vanguard Republican district leaders in New York City. Tina's echoed the famous refrain, "You should talk to Fred." She either was not aware of the political intrigues and machinations already underway, or was in state of clinical political denial. Whatever the case, I was not going to raise the issue and put our potential relationship at risk. I listened to her constant refrain in the course of our work together. "You should get with Fred."

I answered her accordingly; "I am still working on it."

The Brooklyn organization was weak at best. The Vice President of the borough was William Hanks. I was never quite certain whether his name was William Hanks, or Hank Williams. Interestingly enough, no one else seemed to know either. Hank did not seem to have the skills required to build a strong local organization. Apart from his organizational deficiencies there was a formidable opposition in Brooklyn to Fred Brown's leadership, and the National black Republican Council Structure. The opposition to Fred's leadership and the NBRC structure came from three well-established Republican Party leaders in particular: "BoBo" Garfield, a nationally renowned personality and Brooklyn Republican District Leader; Arthur Bromwell, a well established Republican District Leader; and Mrs. Lugenia Gordon, the president of Freedom Republicans, an activist group supported by the Rippon Society, and based in Brooklyn. Each had their own unique reasons for opposing Fred's leadership and entrance into local Brooklyn politics. As a consequence of this political dynamic, Fred Brown, et al., did not take root in Brooklyn.

Fred Brown was a Republican District Leader in the Bronx, under the late John Calandra, Chairman of the Bronx County Republican Committee. Fred solidified his leadership in Harlem at the Independent Republican Club, which served as the informal headquarters for NBRC. The Independent Republican Club was the hub of Republican Party community based politics of the time, which was not a grassroots enterprise. Fred Brown seemed to be the bell of the ball in Harlem, and the Vice President of Manhattan NBRC, Cyril Brown seemed well disposed to his role as Fred's Lieutenant. In the heart of "Strivers Row," 138th Street and Seventh Avenue the Independent Republican Club was a well appointed storefront operation and accommodated the likes of the black Republican "elite." The Harlem organization was the most visible and active Republican community based operation. The Independent Republican Club apparently had the approval of the Manhattan County Republican Chairman, New York State Senator Roy Goodman. The Independent Republican Club predominated the GOP activity in Harlem; however, there were other individuals and organizations that played a significant role in the political mix. Florence Rice a renowned consumer advocate, Vivian Hall a leader of the Manhattan Republican Club, Vincent Baker a Republican historian, Arlene Avery a district leader, Keith Lonesome district leader, Andy Gainer a popular businessman, Charlie Vincent the developer of 55 West 125th Street, and Honorable Lionel Hampton are several that I had the opportunity to meet.

My former Bailiwick, Queens New York, had its own unique Republican Party political environment. In addition to Nat Singleton another significant Republican Party player of the time was Mrs. Geraldine Jones, a Republican District Leader in the 29AD. Mrs. Jones had a formidable organization and an entrenched leadership. In fact Geraldine Jones had an active citywide structure and infrastructure that competed with Fred Browns organization on various levels. The Queens Republican Party situation had any number of elements that generated an interesting if not intoxicating political cocktail. My newfound political relationships on the Executive Committee of Queens NBRC was not the least of these dynamic elements. My membership on the Queens branch was based on my residency in Queens, and my realization that I needed to work with a local organization in order to achieve my objective, following the aborted voter education symposium. I felt confident that I could work through the organizational process and accomplish the political imperative, as I perceived it to be.

The Queens NBRC was essentially a vest pocket operation of Tom Archer's, the area Vice President. Tom was a middle-aged guy, a journalist by trade, who sported press credentials that enabled him to move in and out of high-level political events. Tom was particularly fond of mingling with the diplomatic community at the United Nations, where he would frequent the pressroom. He had a striking appearance with a broad deep gray mustache, his preliminary move to impress was an invite you to lunch at the United Nations Dinning Room. Tom was absolutely intrigued with Fred's ability to maneuver and negotiate his way into power positions. However, fifty percent of the time, Tom was disillusioned by Fred's failure to deliver the bacon to the loyal troops, and Fred's apparent betrayals and practical failures. Yet Tom remained hopeful that at least he (Tom) would be able to negotiate a deal with Fred to have his wife sing at a Presidential inaugural ball. Tom published a newspaper on an irregular monthly basis, filled with photos of high-level political people, events and sports figures. The newspaper in conjunction with his individual techniques, vis-à-vis, and a camera around his neck was used to leverage his position with his target objective. Tom was a skilled infiltrator, destabilize, and political intelligence operative. Tom and I ultimately developed a good working relationship based on mutual respect and necessity. However, in the process of getting to know one another was indeed an intriguing exercise. The process was engaged, and I was prepared to play my role as a member in good standing with the Queens branch of the National black Republican Council.

Vernell Thompson was the other member of the Queens NBRC Executive Committee. Vernell was quite a character in more ways than one. Well dressed, well groomed and manicured, dark skinned with a beautiful set of pearly white teeth, he had the proverbial gift of gab and was a ravenous reader. Vernell claimed to be a Real Estate developer, yet he never was able to point to a project that he had completed. Vernell and Fred had a special relationship, just as Fred was able to maintain a special relationship with his other people. Fred was an astute student of human nature, a master ventriloquist, and a member of a "secret society." Notwithstanding the profundity of their master ventriloquist Fred, Tom and Vernell had talents of their own. And collectively, they presented a clever political sandbag routine that would destabilize most political agenda's. These were the primary players in my new political environment, and I approached the process with my typical gusto. Unfortunately, my gusto was not matched by my practical facility, since I had lost my office operation in Queens and hardware. If my office operation had been in place Tom and Vernell would have been sufficiently impressed with my capacity and my position of strength would have been apparent. But all of that was gone and I was working from out of a dubious domestic situation and my new political associates were off limits. Since these new political associates had no knowledge of my background and capabilities, their perception of me and my contribution.

During the first few Executive Committee meetings, I remained low-key so as to appreciate the agenda and issues that this new political relationship presented me with. The first two meetings were held in a meeting room at the Hotel Marriott, near LaGuardia Airport in Queens, New York. Tom enjoyed a good business relationship with the management of the Marriott. They supported his newspaper with advertisement and provided him with a few perks. There was no doubt that Tom had the best part of the deal. The next round of meetings took place at a diner on Merrick Blvd. in Springfield Gardens. At this point I began to insert my projects because it was clear to me that Tom and Vernell had no perceptible agenda. All meetings were essentially rap sessions with no specific agenda or structure. The meetings would continue on and on until Tom felt that it should be closed out. As a result of these rhetorical exercises, I determined that Tom and Vernell were satisfied with maintaining a holding pattern in their political positions waiting for Fred to cut them into a deal. Each would constantly lament the amount of time and energy they had already put into the organization without receiving any personal largess, yet they remained faithful and hopeful. The holding pattern that Tom and Vernell maintained was beyond my capacity to appreciate and understand. I was motivated and trained to deal with the resolution of problems and issues that impact the community. Since there were no other projects for consideration than the ones that I had advanced, I managed to get them on the table. There was an aggressive attempt by Vernell to modify my program plans but Tom was neutral, therefore my success was assured. Voters Anonymous, Political Education Organization and the Entrepreneurial and Micro Business Development Information Center, were projects that were developed before the demise of my office operation.

The two projects were solution oriented community based applications that addressed the fact of political and economic impotence in the black community. Brochure drafts were already prepared when I presented the projects; therefore opposition was confined to editing the brochure. There was no noticeable enthusiasm that I detected from Tom or Vernell about the programmatic potential associated with the projects. In fact Tom and Vernell demonstrated a kind of ambivalence that caused me to wonder about their political motives. I was not affected by their lack of enthusiasm, particularly because I intended to honcho the projects myself. I knew better than to rely on others to make things happen. On the contrary, the third project that I introduced generated abounding enthusiasm, and their voluntary activism. The third project that I proposed was to run a candidate for the Republican District Leader in the 29th AD, against the incumbent Geraldine Jones. The excitement of Tom and Vernell was obvious and could not be contained. Vernell volunteered to be the campaign manager and Tom volunteered to be the media and communications coordinator. Some weeks earlier Nat Singleton mentioned that he would be inclined to support my efforts in the 29th AD. I was serious about the challenge because I was convinced that black political empowerment had to be achieved by generating strong black participation in the Republican Party primary election, and a multi-party strategy in the general election. Tom and Vernell were both animated by the political prospects and all of a sudden it seemed as though we had the bare bones of a vanguard structure to promote Republican Party grassroots activism.

The local political activity in Queens began to pick up and intensify. I signed up a few people into the organization and started positioning for a primary election challenge for the Republican Party District Leadership in the 29th AD. As things picked up, Tom and Vernell were still animated, however, I sensed the possibility of a developing political intrigue. Sure enough the intrigue was revealed during an executive committee meeting. Although the organization now had a growing membership, the new members constituted the membership committee and could not participate in executive committee meetings. As a consequence I had to deal with Tom and Vernell singularly, and in the context of their emerging political machinations. On this particular occasion Tom opened the executive committee meeting as usual. The corner right side of his mouth was untypical stiff and curled downward.

Then Vernell spoke, saying, "Tom and I have been looking over this district leadership race, and it seems as though your man is not the strongest candidate. We need money to run a campaign; we talked to your people, and they don't have the money to invest in your campaign."

"Are you going to put up some money, Vinnie?" he asked.

Then Tom came back in, "Vernell and I have been talking with James Degriff; he's got the money, and he is ready to run. We are talking to you as a matter of courtesy. You need to consider the role that you plan to play in this campaign and let us know accordingly." Tom continued, "If you can raise some money for this race, then we will roll with you and your people; that's the best deal you can get."

I could see that a background for future political machinations was being put in place. I knew that I had a limited amount of time to solidify my political position and secure my candidacy, as the political double cross was apparent to me now. It was my turn to speak and I began.

I said, "Thank you for the political courtesy guys, but I must confess that I have some second thoughts about running for the seat, particularly because of the lack of money." As I continued I could see confusion among them.

Both Tom and Vernell thought that I would take a hard line and argue the issue. I continued, "Yeah, man, I told you guys about my recent business setbacks, so as a practical matter, I have to rethink the feasibility of my involvement in the campaign. After the holiday season, I will be in a better position to confirm my decision, but at this point my gut feeling is that I am not going to do this one."

Tom and Vernell were looking at each other smiling, yet obviously completely baffled. As I reflected on the executive committee meeting substance, the political revelation came to me. Since I did not really intend to withdraw from the Republican District Leadership in the 29th AD, I had to solidify my political position. I had the tactical element of surprise on my side because Tom and Vernell believed that I was pulling out of the race. I began to call on my political writing skills and prepared a press release and news article and disseminated it. Fortunately the New York Voice published both the press release and the news article, with a portrait photo of me.

The press release read:

Queens Coordinator

Vincent Burton was recently named Queens Coordinator in the 29th AD, for the National black Republican Council by Tom Archer, borough vice president. Burton has been active in community politics since the 1960s and early '70s when he was staff organizer for the National Welfare Rights Organization, under Dr. George Wiley, and board member of many community-oriented agencies and organization. He worked as a consultant and project director for Long Island Jewish Hospital/Queens Hospital Center, between 1973 and 1978, as the Director of the Sickle Cell Disease Education and Screening Clinic, then he started his own consultancy and pest-control company.

This news article was headlined: **It's Not Too Late!** With my name on the by-line.

The Democratic National Committee Chairman stated that it's too late to change the party rules, which discriminate against black and minority presidential candidates. The recent history of Democratic Party politics vis-à-vis, the Mayor Daleys, the Governor Wallaces, the Voting Rights Bill, Fanny Lou Hammers, the 1968 Democrat primaries in the South, and as recent as 1975, and this statement by the present Democrat National Committee Chairman, Manatt represents a business-as-usual policy with the Democratic Party. Presidential candidate Jesse Jackson raised the issue of discrimination and accused the Democratic leadership of playing with a stacked deck. Interestingly enough, the infamous Bert Lance, the Georgia State Committee Chairman, held several meetings with Jackson, trying to stop him from raising the issue at the national level. On the other hand, Senator Gary Hart, Senator Earnest Hollings, and Senator George McGovern agreed with Jackson that the present rules favor Vice President Mondale and Senator John Glenn. How should the black community respond? Is it really too late, or is it ever too late for the American two-party system? The American political system has historically provided a framework for the attainment of "ethnic ascendancy." The Irish Catholic President John Kennedy is a classic example of the possibility of "ethnic ascendancy." Nevertheless, ethnic ascendancy has eluded America's largest ethnic minority, the black community. It will always be either too late or too soon according to the political party leadership of both parties. The time will be right only when the black community develops a strategy for dealing with the Democratic Party and a strategy for dealing with Republican Party. Eternal vigilance and a bi-partisan primary election strategy may be the only route to "ethnic ascendancy" in the black community. The imperative of an effective bi-partisan political strategy is impacting the primary elections within the two parties. It is not too soon; it is not too late. The time is NOW. The political salvation of black community is a bi-partisan issue, of primary *importance.*

Due to the holiday season, the next meeting of the executive committee was the first week in February 1984. I made extra copies of the press release and news article for Tom and Vernell and prepared to advise them of my intention to enter my candidate in the 29th AD Republican District Leadership race. I prepared my troops for potential internal battle lines that were about to be drawn. The February meeting proved to be the proverbial Mexican standoff, with dynamic follow-up dimension. The opening of the meeting was cordial and light. I distributed the news article to Tom and Vernal, and they made their respective comments based on what they understood was the current situation. Tom thought that the media coverage was good for the Degriff campaign. Tom was surprised by my writing ability and suggested that he could get me some press credentials if I wrote four articles for his newspaper. Then Tom started to mention the people that he new at the New York Voice, such as Jimmy Hicks, the Editor, as well as the publisher Kenneth Drew.

He said, "I know Jim and Ken real well, and they know and respect me. In fact," Tom concluded, "they probably published you on the strength of your mentioning my name in the piece."

I listened to Tom without making a comment, then I listened to what Vernell had to say.

Vernell said, "This is a pretty nice piece, man, but the next time you need to bounce it by me or Tom for comments and input before you send it out. But it's cool, man, although I would have liked Degriff's name to have been mentioned in some oblique way."

I said, "Yeah, man, you know, I thought about using his name, but I decided against the idea because my people are not disposed to supporting him in the 29th as initially planned."

Tom and Vernell were livid. Tom raised his voice and balled his mouth up as he spoke saying, "What did you say, man? What do you think this is, man? Musical chairs? You can't just jump up and down to the tune you're whistling to yourself and nobody else can hear."

"Do you have the money, do you have the money, man?"

I raised my voice as well and said, "I got my people, and we will get the money. Are you down or is something else happening? Please advise, Tom."

Then Vernell interjected, "Jim D. has got the money in hand to run, and I am not counting on what you think you may have in the bush, Vincent."

I closed out by saying, "Sorry, my brothers, that I can't stay and indulge you, but I got to go, 'cause I got a campaign to run." I concluded, "Mr. Chairman, please excuse me."

The March meeting was a brief one. I was prepared to stonewall my position relative to running my candidate for Republican District leader. The news coverage gave my effort a momentum and credibility on which I was eager to cash in on. I expected that there would likely be two candidates in the race against the incumbent leader Geraldine Jones, which would be a healthy political exercise. However, I was absolutely surprised by the tactic employed by Tom and Vernell.

Tom began the meeting with a long monologue and concluded this way, "In order to focus on the intensity of the upcoming campaign and also to avoid any potential damage to the organization I am going to suspend the organizational meetings until after the campaign."

I responded by saying, "What are you talking about, man? You can't just suspend meetings at will. This is a formal organization with by-laws and a structure. What are you really about, Tommy Gun?"

Vernell jumped in. "Hold it. Hold it, fellas, I am the peacemaker here."

"No, brother, you can't mediate peace because you and Tom are on the same side, in opposition to me. Come on guys, I can't go for that political maneuver," I said.

The intensity of the controversy ebbed and flowed for too long and then ended in a stalemate. Ultimately, Tom and Vernell resigned from the Queens Organization. They may have been under the impression that their resignations would hamstring my organizational and campaign effort. I went to work immediately, and they soon found out that their maneuver failed to achieve the objective.

The New York Voice again published a news release of mine on Saturday March 31, 1984:

New Chairman of Queens NBRC

Vincent Burton has been elected Chairman of the Queens National black Republican Council. Other officers include Vincent Burton Co-Chairman, Joanne Davis Secretary, and Ethel Archer Treasurer. The group will spearhead local education and registration activities. The National black Republican Council is an auxiliary organization of the Republican National Committee. Burton is also Chairman of 21st. Century Independent Republicans, a citywide organization, President of New York Minority Entrepreneurs and Contractors Association, (NY MECA) and Chairman of Voters Anonymous a bi-partisan political education and research organization. The Queens National black Republican Council will announce its endorsement of candidates for the 29th AD, and the 32 AD District Leadership positions subsequent to the March 31,1984 meeting, Brown said.

The battles lines were clearly drawn. Tom and Vernell had made the decision to close me out. Therefore, I dug in deep and began to stretch out and establish a citywide presence. I was certain that Fred Brown was kept abreast of the developments; however, the origin of the plot was irrelevant. Since I was in the process of developing a base in Harlem, I began to focus on building a Harlem political operation. Apparently, the people at the *New York Voice* newspaper liked what I was doing so I dispatched another press release and news article.

From the vantage point of the newly formulated 21st Century Independent Republican Organization, I appointed Joseph Gibson to the position of Harlem political coordinator. Joe Gibson was the cousin of an associate of mine. Gibson was in his mid twenties and was a recent graduate of Albany Law School. He had begun to take a keen interest in my political agenda, so I began to get him up to political speed. On February 4, 1984, *The New York Voice* published my press release entitled:

Harlem Political Coordinator

Joseph Gibson, a graduate of Albany Law School, has been named Harlem Political Coordinator for the 21st Century Independent Republicans by Vincent Burton its Chairman. Gibson is the Executive Director of Voters Anonymous, a bi-partisan political education and research organization, and is presently researching a potential class-action suit against the Taxi and Limousine Commission on behalf of the coalition of Gypsy Cabs and Associations. He is also heading up Voters Anonymous, Harlem Public Interest Research Group, as a follow-up mechanism for the investigation he is performing as a resident of the city's shelter for the homeless.

The news article was headlined: ***Burton, Developing GOP Slate in Queens***. The contents read:

Vincent Burton, Chairman of Voters Anonymous, bi-partisan political education and research organization, and executive committee member of the Queens National black Republican Council is holding meetings to develop a slate of candidates to run for District Leadership in the 29th, 32nd, and 35th ADs. We are seeking independent Republican candidates in these districts. If we win these districts we can develop a bi-partisan strategy on a local level with Democrats in the respective Assembly Districts. With a bi-partisan strategy ethnic ascendancy is achievable for the black community.

The citywide organizational initiative was taking root. I received a letter at my Harlem address from the Reagan-Bush, '84 campaigns, dated April 20, 1984, over the signature of Roger Stone Jr., Eastern Regional Campaign Director. The letter read:

Dear Mr. Burton,

I have received word from the White House of your interest in helping in the president's reelection. We appreciate your generous offer of support. We are building a strong organization in your state

166

and would like to see your group involved. I have taken the liberty of passing your qualifications on to our Executive Director in New York, Mr. Charles Gargano. I trust he will be in touch with you soon. Again, thank you for your support and enthusiasm.

Sincerely, Roger J. Stone Jr.
Eastern Regional Campaign Director

I contacted Charles Gargano's office and was directed to appear at the Roosevelt Hotel, at which point the Reagan-Bush, '84 Campaign opened in New York. At that event which was attended by many GOP notables. A news reporter for *The New York Tribune*, Mr. Dirk Anthonis, quoted me and it was published in the May 30, 1984 edition of *The New York City Tribune*:

Vincent Burton, Chairman of the New York City branch of the National black Republican Council, said, "Reagan and the Republican Party present the best opportunity for the black and minority community to attain ethnic ascendancy."

On July 4, 1984, the same reporter published an interview with me in *The New York City Tribune*. The interview also appeared in *The Harlem Weekly*, as a front-page feature.

Black GOP Leader Surveys Road Ahead

Vincent Burton, recently named the New York City Chairman of the National black Republican Council (NBRC), has been active in community politics since the 1960s. He has been a staff organizer for the National Welfare Rights Organization and Board member of many community-oriented agencies and organizations. Burton is also the founder of Voters Anonymous and President of the New York Minority Entrepreneurs and Contractors Association. In an interview with New York Tribune reporter, Dirk Anthonis, Burton discusses political issues as they relate to the black community.

Q: What are the most important needs of the black community today, and how does the NBRC intend to meet those needs?

A: The most important needs of the black community are political and economic enfranchisement. Political enfranchisement would enable the black community to positively impact the state of education, the delivery of social and health services, community economic development, etc., in our local communities. The achievement of political enfranchisement requires citizen activism and a bi-partisan strategy on the part of the black community. Economic enfranchisement requires that we transcend the so-called "good-job mentality" and begin to develop the individual skills that enable us to establish businesses, economic development projects, and new systems of employment peculiar to the needs of our community. The NBRC has the capacity to dynamically impact the political and economic state of the black and minority community in a positive way. Politically, the NBRC provides a framework for the local community control, and economically it provides a network of business and community development resources, vis-à-vis, the Republican Party.

Q: How in your opinion does the "good-job mentality" affect the chances of the economic enfranchisement of the black community?

A: The fact is, the proverbial "good-job mentality" does not insure the blessings of economic enfranchisement in the black community. The goal of obtaining the good job has resulted in relative slavery in most instances, while providing a minimal amount of mobility and zero growth potential. Notwithstanding the various professional careers, the black community for the most part is relegated to a marginal economic status with ultimate retirement to virtual poverty. The expectations of the "good job" tend to be illusory and self-defeating in the long run. A "good job" must be viewed as a stopgap measure in the transitional process toward a career goal or business enterprise. The short-term benefits of a job must be seen in contrast to the broader long-term benefit of an economic enterprise. Since America is structured to benefit free enterprise, the black community must explore more fully the application of the individual and collective corporate forms to achieve economic enfranchisement.

Q: Black Americans are overwhelmingly conservative as far as moral and family values are concerned. Why then are they overwhelmingly affiliated with the Democratic Party, which by and large rejects many of the conservative viewpoints? How realistic do you think it is that the black community will return to its conservative roots in the Republican Party?

A: It is true that the black Americans are overwhelmingly conservative as far as moral and family values are concerned. The fact that blacks are overwhelmingly affiliated with the Democratic Party is on one hand the result of developments in recent history. On the other hand, it is characteristic of the many political contradictions that exist in the black community. The Democratic Party was instrumental in advancing the issues of the black community from the days of President Franklin D. Roosevelt up to approximately the 1970s, the zenith of the anti-poverty program. During this period, many liberal, progressive, and radical student movement lived and died that were associated with Democratic-Party politics. These movements were positive vessels for the aspirations and political growth of the black community. The paternalism characteristic of these essentially Democratic-party movements was beneficial at the time. However, as the black community is growing more and more toward sophistication, this paternalistic mentality is becoming more and more irrelevant for the further emancipation of blacks in America. Paternalism does not stimulate the dynamics of individual and collective development of the black community and tends to overly rely on legislative provisions, employment, and social programs which are ad hoc, short range, and short lived. The needs of today render Democratic-Party paternalism irrelevant to a strategic political empowerment in the black community. For this reason, I believe that the black community will return to its conservative roots in the Republican Party. The nature of the Republican Party as it relates to individual entrepreneurship and business and community development enables the black community to minimize the problems inherent in paternalism.

Q: You predict that within the black community there will be a shift in political preference toward the Republic Party. How soon do you expect that to happen?

A: I believe that the black community is becoming more sophisticated politically as it relates to how to maximize the impact of the vote. With that sophistication, there will begin an application of the two-party systems in the black and minority community. If the Republican Party implements a clear program for political ascendancy and outreach to the black community it will soon rekindle support for the GOP to the extent that it could have a significant impact on the 1988 elections.

Q: How successful, in your opinion, has Jesse Jackson's run for the Presidency been, and how will it affect the November elections?

A: Rev. Jesse Jackson's run for the Presidency has so far been a great success in the sense that he has raised the level of voter participation in the black community. It remains to be seen how sophisticated these neophyte voters are as it relates to the tactical application of their votes, particularly in the November elections. The ultimate outcome of the Democratic National Convention in terms of how the party deals with the issues expressed by Rev. Jackson will have a dynamic effect on the November election. I believe that the National Democratic Party will take the hard line and concede nothing to Rev. Jackson. I think that the majority of the neophyte voters will be disillusioned by Jesse's ultimate compromise and decide not to vote, while a significant number of more adept Democrat voters will defect or a least consider the wisdom of defection. Therefore the effect of his campaign on the November election will be rather limited.

Q: How would you rate Reagan's performance on minority issues?

A: President Reagan's performance on minority issues from a minority perspective is poor. Generally speaking, the minority community is concerned with immediate impact and short-term benefits, while the president is concerned with long-term solutions, which may sacrifice short-term benefits. I am convinced that as the Republican Party invests more in outreach and education on a local level, the perception of the minority communities regarding the Republican Party will change in a revolutionary way. Despite what others may be saying, I believe that President Reagan's policies embody what is beneficial to the black community and may even usher in a second reconstruction.

Q: How do you position yourself in the ideological and political framework of the Republican Party?

A: Philosophically, I subscribe to the notion that the individual has the bottom line responsibility for the improvement of his or her lot, in spite of the conditions of racism, and gross inequities across the spectrum of American society. The individual must develop the personal skills and moral character to master his condition and inspire others to do likewise. Politically, I believe that the Republican Party at present provides the best opportunity for the black individual and community to develop and attain political and economic ascendancy. The rebuilding of our communities requires that we begin to make our decisions on how we relate to power imbalances. The needs of today require that we re-evaluate traditional relationships and strategies and charter a new course of activist Republicanism, independence and bi-partisanship.

Q: Do you have plans to raise the awareness of black Americans to foreign policy issues?

A: My priorities have to do with local control of the black and minority community by blacks and respective minorities. The purpose of local community control is to significantly impact domestic policy and improve the condition within the black and minority community. Foreign policy is not my priority. However, the extent to which the black community can impact foreign policy will depend on how much it can impact domestic policy.

Q: Could you explain something about the activities of the NBRC and Voters Anonymous?

A: Voters Anonymous is a political education and research organization. The Voters Anonymous concept stresses the need for a two-party political strategy in order to achieve ethnic ascendancy for the black and minority community. By using a bi-partisan strategy, we can exert leverage on both sides of the political aisle. Right now, the black community is registered disproportional in the Democratic Party, which lessens the possibility of exerting significant leverage on both parties. The Democratic Party has controlled New York City Politics since the time of "Plunkett of Tammany Hall," yet New York has deteriorated, the minority communities in particular. In all areas of New York, Democratic candidates are running against each other, expressing cosmetic differences while never challenging the institutional and patent inequities. Since all of our minority politicians are Democrats, we cannot expect them to discuss the need for a two-party electoral concept in the black community. The purpose of Voters Anonymous is therefore to promote this bi-partisan concept and develop educational materials, forums and programs to stimulate citizenship activism and raise the political consciousness. As for the National black Republican Council, it was established in 1972, by an amendment to the party rules of the Republican National Committee. It was founded by people like Gerald Ford, Robert Dole, Henry Lucas, Art Fletcher, and Ed Bivens, for the purpose of providing a mechanism for black participation in the National Republican Party. Its national Chairperson is Legree Daniels. The New York City black Republican Council is presently implementing a comprehensive and on-going voter-education and registration program in conjunction with Voters Anonymous.

Developments seemed to have positioned me well to address the immediate political battles. The newspaper coverage provided documentation of activism and strength. In addition, the correspondence from the Reagan-Bush people provided the credibility for conducting broad-based organizing. As I reflected on my current political positioning, I felt confident that we could make a credible showing in the district leadership race. It also seemed clear to me that my position as Queens's area Vice President of the National black Republican Council was pretty secured. At this point I prepared to attend the statewide conference of the New York State Council of black Republicans. Fred Brown was the president of the New York State

Council of black Republicans, as well as being the president of NBRC. This was my maiden voyage in terms of black Republican Conferences, although I had already been acquainted with Fred Brown. However, in contrast to our first meetings, I was now a member of my local organization in good standing. In fact, it was my skill and tenacity that enabled the Queens NBRC to survive and grow in the wake of Tom and Vernell's resignations. To my local people I was somewhat of a hero, for sustaining the organization. Since this was my maiden voyage, I was concerned with making a good impression at the conference. Therefore, I prepared a written report for distribution and included various news articles for substance.

To my surprise Tom attended the conference but was apparently not interested in being a part of the Queens delegation. When my opportunity arrived to give a report, I confidently rose to the occasion. I felt particularly proud because I was the only one thus far with a written report.

After I delivered my report, Fred Brown approached the lectern, then said, "Everyone, please give Brother Burton a rousing round of applause for his magnificent effort." When the applause stopped, Fred spoke again, "I want to personally thank you for a marvelous work. At this point I would like to appoint Morris Lee, as the new Queens-area vice president."

I was stunned to say the least, and so were many in the audience.

As soon as what seemed an eternity was over, I pulled my things together with as much dignity as possible then made my way back to New York City. Fred Brown had abruptly and without cause pulled the rug from underneath my feet. There was no way that I was going to resign my effort to Morris Lee, who I knew from earlier political challenges, and was never impressed with his skills or independence. In fact, I knew Morris Lee to be a typical political hack that was often juxtaposed to me in similar situations. It was clear to me at this point that I had to perish politically or establish a presence independent of the Brown apparatus, vis-à-vis, the National black Republican Council, and the New York State Council of black Republicans. My only impulse was to move my agenda forward.

The following Monday, I learned that a small group of Brown supporters left the conference in protest to what had occurred. That afternoon I received a phone call from a person who identified himself as Andrew Gainer. I agreed to meet with him at his office On 116th Street and Eighth Avenue, in Harlem. Present at the meeting were Andy Gainer, Alex Prempah, and Bill Hampton.

Mr. Gainer opened the meeting and discussed his displeasure with the way in which Fred handled the Albany conference. Andy continued, "I want you to know, young man, that I do not support what took place in Albany over the weekend. I want you to know that I have been a strong supporter of Fred Brown, and as a result of this event I am withdrawing my financial support."

Mr. Gainer was in his mid 60s but looked a bit younger. Andy Gainer was a well-known businessman in Harlem and a long time member of the Republican Party. Bill Hampton was in the same generation as Andy. Bill Hampton headed a consulting firm in the Teresa Hotel, on 125th Street and Seventh Avenue, and shared the office with Alex Prempah. I was advised that Bill was the brother of Lionel Hampton and the Alex Prempah was a confident of the late Adam Clayton Powell. All in all I was honored and impressed to be in the company of such esteemed brothers, and I was greatly appreciative of their candid remarks.

While it was abundantly clear that Fred Brown, et al., was a formidable political adversary, I had personal confidence in my skills and a growing citywide grassroots constituency. My constitution would not permit me to disappear into political obscurity because of Fred Brown's opposition to my agenda. Therefore, I dug in deep for the long haul. The similarity between my black opposition in the Republican Party now and the Democratic Party opposition that I had experienced in the 1960s and 70s was indeed noteworthy. In both instances, the black (elite) leadership thwarted and undermined grassroots activism and leadership. Yet, neither the black ruling bulls in the Democrat or Republican Party had addressed the issues of political and economic empowerment in the black community. Both Republican and Democrat ruling black elite seemed to be satisfied with the status quo, and feathering their egos and nests. The general lack of black Republican visibility on the local level added to the feasibility of my objective to organize a meaningful grassroots presence. The status of the Fred Brown organization aided my cause as a result of the disillusionment among some of his heretofore supporters.

Tom Archer approached me and confessed that he had delivered me to Fred at the Albany conference for a "special" kill. Tom said, "I rolled over on you, man, and I am sorry about that. That damned Fred knows how to use smoke and mirrors, man," he concluded.

Gradually, Tom became a trusted ally. Vernell and a few other "so-called Brownies" began to intersect regularly with my political orbit as well.

Another process that was strengthening my political position involved some new relationships with an interesting group of young professional Republicans that I came to know through Joe Gibson. Joe was about fourteen years my junior. He introduced me to a dozen or more members of his peer group. All were university educated young and impressive professionals, of varying disciplines. Among them were Joseph Holland, Jackie Patton, Leslie Walter, Hasan Farrah, Helen Downing, just to recall a few. The constellation of these knew elements added to my general optimism of political success.

Also, an interesting proposition was laid out for me by Alex Prempah, the colleague of Andy Gainer that contributed substantially to my growing presence in Harlem as a controversial figure.

During a follow up meeting at Andy Gainer office, Alex Prempah said, "There is a Republican District Leadership opportunity in the 69th Assembly District. If you are interested, I will arrange for you to meet the people involved."

Although Fred Brown cut my organizational relationship in the Queens NBRC, my Harlem operation was now substantial enough to make a political base transition. At this point I positioned Harlem as the citywide headquarters of the newly founded "New York City black Republican Council." The district leadership proposition seemed increasingly attractive to me; therefore I decided to explore the situation further. Alex Prempah gave me the background briefing on the district leadership position, than advised me to get in contact with Mrs. Louise Garcia, the District Leader of the 69th AD.

I contacted Mrs. Garcia, and arranged to meet with her at her home in Esplanade Gardens. The meeting with Mrs. Garcia went well, I thought she was very cordial and warm. She said her Co-leader was ill and was not likely to be able to return therefore, she was interested in identifying a potential replacement. I felt that she provided a pretty full disclosure of the pertinent matters. The meeting was a one on one situation, and it ended with an agreement to meet again in the near future so that I could become acquainted with the members of her political club. During the meeting Mrs. Garcia explained that the process of my appointment concluded with a meeting at the Manhattan County Committee level, wherein, Senator Roy Goodman, the Chairman of the New York County Republican Committee would confirm or reject her recommendation of me. She made the point that the County Committee leadership preferred to avoid the internal competition of a Republican Party primary election wherein District Leaders are elected. Therefore the district leaders and co-leaders were appointed by the County Committee system. I parted from the meeting very inspired and I looked forward to the follow-up meeting at which time I would meet the members of the club. In the interim, I received many phone calls from Mrs. Garcia about local issues and concerns. It seemed apparent to me that Mrs. Louise Garcia was just as inspired as I was. I continued to make my contribution to the Reagan-Bush re-election effort. Following the election victory I wrote an article that was published in the November 29, 1984 edition of *The New York City Tribune*. The headline read: **Black Leaders Still Fixated on 60s Protest Politics**. The article read:

> *In wake of the president Reagan's earthquake victory; many black Democrat leaders are still advocating protest politics. All information indicates that the black community was the only ethnic community in the country that essentially unanimously supported the Mondale-Ferraro ticket; consequently the black community is the only ethnic community with virtually no political leverage with the president or the Republican Party. There is a great lesson to be learned as a result of analyzing the process and outcome of the 1984 Presidential election. However, the rhetoric of the black leadership obscures the abounding practical wisdom. While the black community should pride itself in the percentage of the voter turnout in this election as compared to previous presidential elections, we would be well advised to seriously question the political strategy and tactics promoted by the black Democratic leadership.*
>
> *It is unfortunate that the black community is unable to translate the high voter turnout into practical political muscle. Now that we have proven to ourselves and others that we will turn out and exercise our voting responsibility, we must now demonstrate an ability to leverage the American political system and rebuild our community. It is regrettable that our black Democratic leaders who advocated blind loyalty to the Democratic Party are now advocating reactionary politics, vis-à-vis, "demonstration, resistance, and protests." The Rev. Jesse Jackson, the impetus for the massive voter registration, has stated, "Under no circumstances should the black community vote Republican. We must now organize to resist the Reagan Administration." New York City's Rev. Herbert Daughterly has said, "We must now take to the streets and demonstrate and boycott." I would challenge these strategies and tactics of the 1950s, 60s, and 70s as inappropriate and ineffectual for the 1980s. The protest period is over as it relates to a strategy for political and economic ascendancy*

in the black community. Those black political leaders who suggest that political empowerment can be achieved by voting for a Democratic candidate singularly must be challenged as politically naive and monolithic. The political empowerment of any American community can only be achieved by utilizing a two party strategy in the primary election and a multi-party strategy in the general election. Both political parties must be leveraged by a coherent black political strategy. Resistance, protests, demonstrations and boycotts may have an effective economic empowerment application, but at this point in the post civil rights era, there political application is dubious at best.

The Road Ahead

Although many in the black community view the re-election of President Reagan as an odious machination, it may be ultimately a blessing in disguise. Since necessity is the mother of invention, perhaps we should look internally for new political and economic applications and innovations. The black community will need to develop an independent electoral political dialectic and a bi-partisan voter education and registration strategy. An independent electoral dialectic provides a framework for a leveraging strategic posture. However, that leveraging posture must necessarily be founded on voter education and registration in the two major parties. Without substantial education, registration and application in both political parties, we will continue to be unable to leverage the political process. Until this condition in the black community is positively impacted, vis-à-vis, the strategic application of the vote, we will relegate our political potential to the superficial popularity contest of the general election. The situation is compounded when we continue to vote as a monolith without receiving a quid pro quo, and the black partisan leadership continues in insult our political intelligence.

The Democratic Party is not a panacea or paternal savior of the black community. Only when the black community begins to participate significantly in the local primary election politics of both the Democrat and Republican Parties will political leverage and ethnic ascendancy be achieved. Only when the black Community begins to vote in the local primaries will Republican or Democrat "insensitivity" change for the better. Unfortunately for the black community, all of the visible political leaders are Democrats, and it is

177

not within their political self-interest to advocate "holistic politics."
In fact the black community expects too much truth from the
traditional political leadership.

Concomitant to the unfolding Republican district leadership controversy an insurgent electoral activism was being generated. Joe Gibson had been talking very enthusiastically about a group of his peers; he called "Harvard Cats." Gibson would always talk glowingly about this group of "Harvard Cats," in the context of his current role as Harlem Political Coordinator, of the citywide agenda. Gibson invited me to a meeting sponsored by members of the group that called themselves "Radical Republicans." I got the impression from Gibson that he may have been talking to them about electoral politics and he got over his head, therefore he decided to interface me with the group at this point. I came to this conclusion because he told me in advance that he was not going to attend the meeting, I would have to go and introduce myself. His only point to me was that the group intended to advance their agenda into the area of electoral politics so he mentioned my name and the invitation was made.

Gibson said, "My point to them was that you may be able to provide them with some useful information."

Sure enough Gibson did not show up to the meeting, so I introduced myself, organization and what I was about. I was thoroughly impressed with the group, their expertise and agenda. We exchanged information following the meeting and I subsequently began consulting with the group. The key contact person was Joseph Holland, Attorney, entrepreneur, writer, and political activist. Holland had recently set up his law practice in Harlem on 126th Street. The office was shared with his business associate, Hasan Farrah, and another attorney in his late 60s. Joseph Holland and his peers were in their mid twenties about a dozen years my junior. The group's agenda included organizing a grassroots political apparatus to elect independent candidates to political office. Holland had some personal political ambition and consequently we developed a political relationship in that regard.

While my relationship with Gibson and his group developed and electoral prospects for the future were kicked around, events conspired to provide for a dynamic electoral Republican Party initiative. The untimely death of the Honorable Leon Bogues, Harlem representative of the New York State Senate, set the political stage for an unprecedented grassroots Republican electoral campaign. As a result of the unexpected event a Special Election was scheduled to fill the vacant seat of the later State Senator. Although it was a practical political impossibility for a Republican candidate to win the classic victory in Harlem, particularly in an abbreviated Special Election we engaged the process. Joe Holland believed that he could make a credible impression and I agreed to work on the campaign team to that end.

The campaign executive committee was a triumvirate that included myself, Joe Gibson and the candidate Joseph Holland. The campaign organization comprised fifty or sixty volunteers who were committed and disciplined. Holland's Democrat opponent David Patterson was the son of the famous New York State Senator Basil Patterson, and a virtual electoral shoe-in. Bill Lynch the preeminent Democrat guru managed the Patterson campaign. There was a third candidate in the race, Gaylin Kirkland, the candidate of the Liberal Party. All in all these impressive three young men provided the black community with a stimulating campaign and a preview of the future black political talent. The final election result was anti-climatic and David Patterson won a convincing victory. However, Holland was an impressive candidate and we developed an impressive campaign organization in spite of the short time period. In the final analysis, Holland was able to land an impressive and influential appointment as the Chief Counsel to the New York State Senate Housing and Community Development Committee. In addition the campaign served notice to the New York City political establishment that an insurgent initiative had been undertaken, outside of the traditional political framework.

Following the campaign, I set my consulting company up in the rear street level office in the Brownstone along with Holland as I was able to negotiate a deal with the property owner. With a reasonable office function in place, I began to consider how to best take advantage of the new political positioning in the Republican Party. The quality of the organization that was put in place generated some interest in significant Republican quarters. Members of the staff of the Senate Majority Leader the Honorable Warren Anderson, Tom Slater and Steve Rice, contacted me and articulated the support of the Senator. The Senator provided significant support for the Holland campaign, and suggested that following the campaign they would interface me with the appropriate people at the New York Republican State Committee. I was introduced to Chairman of the State Committee, Anthony Calavita, and the Executive Director Ed Lurie, during a downstate meeting of the new organized Black Republican Taskforce, under the auspices of the New York Republican State Committee. Tom Slater, Ed Lurie and I had extensive discussions as Slater was recommending me to the State Committee as the person to spearhead the State Committee's Black Taskforce, that Ed Lurie was apparently having some difficulties implementing. We finally agreed that I would prepare a Black Republican Taskforce proposal for implementation. I prepared the document, Tom Slater critiqued it and the Black Republican Taskforce proposal was submitted and accepted by State Committee. The Republican State Committee seemed interested in the proposal, however, implementation became problematic.

My political fortunes seemed to be on a fast curve. I was beginning to generate a presence on the Republican Party State Committee level, and my local positioning, vis-à-vis the district leadership in the 69th AD, was undoubtedly generating a spectrum of controversy. The controversy with Fred Brown became peripheral if not eclipsed by the controversy at the level of real-time black and white political power relations in the Republican Party. Mrs. Garcia had her own problems with Fred Brown, the New York State Council of black Republicans and NBRC. She, (Mrs. Garcia) was a member of the Geraldine Jones citywide network and had recollections of an epic political battle between Fred Brown and Geraldine Jones that Fred ultimately got the better of. The confrontation that Fred had with Geraldine Jones did not set well with many blacks in the Republican Party. My follow-up meeting with the members of her political club went well therefore I was looking forward to the confirmation at the New York County Committee level. The meeting at the County Committee office took longer than I had anticipated. However, the moment was at hand and I was looking forward to completing the process. I waited in the conference room on the offices of the County Committee for Senator Goodman, the Republican County Chairman. Present was Mrs. Louise Garcia and two members of her club, Mrs. Gertrude Parker, executive assistant to Senator Goodman, and Stuart Wershub, administrative assistant to the senator. After a long wait a brother that I recognized from the general Harlem neighborhood came in and sat down along with us at the conference table. After a brief introduction and Mrs. Garcia's acknowledgment of him, it soon became clear that the brother was present for confirmation as co-district leader. Although I was absolutely surprised, I managed to maintain my poise as I saw the maneuver operating before my eyes. I closed my remarks by offering my support of the new leader, and gave my blessing to Mrs. Garcia and the group for their effort to strengthen the county with young energetic black men. As everyone paused practically speechless, I excused myself and made my exit. The young man was familiar to me; as I knew that he played tag with drugs and had an alcohol problem.

It was two or three weeks later that I received a call from Mrs. Garcia, who told me that she got some negative feedback from the county committee leadership to the effect that I was too controversial therefore she was pressured to drop me. I was not surprised by the rumor and innuendo, because I was baptized with it during the Campaign with Holland. Rumors and innuendo was circulated about Holland as well as me that were generated from high places. Meanwhile, the New York Republican State Committee and the implementation of the Black Republican Taskforce were static. According to the State Committee Executive Director, Ed Lurie, the Chairman Anthony Calavita, was debating whether to fund the Black Taskforce in view of the "upstate vs. downstate dichotomy." I knew that there was some truth to that assertion, but I also knew that there were other issues negatively impacting on the Black Taskforce initiative. I was aware that Ed Lurie, also had a problem with the taskforce being located in the upstate office as it would encroach on his bailiwick, as well as there was a under current resistance to reaching out in the black community. The downstate resistance to the Black Taskforce was just as intractable as the local Republican county leadership was opposed to the State Committee, imposing the taskforce and its controversial leadership on the esoteric, stealth political power relationships that manipulate New York City politics. The Black Republican Taskforce was between a rock and a hard place and I had to be careful that I did not get played out of position in the balance. The New York Republican State Committee outreach effort deteriorated to the superficial, then I dropped out.

CHAPTER 12

Mr. Robert Dolphin broke my trance as he approached me while I was standing at the door of the print shop. "My brother, how are you feeling today?" he asked.

"Pretty good, I feel pretty good, Mr. Dolphin, in spite of my daily bread," then he followed me as I walked into the shop. Mr. Dolphin was a senior citizen in his early 70s, and a long-time member of the New York Republican County Committee, and officer of the West Side Republican Club.

Mr. Dolphin began, "Well, Brother Burton, I thought that I would stop by and bring you some information and some documentation. I was up to the county office today, and we have a club meeting later. Mrs. King and I have to deal with a major problem concerning the club, and we may have to change our location. My District Leader, Joe Roberts, as you know, Brother Burton, is on the staff of the Democratically controlled Uptown Chamber of Commerce. Therefore, me and Mrs. King are the only ones to carry the business of the club, including the petitions. I'm getting sick and tired of it, because it is not going anywhere and not accomplishing very much. Brother Burton, I have come to the conclusion that the County Committee leadership is afraid to deal with you because you will shake things up."

I answered, "Well, Brother Dolphin, I suspected that for a long time, ever since the Louise Garcia, District Leader, scenario. And more recently, it is clear to me that Leroy is avoiding me deliberately. The County Chairman tells me continually that Leroy Owens will represent the county in conjunction with my 'grassroots' initiative, yet Leroy never keeps his appointments with me to discuss the project."

Mr. Dolphin continued, "In fact, Republican District leader John Woods has confirmed to me that Leroy was specifically instructed not to work with you. John would not confirm whether Fred Brown or county that gave him the instruction."

"Mr. Dolphin," I said, "I wouldn't be surprised if both the county chairman and Fred Brown have influenced Leroy to stay out of my political orbit." I said, "During the O'Rourke gubernatorial campaign, the County made it abundantly clear that they would play political hardball with me. So I have focused on my economics and other grassroots political components necessary to move the agenda forward."

"Well, Brother Burton," Mr. Dolphin said, "I had hoped that after the O'Rourke campaign, the county would embrace you and the taskforce. But that obviously never happened, and some people wondered why.

"It was about in 1989, after you were a Delegate for Jack Kemp during his bid for the presidential nomination. Following the election of President George Bush, the objective on the county level was to isolate you from the District leaders. The county is not interested in building a competitive party against the Democrats. As you know, politics makes for strange bedfellows, and it seems as though the Republican leadership prefers to deal with the designated black Democrat leadership. The only way that the political power equation will change in the black community is to replace the current black leadership across the political spectrum. I am an old man now; maybe I will see it happen and maybe not, but I want to make a contribution to it, so I brought you some documentation about the County structure. I don't know how, or if you can use it, but I am sure that you will find a way. I am tired of carrying the club alone with Mrs. King, and I am tired of lollygagging on the Republican County Committee. I know what you are trying to do, and the county knows too. The main problem is that the two main District leaders in Harlem, Leroy Owens and Joe Roberts, don't have any backbone. They let Fred Brown, the District leader in the Bronx, dictate Harlem politics."

In addition to the documentation on the County Committee there was a commentary on race politics that I read with interest:

> *From the very founding of America a racial dichotomy (white and black) and juxtaposition was the philosophical construct of the political, economic and social system. Although the notion of racial distinctions had no scientific and factual basis, racial superiority vs. inferiority continues to be the operative social construct in virtually every aspect of American life. While the truth relative to the falsity of racial distinctions has been known for many decades, recent advances in science coupled with archeological finds have unequivocally established the fact that human beings are essentially one race, which originated in Africa.*
>
> *The race juxtaposition in the framework of the inferiority of African American slaves was the principle factor that caused the Civil*

War, and the race dichotomy continues to be the emotional trigger that energies and animates the political and electoral process. While the North in the context of the Union Army won the Civil War; the South, for its part, won the battle, in that de facto segregation became common law in the South until the modern civil rights movement. Despite the advances of the civil rights movement in desegregating the South, a presidential candidate must currently have a successful Southern Strategy in order to prevail whether he or she is a Democrat or Republican.

A substantive and sustained change in how the black community is organized and deployed in the framework of the Democratic and Republican Parties is the road to "Black Power." Heretofore, black folk have played the either/or-political-party game because of the way they (black Americans) were organized by white Republicans in the nineteenth century and by white Democrats of the twentieth century during the modern civil rights movement. In order to achieve "Black Power" in the twenty-first century, the black community must be the priority, not "all people of color" or the "minority" community. Politics and the electoral process are not magnanimous exercises or games of friends and enemies. There are no permanent friends and enemies in politics, only permanent interest is the perennial quote. And the process of give and take is termed political "hardball." Black folk have been organized to play political "softball" only.

Political parties, labels, slogans, and personalities do not embody, embrace or have a particular relevance to black Americans. The achievement of "Black Power" requires that black folk organize and deploy themselves among the political parties strategically.

Mr. Dolphin said, "Oh, I forgot to ask you about this a couple of months ago. I saw Joe Gibson, and he looked terrible. What happened to him? He looks like a bum."

I answered, "Well, Mr. Dolphin, I am baffled by the transition of Joe Gibson. Gibson is on crack, homeless, and he has been that way for more than a year."

Mr. Dolphin looked perplexed then said, "But, Vincent, he is a lawyer and not even thirty years old. I still smelt him after I got a block away. He asked me for three dollars, and I gave it to him. It hurt me to my heart to see him like that."

"Well, Mr. Dolphin, I know what you mean," I said. "It's a hurting thing. Just a minute, Mr. Dolphin, let me go up front and see who came in. Hopefully it's somebody with a five-thousand-dollar job."

"Hey, how are you doing, Johnny, baby?" I shouted as John Wood came on into the print shop.

Seeing Mr. Dolphin, Wood said, "Hi, hello again, Mr. Dolphin; it seems like I see you everywhere I go. At the County, in the community, and with my political consultant Vincent Burton."

"John Wood, my friend, yeah, hello again," said Mr. Dolphin. "I thought that this address was off limits to all black Republican District Leaders."

"No, not me, Mr. Dolphin. I value Vincent's political perspective. I am fairly new to politics at the District Leadership level, and Vincent helps me negotiate the various political currents. I'm trying to find out why Fred and Leroy and Vincent can't get together. I want to see some unity and progress so that we can beat some of these do-nothing Democrats. That's what I am about. Right now I am working a Souvenir Journal for Fred Brown's New York State Council of black Republicans. Fred Brown is riding high; and the word is that he is getting blacks appointed to the Pataki and Giuliani Administrations."

Wood continued, "I heard that Fred was instrumental in getting Joe Holland appointed as Pataki's Commissioner of Housing and Community Development."

"Hold it guys; let me check the door again." I responded, "Who told you that news, Johnny baby? Leroy, Fred, or Joe?"

Mr. Dolphin said, "I'm on my way out, Vincent; we'll pick up the conversation again on the next time."

"I'll walk up front with you," I said.

Wood said, "Me too, Vincent, I'm out too; I just dropped by to check in. I'm out along with Mr. Dolphin. Maybe we can figure out how to unify the crazy political situation."

"Okay, Mr. Dolphin and Johnny baby, see ya." I concluded.

It was the coach at the door. "Hey, Coach, what's happening, man?"

"Everything is cool, B.; he said, I want you to meet a long-time buddy of mine, Johnny Crocker, alias the Indian, or rather Hacksaw. Johnny works around the corner on 125th Street, at the Department of Labor. Johnny and I go back damn near to single digits. I was on my way here, and I ran into him right outside of the Department of Labor. Johnny is a real-time organizer. He took a fall and did 15 years in the joint, and earned a master's degree. You guys need to network and put it all together and take the power. We got all the necessary talent within."

Johnny said, "Yeah, I am glad to meet you, Vincent; yeah, this dude and me go way back. Yeah, I'm a counselor with the Department of Labor, and I do employment counseling, placement, and transitional service referral. My pleasure meeting you, brother, especially since you come so highly recommended."

I replied, "Glad to meet you. And the time is perfect, because my son is in trouble with the law in Florida, and I'm making arrangement to go to Florida."

Coach remarked, "Damn man, you don't need that shit. What kind of beef is it?"

"Well, man," I said, "It is drug related, but I won't know the real deal until I go there and check it out."

Coach looking disappointed said, "Well, I wish you the best on that situation, man. What are you going to do with the shop, close down?"

"No, man," I said, "I can't afford to close down. My partner Harold Williams is going to handle the printing contract deliverables, and keep a modified retail schedule until I get back."

Coach repeated, "Damn, B., please keep me on top of the situation."

"Okay, Coach," I said, "I will do that, and yeah, Johnny, we will get together when I come back."

The prospect of losing my son to the prison industrial complex, on the heels of the murder of his brother seemed more than I could bear. As I composed the letter to the judge, the hurt and pain tightened around my neck and throat leaving my mouth like dry desert sand. I couldn't swallow, I'm going to choke I thought. As pulsating rhythms of hurt and pain crescendo throughout my body and very soul, I closed my eyes and could graphically visualize my parents who were long since deceased. The spirit of my deceased parents had always comforted me throughout my tumultuous and controversial life. This time there would be no comfort or rest from my agony and weariness, by way of the spiritual realm of my beloved parents. My suffering was compounded by the belief that my parents were in fact disappointed with me. My inability to keep my son from being fodder for the criminal justice system means that I didn't do a good job in raising him. As devastated as I was by the overwhelming circumstances of my loss, I knew that I ultimately fell short of my parents expectations and pride in me. My son's criminal behavior was totally unacceptable to my parents and I will be held accountable to them for his transgressions.

Why was my generation then so much different from the young generations of today? I could not avoid reflecting on the various generational differences between my experiences growing up, compared to the young men of the present era. Addictive drugs were always accessible in the black community and the informal economy has always been perceived if not positioned as an attractive career option for inner city youth. Whereas my generation had to only contend with the addictive drugs of heroin and cocaine, today's generations have the addition of crack, ecstasy, and crystal-meth amphetamines, among others. The complexity and sophistication of the present day drug crisis has over run the New York inner city, and expanded to the suburbs and across economic and class lines. Apart from the proliferation of the drug culture, there is a general lack of respect by youth for authority, to parents, elders, themselves and virtually everything else. This strident indifference on the part of today's young people was unheard of back in the day. Plus, there were open lines of communication between youth and adults in my day, but today there are absolutely no open lines of communications to the youth from any quarter.

Haunting visions and memories of my recently-murdered godson, Johnny, were being superimposed on the kaleidoscope of images of James disappearing into the prison environment. I recalled the morning after receiving the news that my Godson had been murdered. A thin blanket of snow on the ground reflected the blinding brilliance of the morning sun. The return train ride from the morgue at the Queens Hospital Center was long and reflective and deep. Growing up in the South Bronx, back in the day was rough and hazardous to say the least, but compared to the hazards of today we were like Cub Scouts. The neighborhood of my day embodied an extended family infrastructure of adults who would exercise parental authority on my butt, family or not. And they would report my activities to my parents that might result in another beating or punishment. As a consequence of all the eyes and ears directed to me, I had to be mindful of my behavior and language, especially around elders. During my day there was a sense of connectedness to the neighborhood and community in the consciousness of the youth, and an abiding respect for elders and authority.

Youth and young adults of today do not have the benefit of an extended family infrastructure in the neighborhood to curtail irresponsible and anti-social behavior. Parental authority has been compromised by many factors, such as poverty, unemployment, underemployment and drugs as well as social policy among other socio-political issues. The situation is completely out of control now. But, then I thought the situation was also out of control during my day on the block. The main difference between then and now is that we had a sense of respect, order and discretion. Whereas now there is utter chaos, and the neighborhoods are, in many instances, managed by drug kingpins and the anti-social behavior of popular culture.

I reviewed the period of my youth and development into adulthood in the Bronx and analyzed the impact that drugs and the environment of poverty had on the young men in my family. Of my thirteen male cousins, nine died prematurely as the result of drug addiction, and a few of my remaining cousins are in at risk situations. The extended family neighborhood infrastructure that was the backbone of my development as a youth broke down during the succeeding generations. The neighborhood and sense of community held by the residents deteriorated dramatically in the wake of the heroin epidemic in the 1960s to date. The drug culture and informal economy took control of the neighborhood and succeeding generations came under its influence. Coupled with the lack of employment and economic opportunities within the larger society, many fell victim to the abyss and paid the ultimate price. As I reflected on my peers in the South Bronx, I realized that better than 50 percent of my "home boys" were dead due to drug addiction, or neighborhood crime and violence. Obviously, the extended family infrastructure of my day was not able to save the multitudes of my contemporaries from the abyss of drugs and attending criminal activity. In retrospect it is clear that the proliferation of heroin in particular in my youth was the critical factor that undermined the family, neighborhood and community system. My brother four years my junior and the majority of his peers became addicted to heroin. All of my brother's friends and associates were basketball players in high school and most of them got strung-out on smack (heroin) before they got to college. Others got strung-out while in college and even at the professional basketball level. I estimated that 70 percent of my brother's peers became addicts and most of those that are still alive are addicted to legal drugs. I guess the real difference between then and now is only a matter of degree. Finally, the train pulled into the 125th Street station and I exited.

As I rounded the corner of 5th Avenue and 125th Street in Harlem, on the northeast side facing 126th Street, I looked toward my printing shop across 5th Avenue on the west side between 125th and 126th Street, and saw Wilfred Toppin, who was apparently approaching my shop.

"Yo, Wilfred," I called as I started walking diagonally across the street.

Wilfred was one of my first friends, we were the same age and he lived in the apartment building across the street of 167th between Prospect and Union Avenues. We both attended Public School 99, Junior High School 40, and Morris High School. I was always tall for my age and Wilfred was perhaps the shortest guy on the block in our age group, but we were best friends. From time to time I would need to take up for Freddie when he was bullied by peer's especially Jimmy Lee, who was also our age and lived in the same apparent building as Freddie. Freddie was also the oldest child, and he had a brother and a sister.

"Hey, man, what's happening?" I said, as he approached.

"Ain't nothing happening till you start something," Wilfred answered. "You know how that goes. But everything is cool; I just figured I'd stop by and chill for a few. I'm on my way to a gig; you know how we do."

I continued, "Yeh, I can dig that, but it's really not what we do, as much as it is what you have done, my brother, that is such an inspiration to all worthy studs. You are the only cat that I know to wait until he is 50 years old to get married. Your patience and perseverance is of biblical proportions, rivaling Brother Job."

We both laughed hysterically then went inside. "So, Wilfred, how is your father doing?" I asked. His father had a stroke a couple of years ago that left him partially paralyzed. Every Saturday Wilfred goes to his father's house on Long Island and spends the day with him. He bathes his father and runs all types of errands. His respect for his father and commitment to his father was unconditional, and a testimony to the values that many in my generation grew up under and continue to practice. His dedication to his father was particularly exceptional because as we were growing up his dad never spared the rod on Freddie's ass -just because. Wilfred's mother and father separated many years ago, but Freddie remained dedicated to them both.

"So Vincent," he said, "what's up, what's news?"

I cleared my throat and reach for internal strength then said, "Well, brother, I had a terrible night and a bad morning, but you have made my day." As I spoke my mouth again began to get parched and dry, and the pain and tightness in my throat began, as I labored to pronounce words and express myself. Almost inaudibly I uttered, "Just returned from the Morgue at Queens Hospital Center to ID the body of my Godson, Johnny Davis."

Wilfred's face got serious then he said, "Oh, man, that's a drag. Wow. I am sorry to hear that, man. My condolences to you and his family. How did it happen? I never met him, but I heard about the young brother from Willie. Is there anything that I can do?" he said.

I responded, "You already made my day by your presence at this most critical moment." Just as I was about to digress, the door swung open and in walked Willie and Van.

"Yo, yo," they both yelled in unison, "is any business being conducted in this establishment today?"

Recognizing the voices, Wilfred responded, "No, this establishment is closed for the day as the Bronx-ite block reunion conducts a meeting in Harlem."

Willie's voice was the loudest, as he spoke, "Now ain't this a bitch, my man, Wilfred; I haven't seen you since the first Sunday in August a couple of years ago at Cratona Park during the Bronx reunion event."

Then Van cut in, "Damn, man, I haven't seen you since your family moved to Queens from the block in the late 1950s."

Wilfred replied, "But you need to come to the reunion during the summer in Cratona Park; you'll see all the survivors from the neighborhood and their progeny."

Van said, "Vincent, will you tell this cat what's up. I come to the reunion every year; I missed last year because I had to visit my father and do some things for him, but last year is the only one that I missed."

We moved to my back office and began to reminisce and laugh.

The session with my homeboys was therapeutic, and it gave me some perspective in terms of context and the larger picture. We all had a similar background and a single relationship, growing up on the block. All of our families moved from the block within a few years of each other. Willie's family was the first to leave the block, during the late 1950s and '60s. Willie's oldest brother was nick named Rip and he was five or six years our senior. Rip was in the first group that started experimenting with heroin. Soon after his parents found out about his forays into the drug culture they moved from the block and bought a house in St. Albans Queens, New York. The move apparently saved Rip from the grim fate of his contemporaries, and he ultimately got married and lived a family life in Rochdale Village in Queens.

My Godson lived a short life in St. Albans Queens New York from 1967 to 1993. While Southeast Queens was an oasis of working class people, home ownership and quality of life stability at one time; by the 1970s that oasis was rapidly drying up and giving way to encroaching heroin epidemic and the associated crime and violence. The speed in which the transition was taking place was a stunning revelation to me. I had witnessed a similar transition process ten years earlier growing up in the South Bronx. Beginning with the proliferation of heroin addiction, and prostitution and the allure of the informal economy neighborhoods suddenly locked onto a downward trajectory of self-destruction. Growing up in the 1950s and seeing my neighborhood idols and peers falling victim to the insidious heroin culture prepared me as an expert witness to the malignant and terminal process as it began to unfold in Southeast Queens. The process had an absolute stealth quality to the uninitiated eye. Therefore it was not seen or noticed until it was in epidemic proportions and virtually too late. However, once the neighborhood was infected, it was never cured of the problem. Heroin and drug addiction had morphed into an industry that employed and facilitated the working class people who managed and maintained the people dependant on chemical substances and who worked in the prison industrial complex. When the heroin problem ultimately surfaced in Southeast Queens it was already pervasive and prolific and too late for damage control techniques. Most of my peers who grew up in Queens and had no background in the Bronx, Manhattan and Brooklyn, were completely blind sided and fell victim to the drug culture. Sons undermined heretofore strong and stable families internally and daughters who played tag on the weekends with heroin and cocaine and ultimately got caught up in addition. Sons and daughters began stealing from mothers, fathers, grandparents, relatives, neighbors and the community at large. Then petty crime escalated to hardcore crime and violence. Hard-working fathers, mothers, and relatives were unknowingly victimized by the clever manipulation of a drug-addicted mind. Ignorance, denial, embarrassment and delusion on the part of many family members insulated the festering cancerous malignancy. By the 1980s Southeast Queens had succumbed to a full-blown epidemic of drug addiction and informal culture of crime and violence. Southeast Queens became competitive with the Bronx, Manhattan, and Brooklyn as a venue to embody a full range of the drug culture.

Addiction to heroin and cocaine contributed mightily to crime, violence, prostitution, family and neighborhood deterioration. Coupled with abounding unemployment, institutional racial discrimination and draconian social welfare policy, the options for young poor blacks were few. My Godson Johnny was not involved in the drug culture, nor was he a victim of police brutality that was also too prevalent in the black community. He was not a victim of random violence or gang banging activities. Johnny fell victim to the social complexities of the popular mob-criminal, bad-boy culture that seemed to have captured the minds of inner city youth. As a graduate of

Brooklyn Technical High School, one of the highest rated schools academically in the city of New York, Johnny had myriad opportunities for higher education and economic stability. His interest in raising a family was premature and subsequent to his wife giving birth to their second son, Johnny realized that due to his lack of education he was relegated to menial under employment, when employment was available. His salary as a security guard was not sufficient; therefore, he was forced to take a second job. Ultimately, fast and easy money became an attraction, as the result of associating with his childhood friends. Unfortunately, Johnny was not as streetwise as most of his childhood friends. Some of his peers and associates had already done time in the joint and adopted the criminal mentality. After making a ten-thousand-dollar investment in a collective barber shop enterprise in St. Albans, and realizing that he was being taken advantage of, Johnny began to get disillusioned. In addition to his concern that he was getting beat for his bread, he was involved with them in a credit card scheme that was now under investigation. Johnny was questioned by the detectives investigating the case, and his cohorts became unnerved that Johnny might turn and give state's evidence implicating them. Johnny and his boys went out clubbing on Saturday night, and when he returned home after driving others to their destination, Johnny parked his car in front of his apartment. As he walked to the side door of the one family house, he was approached and shot at close range by a 22-caliber pistol. Johnny paid the ultimate price for wanting to be accepted by the wrong group of individuals.

CHAPTER 13

I was seriously wounded by the situation with my son in Florida. My son was facing a 5-year mandatory sentence for the sale of crack cocaine. Getting back to New York and resuming my work routine would be therapeutic; therefore I overwhelmed myself with the business at hand. The reality of my son's situation bridled my hopes, dreams and aspirations, and it generated an anxiety in me. As I settled into the routine of the print shop during the first days of my return, the coach and Johnny Crocker stopped by.

Coach said, "Yo, B., glad to see that you're back. Johnny and I were just having some lunch, and decided to check to see if you were back."

"Yeah," I said, "I'm back at them; glad you guys dropped by. Hi, how are you doing, Brother Johnny?" I continued, "Yeah, I just got back a couple of days ago, and I figured that I would come in and jump right to work. I need the money, and I need the therapy. It looks like my son is going to have to do five years, mandatory. He is charged with the sale of $20 worth of crack."

"Damn, Vinnie, I know that it hurt and disappointed you. But the bottom line is, as I'm sure you understand, he made a bad decision, and you can't support what he did. I know that it hurts, but you got to be rough on him, B. You got to make sure that he understands that if he goes to jail for defending himself or the family, or some principled situation you could support him. He needs to know that you cannot, under any circumstances, support or condone the sale of crack. I know that you love your son, and I love him too. But I am more concerned about you. You have to take care of yourself and your health in particular, because we got a lot riding on you. It remains to be seen whether your son will come to his senses, or get trapped-off by the tricks of sophisticated American society. Think about it, B., you know the real deal. Come on, let's move forward and get it on. You said it yourself, B., this is a rough camp."

I smiled at Johnny and said, "Do you hear this stuff, Johnny? The coach is in preacher mode today."

Johnny, answering said, "Yeah, I hear him, B. But the coach is preaching a strong sermon; therefore we have got to listen."

"Well, Vinnie" he continued, "when Trevor (Coach) introduced us he mentioned my background. I did fifteen years in prison, and made constructive use of my time, earning a master's degree. I learned that it is more important how you spend your time, as compared to *where* you spend your time. I would like the opportunity to meet your son, James, in the future, but more importantly I would like to share with you the program that I am promoting under the auspices of **Future Directions**."

Introduction

Future Directions is a course of study designed for use with prisoners in correctional facilities. Although it may be adapted for use in other settings, this manual has been structured for group work inside jails and prisons. It deals with the prisoner, as he is, where he is. We developed Future Directions as community volunteers working inside state institutions for over ten years. As professionals in human and community services, we had considerable experience in areas of the criminal justice system in the outside community, working often with the ex-offender. The volunteer work inside the facility brought into sharper focus many of the problems faced by the released prisoner. While in imprison, a person is not only removed from the community, but often from his own humanity. Therefore, if a man is alienated from society to begin with, his alienation is made more complete by his confinement. As total institutions, prisons do tend to breed inhumanity, and because they are cut off from public scrutiny, they are even more inhuman than most other institutions. It is our belief that restoring a person to full humanness should be the honest intent of rehabilitation.

Future Directions endeavors to provide the insights by which the prisoner may remain "in touch with himself" or to "rediscover his humanity." These insights will enable him to relate to himself and others in an authentic manner, and thereby make possible an atmosphere of "community" inside the prison. It assumes, by its basic philosophy, that we are not merely "keepers," that a person has the power to take control of his own life. By learning to better understand himself, to accept the fact that he is a person of value and worth and to accept the "acceptance" offered to him by others, he can come to make decisions and choices which will benefit him and those he cares about, and the total community as well. This type of learning is possible in a group setting in an atmosphere of openness made possible by leaders who are accepting of both self and others, who have the capacity to care, and who are authentic in the relationships.

Carl Rodgers' theory of man's ability to grow into "personhood" has been the basis and inspiration for our program efforts. We have been significantly influenced by Thresholds, a program of correctional counseling created by Milton Burglass and some of the material has been contributed, refined, or structured by the participants themselves, prisoners and leaders, in the process of development. This background, plus our on-the-spot observations and experiences served to further strengthen our belief that love and caring are the only things that work to create wholeness in the individual and in the society. While the course combines both cognitive and affective learning, it is, by design, largely experiential. The prison, as an unloving, non-caring, inhumane institution, therefore, is a formidable roadblock between the person and the supportive community. No one program can serve as the resource to overcome this handicap. We must work to build a caring community so that the present costly, ineffective, hurting prison system, as we know it, can be abolished. We must give the prisoner "hope" while this building of the community is taking place; in truth, he himself, must be a part of the process.

Future Directions is an "enabling" program. Its purpose is to enable the prisoner to become the object of his pawn awareness so that he can become a contributor to the caring community. While it is helpful for the ex-offender to have certain skills and training, to have a career counseling and formal education, it is even more important that he be a person of dignity, capable of commanding respect. Future Directions is a caring, supportive, learning program to be used inside facilities. It is not therapy, encounter, nor a tool of pacification. Neither is it "prison reform." It is merely a first step in the process of enabling the prisoner to take hold of his life so that he may re-enter the community in a positive and constructive manner.

"Thanks a lot, Johnny, your program is right on time.

Coach said, "I told you, B., that he was a bad dude inside and outside of the joint. We got all of the pieces necessary. B., we're going to cut out of here so you can catch up on your work."

A few minutes after the coach and Johnny left, Preston Smith came in the shop, with his son Jason. Smitty, was a close associate of mine going back to the Parent Youth Organization (PYO), the Southeast Queens Community Corporation and South Jamaica Steering Committee scenario. In fact he was my closest confidant during those formative days and was indicted along with me in the political take-out. Smitty was always an entrepreneur and business-man, in fact he was a majority partner in a well established dry cleaning business in the community when we met. It was his entrepreneurial spirit at that time that motivated him to make a significant financial investment to the community-based enterprise. Although Smitty remained in Queens managing his company we maintain contact, as a result of our mutual interest in the greater good and concern for the lesser of these. Along these lines we were working on an entrepreneurial and economic empowerment application to address the need for creating a business culture in the black Community. We were working on a concept called The Millennium Group (TMG) to introduce a business experience to target members of the black community. So I was happy to see him to review progress on the concept as well as to share my personal situation with him.

The Millennium Group
"Dedicated to building a business culture in the black community"

The Millennium Group (TMG) is in the vanguard of providing transitional services to people seeking to enter the entrepreneurial/ business world, and global economy. TMG provides a broad range of services to new as well as existing businesses and entrepreneurs. TMG has targeted traditionally working people as a primary market for transition into the formal corporate format. In order to achieve this goal TMG has outlined the following purposes:

To act as an information clearinghouse for individuals interested in exploring an entrepreneurial and business environment

To promote and create opportunities for black Americans to participate in the business world on a local, national and international level.

To promote entrepreneurship in the framework of transforming the individual and family to the corporate form, and provide technical assistance to those seeking to make the transition.

To sponsor symposiums, seminars, conferences, workshops and educational materials for the purposes outlined.

Executive Summary

Economic ascendancy requires that the black community transcend the so-called "good-job mentality." Concomitantly, what needs to also begin are personal skills/talent development and business exposure. Exploring businesses, enterprise-development ventures, and alternatives of employment peculiar to the needs of the black community and family. The fact is, the proverbial "good job" does not insure the blessings of economic ascendancy for the black family and community. The goal of obtaining the "good job" has resulted in relative slavery in most instances, while providing a minimal amount of mobility and zero growth potential. Notwithstanding the various professions and careers of educated black Americans, there is relegation to marginal economic status with ultimate retirement to virtual poverty for most black Americans. The expectations of the "good job" tend to be illusory and self-defeating in the long run in too many instances. A "good job" must be viewed in contrast to the broader long-term benefits of an economic enterprise (entrepreneurship). Since America is structured to benefit free enterprise and not the "worker," it is the responsibility of the visionaries and creative people in the black community to explore more fully, the application of the individual, family and collective corporate forms of business enterprises in order to achieve economic ascendancy.

As we stand on the dawn of the twenty-first century, the industrial revolution and its traditional concepts of labor, management, and community have effectively been displaced by the age of technology, for which no models exist. As a consequence, the standard solution of "retooling" in order to save industries and jobs may be irrelevant. Therefore, the black community must necessarily adapt and develop appropriate entrepreneurial and corporate forms for family survival and prosperity. It will take new business relationships to rebuild the world. It is the business of the black community to be an active player in all of this business

CHAPTER 14

I could not help but think what Mr. Dolphin said about seeing Joe Gibson. For the past year or more, I would see him from time to time walking aimlessly. On a few occasions I saw him coming out of a known "crack house." I was indeed perplexed by Gibson's transition, as I thought that he had a lot going for him. Not the least of which was Law a Degree form Albany Law School. Gibson would acknowledge me with eye contact when he saw me. At one point upon seeing me he put his hands together as if in prayer, then bowed oriental style from the waste down, when he passed in front of me. This occurred when he walked by the print shop while I was standing out side in front of the door, in the "war zone." We never exchanged words during these brief encounters other than my greeting of hi, Joe. I recalled the last conversation that I had with him, a year or more ago. Gibson was allegedly doing some investigative research on the city shelters and homeless populations. I had recently appointed him to a taskforce to study the gypsy cab situation and the mini-van proliferation in conjunction with the Taxi and Limousine Commission controversy.

Late one evening I received a phone call from Gibson that I was never able to decipher to any satisfaction. As I recalled, Gibson said, "You're going to get slammed against the wall, and you are not going to destroy my potential career."

"I am on my way to Paris."

A couple of days later an associate reported to me that he saw Joe Gibson, dressed formally in a shirt and tie. I heard about other similar sightings of him, and then he apparently dropped from the scene for a month or so. Then finally the report that I received relative to the next sighting of Gibson was that he was cracked out.

Several days following the departure of my South African guests, I ran into Joe Roberts, a Republican Party District leader, as I walked on 125th Street. After we greeted each other, he advised me that Mr. Dolphin had gotten sick and passed away some weeks earlier. I was shocked to learn the news, and understood therefore why Mr. Dolphin was not present at any of the venues with my South African guests. When I returned to my office, I continued to think about Mr. Dolphin, so I went to his file and reviewed the information that he had given to me about a year ago. Two of the document immediately caught my attention: 1) Rules and Regulations of the Republican County Committee of the County of New York. 2) Executive Committee of the New York Republican County Committee.

As I reflected on the various political conversations that I had with Mr. Dolphin, I was inspired to focus on developing a coherent political empowerment strategy that addressed the pathology of political impotence in the black community. Following the 1986, Gubernatorial campaign and the 1988 presidential campaign, I was concentrating on developing the economic and social components and infrastructure to move the black community from point A to point B in the context of political empowerment. As a result of the relative success of these campaign efforts and the support and participation that was generated, it was now time to put the political component on line. Moreover, the current state of the black community at large was worst than ever, and the black political ruling elite, was as removed from the reality of the black masses as ever. I was more certain than ever that a grassroots, bi-partisan political empowerment strategy had to be implemented to displace the ruling political elite, in both political parties. There were some grassroots activists Democrats who seemed to be addressing that internal process. I was inspired to mount a challenge from the Republican Party structure. Following the reading of the Rules and Regulations of the Republican County Committee of the County of New York, I highlighted Article II—The County Committee, and Article VI Assembly Executive Districts.

Section I:

The County Committee, a voluntary, unincorporated association, is the representative body of the Republican Party in New York County. It shall take care of the interests, and be charged with the governance, of the affairs of the Party in New York County as well as with the promotion of the efficiency, welfare and success of the Republican Party at the state national levels.

Section II:

The County Committee shall consist of two members elected from each Election District within the County of New York. Each member must be qualified in accordance with the provisions of the election law, be an enrolled Republican, and be duly elected to the County Committee at the Primary Election or duly chosen to fill a vacancy.

Section III:

The members of the County Committee shall be elected biennially at the Primary Election in each odd numbered year, and shall hold office until the next Primary Election in the succeeding odd numbered year. Should the provisions of the Election Law of the State of New York allow the election of County Committeemen for a term of greater than two (2) years, then in such event the members of the County Committee shall thereafter be elected for the maximum term so provided for and permitted by law.

Article VI—Assembly Executive Districts

Section I:

The Chairman is hereby empowered to divide each Assembly District into separate Assembly Executive Districts to be designated by the Assembly District number and a geographic appellation (North, South, East, West or Middle as the Chairman may choose)' or to designate an entire Assembly District as an Executive District, or to consolidate one or more Assembly Executive Districts within the same Assembly District.

Section II:

In each of the said Assembly Executive Districts, an Assembly Executive District Leader and an Associate Assembly Executive District Leader shall be elected biennially at the Primary Election in each odd numbered year and shall hold office for a period of two years or until the election of their successors. Each Assembly Executive District Leader and Associate Assembly Executive District Leader shall be an enrolled voter of the party and reside within the Assembly District, which includes the Assembly Executive District they represent. The Republican voters in the Assembly Executive District, which they represent, shall elect each Assembly Executive District Leader and Associate Assembly Executive District Leader. A duly registered Republican can solicit signatures on petitions in any part of the Assemble Executive District he or she may reside in. The duties, powers, and functions of each Assembly Executive District Leader and Associate Assembly Executive District Leader shall consist of service on the Executive Committee and such other duties, functions, and powers as the County Committee and Chairman shall provide.

200

The information that Mr. Dolphin provided me with was significant and would establish a basis for a major challenge to the black Republican District leadership as well as the County organization. As I reviewed the Executive Committee membership and structure, I counted about eight assembly districts and district leaders worthy of a political challenge, which included a total of 274 election districts. Although the political objective was clear, the ways, means, timing and feasibility were open questions that required answers. Nevertheless, the political objective was an imperative in order to move plantation politics to empowerment and leverage politics. The election primary was the determinant of the district leaders. However, the election primary was never promoted to the general Republican and Democratic electorate. The party ruling elite kept the election primary pool of voters small in order to manage and manipulate the process at various levels. By thwarting or controlling the primary election process the local Republican and Democratic County Committees, undermined independent insurgent candidates, and usurped the will of the people. They minimized and undermined mass participation in the election primary in favor of promoting the general election popularity contest. Consequently, only 15 percent of the electorate participates in the primary election process. The tactics and strategy of the black ruling elite continued to insult the political intelligence and sophistication of the black community at large. Yet, there were insurgent grassroots challenges to the Democrat power elite underway, despite the advantages and incumbency. There were many encouraging signs that the time is right for a comprehensive bi-partisan political empowerment initiative. However, a successful campaign to challenge and defeat the black ruling elite would require significant resources plus the power of the people. Voter apathy is pervasive and plays into the hands of the "elite" leadership. A critical mass would have to be achieved in order to facilitate the triumph of the emerging black political bucks.

Following generations of political monopoly, by the black ruling elite based in Harlem, a Brooklyn black political based emerged in the 1970s. Since the advent of the Brooklyn "vanguard" there had been an on going rivalry between the "vanguard" and the Harlem "old guard." Unfortunately the rivalry of the two black Democrat camps had, over the years, marginalized the effectiveness of each respective camp, and had nullified the prospect of political empowerment and leverage. Due to the lack of a coherent political empowerment strategy for the community, there was a growing dissatisfaction among black voters with the status quo of the respective Democratic camps, generating serious attrition. More significant however, was the fact that a "silent majority" existed within the black Democratic constituency that could potentially change the way political business was conducted in the city and the state. The deplorable state of the black political leadership in the city and state had in deed paved the way for insurgent political bucks to emerge. In recent city and state election campaigns, the Reverend Sharpton and his grassroots movement had stacked out and solidified a political and electoral base in the Democratic Party.

In spite of tenacious overt, covert, legal and not so legal political maneuvers, the Sharpton forces had negotiated a place at the political table and contract room with the "old guard" and the "vanguard." Apart from the political and mobilization skills of the Sharpton's political movement, there was a leadership void that helped to make his political positioning successful. The Brooklyn and Manhattan black political elite unsuccessfully deployed the usual tactics to squash the Sharpton challenge, but attrition and defection within their ranks coupled with a growing political sophistication among the grassroots as well as new voters, firmly established Rev. Sharpton as a major player. As black political empowerment was an on-going, interactive, and dynamic process, it remained to be seen as to how the Democratic Party power dynamic would shake out. The present and immediate political future in the black community was fluid. In view of the increased level of political and voter sophistication, and the deterioration within the city, the influence of the black Democratic ruling elite may have ebbed.

The defeat of Mayor David Dinkins by Republican Party candidate Rudy Giuliani may have closed a chapter in the context of black politics in New York City. Although the "old guard" remains in relative control in the context of the Manhattan Democratic County Committee system, there were new players at the citywide political table and an effervescent grassroots community growing in sophistication. The Brooklyn political "vanguard" was significantly weakened with only a few elected officials tenuously clinging to office, by a depleting political base. As political power and influence continued to diminish within the ranks of the "old guard" and "vanguard," the emerging power of the Democratic political bucks were destined to clash with the ruling bull elite's. On the surface the major black Players in the Democratic Party were abounding with utterances of political correctness, due to the broad grassroots constituency of the Sharpton base. On the other hand under the surface the game was hardball and was comprised of strange bedfellows. As a consequence the foreseeable political future is dynamic volatile and uncertain. While the inevitable cathartic process of political purging and growth continues and increases in intensity, the major white power players in the Democratic Party will require that some black political elite players carry their water, and discard other blacks that have out served their practical usefulness. Unless the emerging black bucks establish a new political paradigm, rhetoric and organizing technology that embraces the new international diversity that constitutes the current New York City black population.

There has been a major change in the New York City black community demographic. The African American generations of the 1930s, 50s and 70s have been devastated perhaps at a level of 80%, by a complex and comprehensive lethal process that is both external and internal. The external sophisticated system of evil called "racism" is compounded by the internal process fratricide has left only a small remnant of three generations to be expert witnesses. Following the virtual demise of pre-war, baby boomers, and post-war generations due to the pathologies of the inner city, immigration from the Caribbean, South and Central America and Africa facilitated a new black American. The "new immigrant black American" is not inclined to respond affirmatively to the traditionally partisan political organizing techniques and applications. The current black ethnic mosaic presents major challenges to organizing the black community to achieve political empowerment in the new millennium. The new black demographic challenges all of the black leadership factions within the Democratic Party equally. My contacts within the respective echelons of the black Democratic Party electoral and activist sectors suggest that the prevailing "African American" political nomenclature, rhetoric and policy orientation does not consider the new diversity that constitutes the black community, vis-à-vis, Caribbean, South American and African US citizens. Hopefully the new diversified black community will not be devastated by the unconventional, chemical and covert operations that emanate from the poor quality of political leadership and elected government and the permanent government et al.

Darryl Brown was in the print shop talking with me, when Alton Chase came in. "Salaam Aleikum acqui," said Chase.

I responded, "Aleikum Salaam, my brother."

Chase, acknowledging Darryl Chase again said, "Yeah, Salaam Aleikum, brother Darryl; I haven't seen you for a little while."

Responding, Darryl said, "Yeah, peace there, Brother Chase."

Chase stood at his full 6 feet four inches height, with a particular gleam in his eyes, and continued, "Yes, brothers, I'm getting ready for the anniversary of the Million-Man March, Day of Atonement. A contingent of my organization, the Star Alumni Association, Inc. will be present at the United Nations."

Chase continued, "Vinnie, I know that you have a major meeting to pull off at the South African Consulate, so it will be difficult for you to get there, so I will represent you and our comprehensive initiative. But what are you going to do, Darryl? Are you going to be at the United Nations?"

Darryl took a step back to strengthen his portly stature and spoke with confidence, "No, Chase, I'm not going to be there. I did not attend the first Million-Man March last year either. But don't get me wrong; I support the work of the Nation in the community. I just don't believe that the Nation is political enough. If the Nation got involved in grassroots politics, they could change the political power equation in New York City and in critical cities around the country. They should get involved in political activism and community based politics. That's my problem with the Nation in general and the Million-Man March in particular, you know what I'm saying, man. And the Million-Man March was heavy in it self, you dig? Now just imagine if there was a political agenda linked to the March, man, there would have been a sure enough political revolution by this time. I think that the Nation blew a major opportunity to take these jive black political leaders out. I don't believe that the annual events will have as much impact or demonstrate as much potential as the first one did."

Chase replied, "Okay, I hear you, my brother; I see that you have very strong political feelings about the Nation and the March."

Darryl replying said, "Yeah, man, I have strong feelings about the Nation and the March, but I also have strong feelings about Minister Farrakhan. Minister Farrakhan is the only black leader in my opinion with the independence, infrastructure and credibility across the board that could pull off the march, and the minister is one of the few black leaders that can pull off a serious political movement."

Chase continued, "Well, brother, the Minister and the Nation can't do everything. They have successfully turned criminals away from a life of crime and incarceration, and they operate a successful drug-free drug rehabilitation program, as well as a successful economic self-reliance and empowerment plan. But I could dig where you're coming from, although I like to think in terms of what the brother *is* doing good as opposed to what he *ain't* doing or *could be* doing, you understand what I'm saying?"

Darryl concluded, "Yeah, I hear you, Brother Chase; I could relate to that. I know how the Nation turned Malcolm out. Yeah, I hear that my brother. What about you, Vinnie? How do you line up on the Farrakhan, Million-Man March, and the need for new independent black political leadership?"

The exchange was getting good, and I made my contribution, saying, "Well, man, I agree that Farrakhan, and the Nation of Islam, is the only black independent entity with the integrity, infrastructure, financing, vision, and confidence to put the march idea out there and pull it off. However, I view Minister Farrakhan as a religious leader, and the Nation of Islam as a religious and social program. The Nation never got involved in electoral politics under the Honorable Elijah Mohammed. In fact they advocated non-participation and separation of the American government. Farrakhan, in my view, has not substantially moved from that apolitical position. I believe that Farrakhan sees himself in a prophetic context. I think that the question really becomes, to what extent are the members of the Nation of Islam registered voters and to what extent do they vote. My guess is that the members of the Nation for the most part do not participate in the political process.

"On the other hand, if, in the unlikely event that Minister Farrakhan had a political objective or motive, what would he tell his membership to do? Would he tell his people to vote Democratic, Republican or Independent at the Million Man March anniversary? Do you think that Farrakhan should run for the presidency, or the senate or for governor of Chicago? No, I don't think that politics is on Farrakhan's agenda."

Darryl injected, "Well, I think that the Minister and the Nation have the credibility and resources to start a black Independent Political Party, and take control of target cities around the country. I'm talking about real independent black political power, you know what I am saying, man."

I said, "Yeah, D., that sounds great, but there will be no mass independent political organization in the black community that could survive sophisticated infiltration and subversion. We learned that in the 1960s and 70s. Independent black political Party sounds hip, but American party politics is complex, sophisticated, and cannot be leveraged by external, independent techniques. In order to master American Party politics a critical mass or magical number must strategically infiltrate and leverage the prevailing electoral and political party process. Unfortunately, the black community has not yet demonstrated the level of voter application and political sophistication to leverage the political process on the most basic level. We have relied too much on the black political elite to deliver the masses, but they have failed us. Now it is up to us to be the leaders."

"Yeah, I buy that, Brother B; it is up to us to make it happen." Darryl concluded, "Chase, what is your organization, the Star Alumni Association about?"

Chase gave an overview of the program, he said, "The Star Alumni Association, Inc., is a support group of recovering addicts, who have completed the Star Program. The Association joins together with family, friends and supporters in a comprehensive and collaborative effort to maintain a continuous bond of support and infrastructure, between graduates and residents of the Star Program. The Alumni are committed to the development, enhancement, empowerment and the continued financial support for the Alumni and the Star Program. We, the Alumni, view ourselves as positive role models, and to respect ourselves as well as those that we encounter. We provide a support network of services to Star Program residents, and the community, through education, training, and out-reach services. We do public speaking about the program services and activities. We also have the 'Star Choir' who perform at special events."

I first met Darryl Brown few years earlier, when I was the state coordinator for the Republican Party Gubernatorial candidate Andrew O'Rourke. Darryl was around thirteen years my junior, and was a popular local community activist and entrepreneur. He recently moved from Harlem to the Bronx, but maintained communication with his contacts in Harlem. Darryl was aware of my political and economic empowerment strategy, and expressed an interest in playing a role when the plan got to the implementation and application stage. I let him know that I was in the process of developing a final solution scenario; therefore, he should keep lines of communication open.

CHAPTER 15

"Yeah, Vinnie," said Darryl, "I know where you are going with that concept. The term, 'new-world African' embodies blacks from the Caribbean, North and South Americans, and the entire African Diaspora that emigrate to the United States. I agree that unifying the general nomenclature may serve to minimize the continuing internal ethnic dynamic generated by African Americans, and blacks from the respective Caribbean countries and South America. Yeah, man, I'm with that idea. Yes, man, I think the concept is pretty deep because it also maximizes the potential political unity dynamic relative to the African in Diaspora, and focuses on the continent."

Smitty said, "I'm glad that you mentioned the word 'politics' because it's about time that the political empowerment component that we've been working on for so long be implemented. All of the necessary pieces are at hand. Everything is in place, man, but it is supposed to follow the political initiative. What are we waiting for, my brother? We have a viable political application alternative formula to organize on the ground ready for testing. The black political leadership are foundering, and the community is tired of these emotional rallies, demonstrations, and marches that do not achieve political power or leverage. The black community is ready to engage in a broad-based political discourse and strategic plan to change the political status quo. I say we move now!"

"We are not ready just yet," I continued. "You know the real deal, man, because we've done this operation a couple of times before. We can't just jump out there. We're in the fourth quarter, man, and this may be our last shot. True, everything is in place, and we are almost ready. But it ain't soup yet."

Smitty, getting adventurous, said, "Vinnie, if I didn't know you so long, I would think that you are getting gun shy in your old age."

I snapped, "Gun shy. What do you mean, gun shy, man?"

Smitty reacted, "Take it easy; I am with you, as usual, but remember what you told me over 20 years ago. You told me something that I continue to believe. Do you remember, man? You told me that we couldn't wait until we are ready. If we wait until we are ready, we will never move on the agenda. You said, 'we must move before we are ready, and have the ultimate faith that we will achieve our objective.' I understand your concerns, particularly since you will honcho the political piece, but we've got to jump out there and force the issue and engage the political process. Anyway, I have to cut out, and I will see you again on Saturday."

Changing the subject, Darryl said, "Vinnie, what's up with Ron Taylor, the white guy that seeks you out to do his Congressional campaign every two years? Is he down with the final political solution? You remember the white guy that wanted you to do his campaign for the US House of Representatives against the incumbent, Steve Solars. Have you seen him?"

"Oh, yeah, D," I said. "I got some news about Ron Taylor the other day."

Smitty stopped in his tracks and said, "You mean the Ron Taylor, your FBI-spy friend? Where has he been? Whatever happened to him, or is it the spy disappearing-and-reappearing act again? You know that I never thought that he was serious about running for congress; it was just a front and cover for the real objective of intelligence and surveillance on you and our activism, B. I told you that you are one of his operations because your political activism represents an agency of revolution."

"Well, D.," I said, "I have always believed that Ron was an intelligence officer, but I also believe that he was serious about running for Congress."

Darryl saw his opportunity to make his point, "Yeah, B., he was serious all right, he was serious in 1982, '84, and '86, but never became a real-time candidate; then he disappeared in 1988. Yeah, B., he never ran, but he took copious notes relative to the whole operation."

Trying to put the conversation in political perspective I said, "But guys, you know as well as I do that infiltration, subversion and co-option are occupational hazards when engaged in political empowerment initiatives for black people. But, anyway, I didn't hear from him directly; I heard from his mother. Apparently Ron has been very ill, I understand, and I've been told that he is in the hospital. His mother Jean said that he asked her to get in touch with me, because he wanted me to visit him. And his mother said that she wanted to meet me as well, so I arranged to visit them in Clifton New Jersey in a couple of weeks. She did not tell me what his illness was nor his condition, but it is clear that his situation is serious."

Smiling broadly Darryl said, "Well, be sure to give him my regards, and tell him that I am eager to work on his next campaign."

I closed out, continuing to make my point, "I want to reiterate the point to you guys that I am not gun shy in the political context. The fact is that we need a public relations component in order to inspire and facilitate a broad-based political discourse in the black community concerning the road ahead. If we don't have an effective public relations function we will be steamrolled by the prevailing rhetorical political inertia, the fact that black and white Republicans and Democrats are for the most part our adversaries in this political-empowerment exercise cannot be over stated. We have a formidable political foe that will stop at nothing in order to maintain the political status quo. Having said that, I want to share this with you and I look forward to your comments on it next Saturday. This is the substance of the requisite public relations function. Read it, and let's talk about it."

The ongoing quest of black Americans to achieve political, economic, and social equity are characteristic of a perpetual serial drama with the full range of successes, failures, intrigues, expectations, detractors, trials, challenges, and tribulations. Apart from the seriousness of the past and current situation that plagues the black community at large, the plethora of stories and circumstances have an entertainment factor in retrospect that is both engaging and enlightening to all interested observers.

For more than four hundred (400) years Africans enslaved in America provided a rich and colorful trail and sequence of events that chronicles their legitimate attempts for full enfranchisement as citizens of the "New World." This odyssey comprises classic American history as well as informs the global community relative to the sophistication of the American political, economic and social system. Needless to say, the American political, economic and social system is, in many ways, a microcosm of how the world operates and the lot of black folk wherever they are.

Paradoxically, this is the first decade of the twenty-first century, and many of the issues and conditions that beset black America in the nineteenth and twentieth centuries remain. Despite advances and victories on many fronts, during the period of Reconstruction following the Civil War and the modern civil rights movement, the political, economic and social conditions are virtually unchanged for black Americans at large.

Subsequent to the Emancipation Proclamation (1862), black Americans were the only "racial minority" of numerical consequence in the country. Black Americans are still arguably the largest "ethnic minority" in the country, although there is a broad range of other ethnic minorities that constitute today's citizenry. Yet the black community at large is the weakest community in terms of political power and leverage, compared with all other minority groups. What accounts for this dilemma that continues to plague the masses of black folk? In view of the profound achievement of the very few black Americans, some suggest and attempt to prove that there is an inherent deficiency associated with black folk in general.

When one makes a cursory observation of the global black community, the black American political, economic, and social dilemma becomes ubiquitous. What are the elements and factors that perpetuate this situation in black America? How is the status quo of black America maintained? What are the elements and factors that keep the global black community in political, economic and social poverty?

Toward the end of the modern civil rights era, perhaps about 1966, Kwami Toure (Stokely Carmichael) popularized the phrase "Black Power." Kwami Toure was the Chairman of SNCC (Student Non-violent Coordination Committee), a youth movement that was more often than not at odds with tactics of the civil rights movement leadership. The phrase "Black Power" was embraced by the various youth organizations and components; but the civil rights and elected black leadership denounced the phrase and its youthful proponents as too radical. The "Black Power" movement and the war in Viet Nam became two wedge issues that separated the youth and adult political movements in the 1960s.

The late and great Congressman Rev. Adam Clayton Powell Jr. was virtually the only black elected official to embrace Kwami Toure and the concept of "Black Power, and provided the public an analogy of the phrase. The glib Congressman Powell put "Black Power" in context and made the point to news reporters that "Black Power" was no different than "Polish" or "Jewish" power. And Congressman Powell Jr. was sensitive to the war issue as well. Rev. Dr. Martin Luther King Jr. did not embrace "Black Power" but ultimately became an anti-Viet Nam War advocate, a central "Black Power" issue. Kwami Toure also played no small part in Rev. King's conversion on the war question. Both Congressman Rev. Adam Clayton Powell Jr. and the Rev. Dr. Martin Luther King Jr. were widely criticized by their peers for their respective political positions. Hence the phrase "Black Power" became a politically radioactive a term, not to be uttered by "responsible" or "mainstream" black political leadership.

During the mid 1970s the phrase evolved to "black empowerment" and then it spit in two to form "political empowerment" and "economic empowerment." Finally, "black empowerment" was positioned as a black "racist" idea and has virtually disappeared from the political lexicon. During the process of translation the essential identity of the power to be achieved was lost and "political" and "economic" empowerment became an individual or elitist black achievement. Perhaps with the light and wisdom of hindsight the concept of "Black Power" and its various political, economic and social elements and derivatives should be revisited.

With the benefit of hindsight this historical perspective and context to explore the political, economic and social dynamic that reinforces the black American dilemma of poverty and powerlessness. The exit strategy from this political, economic and social quagmire will require the application of "Black Power" consciousness and not the rhetoric of a vague slogan or articulation of "hip" phrases. The question of whether the objective of "Black Power" is politically correct or racist is superfluous political subterfuge. The requisite black political, economic and social power must be a synthesis of the historic as well as real-time situation that challenges the black community at large.

Hopefully, a comparative assessment and analysis of the various institutional components, how they intersect and facilitate a redundancy that seems to reinforce perpetual poverty. Fortunately, an exit strategy from the dilemma is in the grasp of black Americas irrespective of their current station in life. Obviously, black folk are going to have to do things differently in order to achieve a different and desired result. Of the many things that must be done differently are long range planning, preparation and application in all relevant areas. The planning should be preceded by an in-depth study and analysis of how the American political, economic and social system works.

CHAPTER 16

I opened with a written presentation and passed it out among the assembled. "Black politics is in crisis for any number of reasons that are beyond the scope of the partisan leadership to effectively deal with. There is, in fact, a leadership vacuum at all levels in the black community, and nature abhors a vacuum. Apart from the fact that political correctness, race demagoguery, and protest politics has outlived their usefulness, the last decade in New York City has ushered in a new demographic in the black community, rendering African Americans a minority among the range of black Americans. Additionally, there is an emerging political paradigm shift in traditional voting patterns that has facilitated the election for three consecutive terms a Republican mayor of the city and governor of the state.

"Black politics is in crisis, and accordingly Congressman Charles Rangel may be the last black American to represent Harlem, the world's most popular black community in the United States House of Representatives. Where does the black community go from here politically, or do we remain the political weakling among America's ethnic minorities despite our overwhelming numbers?

"This is the subject of this Saturday's political roundtable. But we are not going to kick that question at the table this Saturday. This Saturday we will endeavor to study and analyze the crisis in black politics. To help us to study and analyze the status of black politics, I'm going to distribute this material.

"This is a commentary published by the Grassroots Political Taskforce, a political action committee focused on helping to finance and facilitate electoral campaigns targeted to the black community irrespective of political party affiliation or ethnic background. And it is entitled 'Black Politics in Crisis.' 'Black Politics in Crisis' is a voter-education tool that promotes dialogue and critical analysis relative to electoral politics in the black community in general and New York in particular.

"We won't discuss the material today; we will in follow up sessions. Today I only want to introduce and distribute it. In closing let me just say that before we roll out the empowerment initiative our political database must be in place.

"The strategic plan of the Grassroots Political Taskforce relative to New York is the application of a multi-party electoral strategy in the general election and an increase of black American affiliation with the Republican Party to 35 percent. The general objective of the taskforce is maximum feasible participation of black Americans in the political process in the context of an 80-percent plurality in the respective party election primaries and general election.

Overview

The recent election of the Republican Party candidate for mayor of the city of New York, businessman and political neophyte Michael Bloomberg, has highlighted a pervasive crisis in conventional black politics. The 25-percent plurality that black voters gave Bloomberg represents a 16-percent increase from the 9 percent vote given to the Republican Party when Mayor Giuliani was the GOP candidate four years ago. The factors that have led to this unprecedented surge in the black vote for the Republican candidate is generating intriguing speculation from all quarters.

Many are touting the wisdom and political sophistication of the Latino community who virtually split their vote between the candidates Mark Green, Democrat, and Michael Bloomberg, Republican. In the previous mayoral election, the Latino community gave the Republican candidate, Mayor Giuliani, 44 percent of its vote, therefore, the 47 percent that Latinos gave to Bloomberg represents only a 3-percent increase as compared to the 16-percent increase of black voters. Therefore, the momentum is with the black community in terms of constituency growth-rate potential. As a consequence, future Republican Party candidates are well advised to target the potential groundswell among the emerging black electorate. Apparently, Mayor-elect Bloomberg has taken the initiative and reached out to both the black and Latino communities, which has set a constructive and visionary tone for his new administration. Does the Bloomberg outreach initiative to the "minority" community burst the bubble of the high profile, "black and Latino coalition"? Was the coalition political rhetoric, smoke, and mirrors in the first instance is a lingering question.

Since the late 1960s, black and Latino voters in New York have been a dynamic potential factor in terms of the way political business is done on a local and national level. Individually and collectively the black and Latino communities have factored into the electoral strategy of Democrats as well as Republican Party candidates. In this context, race and ethnicity have played a role, more or less in local and national election strategies of the Democratic and Republican Parties. Primarily, the white leadership (majority community) with the acquiescence of the black political leadership manipulates and controls the relative terms of "minority" participation in the electoral process. On the other hand, the black and Latino (minority community) political leadership utilize their respective indigenous and divisive tactics to achieve relative hegemony within the Democratic Party leadership. Moreover, in each community black and Latino are consistently in turmoil among their own ranks. For example, the black political leadership is divided among various camps, such as the Manhattan group, Brooklyn group, and Queens group, and the camps of Rev. Floyd Flake, Calvin Butts and Alfred Sharpton among others.

Yet, the fabled, but popular black and Latino coalition continues to generate political currency despite its shortcomings and historical failures. Born during the days of the civil rights movement the black and Latino coalition continues to sound politically correct and hip, but as a matter of fact it had no practical application heretofore, beyond political organizing, and tactical rhetoric and majority rule, "democratic" political theory. Practical political history in New York speaks volumes relative to the application of the "black and Latino coalition" when a black and Latino candidate both competed for the Democratic nomination for mayor, in particular. We need only review the contest between the Honorable Percy Sutton and the Honorable Herman Badello during the 1970s and the contest in the 1980s between the Honorable Herman "Denny" Farrell and the Honorable Herman Badello to evaluate how effective the coalition has been.

While the internal dynamic between blacks and Latinos is dubious regarding the practicality of an electoral "minority coalition," the white political leadership deploys sophisticated electoral strategies and tactics of a racial nature that polarize and divide all communities and mitigates the prospects for a black and

Latino coalition. The application of the race card is standard practice in terms of emotionally charged buzzwords and wedge issues that have been used with general success by the two major political parties. Apparently, the "race card" as applied by the Mark Green electoral strategist has demonstrated that racial tactics and stereo types may have outlived their usefulness. Although Green was perceived by many in the grassroots community as expressing a glib arrogance, if not a sublime contempt for some in the black and Latino community, the race card application that implicated his campaign sealed his fate with "minority" voters.

It remains to be seen if future white Democratic candidates will repeat Mark Green's mistakes. Sending surrogates to appear on "minority" radio shows as opposed to appearing personally, and the use of racial code words and phases were perhaps the most critical errors. However, the challenge to upgrade the political rhetoric and electoral strategy falls on the political party as well as the candidate. Unfortunately, the statements of the Democratic Party leadership and former Democratic Party State Chair Judith Hope are not encouraging for the immediate future. The suggestion that one of the two announced candidates for the party's gubernatorial nomination in 2002, Honorable Carl McCall and Honorable Andrew Cuomo, should drop out in order to avoid a contentious primary election is absurd and characteristic of the real-time political problem in the party, vis-à-vis, backroom politics.

The party election primary is a healthy process that exercises and ensures the vitality of the party and democratic process. It is the responsibility of political leadership to promote and engage the process in order to stimulate maximum feasible participation of the citizenry in the electoral process. Apparently, the Democratic political leadership, symbolized by the former state chair, takes the position that a party primary between strong black and white candidates for the gubernatorial nomination will necessarily be divisive and minimize the party's opportunity for victory in the general election. Hence, one of them should drop out, implying the need for the proverbial smoky-back-room-deal scenario. In view of the state of confusion within the Democratic Party leadership and follow-ship, it is reasonable to conclude that the chickens may have come home to roost. Specifically, the race based electoral strategy, local and nationally, may have come back to haunt the party if not tear it apart. In addition, the party's black leadership has been preoccupied with internal rivalries and manipulating a constricted electorate that effectively thwarting the democratic process. The voter education and political sophistication of the masses has been left to the hazards of trial and error and the obstacle coarse of ballot access, imposed by the political leadership. Obviously, if a white billionaire such as Mayor Bloomberg had to drop out of the Democratic Party and join the Republican Party in order to get on the ballot, then what are the chances for a "minority" person of marginal economic means to become the Democratic Party nominee?

Some astute observers suggest that the political gene has emerged from the confines of the lantern, evidence being the 25-percent vote that the black community gave to the Republican Party candidate Michael Bloomberg. It remains to be seen whether the black vote is moving toward an unprecedented level of political sophistication and application. Perhaps the 2002 gubernatorial contest will determine if the black vote for the Republican candidate was a political aberration or the beginning of a paradigm shift. Needless to say, the Democratic Party leadership, black and white, are challenged to rise to the occasion. The new Democratic Party State leadership must discard the heretofore race-based electoral strategy and begin to reconcile the internal rivalries among competing black leadership camps. Concomitantly, the party must aggressively reach out to engage and educate a new generation of voters who will not be persuaded by the conventional civil rights political organizing rhetoric and strategic racial techniques.

The Honorable Herman "Denny" Farrell, chairman of the Manhattan Democratic County Committee and the new leader of the New York State Democratic Party, is charged with bringing a semblance of order to a political party in crisis. The Honorable Assemblyman Denny Farrell is a veteran politician and is a formidable factor among the "old guard" characterized by the Harlem-based leadership contingent. Now that Assemblyman Farrell is elected to the post of state chairman, we will have the opportunity to appreciate his vision for the future of the party and his skill and ability to achieve that vision. As the new state chair, he will inherit the good, bad, and the ugly, but it must be noted that, as a veteran politician he has played a role in all phases of the status quo including the current crisis in conventional black politics. The Assemblyman brings to the table a working knowledge and personal insight relative to the Herculean task at hand.

The mandate for the new state chairman is straight forward, vis-à-vis, the 2002 gubernatorial election. But, the abounding internal dynamic will likely generate some unseen curves and obstacles and out right challenges to the prospects of a coherent process and successful outcome. Can the Honorable Herman Farrell navigate the state party out of the New York City municipal and New York State wilderness? This is an open question. Not surprising is the fact that the prospect of the Assemblyman ascension to the state party leadership received mixed reviews. The veteran Assemblyman has already begun to get the state party clubhouse in order by initiating a broadside attack against Rev. Al Sharpton. "Sharpton represents the extraneous wing of the party, and he (Sharpton) is not a leader of the Democratic Party," said Farrell.

According to many in the grassroots community (black and Latino), Rev. Sharpton fills a political leadership vacuum on issues that are perceived as the traditional issues of the Democratic Party in general and the civil rights leadership in particular. In this context Rev. Sharpton has negotiated a converted position of leadership within the party that rivals and competes with many black elected officials. Therefore Rev. Sharpton's endorsement is enthusiastically sort after by political candidates black, Latino, and white for local as well as national elections. Many in the grassroots community suggest that elected officials, for reasons of political correctness, genuflect before Sharpton on one hand while being contemptuous of his popularity and influence with the party and media on the other hand. Apparently the die has been cast, and Rev. Sharpton is likely to become the object of speculation and accusations, particularly regarding the Mark Green loss to Mayor elect Bloomberg. The crisis in the Democratic Party, in general and the black leadership in particular, may require radical surgery to ameliorate the crisis and racial cancer in the party. However, the Sharpton factor may ultimately be proved to be malignant.

The Sharpton Factor

As a relatively recent transplant to Harlem from "The Peoples Republic of Brooklyn," the Rev. Alfred Sharpton has successfully negotiated a coveted position among the black political ruling class in America's most well-known black community. Rev. Sharpton's success in penetrating the Harlem ruling elite is particularly noteworthy in view of the ongoing rivalry between the Brooklyn and Harlem political leadership contingents. The Harlem-based ("old guard") and the Brooklyn ("vanguard") have dominated black electoral politics in New York since the late 1960s beginning with the Ocean Hill, Brownsville (Brooklyn) and IS 201 (Harlem) community control controversy regarding education. Following the civil rights and black political empowerment movements of the late 1960s and 1970s Brooklyn elected a contingent of black politicians lead by Assemblyman Al Vann, Congressman Ed Towns, Assemblyman Roger Green, and others that challenged the sole political leadership of black New York by the Harlem based organization.

Prior to the advent of the civil rights and black political empowerment movements, black politics in New York City was dominated by the Congressman Adam Clayton Powell Jr., who reigned across borough lines and was, as a matter of fact, a towering national figure and leader. Congressman Adam Clayton Powell Jr. was succeeded in 1970 by Congressman Charles Rangel, who is now the dean of the Harlem-based political leadership and senior member of the black Congressional leadership. Concomitantly, following the political demise of Congressman Adam Clayton Powell Jr, the Brooklyn-based black political leadership emerged to compete for political hegemony within the Democratic Party. In the framework of the political-leadership dichotomy between Brooklyn and Harlem, Rev. Sharpton has successfully transitioned to Harlem and emerged as a formidable political factor to be reckoned with by the Harlem leadership and the Democratic Party, both black and white.

Under the surface of the Sharpton move to Harlem swirled a constellation of controversy that culminated with a rift between Rev. Sharpton and the political-activist orthodoxy in Brooklyn. From the outset Sharpton was the boy preacher and mascot of the Brooklyn based political-activist orthodoxy that included people like Jetu

Wausi (Les Cambell), Abu Badeka (Sonny Carson), Rev. Herbert Daugherty, Councilman Al Vann, Assemblyman Roger Green among others. Ultimately, Sharpton was effectively isolated from the inner sanctum of the political-activist orthodoxy and his Brooklyn mentors. Some in the grassroots community suggest that Rev. Sharpton left Brooklyn under duress and established an independent base in Harlem.

Fortunately Rev. Al Sharpton, the boy preacher and political prodigy, had acquired formidable contacts and skills in community organizing, civil rights political activism, public speaking and media manipulation. As a mascot in the civil rights and black political empowerment movements, Sharpton also interned and was a trainee under the tutelage of national black leaders such as Congressman Adam Clayton Powell Jr., Rev. Dr. Martin Luther King Jr., Rev. Dr. Wyatt T. Walker, and Rev. Jesse Jackson among others. As a consequence Sharpton was able to generate his own political thunder and lightening, despite his ouster by the Brooklyn political-activist orthodoxy.

On the other hand, Rev. Sharpton was viewed by many black elected officials as a creation of the media and a political hoax. Since it was common knowledge in political leadership circles that Sharpton was alienated from his Brooklyn base some elected officials believed that he could be easily dispatched by ignoring and minimizing him. Therefore, Sharpton did not initially have access to the black elected elites, particularly in Harlem. Although Sharpton had established links to some Harlem political power players like the Honorable Basil Patterson Sr., Honorable Percy Sutton and Honorable David Dinkins, he was considered a political liability in the electoral context in view of his controversy and dubious political longevity. To the chagrin of many, Rev. Sharpton was able to assemble a significant base of support from some members of the political-activist orthodoxy and supporters of black elected officials who were disillusioned by the internal political rivalries and lack of effective leadership on critical issues from respective quarters.

In addition to the grassroots support that accrued to Sharpton from the disaffected grassroots and electoral constituencies, the Sharpton's political inertia attracted the support of two Attorneys, Alton Maddox and Vernon Mason, who recently came to New York to practice law. Collectively, Sharpton, Maddox, and Mason, ("the Three Musketeers") would crusade issues that impacted the black community such as racism, police brutality, racial equity in the judicial system, racial profiling, economic and political empowerment among other issues. As the lightening rod for these and other "minority" issues, the "Three Musketeers" gained much media notoriety, and generated controversy pro and con. At the end of the day media coverage of the Sharpton triumvirate and its community activism eclipsed or overshadowed the role of black elected officials and the political-activist orthodoxy.

Amidst the constellation of controversy, personal and political rivalries, and competing agendas the Sharpton, Maddox, and Mason trio, and the political-activist orthodoxy staged a major demonstration of unity and solidarity under the umbrella of the Day of Outrage, civil disobedience and direct action which virtually shut down New York City during the Ed Koch administration. Following the Day of Outrage during an interview with some of the role players and stakeholders on the Gil Noble show, Like It Is, the thread that precariously linked the various activist camps seemed to be strained and would soon be unraveled. However, the loosely linked grassroots coalition did not breach until after the initial phase of the Tawana Brawley incident and legal case. Well-placed sources report that it was Sonny Carson who initially introduced the Tawana Brawley incident to Alton Maddox and suggested that he (Maddox) get involved in the Brawley case. Interestingly enough, it seems to have been the Brawley case that finally fractured the dubious relation between Sharpton et al., the political-activist orthodoxy and the black elected officials (Brooklyn and Harlem). Even the Harlem-based political-activist orthodoxy such as Elombe Brath, Lloyd Douglas, and Rev. Charles Kennetta, seem to distance themselves from Sharpton, Maddox, and Mason. Some argue that it was the "Sharpton kiss of death" that isolated Ms. Tawana Brawley and compromised the prospect of support by the mainstream political leadership. Likewise, the Maddox and Mason legal team were isolated by their peers in the legal profession and "responsible black leadership."

Despite various political and legal hits, Rev. Sharpton with the support of his local base people such as Hilly Saunders, the late Roy Canton, Dr. Barbara Justice, Norman (Granddad) Reedy, Imhotep

Gary Byrd and the legal team of Maddox, Mason have prevailed and organized a formidable political and economic base and infrastructure. As the result of Sharpton's impressive electoral campaigns for New York Mayor and US Senator, he has proven that he has a viable voting constituency that holds his detractors at bay, particularly the elected officials. Rev. Sharpton's detractors have been heretofore unsuccessful in their attempts to dismiss him as a political charlatan and hoax. At this point, the Sharpton national political agenda in the context of his presidential aspirations may destabilize further attempts by his political adversaries to play him out of position.

As a practical matter, the Sharpton, Maddox, and Mason triumvirate has fragmented into individual scenarios and Sharpton is apparently secure in his Harlem base in the framework of the National Action Network (NAN). Sharpton has gained the apparent support of many elected officials and his community support seems to be gaining ground. On the other hand, his legal team, Maddox and Mason took some political and economic hits that they have not yet recovered from. Some informed sources suggest that Sharpton's success at thwarting personal political hits are due in part to the level of complacency and fragmentation within the Democratic Party leadership. Moreover, their strategy to take him out and discredit him politically was too little too late.

In the wake of the stunning defeat of Honorable Mark Green by Mayor Michael Bloomberg, the Democratic Party is in crisis mode, and the leadership is beginning to purge the party of destabilizing factors. It remains to be seen if Rev. Sharpton will survive the impending purge of the leadership ranks as the new state party leadership emerges. The 2002 gubernatorial race is underway and the state party chairman, the Honorable Assemblyman Herman "Denny" Farrell seems prepared to make some calculated tactical sacrifices in order to make the party competitive next November 2002. Without question, Rev. Sharpton et al., is a major factor under serious consideration by the new leadership in terms of "What if?" But there are other factors of great concern to the party leadership as well such as the black and Latino vote respectively, non-racial electoral strategy, resolving internal conflicts, avoiding a primary if possible, just to name a few. The state chair may have given a hint of his course of action by indicating that he will seek to regain the "Giuliani Democrats" that constitute the 65-percent white vote that went to the mayor Bloomberg.

Perhaps complacency fragmentation and rivalries among the black political leadership were undoubtedly a factor in the Sharpton rise to power and fame, but he also skillfully organized his way through the leadership vacuum generated by the Harlem vs. Brooklyn political deadlock. According to well-placed sources in the Democratic leadership, "Sharpton may be sacrificed in the context of an electoral strategy to win the gubernatorial election in 2002. The theory behind sacrificing Sharpton is to neutralize him on one hand and to minimize the opportunity for the electoral opposition to use him as a racial wedge issue." There is another school of thought that believes Rev. Sharpton can be bridled for the short term in view of his objective to compete for the party's Presidential nomination in 2004. Whatever the final political scenario will be, it is obvious that Rev. Sharpton is a factor of considerable deliberation among various leadership echelons in the Democratic Party.

The outcome of the political machinations underway will be revealed as the gubernatorial contest of 2002 gears up. Some grassroots political analysts suggest that Sharpton has tailored a political strategy that takes into consideration the hardball nature of the current political and electoral situation. One of Rev. Sharpton's supporters said, "the election of Assemblyman Denny Farrell as the new state chair of the party is not a done deal. "Pressure can be brought to bear on the new state chair at any strategic point. There may yet be substantial opposition to his leadership for any number of reasons, past and present." Therefore I am surprised that the Assemblyman would speak out so directly against Rev. Sharpton unless he was setting off a political trial balloon.

While some are exploring the "What if?" political-sacrifice-outcome scenario, others endorse the notion of political compromise. What if Assemblyman Denny Farrell and Rev. Al Sharpton agree to agree and agree to disagree? In that instance both stalwarts of the Democratic Party leadership may have the best of both worlds, and the party may be able to navigate through the black and Latino political undercurrent without self-destructing during the 2002 elections. For the sake of potential stability and party unity for the short term, discretion may be the better part of valor. It remains to be seen how the politics will be played out, but nevertheless, the Sharpton factor is a significant and ongoing political quantity.

As usual the political personality dynamic seems to be overshadowing the significance of the real arbiter of the political dilemma, vis-à-vis the will and movement of the people. Notwithstanding the outcome of the party's leadership purge, the Latino community and the black community have demonstrated their political independence and voting sophistication. The lessons gleaned from the New York City municipal election of 2001 has highlighted a growing disconnect between the black political leadership and the emerging electorate. While the black leadership continues to be preoccupied with "ethnic cleaning," a new generation and demographic is emerging from an increasingly sophisticated electorate. Approximately 45 percent of the population of New York City are relatively new minority immigrants and the emerging generation of voters who have no affinity or connection with a civil rights and political empowerment consciousness.

Black Politics in Crisis
What Is a Black Republican?

Names and phrases such as Uncle Tom, handkerchief head, House Negro, oreo cookie, and other pejorative terms have long been associated with black folk who are affiliated with the Republican Party. Other references like conservative, right-winger, reactionary, and racist have negatively politicized the Republican Party in the political consciousness of the black community. As a consequence of the political rhetoric, hyperbolic and pathetic stereotypes associated with Republicans, many black folk have an emotional reaction against all Republican Party candidates and registered voters. Despite the overwhelming political opposition within the black community the Republican Party (GOP Grand Old Party) leadership and some black Americans stood behind their conviction and affiliated with the GOP. In general black Republicans constitute two groupings vis-à-vis, grassroots activist and the assimilation wings of the party.

For the most part, black Republican Party district leaders and candidates for elective office are appointees and are anointed to their

223

respective positions by the party leadership. For example, in Harlem, New York, black Republican district leaders are first appointed by the county leadership and thereafter the district leader and co-leader are responsible to stay in office by managing the primary election petition process. However, the district leader continues to serve, essentially, at the pleasure of the county chairman who may summarily seek a replacement. Similarly, candidates for elective office become the party's designee by virtue of negotiations with the county leadership. This internal process compromises the significance of the party election primary. It is common knowledge that the practice of the Republican Party in New York is to avoid the primary election process to what extent possible in municipal, state and national elections. The consequence of the habitual backroom political arrangement is that black Americans and the minority community are effectively locked out of leadership roles in the party. It was not until the 1990s that long-time Brooklyn District leader, the Honorable Arthur Bramwell, was able to rise through the ranks and get elected as the Kings County Republican Committee Chairman. Bramwell is currently the only black or "minority" Republican County Chairman in the 62 counties that comprise New York State.

The structured exclusion of black folk from leadership positions in the Republican Party exists on the local as well as national level. Both the activist and assimilation wings of the GOP subscribe to the general philosophical perspective of the party in terms of, minimum of government involvement, maximum individual responsibility, entrepreneurship and business culture, conservative family values, free market economy, and social responsibility. In addition to the philosophical synergy between many black Americans and the Republican Party, some argue that it is politically astute and demonstrates electoral sophistication for the black community to participate in both sides of the political aisle. They argue that the important thing is leveraging the political process by utilizing a bi-partisan strategy because both parties operate in the context of the "club-house gang." Also, black Republicans are motivated by the same considerations as black Democrats to affiliate in their party of choice. These considerations include, political and economic ambition, the pursuit of public service, opportunity and power are characteristic of entry level considerations. Hence, the black political crisis cuts across party lines, Democratic and Republican equally. The black leadership in both parties essentially operate as an elite group disconnected from the community at large.

On the national level, in the context of presidential election politics, black Republican Allan Keyes has made a couple of attempts at the GOP Presidential nomination. Interestingly enough, while Allan Keyes is as dark as the ace of spades in his campaign rhetoric, he argues that he is not a black American seeking the Republican Party's Presidential nomination. Keys argues that he is an American and his phenotype is irrelevant and inconsequential to his political objective. Many in the black community appreciate the concept and merits of the Keyes argument relative to how he views himself. But how he views himself is not at issue nor is it relevant to the campaign. What is the critical and relevant issue and factor in electoral politics is what people think you are and how they view you, vis-à-vis, how "white people" viewed him and how the media spins the campaign coverage. At the end of the day Keyes is what the people think he is: a black man, and will be treated accordingly. Theoretically, the Keyes argument is sound and intellectually and politically astute, but as a practical matter it is unrealistic and diversionary. With respect to the impressive oratory and debating skills of Dr. Allan Keyes, one gets the impression that he is providing a political service and not seriously seeking the GOP Presidential nomination. As a result of the perception generated by the Keyes electoral strategy his campaign never developed political legs.

The GOP presidential nomination campaign of 2000 was the second attempt for Keyes to become a viable candidate. The grassroots-activist wing of the black Republican contingent outlined a strategic plan in order to assist the Keyes campaign, the plan was for Keyes to become a political factor in the nomination process by generating an organization at the local level. The plan offered by the GOP activist wing was to target several southern states and launch a grassroots organizing effort in those target states including in New York. Since all politics is local, the objective was to establish local, issue-based organizations. However, the Keyes campaign rejected the plan in favor of participating in the national debates and speaking circuit political scenarios. This non-tactical strategy raised serious questions as to the motives and objectives of Dr. Keyes as a viable

GOP Presidential nomination aspirant. The strategic political racial implications of the Keyes campaign relative to the black community was questionable at best. Although Dr. Keyes excelled during the debate competition and intellectual exercises with his Republican Party colleagues, his campaign never established a local presence in any state.

Unquestionably, neither party, Democratic nor Republican, has a monopoly on racial divisiveness and racially oriented electoral strategies. Both political parties equally share a legacy of emotionally charged and race-based political strategies and tactics. Of equal significance is the role that black political leaders in the Democratic and Republican parties share responsibility for the political status quo of black America. Ultimately, history will be the judge and commentator relative to the character and quality of the black political leadership of the contemporary period. However, it is constructive to critique leadership in order to exact the best parts and formulate the synthesis for the road ahead.

The political advances that have been achieved during the civil rights and black political empowerment movements are impressive and legendary. Voting rights, civil rights, affirmative action and racial integration are among a plethora of victories that characterize contemporary history, the black American and "minority" community. The manifold increases in the number of black elected officials in communities of the North and South. These give profound testimony relative to the apparent successes of the black American political leadership and follow-ship over the years. Yet, the vast increase in the number of elected black political officials has not translated into improved lives for black Americans and for the poor black citizen in particular. Instead of an enabling process to help the black community access resources and empowerment, the community has inherited an elite leadership that is locked into the political and community organizing techniques of the civil rights era and protest period.

There are no distinguishing features and characteristics between the black leadership in the two major political parties. It is not an accident that no viable black Republican candidate has emerged to compete for local office against the Democratic candidates. Black Republican officials at the district leadership level continue to allow the party leadership to dictate the terms and conditions of black participation in the process. In addition to the general lack of competent leadership on the part of black Republican officials, some prominent Democratic officials have the benefit of esoteric political relations with the Republican Party leadership. In Harlem for example, Congressman Charles Rangel until very recently ran for office as a Republican despite his status as the dean of the Democratic Congressional delegation and titular head of the local Democratic Party.

Perhaps one of the best-kept political secrets in New York is the grassroots activist wing of the Republican Party. Political sins of omission and a conspiracy of silence by some Republican Party officials (black and white) facilitated the political secret. On the contrary, other party leaders who are white Americans made noteworthy outreach efforts to expand the political base in the black community. The outreach began in the early 1980s with the Honorable Warren Anderson, former New York State Senate majority leader, President Ronald Reagan, the late Honorable Lee Atwater, former chairman of the Republican National Committee, Honorable Ned Regan, former New York State comptroller, Honorable Anthony Calovita, former New York State Republican Committee chairman, Honorable Andrew O'Rourke former Westchester County executive, Honorable Roy Goodman, chairman of the New York County Republican Committee. The result of the unprecedented GOP outreach in the black and Latino community was the emergence of a cadre of quality candidates to compete for local office between 1984 and 1990. The candidates include Joseph Holland, NYS Senate (Harlem); Dr. Delois Blakely, NYS Assembly (Harlem); Dr. Joan Dawson, NYS Assembly (Harlem); Nelson Rodriquez, US House of Representative (Queens); Alton Chase, NYS Senate (Bronx); Francis Potts, NYS Assembly (Bronx); Melanie Chase, US House of Representatives (Bronx); Elvira LaBrone, NYS Senate (Bronx); Said Al-Khaldin, NYS Senate (Brooklyn). Unfortunately, a few black Republicans district leaders dropped the ball after playing a few softball games.

There is a contemporary legacy of black Republican participation in New York City and State worthy of mention. Much of the contributions of these black political stalwart activists are *obscured by the political machinations of organizations such as the New York State Council of black Republicans, the National black Republican Council (NBRC) and district leaders like the Honorable Fred Brown (Bronx), Honorable Leroy Owens (Harlem), Honorable Morris Lee (Queens), and Bobo Garfield (Brooklyn), just to name a few whose record speak for themselves. The great contribution of contemporary black Republicans such as, Honorable Vincent Baker (historian), Charlie A. Vincent (as in the CAV building) Andy Gainer (entrepreneur), Honorable Keith Lonesome, Honorable Robert Dolphin, and the great Lionel Hampton, among others also deserve an honorable mention.*

In addition to significant male figures in the contemporary history of black Republicans in New York City, there is a great tradition of great contemporary women who continued to carry the torch of freedom. In this context, black Republican women in New York City and State provide the shoulders that we currently stand on and claim for ourselves. It was the Honorable Geraldine Jones, GOP District leader (Queens), who pioneered a city-wide network of Republican Party leaders, and established a power base in New York State during the 1960s and 70s. With allies in Manhattan, her network included others. Honorable Mary Louise Garcia District leader (Harlem) and the Honorable Tina Josephs in Staten Island constituted a formidable presence. The Manhattan Republican Club, the oldest Republican Club in New York, has a colorful history as a result of leaders like the Honorable Aileen Avery District leader (Harlem) and the Honorable Vivian Hall. In Brooklyn, the Honorable Lugena Gorden the president of Freedom Republicans successfully challenged the "plantation politics" of the Republican National Committee (RNC) in the 1990s by getting a ruling from the courts that the black auxiliary organization established by the RNC, vis-à-vis, the National black Republican Council (NBRC) was unconstitutional as it defied the one-man-one vote principle. The Honorable Lugena Gorden is the mentor of the well-known, Harlem-based consumer advocate, the Honorable Florence Rice, a contemporary of the great women mentioned. Mrs. Florence Rice continues to advocate on behalf of the consumer, and continually wins battles against many macro powers that be.

In sum, a black Republican is one of the factors that account for the political status of the black community and may be of increasing political consequence and significance as the electoral voting paradigm in the black and "minority" community begins to shift.

Black Political Crisis
Jackasses and Rogue Elephants

Third-party or splinter-party politics is a growing phenomenon in New York City and State, despite the fact the voting plurality has deteriorated substantially. In 1969, during the high point in the civil rights and political-empowerment movements, the turnout was 81 percent of the registered voters. Since that high point, voter participation has steadily declined. Hence, during the first municipal election of the third millennium in New York City (election 2001) less than 50 percent of the registered voters participated in the process. Paradoxically, there are more political parties now than 30 years ago yet, there are fewer people participating in the electoral process. What is the responsibility of political leadership relative to the 50 percent decline in voter participation? Also, what is the nature of political leadership that promotes splinter-party politics while minimizing the primary election process and tolerating a constricted electoral base?

The two great political movements of African Americans (from slavery to emancipation and segregation to integration) were essentially organized and facilitated by white Republicans and Democrats, respectively. Although African Americans were self-motivated and inspired individually and collectively to pursue their civil rights, human rights, and legitimate aspirations, white Americans provided technical assistance and the fundamental material resources. As a consequence of being organized by white abolitionists (Republicans) and white integrationists (Democrats), in the nineteenth and twentieth centuries, the black community has been relegated to the vision and leadership archetype of the paternal masters and political mentors. In this context the African American community has inherited a political leadership elite and an electoral paradigm. Therefore, it is no surprise that African Americans would eventually outgrow the political parameters and paradigms that the black leadership were taught and the black community inherited. It is only a matter of time before the African American community begins to organize itself from the grassroots level under their own terms and vision.

The results of the first election of the third millennium in New York City wherein an emerging groundswell of black voters has departed from the traditional political leadership and voting pattern. Some are suggesting that there is a political paradigm shift underway, and election 2001 was the tip of the iceberg. However, the self-destructive strategy and tactics by the Mark Green campaign and the victorious result of the Michael Bloomberg strategy are no evidence of a political and voting paradigm shift. The results of the gubernatorial race in 2002 and the presidential sweep steaks in 2004 will be a better yardstick to determine whether a seismic political shift has occurred in the black community. There have been many attractive opportunities for one or the other party to make meaningful and substantive inroads into the black community to advance and strengthen their respective positions. Both parties share a history of missed opportunities and continue to superficially juggle the same group of black political and religious leaders in advertising spots and cameos. There is no reason for the black community to believe otherwise at this point.

"We are our own problem" or "We are in our own way" are typical refrains during informal conversations among black Americans. The lack of political accountability by black elected officials and the lack of effective leadership at the grassroots level has precipitated a general political apathy that some suggest is in transition. "The black community must take political power from the black leadership because the leadership has evolved into an elite class of operatives that manage the political status quo." The disconnection between the leadership and follow-ship is complicated by the idea of a messianic expectation in the minds of black people. Black folk are conditioned to expect and respond to the charismatic personality upon which to confer political leadership and deliverance. Since the black electorate in New York City has not had a charismatic political leader to inspire the masses to turn out the vote since the late Honorable Congressman Adam Clayton Powell Jr. the masses of black citizens remain disengaged, disillusioned and apathetic. However, under the surface a new generation of voter is emerging, challenging traditional notions of leadership and redefining political leadership in terms of the first person singular in terms of citizen power. The emerging generation is defining leadership in the context of citizenship, and the responsibility of citizenship is to be an informed voter.

230

Too many black political leaders perform as jackasses and rogue elephants in the face of challenges and opportunities. Irrespective of political party affiliation, an elite clique of political leaders have highjacked the electoral process from the grasp of the people. While there is a growing consciousness at the grassroots level that citizen responsibility and action can stop the tail from waging the dog, it remains to be seen when the critical mass in the black community will be generated to make it happen. Considering the nature of political leadership it is not realistic to expect elected officials will make an intellectual decision to alter their coarse, however meritorious the argument. Elected officials will only respond positively to the actions of the electorate that is organized and has demonstrated a capacity to vote for the opposing team. Other tactics such as protests, rallies and demonstrations can be manipulated until that fateful Election Day. But heretofore, the black voters have been predictable and pose no real threat to the prevailing political leadership.

Liberation from the self-imposed political bondage managed by African American jackasses and rogue Elephants is the final solution. The strategy for political liberation and community empowerment embodies substantially increasing the level of voter participation in the primary as well as the general elections. Also, less than 50 percent of eligible black American voters are registered to vote. The massive voter education, registration and application process of and by the people is required for political liberation to occur. Political liberation and empowerment cannot and will not be undertaken by the elite black political leadership. A grassroots citizen movement lead by self-motivated Democrats, Independents and Republican voters focused on citizen empowerment is the strategy to achieve political liberation. The political liberation of black Americans includes release from the notion that only black elected officials can best represent the issues and interests of the African American community. When the black community is politically organized based on local Assembly Districts (ADs) black Americans will be able to hold all elected officials and political parties accountable, notwithstanding an elected official's race or political party affiliation.

For the most part, racial dichotomies have been discredited by the latest scientific findings relative to the singularity of the human race. Although ethnic and cultural distinctions abound among peoples

231

of the world, there are no essential differences between peoples of the various human phenotypes such as black, brown, red, yellow and white people. The conversation and consciousness pertinent to the current scientific data relative to the human family has not yet emerged in the public discourse and political arena. Nevertheless, the conventional race-based political and electoral strategy has generated a strong adverse reaction among black and Latino voters that may have cost Mark Green the mayoral election. Unfortunately, political parties, leaders and elected officials, as a rule, do not learn very easily or quickly; therefore, it may take them some time for them to catch up with the people. But the people have spoken, vis-à-vis, election 2001, and the political conversation is continuing at the grassroots level.

A clarion call has been issued at the grassroots level for maximum feasible participation in the electoral process. The Clarion Call has been issued to infiltrate the Independence Party as well as the Democratic and Republican Parties with a new generation of voters. Apparently, the Independence Party is not viewed by many in the context of the traditional "splinter group" of one of the major parties at this point. There are many open political questions to be resolved as Americans and the world engages the third millennium. In particular, it remains to be seen if the black community will constitute a new generation of leadership that will formulate and implement a sophisticated political and economic-empowerment strategy to benefit the community at large.

CHAPTER 17

"I thought Rev. Sharpton was finished after the wire incident and the fact that he was denounced by the Brooklyn political leadership, Rev. Herbert Daugherty, Sonny Carson, and the elected leadership." Darryl continued, "They actually ran the brother out of Brooklyn."

"Yeah," Chase injected, "The brother was down politically, but he seems to have rebounded with the help of his Southern Strategy, vis-à-vis, Attorney's Alton Maddox and Vernon Mason. But the wire episode was heavy stuff, brother. The black political insiders and seasoned community activists have cut him off."

Darryl injected, "The political insiders and community activists have cut him off but Sharpton is generating his own constituency because of all the media coverage plus the fact that political insiders, black elected officials and community activist, are losing community support and are experiencing a dynamic attrition rate."

Chase, responding, said, "Well, he definitely had help from Maddox and Mason, but he had some serious help from the media too. The fact that he gets the media infuriates his detractors. The media helps him, and he helps the media. It's a very complicated thing because it perpetuates a comedic and stereotype of black folk. It's what I call 'Calhoun politics.' The bottom line is that it all amounts to a joke. Black folk are perceived as a political joke, because of how the media politically positions Rev. Sharpton, and how the black political leadership plays their cards."

I jumped in asking, "What do you mean, Chase, when you say Calhoun politics?"

Chase answered, "You know, brother. Calhoun, like in *Amos and Andy*. You dig? black folk are not serious. And that's how the media portrays us to the world. Black folk are funny people, comedic. And that's how we play our politics. Look, at black politics in New York City. You got divisions between Brooklyn and Harlem leadership and now the Sharpton phenomenon. This stuff makes for quite an engaging black political soap opera, real-time."

Laughingly, Darryl said, "I didn't understand the 'day of outrage' action to shut the city down. Then what? These guys are talking about a perpetual revolutionary process that is based on some Marxist ideological bent. I'm sure that you noticed their lack of support from the general public. Rev. Sharpton was smart to break from them."

"I don't think Sharpton had a choice because the wire episode discredited him with the political players in both boroughs." I continued, "The Brawley case and his two attorneys breathed new life into him, and he was skilled enough to make the best of it politically. The bottom line is that despite the increasing number of black elected officials in New York City and community activist, the condition of black folk has not changed, and there is no change on the political horizon. And you can apply that reality to any black community in any state of the country."

Darryl added, "The black political leadership in New York City has become elitist, interested only in perpetuating their leadership. Now we have a political leadership class that has distinguished itself from the aspirations of the people. The leadership is plagued with internal strife, and now we have two distinct political camps, one in Harlem and the other in Brooklyn. And Brooklyn is positioned as the political vanguard and headquarters of the community and political-activist orthodoxy."

"I agree with your assessment about the deteriorating state of the local political leadership and their dynamic loss of support and credibility." I said, "But just like we know this, Rev. Sharpton is hip to it also, therefore his move to go for himself was a good strategic decision, and it was tactically successful. Now we have the "old guard," "vanguard," the "community activist orthodoxy" and the Rev. Sharpton, et al."

Chase observed, "Sharpton has the media, and they are covering all of his community and political exploits. He is dealing with police brutality, racial profiling, and none of the other leaders are dealing with these serious issues that affect the black community."

I said, "But mass rallies, protests, and demonstrations don't effectively deal with police brutality and racial profiling. Let's face it; these taking-it-to-the-streets maneuvers are pep rallies to promote the conveners; they exacerbate the problem and are politically diversionary."

Chase agreed, "That's right, brother; only the black political leadership is engaged in protest politics, and look where it has gotten us. We have the political numbers, yet black folk are the weakest of all the so-called 'minority' communities. The Jewish community, Asians, gays, women,

Latinos are all in a stronger political position than we are, despite that fact that the civil rights movement was based on discrimination against black folk."

Darryl commented, "That's what I'm talking about, man; the other 'minority' communities make phone calls and push buttons. They've got interest groups, think tanks, lobbyists, media, and a business and entrepreneurial culture directed at addressing their political situation. We have no institutions and organizations of empowerment beyond the rhetorical exercise. All we have is the Harlem 'old guard,' Brooklyn's 'vanguard,' the political and community activist orthodoxy, and Rev. Sharpton, et al."

I said, "Both of you guys make the point that we as a community need to do our politics different if we intend to get a different result. And for one thing, we need to look at the political process as a tool. Not in terms of friends and enemies, it's obviously more complicated than that. But the reality is that we can't rely on the current crop of political and elected leadership to approach the process differently. They have their partisan and parochial interests to safeguard. And their vested interest and role is to lead us. Or at least make believe that they lead us."

Chase, reiterating, said, "Well, as I mentioned before, I think the black community is ready to consider new ideas to achieve political and economic empowerment, and so I'm ready to take it to another level, but I'm not going to roll out there like I used to do because in my maturity I realize the change is complex and comprehensive. We can't do community organizing as we did in the past. This time we need to educate the community on a much more sophisticated level of political action. That's why I like your idea about putting together a political database for public consumption and a public-relations component. The fact is, in practical application electoral politics become poli-trix."

"We are all on the same page." Darryl said, "I read the 'Black Politics in Crisis' piece and I think it is required reading for the community organizing initiative. There are major forces within and without to maintain the status of the racial political paradigm. And let's face it; the current political leadership is in place at the pleasure of the white paternal political masters for the purpose of managing the people. And that surrogate leadership includes the Rev. Sharpton."

Chase said, "Well, my brothers, I read the 'Black Politics in Crisis' material and I think it is on point. And you know me, V; I'm down with the database imperative, but I remember the political stuff that we ran into during and following your role in the O'Rourke GOP gubernatorial campaign. I know that the average person would not believe the behind-the-scenes relationship between the local Republican Party leadership and the Democratic Party leadership to control politics in the black community. It is no accident that there is no viable Republican Party candidate to challenge any of the many black Democratic elected officials in Harlem, Brooklyn and the Bronx."

I said, "I'm with you, Brother Chase, that esoteric power relationship between Democrats and Republicans on the local level is included in the database as well. At this point most in the black community are not aware that Congressman Charles Rangel runs on the Republican Party ballot as well as on the Democrat's. But we are going to get to that in context in the near future. In the meantime I want to share with you and the other folk a piece that was published in the Amsterdam News about the Brawley case. I think that the brother may be on to something."

Black Politics and the Brawley Case:
By Vincent Burton

It is without question that the infamous Tawana Brawley case is in fact a tragedy. Whether the incident as alleged occurred, or whether there were some other circumstances that resulted in the finding of Brawley in a garbage bag, a crime did occur. If Brawley was abducted as she alleged or if she willingly or unwillingly participated in a scenario that contributed to how she was found, it is, in fact, a tragedy. Ultimately, the crime will remain unknown, and we can only pray that something similar will not involve another 15-year-old-girl whatever the circumstances are. However, I pray that Brawley and the others involved in the act and cover up will be touched by the grace of God, notwithstanding the true circumstances.

The hoax, on the other hand, must be exposed, understood, and reconciled in light of historical political perspective in the context of the esoteric and practical political reality. The "Brawley Hoax" has nothing to do with Ms. Tawana Brawley. The so-called "Brawley Hoax" has something to do with an ongoing "black political dilemma." Unfortunately, the "old guard" and the "vanguard" were unsuccessful in discrediting Rev. Sharpton and destabilizing or compromising his political insurgency; therefore the political dilemma is now substantial as Sharpton expanded his political base to Harlem and ran an impressive campaign for the Democratic nomination for the mayor of New York City. The facts appear to suggest that the black political elite were unable to stop or contain Sharpton or cut his political momentum off at the pass.

Now that Sharpton has blown-up beyond their wildest nightmare, the "old guard," "vanguard," and political-activist orthodoxy may have played themselves out of political position. Although the black political power players that positioned Sharpton as a "hoax" and phantom leader to the community at large, and white power brokers, mere rhetoric could not compete with the news coverage of Sharpton crusading the legitimate issues and aspirations of the black community. Concomitantly, an increasing number of community residents and constituents began to question a mute and inattentive black leadership relative to the sensitive community-based issues. Once positioned by the black political leadership as a "hoax" and phantom leader, the tenacious Sharpton has proven his personal and political ability to endure. But the Sharpton embrace was apparently a kiss of death for Brawley, Martin, and Moses, because they have apparently been hurt by the "hoaxster" hype. While the accusations of "hoaxster" and phantom leader rolled off Sharpton as water rolls off a duck, the hoax accusation was successfully transferred to Brawley, Martin, and Moses. No, the "old guard" and the "vanguard" must speak in politically correct terms in the public relative to the Sharpton question.

Sharpton was able to skillfully neutralize the political and economic hits directed at him. At the end of the day, Sharpton is the current victor, as his electoral achievements rival the diminishing voter pool of the Brooklyn "vanguard" and the Harlem "old guard." Therefore, both the black Democratic leadership camps genuflect, in relation to Sharpton, and play the politically correct role in public. Now it appears as though the tables have turned, and the "hoax" is on whom? Sharpton has thwarted and circumvented the attempts to isolate and discredit him by the respective black political ruling elites on the electoral and grassroots activist levels.

On the contrary, Sharpton's attorney confidants took tremendous professional and financial hits, although individual and personal contingencies may have contributed to their destabilization.

Apparently, the black political powers that be were able to maintain a united front in opposition to Sharpton, albeit in vain. While Sharpton et al. was being positioned as a "hoax," leadership by the "old guard" and "vanguard" and political and community activist orthodoxy, the black community at large was being disillusioned by the internal and external political spectacle. The political spectacle suggests a contempt, for the political intellect of the African American community on the part of the political leadership. The idea of a "hoax" was superimposed on the 15-year-old Brawley, and as a consequence the truth may never be known.

The passion, emotion, and anger generated by allegations of blatant racism and rape, in the context of the African-American experience, is without equal. The allegations are indeed surreal and generated extreme reactions from all quarters, and ultimately emotions and politics have eclipsed the need for truth and the search for the facts in the case. In addition, the on-going Sharpton political saga has almost become an entertainment serial, as the media has an apparent synergy with Sharpton's glib one-liners and fiery sound-bite oratory. Moreover, Sharpton has become a convenient pawn of particular white political interests as well as political power brokers who perpetuate race-based politics and electoral-campaign wedge tactics. Hence, Brawley, Martin, and Moses became saddled with the "hoaxster" pejorative and are experiencing relative personal and professional hardship.

On the other hand, Sharpton and his political momentum rolls on. Apparently, everything associated with Sharpton et al., is positioned as a "hoax" in some quarters. The real "hoax" may in fact be the one that is being perpetrated by the black political ruling elite, who would have the community believe their political correctness. When, in fact Sharpton has been the principle object in connection with the ongoing "black political dilemma" that has spun out of control. The "political dilemma" has not been sorted out yet. Therefore, political leadership remains an open, unsettled issue in the black community. In view of the 1998 election campaigns, it is clear that the black political leadership question will move into the presidential elections of 2000—at the earliest.

According to the emerging political sophistication, voting patterns and changing demographic in the black community, the political leadership is not only in question, but may be up for grabs. The inability of the black Democratic leadership to marginalize Sharpton, et al., or play him out of political position speaks volumes as it relates to the state of black political leadership and portends interesting political scenarios for the near future. At this juncture, there are other players and potential players in the unfolding political leadership drama to contend with the Sharpton, "old guard," "vanguard," and political-activist orthodoxy's power scenario. "New guards" are emerging on the grassroots and "middle class" levels to compete for the spoils of political power.

While the political transition process is percolating at the grassroots level, some white candidates and political brokers took the liberty to select a "black leader" in conjunction with their persona; political objectives, Rev. Floyd Flake and Rev. Calvin Butts as a "political broker" and "political candidate," respectively. Perhaps the most interesting connected with these two "neo-black political-leader" hopefuls is the fact of their Republican Party mentors. The fact that Republicans have selected or anointed their favorite black leader for strategic and tactical purposes is not a new phenomenon. But at this point the bi-partisan political power pack is likely to have a dynamic effect on the black political leadership dilemma, as it plays out in the immediate political future, to say the least.

The Republican Party factor in the unfolding black political leadership drama is of particular significance in light of the fact that the mayor of the city and governor of the state are Republican. The present Republican Party domination and control of New York City and New York State government speaks eloquently relative to the state of black politics and suggests dubious leadership, if not a leadership vacuum. In any case, the political leadership in the black community is fluid at best.

The addition of Flake and Butts to the unfolding black political power equation, backed by the Republican Party powers, suggests that the "old guard" and "vanguard" players are on their own and may not be relevant to the ultimate outcome of the black political dilemma, from the standpoint of the white political power brokers. On the other hand, the liabilities associated with Revs. Flake and Butts can possibly play them out of political position as "neo-black political leaders" in the final analysis, as well as back fire on the Republican

Party benefactors. Flake, a former Congressman and personal choice of Mayor Giuliani, has been overstated as an economic and community development entrepreneur. While it is true that Flake stewarded a very impressive community development project under the umbrella of his Allen AME Church community base, it was Flake's predecessor, Bishop Donald Ming, who developed the ambitious plans and laid the political and community groundwork for the plans to be realized. Flake did a great job implementing the blueprints and solidifying and expanding the church base, which leveraged him to Congress. Flake was able to help the mayor with his reelection, but his potential as a future political power broker was remote for a number of reason, not the least of which are his parochial concerns and the controversial nature of his recent political positions. Should Giuliani seek political office in the future, he will need to move beyond Flake. Flake has no significant impact on black politics beyond his congregation and his former Congressional district.

Butts, the stated "friend of Governor Pataki," who is said to have political ambition for the near future, may need to expand his network of "friends" in order to accomplish his ambition. However, there my be some political fallout for Butts and his high-level Republican Party supporters, in view of his visit to South Africa as a guest of the P.W. Botha government. As the gubernatorial and presidential election season approach, the dynamic will no doubt intensify, and other players will emerge into the mix.

The ongoing black political leadership dilemma has been obscured by the Brawley case and other high-profile issues and hype that animate emotions in the black community. A new black political leadership is emerging that may help to provide closure to many outstanding issues relative to the political future of the black community in New York City. However, the Brawley case may ultimately be a catalyst and vehicle that helps to purge and put closure to the black political-leadership dilemma.

Concomitantly, Sharpton's experience as a community organizer positioned him as an attractive media personality and point man on racial wedge issues. In some instances, Sharpton is played as a political wild card, juxtaposed with the "orthodox black leadership" for the purpose of political diversion. Sharpton's personal celebrity and media attention continue to create enmity in some grassroots and electoral quarters. Undeterred by his vocal and well-placed political detractors, Sharpton continues to advocate on behalf of the unorganized masses and particular controversial cases and high profile issues. Following his estrangement from the Brooklyn "vanguard" leadership, Sharpton's association with Maddox and Mason began to develop precipitously. The Sharpton triumvirate began to distinguish itself from the grassroots activist orthodoxy as they assembled new community base support along with some disaffected and disillusioned veteran organizers. While there was an auspicious beginning between Sharpton, Maddox, and Mason, and the community activist orthodoxy in the context of political demonstrations, protests and rallies, the marriage of convenience was soon a messy divorce. The coalition was short-lived, as the attorneys also split with the community-activist orthodoxy following the "day of outrage" demonstration and rally that attempted to "shut down the city." Following the day of outrage it was clear the "activist" attorneys would not be restrained from making statements to the media, above and beyond the scope of the activist orthodoxy's leadership. The outspoken attorneys had a natural affinity toward the style and loose, freewheeling structure of the Sharpton contingent, as opposed to the rigid ideology and hierarchy of the fragmented political-activist orthodoxy. Apart from the tendency of the "activist" attorneys to speak to the media outside of the orthodox leadership contingent, they were considered in some quarters as Johnny-come-lately to the New York style of doing political business. The clandestine internal rifts and fragmentation within the orthodox activist leadership, coupled with the capacity of the triumvirate to crusade its own issues and generate media coverage, community support, and following, was an impetus for the Sharpton, Maddox, and Mason trio to generate their own independent political power and make a formal separation from the orthodox leadership. The triumvirate generated its own political activist movement on an electoral as well as a community-based level. The Sharpton political initiative rivaled, if not overshadowed, the preceding Brooklyn-based community activism and destabilized the ailing Brooklyn electoral vanguard.

A consequence of the success of the Sharpton, et al., political phenomenon is that the political-leadership dilemma is complicated

241

and compounded by his electoral achievements. The media seized upon the exploits of the triumvirate and their brand of activism, and Sharpton became one of the most visible and prominent of the black Democratic leadership in New York, while successfully dodging political bullets and booby traps. Without a doubt the black political elite underestimated the capacity of Sharpton, and the attrition among their own ranks and the changing voter demographic. Although the black political powers that be positioned Sharpton et al., as a "hoax" to the community and the white political brokers, their mere political rhetoric could not compete with the media coverage of the various Sharpton crusades. Perhaps the strategy and tactic of the black political leadership to ignore and/or debunk the problem, expecting the problem to go away, may be coming back to haunt them. Certainly, Sharpton's electoral and community support base renders him untouchable to the "old guard" and "vanguard" political power counterparts by conventional strategies and tactics, as white Democrat electoral candidates tip-toe through the tulips, to avoid disturbing the Sharpton voter potential. The Sharpton political machine would now rival the "old guard" and the "vanguard" dichotomy with a legitimate electoral and grassroots political component and capacity that has created a seat at the black leadership desk in the Democratic Party.

CHAPTER 18

I visited Southern Africa for the first time in February 1991 for 21 days to conduct a fact-finding mission at the invitation of the South African Department of Foreign Affairs. My maiden voyage embodied a non governmental itinerary, (people to people) that covered a broad spectrum of South African society. Contacts included the competing political parties, movements and factions, business, financial, education and interfaith sectors. The visit was comprehensive, exciting, informative and insightful particularly as it related to the similarities of "inner city" and "third world" sustainable-development challenges. New and accessible opportunities for economic and social development had emerged since the geo-political paradigm shift from the East vs. West adversarial relationship, following the demise of the Soviet Union. The emerging North-South geo-political dichotomy in the context of the developed vs. developing economies favored the development process in the "third world" though major challenges existed.

Three weeks away from the daily business grind of the print shop operation, and the abounding political machinations was refreshing and helped me to put politics and my current situation in perspective. Apart from the sophisticated political dilemma that besets black folk in America and on the African continent the sophisticated economic dilemma in terms of pervasive poverty was equally devastating. The lack of access to investment capital and international markets relegates both black Americans and black African entrepreneurs and businesses to the traditional ma and pa subsistence economy. Consequently, blacks in America and on the African continent have been unable to establish a business culture beyond the familial subsistence model. In Africa this general situation makes it virtually impossible to escape the inertia of poverty and class distinction. In the United States the inertia of poverty is similar with an interesting caveat, vis-à-vis, job opportunities. Job opportunities for black Americans, particularly in the area of civil service traditionally provided an opportunity to move into the middle class. However, in these days civil service employment is no escape from virtual poverty. The difficulty of developing a business culture in the black community is compounded by the "good-job mentality" which pervades the black community. The few black Americans that succeed in higher education do so with the expectation of a "good job" subsequent to graduation. The conditioning from the larger society reinforces the "good-job mentality" and internal pressures within black society positions a good job as the only viable option.

My emotional and spiritual connection and affinity to Africa was profound and I suspected that many black Americans have experienced similar sentiments when they set foot on the African continent. The psychological complex of being a "racial minority" in America was completely eviscerated when I was transported from the airport to my hotel in Pretoria South Africa. I was in absolute awe seeing so many black people everywhere I traveled in South Africa. From Pretoria, to Johannesburg, Cape Town, East London and the Transvaal, I saw folk that reminded me of people who I knew or have seen in the United States. By the time I settled back into my daily bread on the Harlem front, I was perplexed and felt overwhelmed at the complexity and comprehensiveness of the political and economic state of black folk in American and Africa and our future on the planet in general. Prior to my visit to South Africa, I felt that I had a grasp of the nature of the political and economic challenges that confronted black Americans. But after my maiden voyage to the "motherland" I was not so confident that my political and economic assessment of the state of the "race" and strategy to improve conditions was sufficient. There was a clear correlation between the state of black America and blacks in Africa that completely eluded me prior to my visit.

Darryl asked, "So, Brother B., how was your visit to the motherland? Did you plant some seeds for the global black political and economic movement?"

I answered, "It was an awesome experience, my brother. I am still so emotionally and spiritually moved by the experience that I have not completely absorbed it all yet. I am still debriefing myself as we speak. You might be surprised to know that I saw some people that were, without doubt, related to you."

He followed up. "Are the brothers as bad off in reality as we see on the television and read in the news media?"

"The first thing that struck me," I said, "was the contrast between what we see and hear from the news media and the reality on the ground; the contrast is like night and day. Most of the black folk are indeed poor and live in squalid conditions, but nearby, in the same neighborhood, there are middle-class as well as wealthy people."

"What about the politics?" He continued to question, "Do you think that Mandela and the ANC will be able to unite the black community and take control of the country eventually?"

"Mandela and the ANC may be able to pull off the political victory," I answered, "But there's a little more to it than meets the eye. The real deal is that Mandela and the ANC do not have any control of the South African economy, which is critical to the success of a Mandela and ANC government."

Continuing to query he asked, "Can't a Mandela-ANC government nationalize the economy to address the financial aspects of a political victory?"

I said, "As a practical matter I believe that we need to make some critical adjustments if we are to move from point A to point B."

Darryl said, "I'm glad that you mentioned the sophisticated nature of our political and economic situation because I read a profound article that I shared with Chase about the political and economic aspects of the prison-industrial complex. The information in the piece was pretty interesting, but I was intrigued by a possible connection between the construction of prisons in New York under Governor Cuomo and the demise of our grassroots GOP movement in 1986. The article sheds some light on a possible deal between the State GOP and the Cuomo political forces to take the political steam out of our grassroots electoral initiative in 1986 under the umbrella of the O'Rourke gubernatorial campaign. Brother Chase read the piece and concluded that the O'Rourke campaign and our efforts were marginalized in favor of prison-construction deals in upstate New York. Chase was blown away by the piece and said that it answered some questions that he had concerning why and how we may have been compromised in 1986. Here is your copy. Chase is looking forward to talking with you bout it."

I looked at the article and began reading it:

***Americans Behind Bars—The Majority of Them Nonviolent Offenders—
Means Jobs for Depressed Regions and Windfalls for Profiteers
by Eric Schlosser***

Three decades after the war on crime began, the United States has developed a prison-industrial complex, a set of bureaucratic, political, and economic interest that encourage increase spending on imprisonment, regardless of the actual need. The prison-industrial complex is not a conspiracy guiding the nation's criminal-justice policy behind closed doors. It is a confluence of special interests that has given prison construction in the Untied States a seemingly unstoppable momentum. It is composed of politicians, both liberal and conservative, who have used the fear of crime to gain votes; impoverished rural areas where prisons have become a corner stone of economic development; private companies that regard the roughly $35 billion spent each year on corrections not as a burden on American taxpayers but as a lucrative market; and government officials whose fiefdoms have expanded along with the inmate population.

Since 1991 the rate of violent crime in the United States has fallen by about 20 percent, while the number of people in prison or jail has risen by 50 percent. The prison boom has its own inexorable logic. Steven R. Donziger, a young attorney who headed the National Criminal Justice Commission in 1966, explains the thinking: "If crime is going up, then we need to build more prisons; and if crime is going down, it's because we built more prisons—and building even more prisons will therefore drive crime down even lower."

The raw material of the prison-industrial complex is its inmates: the poor, the homeless, and the mentally ill, drug dealers, drug addicts, alcoholics, and a wide assortment of violent sociopaths. About 70 percent of the prison inmates in the United States are illiterate. Perhaps 200,000 of the country's inmates suffer from serious mental illness. A generation ago such people were handled primarily by the mental-health and not the criminal-justice system. Sixty to 80 percent of the American inmate population has a history of substance abuse. Meanwhile, the number of drug-treatment slots in American prisons has declined by more than half since 1993. Drug treatment is now available to just one in every 10 inmates who need it. Among those arrested for violent crimes, the proportion who are African American men has changed little over the past twenty years. Among those arrested for drug crimes, the proportion who are African

American men has tripled. Although the prevalence of illegal drugs among white men is approximately the same as that among black men, black men are five times as likely to be arrested for a drug offence. As a result, about half of the inmates in the United States are African American. One out of every four black men are now in prison or jail. One out of every four black men is likely to be imprisoned at some point during his lifetime. The number of women sentenced to a year or more in prison has grown twelve-fold since 1970. Of the 80,000 women now imprisoned, about 70 percent are nonviolent offenders. About 75 percent have children.

The prison-industrial complex is not only a set of interest groups and institutions. It is also a state of mind. The lure of big money is corrupting the nation's criminal-justice system, replacing notions of public service with a drive for higher profits. The energies of elected officials to pass "tough-on-crime" legislation, combined with their unwillingness to consider the true cost of these laws, has encouraged all sorts of financial improprieties. The inner workings of the prison-industrial complex can be observed in the state of New York, where the prison boom started, transforming the economy of an entire region, in Texas and Tennessee, where private prison companies have thrived, and in California, where the correctional trends of the past two decades have converged and reached extremes. In the realm of psychology, a complex is an overreaction to some perceived threat. President Eisenhower no doubt had that meaning in mind when, during his farewell address, he urged the nation to "a recurring temptation to feel that some spectacular and costly action could become the miraculous solution to all current difficulties."

The Liberal Legacy

The origins of the prison-industrial complex can be dated to January of 1973. Senator Barry Goldwater had used the fear of crime to attract white middle-class voters a decade earlier, and Richard Nixon had revived the theme during the 1968 presidential campaign, but little that was concrete emerged from their demands for law and order. On the contrary, Congress voted decisively in 1970 to eliminate almost all federal mandatory-minimum, sentences for drug offenders. Leading members of both political parties applauded the move.

Mainstream opinion considered drug addiction to be largely a public-health problem, not an issue for the criminal courts. The Federal Bureau of Prisons was preparing to close large penitentiaries in Georgia, Kansas, and Washington. From 1963 to 1972 the number on inmates in California had declined by more than a fourth, despite the state's growing population. The number of inmates in New York had fallen to its lowest level since at least 1950. Prisons were widely viewed as barbaric and ineffective means of controlling deviant behavior. Then, on January 3, 1973, Nelson Rockefeller, the governor of New York, gave a State of the State Address demanding that every illegal-drug dealer be punished with a mandatory prison sentence of life without parole.

Rockefeller was a liberal Republican who for a dozen years had governed New York with policies more closely resembling those of Franklin Delano Roosevelt than those of Ronald Reagan. He had been booed at the 1964 Republican Convention by conservative delegates, he still harbored great political ambitions, and President Nixon would be eligible for a third term in 1976. Rockefeller demonstrated his newfound commitment to law and order in 1971, when he crushed the Attica prison uprising. By proposing the harshest drug laws in the United States he took the lead on an issue that would soon dominate the nations political agenda. In his State of the State address Rockefeller argued not only that all drug dealers should be imprisoned for life but also that plea-bargaining should be forbidden in such cases; even juvenile offenders should receive life sentences.

The Rockefeller drug laws, enacted a few months later by the state legislature, were somewhat less draconian; the penalty for possessing four ounces of an illegal drug, or for selling two ounces, was a mandatory prison term of fifteen years to life. The legislature also included a provision that established a mandatory prison sentence for a second felony conviction regardless of the crime or circumstances. Rockefeller proudly declared that his state had enacted "the toughest anti-drug program in the country." Other states eventually followed New York's example, enacting strict mandatory-minimum sentences for drug offenses. A liberal Democrat, Speaker of the House Tip O'Neil, led the campaign to revive federal mandatory minimums, which were incorporated in the 1986 Anti-Drug Abuse Act. Nelson Rockefeller had set in motion a profound shift in American sentencing policy, but he never had to deal with the consequences. Nineteen months after the passage of his drug laws Rockefeller became Vice President of the United States.

When Mario Cuomo was first elected governor of New York, in 1982 he confronted some difficult choices. The state government was in a precarious fiscal condition: the inmate population had more than doubled since the passage of the Rockefeller drug laws, and the prison system had grown dangerously over crowded. A week after Cuomo took office, inmates rioted at Sing-Sing, an aging prison in Ossining. Cuomo was an old-fashioned liberal who opposed mandatory-minimum drug sentences. But the national mood seemed to be calling for harsher drug laws, not sympathy for drug addicts. President Reagan had just launched the War on Drugs; it was an inauspicious moment to buck the tide.

Unable to repeal the Rockefeller drug laws, Cuomo decided to build more prisons. The rhetoric of the drug war, however, was proving more popular than the financial reality. In 1981 New York's voters had defeated a $500 million bond issue for new prison construction. Cuomo's search for an alternative source of financing, was the reason he decided to use the state's Urban Development Corporation funds to build prisons. The corporation was a public agency that had been created in 1968 to build housing for the poor. Despite strong opposition from up-state Republicans, among others, it had been legislated into existence on the day of Martin Luther King's funeral, to honor his legacy. The corporation was an attractive means of financing prison construction for one simple reason: it had the authority to issue state bonds without gaining the approval from the voters.

Over the next twelve years Mario Cuomo added more prison beds in New York than all previous governors in the state's history combined. Their total cost, including interest, would eventually reach about $7 billion. Cuomo's use of the Urban Development Corporation drew criticism from both liberals and conservatives. Robert Gangi, the head of the correctional Association of New York argued that Cuomo was building altogether the wrong sort of housing for the poor. The state comptroller, Edward V. Regan, a Republican, said that Cuomo was defying the wishes of the electorate, which had voted not to spend money on prisons, and that his financing scheme was costly and improper. Bonds issued by the Urban Development Corporation carried a higher rate of interest than the state's general-issue bonds.

Legally the state's new prisons were owned by the Urban Development Corporation and leased to the Department of correction. In 1991, as New York struggled to emerge from a recession, Governor Cuomo "sold" Attica prison to the corporation for $200 million and used the money to fill gaps in the state budget. In order to buy the prison, the corporation had to issue more bonds. The entire transaction could eventually cost New York State about $700 million.

The New York prison boom was a source of embarrassment for Mario Cuomo. At times he publicly called it "stupid," an immoral waste of scarce state monies, an obligation forced on him by the dictates of the law. Bit it was also a source of political capital. Cuomo strongly opposed the death penalty, and building new prisons shielded him from Republican charges of being soft on crime. In his 1987 State of the state address, having just been re-elected by a landslide, Cuomo boasted of having put nearly 10,000 "dangerous felons" behind bars. The inmate population in New York's prisons had indeed grown by roughly that number during his first term in office. But the proportion of offenders being incarcerated for violent crimes had fallen from 63 to 52 percent during those four years. In 1987 New York State sent almost a thousand fewer violent offenders to prison than it had in 1983. Despite having the "toughest anti-drug program" and one of the fastest growing populations in the nation, New York was hit hard by the crack epidemic of the 1980s and violent crime that accompanied it. From 1983 to 1990 the states inmate population almost doubled— and yet during that same period the violent-crime rate rose 24 percent. Between the passage of the Rockefeller drug laws and the time Cuomo left office, in January of 1995, New York's inmate population increased almost fivefold. And the state's prison system was more over crowed than it had been when the prison boom began.

By using an unorthodox means of financing prison construction, Mario Cuomo turned the Urban Development Corporation into a rural development corporation that invested billions of dollars in upstate New York and its suburbs. High real-estate prices and opposition from community groups made it difficult to build correction facilities in the city. Cuomo needed somewhere to put his *new prisons; he formed a close working relationship with state Senator Ronald B. Stafford, a conservative Republican whose rural, Adirondack district included six counties extending from Lake George to the Canadian border. "Any time there's an extra prison" a Cuomo appointee told Newsday in 1990, "Ron Stafford will take it."*

Stafford had represented this district, known as the North Country, for more than two decades. Orphaned as a child, he had been adopted by a family in the upstate town of Dannemora. The main street of the town was dominated by massive stone-wall around Clinton, a notorious maximum-security prison. His adopted father was a correctional officer at Clinton, and Stafford spent much of his childhood within the prison walls. He developed great respect for correctional officers and viewed their profession as an honorable one; he believed that prisons could give his district a real economic boost. Towns in the North Country soon competed with one another to attract new prisons. The Republican Party controlled the state senate, and prison construction became part of the political give and take with the Cuomo administration. Of the twenty-nine correctional facilities authorized during the Cuomo years, twenty-eight were built in upstate districts represented by the Republican Senators.

When most people think of New York, they picture Manhattan. In fact two thirds of the state's counties are classified as rural. Perhaps no other region in the United States has so wide a gulf between urban populations and rural populations. People in the North Country— which includes the Adirondack State Park, one of the nation's largest wilderness areas—tend to be politically conservative, taciturn, fond of the outdoors, and white. New York City and the North Country have very little in common. One thing they do share, however, is a high rate of poverty.

Twenty-five years ago the North Country had two prisons, now it has eighteen correctional facilities, and a nineteenth is under construction. They run the gamut from maximum-security prisons to drug-treatment centers and boot camps. One of the first new facilities to open was Ray Brook, a federal prison that occupies the former Olympic Village of Lake Placid. Other prisons have opened in abandoned factories and sanitariums. For the most part North Country prisons are tucked away, hidden by trees, nearly invisible amid the vastness and beauty of the Adirondacks. But they have brought profound change. Roughly one out of every twenty people in the North Country is a prisoner. The town of Dannemora now has more inmates than inhabitants.

The traditional anchors of the North Country economy—mining, logging, dairy farms and manufacturing—have been in decline for years. Tourism flourishes in most towns during the summer months. According to Ram Chugh, the director of the Rural Services Institute at the State University of New York at Potsdam, the North Country's per capita income has long been 40 percent lower than the state's average per capita income. The prison boom had provided a huge infusion of state money to an economically depressed region—one of the largest direct investments the state has never made there. In addition to the more than $1.5 billions spent to build correction facilities, the prisons now bring the North Country about $425 million in annual payroll and operating expenditures. That represents an annual subsidy to the region of more than $1,000 per person. The economic impact of the prisons extends beyond the wages they pay and the local services they buy. Prisons are labor-intensive institutions, offering year round employment. They are recession proof, usually expanding in size during hard times. And they are non-polluting—an important consideration in rural areas where other forms of development are often blocked by environmentalists. Prisons have brought a stable, steady income into a region long accustomed to a highly seasonal uncertain economy.

Ann Mackinnon, who grew up in the North Country and wrote about its recent emergence as New York's "Siberia" for Adirondack Life Magazine, says the prison boom has had an enormous effect on the local culture. Just about everyone now seems to have at least one relative who works in corrections. Prison jobs have slowed the exodus from small towns, by allowing young people to remain in the area. The average salary of a correctional officer in New York state is $36,000—more than 50 percent higher than the typical salary in the North country. The job brings health benefits and a pension. Working as a correctional officer is one of the few ways that men and women without college degrees can enjoy a solid middle-class life there. Although prison jobs are stressful and dangerous, they are viewed as a means of preserving local communities. So many North Country residents have become correctional officers over the past decade that those just *starting out must work for years in prisons downstate, patiently waiting for a job opening at one of the facilities in the Adirondacks.*

While many families in the North await the return of sons and daughters slowly earning seniority downstate, families in New York city must endure the absence of loved ones who seem to have been not just imprisoned for their crimes but exiled as well. Every Friday night about 899 people, mostly women, children, almost all of them African American and Latino, gather at Columbus Circle, in Manhattan, and board buses for the north. The buses leave through the night and arrive in time for visiting hours on Saturday. Operation Prison Gap, which runs the service, was founded by an ex-convict named Ray Simmons who had been imprisoned upstate and knew how hard it was for the families of inmates to arrange visits. When the company started in 1973, it carried passengers in a single van. Now it charters thirty-five buses and vans on a typical weekend and a larger number on special occasions, such as Father's Day and Thanksgiving. Ray Simmons' brother, Tyronne, who heads the company, says that despite the rising inmate population, rider ship has fallen a bit over the past few years. The inconvenience and expense of the long bus trips take a toll. One customer, however, has for fifteen years faithfully visited her son in Comstock every weekend. In 1996 she stopped appearing at Columbus Circle; her son had been released. Six months later he was convicted of another crime and sent back to the same prison. The woman, now in her seventies, still boards the 2 A.M. bus for Comstock every weekend. Simmons gives her a discount, charging her $15—the same price she paid on her first trip in 1983.

The Bare Hill Correctional Facility sits near the town of Malone, fifteen miles south of the Canadian boarder. The Franklin Correctional Facility is a quarter of a mile down the road and the future site of a new maximum-security prison is next door. Bare Hill is of the "cookie cuter" medium-security prisons that were built during the Cuomo administration. The state has built fourteen other prisons exactly alike—a form of penal mass production that saves a good deal of money. Most of the inmates at Bare Hill are housed in dormitories, not cells. The dormitories were designed to hold about fifty inmates, each with its own small cubical and bunk. In 1990, two years after the prison opened, double bunking was introduced as a "temporary" measure to ease over crowding in county jails, which were holding an

253

overflow of state inmates. Eight years later every dormitory at Bare Hill houses sixty inmates, a third of them double bunked. About 90 percent of the inmates come from New York city or one of the suburbs, eight hours away about 80 percent are African American or Latino. The low walls of the cubicles, which allow little privacy, are covered with family photographs, pin-ups, and religious postcards. Twenty-four hours a day a correction officer sits alone at a desk on a platform that overlooks the dorm.

The superintendent of Bare Hill, Peter J. Lacy, is genial and gray-haired, tall and dignified in his striped tie, flannels, and blue blazer. His office feels light and cheery. Lacy began his career, in 1955, as a correctional officer at Dannemora, he wore a uniform for twenty-five years, and in the 1980s headed a special unit that handled prison emergencies and riots. He later served as an assistant commissioner of the New York Department of Corrections. One of his sons is now a lieutenant at a downstate prison. As Superintendent Lacy walks through the prison grounds, he seems like a captain surveying his ship, rightly proud of his upkeep, familiar with every detail. The lawns are neatly trimmed, the buildings are well maintained, and the redbrick dorms would not seem out of place on a college campus, except for the bars in the windows. There is nothing oppressive about the physical appearance of Bare Hill, about the ball fields with pine trees in the background, about the brightly colored murals and rustic stencils on the walls, about the classrooms where instructors teach inmates how to read, how to write, how to draw and blue print, how to lay bricks, how to obtain a Social Security card, how to deal with anger. For many inmates Bare Hill is the neatest, cleanest, most well ordered place they ever lived in. As Lacy passes a group of inmates nod their heads in acknowledgment, and a few of them say, "Hello, sir." And every so often a young inmate gives Lacy a look filled with hatred so pure and so palpable that it would burn Bare Hill to the ground, if it only could.

Big Business

The black-and-white photograph shows an inmate leaning out of a prison cell. Scowling at the camera, his face partially hidden in the shadows. "How he got in is your business," the ad copy begins. "How *he gets out is ours" The photo is on the cover of a glossy brochure promoting AT&T's prison telephone service, which is called The Authority. Bell South has a similar service, called MAX, advertised with a photo of a heavy steel chain dangling from a telephone receiver of a cord. The ad promises "long distance service that lets the inmate go only so far." Although the phone companies rely on clever copy in their ads, providing telephone service to prisons and jails has become a serious, highly profitable business. The nearly two million inmates in the United States are ideal customers: phone calls are one of their few links to the outside world; most of their calls must be made collect; and they are in no position to switch long-distance carriers. A pay phone at a prison can generate as much as $15,000 a year—about five times the revenue of a typical pay phone on the street. It is estimated that inmate calls generate a billion dollars or more in revenues each year. The business has become so lucrative that MCI installed its inmate phone service, maximum Security, throughout the California prison system at no charge. As part of the deal it also offered the California Department of Corrections a 32-percent share of all revenues from inmates' phone calls. MCI maximum security adds a $3.00 surcharge to every call. When free enterprise intersects with a captive market, abuses are bound to occur. MCI maximum security and North American Intelecom have both been caught over-charging for calls made by inmates; in one state MCI was adding an additional minute to every call.*

Since 1980 spending on corrections at the local, state and federal levels has increased about five fold. What was once a niche business for a handful of companies have become a muti-billion-dollar industry with its own trade shows and conventions, it owns web sites, mail-order catalogues, and direct-mailing campaigns. The prison-industrial complex now includes some of the nation's largest architecture and construction firms, Wall Street investment banks that handle prison bond issues and invest in private prisons, plumbing supply companies, food service companies, and companies that sell everything from bullet resistant security cameras to padded cells available in a "vast color selection." A directory called Correction Yellow Pages lists more than a thousand vendors. Among the items now being advertised for sale: a "violent prisoner chair," a sadomasochist's fantasy of belts and shackles attached to a metal frame, with special accessories for juveniles: B.O.S.S., a "body office security scanner," essentially a metal detector that an inmate must sit on; and a diverse line of razor wire, with trade names such as Maze, Super-Maze, Detainer, Hook, Barb, and Silent Swordsman Barbed Tape.

As the prison industry has grown, it has assumed many of the attributes long associated with the defense industry. The line between the public interest and private interests blurred. In much the same way that retired admirals and generals have long found employment with the defense contractors, correctional officials are now leaving the public sector for jobs with firms that supply the prison industry. These career opportunities did not exist a generation ago. Fundamental choices about public safety, employment training, and the denial of personal freedoms are increasingly being made with an eye to the bottom line.

One clear sign that corrections has become big business as well as a form of government service is the emergence of a trade newspaper devoted to the latest trends in the prison and jail market place. Correctional building news has become "Variety" of the prison world, widely read by correctional officials, investors, and companies with something to sell. Eli Gage, its publisher, founded the paper in 1994, after searching for a high-growth industry not yet served by its own trade journal. Gage is neither a cheerleader for the industry nor an outspoken critic. He believes that despite recent declines in violent crime, national spending on correction will continue to grow at an annual rate of 5 to 10 percent. The number of young people in the prime demographic for committing crimes, ages fifteen to twenty four, is about to increase; and the demand for new juvenile-detention centers are already rising. Correctional Building News *runs ads by the leading companies that build prisons (Turner Construction, CRSS, Brown & Root) and the leading firms that design them (DMJM, the DLR Group, and KMD Architects). It features a product of the month, and a section titled, "People in the News." In a recent issue promoted electrified fences with the line, "Don't Touch!"*

CHAPTER 19

After a hectic work day and a marathon Saturday evening political round table session I was hungry and exhausted and decided to have a bite to eat at a local Harlem restaurant before turning in. The marathon political session ended with a consensus to challenge the appointed black GOP district leaders. Without question it is the black GOP gatekeepers and pawns that have hi-jacked electoral process and continues to thwart the primary elections and marginalize black politics. An organic grassroots district leadership would be advocates for local issues as opposed to undermining the legitimate aspirations of the black community. As it currently stands, the "official" black GOP leaders serve as political tools of the modern slave master, vis-à-vis, the county political boss.

Breaking through the political inertia of the New York City GOP county system has always been a critical and fundamental challenge to the emerging grassroots leadership. The National Republican Committee and the Republican administrations in the White House have always demonstrated an interest in party building in Harlem, and the state party to a lesser degree. But, indeed the local party leadership are, formidable obstacles to meaningful outreach and party building in the black American community. At this point it behooves us to link our grassroots activism, directly to the national party. But a challenge to the district leadership in a party primary is not something that the national party would take a position on. Perhaps a congressional challenge of an incumbent by our grassroots electoral initiative would generate interest at the national level, I thought. I revisited correspondence I received from the White House in 1984, which was the beginning of my foray into national Republican politics and my more recent letter from the Republican National Committee in the year 2000.

April 20, 1984
Dear Mr. Burton:

I have received word from the White House of your interest helping in the president's reelection. We appreciate your generous offer of support. We are building a strong organization in your state and would like to see your group involved.

I have taken the liberty of passing your qualifications on to our Executive director in New York, Mr. Charles Gargano. I trust he will be in touch with you soon. Again, thank you for your support and enthusiasm.

Sincerely,

Roger J. Stone, Jr.
Eastern Regional Campaign Director

The national party and the White House have been consistent in maintaining lines of communication with us for the pass 20 years, but on the local level the party only gives us hard time and bubble gum!

July 7, 2000
Dear Mr. Burton:

Chairman Nicholson asked me to follow up with you regarding the launching of your voter education and registration project at www.votersanonymous.org. We have a number of people working on minority outreach here at the RNC, and your pursuits developing the Voters anonymous program are very appealing.

Please keep our team apprised of your efforts. With best wishes.

Sincerely,

Lawrence J. Purpuro
Deputy chief of Staff
Republican National Committee
Cc: Angela Sailor, African American Outreach

As I pondered possible scenarios to interface the national party with our local grassroots initiative, I ordered an oxtail dinner and proceeded to relax and enjoy a great meal. While engaged in deep thought, I recognized a familiar face from back in the days of Southeast Queens and our community center on Hollis Avenue. It was Brother Sharrieff who was apparently associated with management of the establishment as he was obviously holding court with the cashier, waiters and the chef. I first met Brother Claude Sharrieff in the 1960s, and the last time that I saw him was sometime in the mid 1970s. Brother Sharreiff was a peer of Malcolm X in the Nation of Islam, and he was a confidant of Master Moses Powell a 9th degree black belt holder, and founder of the Sanucus martial arts technique. Master Moses, was prominently featured in many magazines associated with Martial Arts, and for his role in training the F.O.I., Fruit of Islam. I met Master Moses, in the early 1960s when I was introduced to him by Ed Sawyer, a co-working at Cosmopolitan Mutual Insurance Company. Ed was enrolled in Master Moe 's School in Brooklyn. The Master and I hit it off very well and became good friends as I studied under him, along with others in my organization. When we opened the Afro-Disiac community center in Hollis Queens, we offered a weekly class in the Martial Arts that was taught by Master Moses, and his black belts. This was the context in which Brother Sharrieff and I met some 20 plus years earlier. Sharrieff was at least 15-years or more my senior, and he looked very good for his years, holding court and negotiating through the expanse of his impressive venue.

"Brother Sharrieff," I called as he whizzed by my table behind the waiter delivering my much-deserved dinner.

As he passed my table I motioned to him. Acknowledging me he said, "Be right with you, brother!" As I prepared to gorge myself, Sharrieff returned.

He said, "Salaam Aleikum, brother."

I responded, "Aleikum Salaam, my brother." He stared at me then said, "Wow! You look so familiar. I know that I know you, my brother."

I responded, "Master Moses Powell, Brother Li'l John, Brother Lumumba. Hollis Avenue Dojo, Big Indian New York, Sis's Horizon."

"Oh, yeah." he said; Vincent, that's right, Brother Vincent or as Master Moses used to call you, Snake or Pretty Feet. I never figured out why he called you Snake affectionately. Damn, man. it's been a while."

Sharrieff and I talked for quite a while and I made it a point to rekindle our relationship for a number of reasons. Not the least of which was the fact that we both were active in local Republican Party politics. While I shared with the brother, my perspective on the state of the party and my agenda to challenge the Harlem district leaders, which I argued was a healthy process because it would stimulate the party primary election process. Sharrieff argued that my radical approach was not necessary in view of his connections with the new district leader in the 70th AD, among others, and the fact that he produced a weekly radio talk show and managed a venue for facilitating community forums. All he and I needed to do was to work together on a mutual agenda. Ultimately, I had no problem with that since we had a history and the resources that he had available vis-à-vis, the radio show and forum venue, were very persuasive assets. Consequently, I became a co-host on the weekly radio show and we began to plan political education forums at the venue. Sharrieff, introduced me to the new appointed district leader in the 70th AD, Will Brown, and others that he felt would be assets to our newly formed political joint-venture. I knew Will Brown's predecessor Leroy Owens who recently resigned the position and Will Brown was installed as his replacement by the county chairman, New York State Assemblyman John Ravitz. Leroy Owens was the previous county chairman's HNIC in Harlem, and we knew each other very well. On the other hand I didn't know the new guy, but my man from back in the day told me that we could work with him. Also, I was inspired to give Will Brown the benefit of the doubt, because of the formidable assets that Sharrieff put on the table.

It became a done deal, when Sharrieff introduced me to Conrad Muhammad, the former minister of the Nation of Islam's famous Mosque No. 7. Conrad was reportedly interested in continuing is community service by considering elective office as a possible option. More importantly, the exceptionally articulate young man was a natural conservative and was touted as a potential G.O.P. convert. Brother Sharrieff made the introduction and Conrad and I met and explored the pros and cons, ups and downs and the ins and outs of Conrad as a GOP congressional candidate. I shared with Conrad my experience and perspective as it related to his entering the electoral process in the Republican Party. We promoted a political forum at the restaurant and invited Ms. Angel Sailor, the African American Outreach Coordinator for the Republican National Committee. We sponsored a program in Harlem in support of the election of Gov. George Bush and Conrad was the Keynote speaker. After the event, during dinner Conrad and I discuss with Ms. Sailor the prospects of Conrad running for congress from Harlem's 15th CD, in 2002. And I also discussed my interest in developing contacts with Republican National Congressional Committee (RNCC) to have New York targeted for financial support and technical assistance.

Both Conrad and I were pleased with the prospects for the future and began to discuss and develop a grassroots strategy to formulate "A Great Race in Harlem" in the context of building Conrad's GOP Congressional campaign.

In July 2002 the New York press published, **"Will Hip-hop Minister Conrad Muhammad Go from No. 1 to G.O.P?"** by Adam Heimlick

Conrad Muhammad is the fastest walker in Harlem. The late afternoon sidewalks are sweltering, but he's wearing a suit and tie, keeping a rush hour pace. Everyone else is doing that unhurried summer shuffle, or else they're stationary, under trees in folding chairs. The former Nation of Islam minister greets them all heartily, many by names. When someone replies with more than a greeting, he turns on his heel without breaking stride to face them. The new perspective might yield a view of someone else he wants to approach, in which case: zip. It's like trying to follow a bumblebee.

"This community needs someone with young legs, who can walk up and down the streets of the district and provide leadership to the people," is the first thing he tells me. He says he walks the streets of Harlem every day. I find out later that by "every day" he actually means every day he's not down in Baltimore, where he was until recently director of outreach for a church, or up in Mount Vernon, where he's employed as administrator of a $3 million grant for city youth programs. There was also some time at Harvard. He did a lot of walking and greeting as part of his old job though. Today, the focus is on what he'd like to be the next U.S. congressman from the 15th District, and it's clear enough that he's no carpetbagger.

He has a youthful face to go with his young legs. He's a natural speaker, with skills sharpened by a decade of preaching and a mini-career in radio, and he's not a bad listener, either. People in Harlem know who he is. To some, no doubt, he's just that fast walking guy with a suit, but Muhammad wouldn't have conducted an interview while walking Harlem's streets if the routine didn't make him appear widely respected. It does. The question is, is he serious? His generational peer across the Hudson, Cory Booker, held political office and enjoyed outside as well as grassroots support, yet he failed to wrest power from Newark's Mayor Sharpe James. Conrad Muhammad may be down with the regular folks, and they might be tired of the old dandy in office, but a demonstration of that is not necessarily as impressive as a campaign plan, some experienced strategists and a volunteer team might have been. Those are not things he has shown, today at least

Muhammad's most intense period of communication with the people of Harlem was plenty serious. He was a successor to Malcolm X, heading the Nation of Islam's Mosque No. 7. Many people still address him as "Minister," even though he doffed his bow tie five years ago. A phantom association with the Nation may be a boon to the candidate's popularity along Malcolm X Blvd., but it's also likely to be the main obstacle between Muhammad and his goal. That's because the easiest way to acquire funding to oppose Democrat Charles Rangel, who's held the House of Representatives' 15th District seat since 1970, would be as a Republican. And the local G.O.P. is cool on Conrad. The party has said the problem is that he's a registered Democrat. Muhammad doesn't buy it.

"May whole career has been talking about self-sufficiency, the African American people taking their own destiny into their hands," he says. He points out that he's a free marketer, that his message is strong on traditional values and that the local G.O.P. regularly endorses candidates far to the left of him. His post N.O.I. work as "The Hip-hop Minister" was undisguised conservative activism. Furthermore, he adds, the Republicans put Rangel on their line in several of his 16 successful races. Calling the issue of party affiliation "a smokescreen, a red herring," he says he and the Republican leadership "shouldn't even be arguing over this. We should be focused on getting the seat."

Conrad Muhammad: "Hey, brother, how are you? You know I'm running for congress?"

Jamaican man on Lenox Ave.: "Yes, I do. I heard it."

CM: "I need your help."

JM: "You Democrat or Republican?"

CM: "Ah, I'm running as a Republican."

JM: "That's not going to work."

CM: "Listen to me: I am a Democrat, but I may have to run as a Republican."

JM: "It's not going to work."

CM: "Remember Bloomberg was a Democrat all his life. He had to run as a Republican because of the system."

JM: "You don't want anything to do with that."

CM: "You don't like the brother."

JM: "Nah, I really don't."

CM: "I have not liked him in the past, but sometimes you see, we got too many people in one club. We got to be in both parties."

JM: "They not gon' change, boss."

CM: "Let me ask you a question: Are you a betting man at all?"

JM: "Huh?"

CM: "Do you bet? Are you a betting man?"

JM: "Yeah."

CM: "You ever go to the race track?"

JM: "Oh, yes."

CM: "When you go to the race track, how many do you bet? Do you bet on one horse, or do you spread your money around?"

JM: "Sometimes three, because sometimes I play the trifecta."

CM: "That's what I'm saying. In politics, you gotta do the same thing. You can't have all Democrats. You gotta have some Democrats and Republicans."

JM: "You have to look at the constituency; you know what I'm saying? These people are not gon' change that easily. You have to come up with something real good for them to do that. I'm telling you. Get with the hip-hop crowd and the old folks and stay in the middle."

CM: "I know what you saying."

JM: "And you will do it, trust me."

CM: "And I can count on your vote?"

JM: "Makes face indicating that he's not ready to vote Republican."

CM: "Laughing. "Okay, okay."

Muhammad is 37, divorced, the father of three. His children reside primarily with their mother in Bethesda, MD, though Conrad shares custody. Despite his comfort in Harlem, his speaking voice is obviously that of a non-native New Yorker. He grew up in St. Louis and Washington DC, middle-class and Christian. He came to politics and black nationalism simultaneously, while an undergrad at the University of Pennsylvania, working on Jesse Jackson's 1984 presidential campaign. "I became discouraged and almost bitter against the political process because I felt that he was disrespected," he recalls, then adds, "but that was my immaturity."

That same year, his 19th, Muhammad joined the Nation of Islam. "I had a lot of faith in the Nation, pretty much because of the message of self-reliance, family values, hard work, discipline, and clean living," he says. Though Muhammad doesn't speak of it, his rise to the top of the local N.O.I. hierarchy suggests that in his 20s he was extremely effective at communicating the Nation's message-which, Nation detractors are quick to point out, has included anti-Jewish and anti-American rhetoric. He was 32 when he and the Nation parted ways.

"I just became frustrated with the direction of the movement," he says. "I believe that as African Americans we can be critical of this country, but we have to embrace our American-ness, and we have to embrace the process. I've really grown to believe that we have the best political system in the world. I've grown to appreciate democracy. And I think the Nation is challenged to embrace those ideas. You may not like the way things are, but you have a right to say it, and in a lot of countries you don't."

One of the stops on Muhammad's greeting tour is Harlem Underground, a custom hat and T-shirt store off 125th St. Outside, we run into Carl Redding, proprietor and chef of the soul-food restaurant, Amy Ruth's. Muhammad introduces us, and I ask Redding if he ever vote Republican. He replies that he has, three times in fact for Reagan, Pataki, and Bloomberg. Muhammad is engaged in another conversation at the moment, so I follow Redding into Harlem Underground, and Muhammad soon enters as well, teasing me about "diving for the air conditioning."

The candidate, who had been more than an hour late for our interview, neglected to mention that it would be conducted while he worked the streets. Redding's suggestion that Muhammad purchase an embroidered "Conrad for Congress" cap at Harlem Underground is what allows an uninterrupted question-and-answer session to take place. While the hat is being embroidered, he's stuck. If keeping a reporter moving shows solid political instincts, Muhammad's performance when literally cornered in Harlem Underground indicated acumen extending still further beyond his ability to connect with the crowd. Which is to say, he was amiably evasive, saying things like, "I absolutely support the concept of gun control."

Here's the distilled version of Conrad Muhammad on the issues: He's for the war and "very supportive" of President Bush's handling of it so far. But he's "concerned" about Ashcroft "overreaching" on civil liberties. He's also with the president on welfare, particularly his approach to "talking about the importance of marriage with regard to welfare." He's against discrimination based on sexual orientation, but would vote "no" on a civil-unions bill. He's pro-life except in cases of rape, incest, or when the life of the mother at stake. And he believes that the constitution guarantees the right to bear arms. All of these, he frames in terms of values. He says he wants a society ethical enough that abortions are rare and citizens feel safe without guns.

In summary, Muhammad gives a statement that wouldn't sound off-key at a Republican National Convention: "I'm a religious man. I think values are important. I've worked in the community a long time. and I know that no amount of government money can change this community if we don't have strong family values." The only hitch is he refuses to indicate from which religion he's currently drawing his values. "We got 'em all here, and I intend to serve all constituencies," he demurs. "I'm a man of faith, and we'll leave it at that."

Conrad Muhammad: "Hey, good brother, what's happening? What going on, man?"

Man on 125ᵗʰ St.: "I'm all right; how you doin'?"

CM: "It's good to see you. How's your family doing? They good? How's Tony?"

M125: "He's great."

CM: "You know I'm running for Congress, right?"

M125: "Congress?"

CM: "Did you hear about it?"

M125: "You wanna be a politician?"

CM: "I think it's time that a good, strong brother gets into the process, you dig?"

M125: "It's all good."

CM: "Now you know me; I haven't changed."

M125: "Don't get there and sell out."

CM: "I won't do that. I'll be the same man I've always been. And you know it. And I'm coming in smokin' just like that."

M125: "Don't sell out, man; don't sell out. The devil is busy."
CM: "If I sell out, you come and get me."
M125: "I'm comin' to get you, yo."

The New York Sun *reported in its July 5-7 issue that Muhammad plans to convert back to Christianity. According to the Sun's Errol Luis, on Sunday near the end of June, Muhammad stood alongside Rev. Calvin Butts at Harlem's Abyssinian Baptist Church and told the assembled that "at some point in the future" he will retake his birth name, Conrad Tillard.*

New York Post *columnist Robert A. George is someone who thinks Muhammad could with Republican Party support, unseat Rangel. In a scathing June 3 editorial headlined "The Grand Old Stupid Party?, he chided Assemblyman John Ravitz, Manhattan Republican Party Chairman, for giving Muhammad the brush-off. George quoted Ravitz saying that the former minister should start on the path to the G.O.P. acceptance by campaigning in Harlem for Gov. Pataki's reelection.*

Muhammad tells me he'd be happy to do just that. "I've endorsed him," he says. "More has happened in this community under George Pataki and Secretary of state Randy Daniels than had happened for a long time." Also he adds, "I think Pataki has done a good deal to help repeal the Rockefeller Drug Laws, which hurt a lot of African-American young people. Young people's lives have been thrown away, and Cuomo didn't do anything about it."

A more likely scenario involves Muhammad devoting the summer of 2002 to campaigning for himself. That's the case even though the local G.O.P. even before George's editorial saw print endorsed Independence Party candidate Jesse Fields for Congress in the 15th. (Fields might be as unlikely a Republican endorsee as Muhammad, or Rangel, for that matter. She's a Harlem doctor who runs single-issues campaigns about healthcare.) Only hours before our interview Assemblyman Ravitz rescheduled a meeting with Muhammad that had been planned for the following day. The candidate said he was taking steps to enact a plan B: to challenge Rangel in the Democratic primary instead. That would be a David vs Goliath struggle to say the least— fighting within a party against a 32-year incumbent. Regardless, his Democratic petition drive was already underway. Conrad's only hope to get on the Republican line was to convince Ravitz, and other G.O.P.

leaders to make a second endorsement and force a primary against Fields.

Assemblyman Ravitz declared this would not happen. Contacted by telephone Ravitz said a primary would "defeat the purpose" of the Fields endorsement, and that "our number-one goal should be to support one candidate against an entrenched incumbent like Congressman Rangel." He refuted the notion that Fields is less likely than Muhammad to win, calling it "a self fulfilling prophecy." He then lauded the Independence Party candidate Jesse Fields and her fellow endorsees in a way that rather pointedly echoed Muhammad's portrayal of himself. "What I'm doing," said Ravitz, "in finding candidates to run for assembly, state Senate and for Congress in Harlem, candidates who really have a community resume, that aren't just people who we decided, Hey, it's be a great idea for you to run for office. These are people who have invested their life, their time and energy into so many different parts of their community that they want to take to the next level and run for office."

Ravitz said there are reasons why the G.O.P. is wary of Muhammad, and none of them are secret. Directing me to the Anti Defamation League's website for specifics, he said, "Conrad knows about the problems with some of the things that he's said in the past. I believe he's going to have to address and deal with them. I think that all of us who are in public life have to be held accountable for our words, and there are a lot of things that Conrad still needs to work with people who are still feeling very hurt about some of his comments." It is possible that some of those people have Conrad Muhammad confused with Khalid Muhammad, however.

A 1996 ADL press release quotes Conrad Muhammad calling Jews "bloodsuckers" and Christianity "a dirty religion," but his search hits don't compare to those of controversy-seeking Khalid, who was fired from his N.O.I. leadership in 1994 and picked a fight with NYPD cops at the Million Youth March four years later.

Whether known as Conrad Muhammad or as Conrad Tillard (D), he plans to go for it. He believes that enough of Harlem wants to send him to Washington. Muhammad says the energy and creativity of his campaign will resonate strongly with the hip-hop generation, with which he has a lot of experience. After he left the Nation, Muhammad founded a movement for C.H.H.A.N.G.E. ("Conscious Hip-Hop

Activism Necessary for Global Empowerment") and started calling himself "The Hip-hop Minister." He decried the mid 90s flood of lyrics portraying black communities as nests of degeneracy. He also publicly shamed the businessmen who grew from rich to richer off them. That earned Muhammad the ire of Def Jam's founding executive, Russell Simmons, but no artists went on record lashing out at him. Some of them, perhaps, were really shamed.

Today, Muhammad characterizes C.H.H.A.N.G.E.'s "Campaign for Dignity" as more of an esthetics campaign than a political one. "I think my challenge to rappers was a critical challenge," he says. "We used to talk about white men in Hollywood that put out images of people in our community as pimps and prostitutes. Now I'm trying to show these young people: Now you are in a position that you control the imagery, and you have to be sensitive to that. You are in power now. What are you going to do with it? You can't say you love the hood, and see the hood listening to your music and going to jail or dying, and not feel some responsibility."

Conrad says he achieved the authority to preach to hip-hop artists by being there when they needed him. Men who grew up in communities where the Nation was a stable presence generally perceived it to be righteous, and when he was a minister, Muhammad mediated between warring rap factions more than once. He settled a dispute between "A Tribe Called Quest" and "Wrecks-N-Effect" with one meeting. He also intervened in the East-West coastal feud, sadly less successfully. "I saw Puffy shed tears up here when Suge Knight was coming down on him," Conrad recalls. Muhammad says he didn't feel a need to speak up when artists' underworld experience started rapping about it, but "I knew that some of the guys who were doing the thug thing, were not from criminal background. I've seen these men offstage, and said to them, "I know you. You may project a certain image, but this is your brother saying to you it's gone too far. Stop it."

It's difficult to think of another link, besides the Nation of Islam (N.O.I) and its offshoots, between conservative ethics and rap-gangsta subculture. An inner-city Republican who brings to the table the success of instilling a sense of responsibility in anti-social young men without the negative baggage of the N.O.I. would seem, at least on paper, to be a strong candidate. After all, the hip-hop generation is bound to elect someone somewhere, eventually. Theoretically,

Muhammad's youth angle could give the G.O.P. an edge on the issues that are of perennial concern to black New Yorkers, such as education and crime. The Republicans already win on taxes and the war. How close is the reality of Conrad Muhammad to this idealized ghetto-G.O.P. candidate? Maybe it makes more sense to ask how close the G.O.P. has ever gotten to Conrad Muhammad.

After our mano-a-mano session, still in the Harlem Underground, Muhammad rejoined Carl Redding, the Reagan-supporting restaurateur. He told me Redding used to work with the Rev. Al Sharpton. We discussed national politics. Redding explained how the Clinton years changed his view of the Republican Party for the worse when "Bush came to Harlem and I took a picture with him," he said. "They were courting me to work on the Bush campaign. handling the African American clergy. This was in January of 2000. I thought hard about it. They offered me six figures. I couldn't do it."

Offers Muhammad, "Now as George W. Bush and Gov. Pataki are talking about inclusion, it's time for a paradigm shift to take place." He explained that Democratic candidates receiving up to and beyond 90 percent of the African-American vote is not in African American people's interest. To Muhammad, it's realistic to aim for a 70/30 spilt. He explained, "It's not about why we should vote for Republicans. The question is, why shouldn't we place ourselves in that party and leverage our influence in both parties?" Fifty-fifty is not realistic. But 70/30 is, in my opinion a winning formula for the African American community. This is because it makes our 70 percent in the Democratic Party a stronger 70 percent, based on the fact of 30 percent of us leaving and going to the Republican Party, letting them know that we're a force they have to reckon with."

As for the rabid anti-Republicanism of supposedly nonpartisan African-American leaders, Muhammad said, "It's immoral in a sense, because our leaders have betrayed you. Our political leaders essentially have a vested interest in delivering black bodies to the Democratic Party. Almost like a slave trade. And so, what it has done is not allowed our community to engage in the free market of politics. If there's only one dry cleaners one 125th Street, chances are you're going to get bad service there. It's a captive market; you don't have anywhere else to go. But let two or three dry cleaners open up. Competition is good in business it also is good in politics."

269

Conrad Muhammad: "How are you ladies today?"
Ladies #1 and #2 outside of a Pentecostal Church: "Fine."
CM: "Did you know I'm running for Congress?"
L #1 and L #2 smile and nod.
CM: "I sure could use your help. I'm running against a great man, but he's just been there too long. I think it's time for him to let a younger man go forward, don't you think so?"
L #1 and L #2 smile and nod.
Adam Heimlich: "What do you think of Charlie Rangel?"
L #1: "He's a wonderful man."
L #2: "He's a wonderful person, and he's done an exceptional job. He continues to do an exceptional job. However, as you say, it may be time for a young man to put forth his efforts."
CM: "I told this gentleman right here—in this community we respect our elders. I would never disrespect Congressman Rangel."
L #2: "Oh, no never."
CM: "You don't disrespect a bridge—
L #2: 6 "that brought you over."
CM: "That's what my grandmother taught me. But it's time for a new generation of leadership to step forward."

Leaving the Harlem Underground, Conrad Muhammad then lead me to Harlem U.S.A. retail complex, which opened two years before and is the keystone of Upper Manhattan's participation in the federal empowerment zone revitalization plan. We stand on 125th Street across from the Disney Store, HMV record store, and the Magic Johnson movie theater, while Muhammad points out another record store, Record Shack, on the next block east of the shopping center.

"That's a business that's been in this community for 30 years," said Muhammad of Record Shack. "A small business, and of course Republicans support small businesses, right? Why would an empowerment zone not give moneys to that store owner, who's been here through good times and bad, and then open up HMV a few doors down, to drive this man out of business? What kind of community development and leadership is that? It couldn't have possibly have been thought through. There is no clearer metaphor for why I'm running than this right here. This man has committed 30 years to this community."

The man Muhammad refers to is Record Shack owner Sikulu Shange. He and his store have an interesting history. They were the lynch-pin of the 1995 controversy that got out of control and ended in a massacre at Freddie's Fashion Mart. It started when Record Shack faced eviction, and ended when a man presumed to be a former street vendor who'd been forced out by revitalization efforts (a development that Shange, reportedly, had supported) entered Freddie's with a gun and a bottle of lighter fluid and committed mass murder.

Muhammad doesn't mention the incident. Instead, he asks me to interview Shange. The deep-voiced man makes an eloquent complaint about local government's failure to involve him in the changes on 125th St. He seems to be against the empowerment zone as a matter of anti-corporate principle, but allows that, "Even if they brought these companies into the community, they should have empowered us to compete."

The encounter with Shange rings a little contradictory, coming so closely on the heels of Muhammad's allegory about competition in dry cleaning. Similarly, some hot air is let out of his grand statement about the limitations of what government money can do for the African-American community when he tells a young mother that he supports reparations for slavery.

Walking past the 125th St. building that houses Bill Clinton's office, Muhammad tells me that rent on the buildings across the street doubled or tripled the day the former president moved in! "Now what kind of leadership is that? You've got to have a view of what the economic consequences are. It got the Congressman good media, but it really wasn't a good thing for the district. At the end of the day, that's exploitation. I believe in the free market, but the political leadership shouldn't speed up the process of people being dispossessed, people being priced out. That's not leadership."

In Newark earlier this year, four-term incumbent, Sharpe James, portrayed insurgent candidate, Cory Booker, as an infiltrator, representing interests antithetical to those of the city's working poor. The mayor seemed to have some success at making this characterization stick, even though at the time of the election Booker resided in a Newark Housing project, as he did throughout his term as city councilman. The tactics Democratic incumbents tend to use in tight contests against upstarts came to pass when Jesse Jackson, for whom Booker volunteered in '88, stopped by Newark to call the challenger, Corey Booker, "a wolf in sheep's clothing," is something

271

Muhammad has been paying attention to. "They brought in all kinds of Democratic leaders," he says of the James campaign. "But even with all they said about Booker, he still got almost 50 percent of the vote. So what that says to me is that the people are ready for a change. The leadership obviously isn't because they have a vested interest." Conrad said.

But they can't say that about me in Harlem," Muhammad continues. "Because this is where I cut my teeth. They saw me out there. I'd like to see Congressman Rangel say that I'm an outsider." And what if he plays dirtier than that and uses Muhammad's N.O.I. background to paint a media portrait of him as a hate-mongering, anti-American radical?

"He's not a bad guy," Muhammad replies. "But I think his style of leadership has served its purpose, and the district needs new energy." For Muhammad to challenge Rangel and not expect the congressman to play hardball smacks of naiveté. If he doesn't drag you into the mud, I suggested, it means you're not a threat. "No," counters Muhammad, "I think what it means is he knows he couldn't get away with it, politically, in the community. If he did that, I'd go straight to Washington on a first-class ticket. The people in this district will not let the media tell them who their leaders should be. And if he tries to paint me as a negative character, people will rally to my side."

Conrad Muhammad: "How you doing? How's it going? Is your brother the one that shoots for the Amsterdam News*?"*

Man #1 at Vendor's Table: "Nah, nah, I'm not the one you're talking about."

CM: "You look just like him! That's not your brother?"

M #1: "Nah, that's not my brother. We're good friends."

CM: "Well, how you doing?"

M #1: "I'm fine."

CM: "Good to se you. You know I'm running, right?"

Man #2 at Vendor's Table: "You running against Charlie? You ganna' bang Charlie in the head?"

CM: "Don't you think?"

M #2: "Man, Charlie's been rolling too long. Too long."

Man #3 at Vendors Table: "Sipping on too many cocktails. Sold out the empowerment zone! C'mon."

CM to reporter: "You see? The only things I'm telling you are what the people are saying to me. I have never met this man. And he just told you exactly what I was just sayin'."

M #3: "Well, you know, Charlie's experienced. You better be ready!"

Adam Heimlick: "Are you ready to pull that "Republican" lever to get this man in and Charlie out?"

M #3: "Well, he gotta' walk the walk, and then he gotta' go straight up with Charlie. I want to see some verbal uppercuts, left-crosses and all that."

M #1: "The Republicans endorse them every time anyway."

CM to reporter: "What did I just tell you? See, don't ask me why I'm running as a Republican. He ran as a Republican for 30 years!"

M #2: "That's right. And he kicks people off the ballot."

M #3: "Which you gon' learn real well!"

CM: "Believe me. We're ready for it."

Conrad Muhammad got into Harvard to pursue two masters degrees: one at the School of Divinity, and another at the Kennedy School in public administration. It was a class in the latter that he read Bernard Crick's "In Defense of Politics," which argues that the democratic process, disappointing as it tends to be, represents the most pragmatic alternative to government by force. Muhammad said, "Crick's book helped me complete my break with the Nation of Islam's opinion of what it means to work within the American system." Crick's utilitarian perspective seems to have also influenced his somewhat-unorthodox view of the Republican Party.

He's currently on hiatus from both Harvard programs. When he applied, Congressman Rangel wrote him a recommendation. "A very strong letter," said Muhammad. Another connection between the congressman and his challenger-to-be, according to Muhammad, is that Rangel is a major shareholder in WBLS, the radio station that broadcast the Hip-hop Minister's hour-long, Sunday Night Live community-issues program for five years, ending in February in 1998.

When I called the congressman's office to get a quote about the brewing race, his assistant put me straight through to him. But Rangel said little of Conrad Muhammad beyond, "I don't know him." After some prodding, he allowed, "When he was with the Mosque I saw him around, but since he left I haven't" he also added "I helped him try to get a job once, but that was by telephone." The congressman concluded our awkward conversation by saying, "There's no indication that he's going to run against me or anyone else. So it would be premature for me to make any comments about non-candidates."

I relayed the conversation to Muhammad, who was shocked. "Are you serious?" he asked. "It's somewhat baffling. If he doesn't know me he's not doing his job in the district. But he does know me, and he's being dishonest with the voters. It's insincere and disingenuous. The community of Harlem will not buy that. It's the wrong approach to a race that the district wants to see. This is Harlem," Muhammad concluded, "and we let the chips fall where they may."

On August 30, 2000 the *New York Amsterdam News* published the following:

Will Hip-Hop Minister Conrad Muhammad Go Republican?"
by Yusef Salaam.

Will Minister Conrad Muhammad, a registered Democrat, switch to the party of the elephant? That was the question buzzing through the audience at a "News and Views" forum and award event this weekend at Windows Over Harlem Restaurant in the Adam Clayton Powell Jr. State Office building. The event was produced by Claude Sharrieff of the WPAT Sunday radio show "News and Views."

Keynote speaker Minister Conrad Muhammad, a former Nation of Islam cleric and WBLS radio host, surprised the audience with his perspective and analysis of the Republican and Democratic Parties. He said that although he is a long-time Democrat, he is currently "shopping" in the marketplace of political parties. As he examines the goods on the racks, he said, "I'm looking for the best bargain."

He charged that black voters have been "led like lambs to the slaughter" in giving 95 percent of their votes to the Democratic Party. The young minister said that no other group— "not Jews, Catholics or homosexuals"—votes in such an "unwise" manner. He suggested that while Jewish people are overwhelmingly Democrats, they make sure that 30 to 40 percent of their people vote Republican, so they can influence policy whichever the party wins. Catholics and homosexuals use the same strategy, according to the hip-hop minister. He advised that no group should put all their apples in one basket in a two-party system. For black people to do so, "we sentence ourselves to political impotence," he maintained.

Muhammad then praised Texas Gov. George Bush, the Republican nominee for president, for "working with blacks, Latino and the Nation of Islam in Texas." Muhammad said voters should remember that President Clinton executed a retarded black man in Arkansas when they criticize Bush for executing Shaka Sankofa.

Muhammad urged the audience to ignore the "fear-mongers" who try to make you think that if you vote Republican or make strategic alliances with the Republicans, you've done something wrong." Also, during the forum, which was chaired by Vincent Burton of Voters Anonymous, awardees Theora Richardson, Lugenia Gordon, and Florence Rice were praised as great community leaders.

Richardson, of the Booker T. Washington Appreciation Committee, took time to trace for guests black electoral politics to the period of Reconstruction. She said, "The main thing that black men during that time forgot to do was organize. They did not organize, so they were turned out of office."

"Years ago," she continued, "black communities had vibrant business districts lined with cleaners, pharmacists, tailors, etc. but we've become so integrated that we walked away from those businesses, and those districts that once were populated by black businesses and are now controlled by everybody except black people."

Lugenia Gordon, 79, said, her family has been voting Republican since 1865. She called for greater unity among African people. "Don't tell me to forget slavery," she bristled. "I'll forget slavery when Jews forget their bondage in Egypt." She added, "I wrote a letter to President George Bush to appoint Clarence Thomas to the Supreme Court, and I wish I had never supported him because he always rules against us."

Harlem consumer advocate Florence Rice, said, "Our children are nothing but consumers. Big companies know this, and that's why they're in Harlem." She said that history shows that elements in white America do not want to see an economically strong black community. "That's why they burned out black Wall Street in Oklahoma and Rosewood, Florida."

CHAPTER 20

A grassroots GOP groundswell was developing in the black community and support was being generated from virtually all quarters and across political party lines. A new generation of voters and activism was emerging inspired by the unfolding congressional campaign of Conrad Muhammad, the Hip-hop Minister. The developing campaign was honored and pleased to get the support of Governor George Pataki, reelection campaign organization, by way of Harold Doley. We had informal discussions on the feasibility of a high profile appearance with the governor in the black community, should Conrad be successful in securing the Republican Party's nomination for congress in the 15th CD. Although there were murmurs of political problems at the county level, we had every reason to be confident because the black district leaders, Will Brown, in particular, were advocates for Conrad's designation in the 15th CD. We had the political inside track and we knew that there was not a better more articulate, well-known, skilled and viable alternative candidate to Conrad Muhammad. Therefore, when we were advised that Conrad's interview with the county committee was scheduled, we started to prepare for the next stage in the campaign with great anticipation.

Our great anticipation was short lived as Conrad's interview with the New York Republican County Committee leadership for the party's designation in the 15th congressional District was short-circuited. The weakness of Will Brown and the black GOP district leaders in their so-called advocacy on behalf of Conrad Muhammad's designation for congress was apparent when Assemblyman John Ravitz, the chairman of the county committee denied Conrad out of hand. The black district leaders and any support that they may have shown for the Conrad designation was swept aside as Ravitz asserted his power. Assemblyman Ravitz resurrected phantom allegations of "anti-Semitism" and referenced statements attributed to Conrad, when he was the minister of Mosque No. 7 several years prior. The black GOP leadership acquiesced and folded under the pressure of Ravitz, leaving Conrad the latest victim of the county committee's political plantation system.

The situation was compounded as Conrad's initial political benefactor, Claude Sharrieff, the person who introduced me to Conrad changed political alliances. Many speculated that Congressman Rangel had considerable political capital (patronage) with the chairman, Ravitz, and the previous county chair, Senator Roy Goodman, and was in fact the clandestine head "Negro in Charge." It was no accident that the Republican Party has never supported a viable candidate to compete against the Democratic incumbent.

Ultimately, Chairman Ravitz insulted and disrespected the Republican Party and its black leadership by giving the GOP designation in the 15th C.D., to Dr. Jesse Fields, an official of the Independence Party. Ravitz's decision to give the party's designation to Dr. Fields in lieu of black Republicans was an egregious compromise of the values and principles of the Republican Party. Moreover, the decision was in fact hypocritical in that "anti-Semitic" characterizations were attributed to the local leader of the Independence Party, Dr. Lenora Fulani. However, Ravitz was the new county leader, massa of the local GOP political plantation and the ultimate arbiter of all matters pertinent to the county's black GOP. Certainly, Congressman Charles Rangel would prefer to have Dr. Jesse Fields as his electoral opponent as opposed to the dynamic, energetic and young Conrad Muhammad. As a practical political matter, the Ravitz decision pre-empted the local Republican Party from a constructive party building mode in the black community, which must necessarily be based on values.

On the other hand, Conrad's enthusiasm and fire in the belly was not diminished by the rejection by the county of his designation. Conrad was surprised but not shocked by the county's ultimate decision denying his congressional designation. When I initially had discussions with Conrad about the prospects associated with him getting the county's congressional nod, I had explained to Conrad that I had good relations at the national level of the party and okay relations with the state apparatus, as a result of my party building efforts. But the real and formidable challenge to GOP congressional designation would be on the county level because of vested political interests between the "white" local Republican Party leadership and black Democratic leaders. The bottom line is that there is no black Republican Party district leadership infrastructure in place. Hence, during elections Democratic Party inspectors, predominate the polling sites. The black district leaders have no organic relationship in the districts they represent. GOP district leaders are appointed and managed by will of the county chairman. The process of perpetuating the anointed black leaders is sustained by circumventing a

Republican Party primary, which could potentially unseat the prevailing official black GOP leadership. I advised that there was a remote chance that what he (Conrad) brought to the table in terms of viability and party building opportunities could tip the scale in his favor. For whatever reason, this was another party building opportunity missed by the local GOP which from my experience was the rule and not the exception.

My assessment of the national and local situation was confirmed to Conrad by Ms. Angela Sailor, the Director of Outreach for the Republican National Committee. Ms. Sailor said that the RNC would be supportive of his future candidacy. Then she recalled, with humor, a national conference-call with the RNC and the national black GOP leadership when Harlem district leader, Ronal Perry disparaged me during the call. This was after Ms. Sailor indicated that she was invited to Harlem by Vincent Burton and my organization Voters Anonymous. Ron had no idea that I was listening to the conference call. I was livid after hearing Ron's personal attack. However, I was pleased to hear Ron's comments repudiated by another GOP Harlem-ite Joan Dawson who was participating in the conference call.

In the face of rejection, Conrad was undaunted. "We need to move forward with plan B," he said.

Plan B was a Herculean feat and a virtual political impossibility, but I understood his political wisdom to move forward despite the odds. The plan was to engage the petitioning process in the Democratic Party to achieve ballot status and force a Democratic Party primary against the powerful incumbent. I viewed the political exercise as gallant and romantic, but unrealistic in the practical political sense. However, at the end of the day, I supported his decision and committed my support to manage the plan B campaign. As futile as the plan B campaign would ultimately be, it served to keep the candidate's political credibility intact after having been summarily spurned by the Ravitz Republican Party leadership.

The Conrad Muhammad/Ravitz, political scenario crystallized the notion that the Republican Party ignores the best interests of the black community. It also graphically portrayed the inner workings of the local GOP plantation system as bequeathed to Ravitz, the new county boss. Conrad's plan B was thwarted in the New York State Supreme Court on technicalities that disqualified a sufficient number of signatures to his designating petitions. Unfortunately, this knocked him off the ballot.

In the wake of GOP County chairman rejecting Conrad Muhammad in favor of Dr. Jesse Fields for congress, and the state of official black political leadership in general, we needed to re-evaluate and fine-tune our strategic plan to advance the cause of political ascendancy in the black community. The nature and comprehensiveness of the political opposition was exposed, and it required that we retool and rethink our approach.

Alton Chase said, "Congressman Rangel is the H.N.I.C., on both sides of the political aisle, Democrat and Republican, case closed. That's how the system works in this town. But at some point you would think that county would have to support a viable candidate, and/or at least a card-carrying Republican against the perceived Democratic opposition."

Darryl Brown made his contribution, saying, "All politics is local, but based on what went down with Conrad Muhammad indicates to me that we need to link our grassroots GOP initiative to a viable presidential candidate and fill out the slate with a congressional candidate as well as candidates for the state legislature. If we don't link to a viable presidential campaign, then the Conrad Muhammad political scenario will be repeated by the county system. But if we link to a viable presidential candidate we may be able to put federal and national pressure on the local electoral situation. I think that federal observers need to monitor this local situation. They must be violating something by conducting political business as they do."

Replying, Alton Chase said, "You may be on to something. If we have a viable Republican candidate for congress in a presidential race, we may have a better shot at leveraging our man for the party designation, or the alternative is to force a primary. I like that idea because what happened in the state gubernatorial race is that we had the articulated support of the state committee, but they are not in a position to enforce their political will. They must go along with the county organizations. On the other hand, if the Feds are involved, pressure could be put on the county organization." I responded, ending with a question, "Yeah, I like your thinking, Brother D. Let me ask you this. Does the viable presidential candidate have to be black?"

Darryl Brown answered, "Come on, B., give me a play. I'm not talking about the "Run, Jesse, run," type thing, specifically. We all know the limitation of black presidential candidates and the reality of the candidates and Southern Strategy that is required to win the presidency. But an attractive black Republican candidate could facilitate a substantial political bridge to the ultimate GOP presidential nominee."

Alton Chase asked, "You got any black candidates in mind, D.?"

Darryl Brown said, "Actually, I hadn't given the idea too much thought prior to this conversation. But since you asked, two names immediately come to mind, and those are General Colin Powell and Tony Brown."

Alton Chase replied, "Well, Colin Powell said that he wouldn't seek the presidency if he only had to run across the street. He knows that he can't prevail because of the Southern Strategy. Who knows? Although I'm sure Tony is not interested in seeking the presidency, he may appreciate the strategic plan and consider the proposition."

Darryl Brown responded, "Yeah, B. You must have links to Tony Brown because he referred to you as a 'prominent' Republican in his book, *Black Lies, White Lies, the Truth According to Tony Brown*. How did that happen, B.? How come he put you down?"

I replied, "Actually I didn't know about it until after the fact. My cousin Roscoe bought it to my attention after he read the book. Interestingly enough I had recommended to Roscoe that he read the book as I intended to read it also. After reading the book, Roscoe called me up and told me that I was mentioned in the book, which was a complete surprise to me. I, of course, immediately went out to buy the book!

"But our interaction began when I responded by letter to a piece he wrote about black American and the Republican Party. Tony responded to my letter with a letter of his own, and apparently decided to publish our exchange. We do exchange e-mail from time to time, so maybe I will introduce that line of discussion with him."

Darryl Brown said, "You got to tell me a little more about this Southern Strategy thing. I heard about it, but I'm not sure I understand it sufficiently. You guys are going to have to develop that a little further for me."

"We're going to get into that." I said "In fact, I am writing a book dealing with the Southern Strategy so I will share the manuscript with you soon because it will be completed shortly. I will give you a hint thought. the North won the war of ideas, but the South won the war on the political ground. And the racial dichotomy remains the subtext of American party politics."

I advised them to check out this piece by brothers.

A Black Paper for White Republicans:
Trent Lott and the Republican Party's Soul
by Tony Brown

Senator Trent Lott resigned his leadership position as of today, but the struggle for the soul of the Republican Party has just begun, and the difficult question of race has taken center stage in politics. The repercussions from l'affaire Lott will be evident for years to come. The

Republican victory in the recent off-year election is now truly history, and new charges of a Republican pro-segregation sentiment could make the losing Democrats the ultimate victors—despite the fact that only 31 percent of voters know what the Democrats stand for.

The arrival of the watershed moment in American racial politics thrusts both major parties toward the last off-ramp before the certain exit of exposure as racist institutions. The political sector of the establishment is at a colossally important juncture, at which the slightest capricious lie about either party's racist moorings will invite an avalanche of probes by the mainstream media, their decades-old enabler. A New York Times *editorial warned that "one of the obvious lessons of the Lott firestorm" is that Republicans must scrutinize the records of those who lead them. If this is a warning of liberal media probes to come, rest assured that the conservative media will be turning over Democratic rocks as well. In short, the days of the media shield that secured the establishment political sector are slowly coming to an end.*

This sorry episode in American history began when the party of Lincoln became the party of the Southern Strategy of exploiting racial inequities for partisan gain by making white Southern racists the descendants of Abraham Lincoln's Freedom Party. A faction within the Republican Party led by moderates such as Governor Linwood Holton of Virginia (1970-1974) lost to the segregationist wing of Richard Nixon (Patrick Buchanan was a Nixon political operative and speech writer.) You saw this crude logic buck-naked when Patrick Buchanan delivered his out-of-step televised speech at the 1972 Republican national convention. It was widely condemned as divisive, mean-spirited and racist. Buchanan alienated white suburbanites, working women, gays, pro-choice advocates, Jews and moderate WASP Republicans. And, of course, it was open season on African Americans. During the season of harvesting the voting crop, Buchanan, an early architect of the party's Southern Strategy, was burning the fields. This scorched-earth policy came home to roost with Trent Lott's remarks on December 5, 2002.

Subsequently, Republican voters in presidential primaries rejected Buchanan's extremist agenda, and now he limits his ranting to the political platform CNN provides for him. But the Republican Party is still plagued by the residual effects of the Buchanan Southern

*Strategy curse, e.g., using racial fears to target white voters. I mentioned my first book [*Black Lies, White Lies, *published in 1995] that the so-called "Southern Strategy" would eventually explode in the face of the GOP, but I had no way of knowing at the time that the Senate Republican leader would be the one to pull the trigger in 2002. In retrospect, you might say that Senator Trent Lott, elected to the House from Mississippi in 1972 with the help of the Southern Strategy, has been an accident waiting to happen for the last few decades.*

The precipitating incident arrived on December 5, 2002 at the 100th birthday celebration of Senator Strom Thurmond, when Senator Lott publicly glorified racism and segregation (which he subsequently called immoral). As it turned out, and contrary to what initially believed, this assumed gaffe was not a slip of the lip in an unguarded moment or a failed attempt at sly humor or due to Lott's over-generous nature to please an old man on his 100th birthday.

*None of those motives are relevant because Lott said that same thing 22 years ago, and has been lauding this and other racist sentiments for decades. "Lott had used almost identical words in praise of Thurmond's segregationist campaign comments in Mississippi, 1980," the *Washington Post* reported. Therefore, his praise of an evil period in American history fits a pattern, rather than being an anomaly. It was a cold-blooded miscalculation. His purpose: divide and conquer the voters along racial lines. It seems that Lott was implementing the Southern Strategy (which is an instrument of power), not making a red-neck case that black people are inferior.*

Lott got caught with his hand in the cookie jar of playing the race card to engender fear of blacks. Tangentially, he magnified the role the Republican legislators have played in opposing modern civil rights legislation. Seizing the opportunity, many Democrats have shoved aside the philosophical basis of Republican opposition to programs such as guaranteed entitlements based solely on race and smeared all conservative idea and all Republicans as racist hate mongers.

The fact that Lott and some of his Republican colleagues have been blind to 40 years of civil-rights progress has made it possible for some Democrats to play the race card and exploit blacks with impunity. Bill Clinton's tactics, for example have been every bit as egregious and demagoguery as Trent Lott's, notwithstanding his appointment of black partisans to low-level government jobs as a down-line to reinforce the fears among blacks with campaigns such as: Republicans are out to take away the right of blacks to vote; Republicans supported the burning of black churches; and President Bush personally supported the lynching of blacks.

There are black Democrats, however, who abhor race-baiting. In his new book, Al On America, *Rev. Al Sharpton rebukes the use of race-baiting politics and offers the example of how fellow Democrat Bill Clinton used the demagogic and racist tactic. "This is what Bill Clinton did to Jesse Jackson with Sista Souljah, and Jesse should have stopped it.*

In fact, you might say that Bill Clinton sewed up the presidency with race-baiting. He used an attack on rapper Sister Souljah during his first presidential campaign to send a message whose intent was clearly to ease the fears of white voters and prove that he could control a radical Jesse Jackson (with whom he associated Souljah) and the blacks would be kept in line if he won the election. He then interrupted his campaign and flew back to Arkansas to witness the execution of a brain-damaged black youth in order to portray himself as hard on crime—that is, on black criminals. His photo op with a national media corps in tow included lining up black inmates in white jumpsuits for his military-style inspection as the white man in charge. This refried liberal was introducing himself to whites as the "New Democrat." Not groveling liberals, who wouldn't stand up to black people's claim for justice.

After those exhibitions of pandering to white racism at the expense of blacks, Clinton was never again behind in the polls. His scam was so perfect that his black victims guaranteed his victory with 82 % of their vote. He later revealed his secret strategy for getting elected and re-elected. Nail down that state's black vote (18%), he explained to an Arkansas state trooper, and let your white opponent scramble "to get his 51% out of the 82% of whites," [Black Lie, White Lies by Tony Brown]. *Thus, the black vote was the guarantor of his Arkansas dynasty, as it would later become for his presidency. That's how the Southern Strategy worked in the hands of a Southern Democrat.*

Clinton's sycophant black propagandists even anointed him "the first black president." I say to these benefactors: Don't soil the record of the first black president (probably a woman) with the shame of an immoral imposter. And if he is black then he is the only one in his Chappaqua, Westchester County, New York neighborhood where the black population is only .03%. This honorary Negro now has the temerity to accuse all Republicans of being racist.

Trent Lott, for years, was just as smooth as his Southern Democratic counterpart, and in the end, just as unprincipled. After being rebuked by President Bush and principled Republicans such as Governor Jeb Bush and Secretary of State Colin Powell, Lott obsequiously admitted, in terms certain to infuriate his Buchanan-esque supporters, to "immoral leadership in my part of the country for a long time." Thus, he fell victim to his own duplicity. But, in doing so, his Samson act exposed the Achilles heel of the Republican Party and forced it to examine its soul. (There's that vision thing again.)

The Curse of Lott's political victims include modern Republicans who believe in equal rights and have, during the last two decades, developed an agenda aimed at benefitting blacks. An agenda including school choice, welfare reform, faith-based initiatives, empowerment zones, etc. As a result of this enlightened approach to empowering blacks, instead of a prejudicial opposition to black interests, the GOP has attracted a broad voter base that includes Elite suburban women who have fled the urban areas, and do not want to be associated with a racist organization; Jewish voters, who because of a history of persecution, are sensitive to bigotry, and "Northern transplants" who know nothing of the Dixiecrats. Racial appeals turn those voters off." (Wall Street Journal, *Editorial,* Dec. 19, 2002) *To win, the modern Republican Party no longer needs a "Southern Strategy" or the southern crackers that Trent Lott was attracting to carry the South or the white voter. However, the Democrats do need racialism as an incentive. Without the race card to scare large numbers of blacks, the absolute core constituency of the Democratic Party, to the polls, it cannot compete.*

At the same time, the Republican Party cannot hold its crucial white coalition together with a racist face and with leaders who are committed to segregation or legislation that ignores the unique needs of blacks (relief from poverty, family disorganization, and poor schools that are in part residual institutions of centuries of White Supremacist persecution). This is because an estimated one-third of the white Republican vote is expected to bolt if the party's leaders do not convince them that the Southern Strategy is a thing of the past. That's why the new politics in President Bush's State of the Union speech in late January is now being hailed by White House insiders as a "healing speech."

The racial politics of the 1960s and early 1970s have expired because the generation of Southern Strategy white racists are mostly dead. There has been a significant demographic change: over half of all Americans alive today were born after 1964, too late to join the segregation bandwagon. Old-school Republican leaders are beginning to realize this fact. If they do not line up behind Bush's call to confront the GOP's racist history head on and to compete with the Democrats for black votes in an inclusive party in the spirit of Abraham Lincoln they will be future Trent Lotts and ex-elected officials.

Whatever one thinks of Trent Lott, he knows the solution. He has previously proposed a Republican focus on economic development and entrepreneurship in the black community as the foundation for better education, stronger families and less welfare—if the economic impact creates jobs. While the Republicans have followed his legacy of Southern racial politics, they have ignored his sage advice about helping blacks build a foundation that secures their future.

After all of the years of giving the Democratic Party over 90 percent of its vote, the black community's chronic social and economic problems remain chronic and unresolved. Real black empowerment and self-sufficiency have never been more than a public relations token on the Democratic agenda. In addition, since business development is indigenous to capitalism, the absence of a Republican Marshall Plan to create economic impact in distressed black communities is a conspicuous omission.

Instead of this sin of omission, the GOP should jumpstart its redemption by listening to blacks interviewed in a recent 12-city survey by the New York Times. Blacks who praised President Bush's firm denunciation of Lott's racially tinged remarks and covert removal of him from his leadership position. However, they made clear that "it would take much more for him to win their support in 2004." Meat-and-bread issues would weigh as heavily, they said, as racial politics. The by product of a truly contrite Republican Party *with a Republican atonement empowerment agenda will help blacks and the nation, but it would also expose the Democrat's racial hypocrisy as well.*

The exposure of the Republican's racist pandering has unfairly hurt modern Republicans such as former Governor Linwood Holton of Virginia. Gov. Holton received nearly 40 percent of the African-American vote in 1969 and put together a winning "coalition of business, labor and African-Americans" in Virginia in the 1960s— only to be marginalized and rebuked by a Buchanan-like clan of political operatives. (See "An End to the Southern Strategy?" guest editorial by Linwood Holton, New York Times, *Dec. 23, 2003). Other new Republicans who refute the racist pandering of the past, have been unfairly hurt by the stereotype of the GOP as a haven for political racists. Furthermore, Lott's behavior has reinforced the stereotype of black Republicans as Uncle Tom's and made victims of their efforts to use the Republican Party as a vehicle to aid the black community.*

Meanwhile, he clumsily (while trying to escape punishment) endorsed the very social programs that are anathema to conservative philosophy. As a convert to affirmative action "across the board," he came perilously close to promising reparations for blacks. In the end, however, the entire Republican Party will be forced to develop a nuanced approach that will solve the problem of the racism that won't go away with equal opportunity programs for all disadvantaged citizens that are carefully drawn to avoid quotas, or demand personal responsibility. This is a soul situation.

That's why it is so important to remember that the soul is eternal. (Republicans, I know you don't want to go there, but that is your new reality.) It is the essence of a person or a thing, and it is not amenable to insincere maneuvers and political slight of hand. And racism, as an immoral act, scars it permanently. Up until the 60s the GOP was the party of Lincoln, and many more Republicans supported civil-rights legislation in the 60s than Democrats—until the Nixon-Buchanan hijackers institutionalized segregation within the Republican Party.

Racism was also the challenge in 1968 at a time when the Democratic Party was the bulwark of segregation in the South. Segregationist and Democrat George Wallace carried Mississippi with 63 percent of the vote and Republican Richard Nixon's political operatives crossed the Rubicon and began the campaign of soliciting segregationist Democrats in the South. This widespread institutional racism and acceptance of a Faustian bargain with racism (selling your soul to the devil, or winning at all costs), remains the subterranean issue and the great danger to the Republican Party's recently acquired political hegemony.

To solve the contemporary Republican predicament and save the soul that was born in the nineteenth century when Republicanism entered the political world as a force to stop the westward advancement of slavery, emancipate blacks from bondage, and give African-Americans citizenship and the right to vote, the Party must refocus on its spiritual, albeit, guiding and founding principles. Republicans can begin by looking to Trent Lott for guidance. He is a quintessential example of the fact that the Southern Strategy is not the soul of the party of Lincoln. Freedom is it's name, and it is the core principle of Republican-ism. The Southern Strategy and racism are imposters in a party that was hijacked by a "sorry Lott."

In everyday terms, it all boils down to this: Do black people deserve to be treated equally as American citizens? If the modern Republican Party has the correct answer, then the path is clear. In that case, it will abandon all appeals to intolerance and pseudo fixes to maintain power and instead be guided by the flight of its soul to a better place. Lott and the GOP (as well as the Democratic Party that has exploited the black vote on behalf of white power) have ignored this fundamental and political lesson because they have rejected a heritage of egalitarianism. The GOP's main obstacle to this liberating achievement will be the Democratic Party's demagoguery and political opportunism.

But if the GOP surrenders to a right-versus-wrong paradigm, race baiting by Democrats will expose the Republican Party as the best choice. Mama taught me that whenever I committed an act that only benefitted me, it was wrong. When I did something that resulted in benefit for everyone, it was right. That is the core value for whatever you call a government program—affirmative action, voting rights, welfare reform.

If the GOP chooses more racism and spiritual fraud, it will not offer the voters a choice. Whether you run off of the left or the right side of the road, you are out of the mainstream. Racism guarantees an accident, as well as spiritual corruption. In that instance, truth becomes the first victim.

In today's perverse climate, the conventional wisdom is that truth has no place in politics and all politicians are expected to be professional liars. Talking about a soul is gibberish. Perhaps, Lott has exposed those myths, not that he didn't try to accommodate them all. He simply could not continue to live a lie without slipping up. This time, he praised Strom Thurmond's segregationist past one time too many. And this time, the ubiquitous C-Span camera was there, along with outraged conservative Republicans whose weblogs and media ignited the Lott controversy with "early, widespread and harsh criticism" of Lott, according to The New York Times *(Dec. 17, 2002).*

The New York Post *editorial page, one of the most conservative in the country, along with the conservative Wall Street Journal, immediately called for Lott's resignation as Senate Majority leader. Secretary of State, Colin Powell, and National Security Advisor, Condolezza Rice, both black, ignored Lott's request to the White House for their assistance in defending him. Later Powell rebuked Lott.*

Mostly, those whites not in favor of desegregation and equal rights—the extremists like Patrick Buchanan and his ilk of racists, like those in Lott's hometown, the whites in Pascagoula (and Grenada), Mississippi, who are worried about the loss of government ports, jobs, and bridges, and about 50 percent of the U. S. white population from areas so insulated from blacks that their attitudes are shaped by a common view that the main problems of America stem from a contentious black population—cannot detect anything offensive about praising segregation and an era of state-sponsored persecution (including public murders) of African-Americans.

In some cases, that phenomenon is due to cultural isolation rather than racism, but it lays the foundation for stereotypes and racism. Many in the aforementioned "inside-of-the-box" groups defiantly still defend Lott's salute to bigotry and deny that it is a bow to America's racist past. Conversely, an outside-of-the-box, racist-free, and denial-free people throughout the world clearly heard and saw Lott encourage a continuation of his party's covert racist appeal: an appeal the mainstream media wink at.

Lott's symbolic message: black people are running wild in our society ("all these problems") and the Republican Party under his

288

own leadership (the solution) is here to put them back in their place and subordinate them. Therefore, I conclude, that his leadership harmed both the Republican Party and the nation. In one brief moment, Lott undercut all of the achievements of the compassionate-conservative wing of President Bush's new Republican Party and re-branded all Republicans as racists.

However, the furor that Lott's unfortunate behavior has ignited is proof that America has somehow moved beyond the politics of racism (a Southern Strategy for Republicans of patronage for a hate program among Democrats) its media enables a race-baiting politicians such as Trent Lott (who was recently reminded by a Mississippi White Supremacist that "the reason you have been elected is because you have been a segregationist"). Even in an attempt to save his political power, a desperate Lott abandoned his traditional racist base and its bedrock principles. He pandered shamelessly and offered obsequious apologies to the group he had hurt the most with a promise (as the then Senate majority leader) that he would "move an agenda that will be helpful to African-Americans." Ironically, his payoff was a poll result that showed 75 percent of blacks urging him to resign.

Racism is not only tricky and immoral, it is a catch 22—a no-win political and economic strategy. Parts of the Old South (which Lott now calls "wicked"), especially Mississippi where racism and segregation were most brutal, have become the regions of the U. S. and the New South that are the last to develop economically. In some cases, the most intensely racist bastions have not grown economically at all. In more pluralistic regions where equal opportunity is prevalent and segregation was historically more benign, all Mississippians tend to prosper more. Many safely speculate that politicians who cling to White Supremacy (or Democratic race-baiting demagoguery) will be America's future "sorry Lott."

As he suffers the torture of public ridicule, Trent Lott, a cultural Southerner, now realizes that he could have been another Lyndon B. Johnson (a courageous advocate of equal rights) or even an ex-Klansman, like Senator Robert Byrd or segregationist advocate Senator Storm Thurmond, who overcame their pernicious racist upbringing and publicly repudiated their former putrid beliefs. By remaining faithful to a racist strategy until he got caught, however, Trent Lott will be remembered as a victim of his upbringing, rather than someone who had the strength of character to overcome it.

If Lott's soul is in need of forgiveness, he is welcome to mine, but it will not change his receiving the consequences of the actions that he has unleashed on the black population of this nation. "For whatsoever, a man soweth, that shall he also reap." Translate this biblical prophesy into an opinion poll, and you get 74 percent of the U.S. population that believes Lott is not only out of step with the New America, but perceives his leadership as jeopardizing the Republican Party's ability to attack the complex problems of unemployment (6 percent nationwide, but 11 percent among blacks), poverty and poor education that afflict blacks more severely than any other group. Equal rights policies will benefit everyone. That fact may be politically correct, but it's still a fact.

If his party sincerely supports the compassionate conservatism of the president it will reinvigorate not only itself, but American-ism as well. While this liberating idea is only in its infancy, it is at least a start. Gradually, most of us will realize that we didn't all come over on the same ship but we are in the same boat. Lott is the catalyst for this emerging public insight.

President George W. Bush made no secret of his unhappiness with Lott. The White House spokesman called Lott's praise-of-segregation statement "offensive and repugnant." In response to Lott's super-gaffe, President Bush stated that racism and inequality are not Republican standards and implied that the Republican Party will no longer remain a haven for closet bigots. He did not make a statement only because he is a moral person, but because he is a practical one as well.

Not only is President Bush aware that he got only 9 percent of the black vote nationally in 2000, but his chief pollster has warned him that 2004 can potentially bring an even more ominous threat from the African-American Democratic bloc. "If we get exactly the same minority vote in 2004 that we got in 2000, we lose by 2 million popular votes and 38 electoral votes" (US News & World Report). *That's because a substantially higher proportion of Latinos will vote Democratic in 2004 (*Wall Street Journal, *December 19, 2002).*

Bush beat Al Gore, decisively, by 54 percent to 42 percent among whites in 2000. No Democratic presidential candidate has won a majority of the white vote since Lyndon B. Johnson in 1964. The proverbial thorn in Bush's side in 2000 was "a 90 percent to 9 percent *landslide among African-Americans." (*Wall Street Journal, *Dec. 19, 2002). Most whites vote Republican, not because of the Southern Strategy, but because they fear taxes, excessive government, and a weak response to foreign threats, and recently because Democrats are mostly offering Republican ideas (Clinton triangulation) because they can't sell their own liberal programs that the majority of blacks, the Democratic Party's absolute core constituency, demands.*

This is true because blacks generally believe that government oversight is necessary for a persecuted minority to safeguard every aspect of life. This is not dependency, it is good reality testing. Only the diminution of institutional racism by the federal government will reduce the conservative vs. liberal polarity between blacks and whites and will allow blacks to judge a conservative position on its merits and not on the basis of a history of bias.

CHAPTER 21

The 2004 presidential election season was upon us, but we're not ready or prepared to engage the process, in the context of the projected grassroots electoral initiative. Although I had completed the manuscript, *Race Politics in Transition* which outlined an overview of American politics from emancipation to the modern era, our lack of boots on the ground and the financing imperative constrained the movement. Our political database and public relations component was in place, which gave us hope for the foreseeable future. Cash flow was the name of the game at this point, from a personal as well as from the political movement's standpoint. This may be a good opportunity for me to explore some of the economic links I developed from my visit to South Africa.

As I pulled out files on my contacts from South Africa, Ms. Keisha Morrisey came into the shop and asked if I would indulge her in a brief conversation. Keisha was the Republican Party candidate for the New York State Assembly in the 70th A.D. during 2002, and the party's nominee in 2003 for the New York City Council in the 9th C.D. In both instances, I managed her campaign, and she had developed confidence in my political acumen and skills. She also confided in me because, as she put it, I was one of the few guys who were not trying to get into her pants.

Keisha was an attractive, 35-year-old single mom, and a new addition to the political process and the Republican Party. I first met Keisha during Conrad's campaign for congress, as she was a volunteer in his campaign and member of his organization. Following the demise of Conrad's campaign, Keisha asked me to manage her campaign because she was given the party's nomination for the New York State Assembly in the 70th A.D. against the incumbent Democrat, Assemblyman Keith Wright.

Keisha came to the Republican Party and her candidacy with great enthusiasm, discipline and commitment. Keisha set out to run a strong campaign and began to focus on financing, organization and other issues in order to make a good showing for herself. By the time of the general election, she became disillusioned because her greatest opposition was from within the party, which was a complete shock to her neophyte political perspective.

During the campaign, I made a special effort not to share my considerable knowledge of how the county officials set GOP candidates afloat, ultimately leaving them facing upstream without a paddle. I did not want to prejudice her perspective in anyway so I let her experience the real political deal first hand, while providing the organizational support and political perspective necessary to modulate the inevitable negative outcomes. Keisha learned first hand from her electoral maiden voyage that the GOP county leadership was only interested in candidates for window dressing purposes only. Keisha became an expert witness to the fact that the GOP district leader infrastructure was seriously compromised to the Democratic opposition, and that the "official" black leaders were the gatekeepers. Despite the admonition from party leaders that she couldn't win, Keisha made every effort to represent her campaign as serious and competitive. Although the result of her refreshing and energetic campaign was a foregone conclusion, I was persuaded that Keisha had a future in local GOP politics.

Following her campaign for the New York State Assembly, Keisha got a political fire in her belly. On one hand she felt deceived, abandoned, and disillusioned by the internal efforts to marginalize her campaign. But on the other hand she felt politically liberated and independent, and inspired to run a competitive campaign in the future. The future came quickly for Keisha as she was the favorite to get the GOP nod for the New York City Council in the 9th C.D. However, in order to secure the nomination for city council, Keisha was required by the county leadership, both black and white, to disassociate her campaign from me. Keisha was forthright enough with me to advise me of the conditions associated with her securing the nomination, and we agreed to disagree. In the context of her campaign for city council, I was to have no official role. Her message to all interested parties was that we were friends and had no current political relationship. Her only request of me in connection with the campaign was to identify an alternative campaign manager, which I did. We agreed not to consider any Harlem based person in order to minimize the inevitable attempts to co-opt the manager and sabotage the campaign.

A contact of mine in Brooklyn was having a political event and I took Keisha with me to meet Harold (Mawu) Straker, a Brooklyn GOP activist who was familiar with electoral politics and had no discernable links with the Manhattan GOP county organization. Several months earlier I asked Mawu to represent me in Washington D.C. at a White House event on the Faith-Based and Community Initiative. He did a good job and returned with the desired information. I advised Keisha of my confidence in him based on that occasion, which was critical to her deciding to take him on board. But from the outset, communication problems between the two developed and she began to lose confidence in him. In addition, she told me that he appeared to be marketing himself, with the white county leadership and the black district leadership for the future. The communication between them deteriorated so much to the extent that the candidate and the manager were moving in opposite directions. Finally, Keisha asked me to intervene because attitudes had set in and I needed to play a mediating role, if the relationship was to continue. My efforts to mediate the impasse proved futile as later that week there was a public spectacle following a campaign event, and Keisha fired him.

Meanwhile, Keisha's Treasurer, Robert Hornack, and member of the Keisha Morrisey's finance committee, Jay Golub, were not convinced that I no longer had a role in the campaign organization. Golub called me on the phone individually and relayed to me the same message, "Vinnie, if you're not involved we can raise $100,000 for Keisha's city Council Campaign."

I assured them that I was not a part of Keisha's campaign and if necessary I would give that to them in writing if it would help them generate the $100,000 they claimed that they could raise. When I told Keisha about the phone call and its substance, she disclosed to me that earlier during a meeting, Robert and Jay said that they were going to call me.

Keisha said, "Rob and Jay said that they could raise $100,000 for my campaign, in the framework of my participation on the 'Urban Platform Agenda' that they are promoting." Now the county leadership and the black district leaders are telling me that you are "blacklisted," and that's why I didn't get their support for the New York State Assembly." She continued, "I just don't understand what's going on."

"Well, I know what's going on," I said, "but it begins before your time, and there was no point then and there is no point now to get into the details of me and the county and the black district leaders."

Keisha was obviously confused by the various clandestine political machinations.

She said to me, "I don't really understand the problem that they have with you, but I see what's going on with them, white and black. They all seem to think that I am some young little weak freak, and most of them are thinking with their lower head. You are the only one that is really helping me, so no matter what they say I'm not going to stop consulting with you."

I responded, "We are on the same page, but in terms of the fundraising, they claim they can accomplish if I'm not involved, let's test them. Let them know you talked to me about it, and I agreed to provide them with a sworn statement if that would help."

Keisha said, "Also, this guy, Thomas Kent Jr., that is trying to date me is giving me the same message that I need to disassociate with you. What's up with all of that? Anyway, this Kent fellow is kind of weird. He shows up unannounced at my door, and I sense this stalker quality in him. Plus I gave him some money to file corporation papers for the joint-venture production company that we talked about doing, and I haven't seen the papers, so I will ask for my money back."

Despite the fact that I was no longer associated with the city council campaign, the promises of financial support and technical assistance from the county district leaders and the Urban Platform. It was obvious to me that her city council campaign was being undermined and the various people around her were inimical to her campaign agenda and political career. Keisha was learning and handling the political reality remarkably well for a neophyte. I understood my role as a political resource and refuge for her during her baptism by fire of the political and electoral process. I kept her briefed on the likely outcomes and reactions to her legitimate inquiries and aspirations and was proven to be right more often than not. With such an outstanding batting average it was in her best interest to seek my advice.

Her City Council campaign never generated political legs, as the candidate was plagued by nefarious political machinations to undermined her campaign and attack her personally. After the city council campaign, Keisha told me that she was going to take some time off and rethink her commitment to public service and party building. Since then we have talked on the phone, but this was the first time I had seen her since. I was glad to see her in good form and high spirits.

"Hi, B., how is it coming?" Keisha continued, "I had a good opportunity to think while visiting my family in Virginia. I left my son there to go to school because things were getting very scary, and for me it became a safety issue. I was particularly concerned for my son, as I was receiving threats of physical harm. I didn't want to disclose this to you at the time, because my first priority was to get my son to a safe environment. Now with him in a place down south I feel confident and ready to battle with these House Negroes."

With a broad smile on her young baby face she said, "Look, at this B. I made a complaint to the DA, and this is the press release that I want to disseminate."

GOP Candidate Files Complaint with DA

Keisha C. Morrissey, a Republican Party candidate for the New York State Assembly in 2002, and New York City Council in 2003 has filed a complaint with the Manhattan District Attorney against leaders of the local GOP. The complaint alleges harassment, threats of bodily harm, and stalking. It identifies leaders and officials in the New York Republican County organization among others.

Ms. Morrissey said, "I reluctantly decided to file a formal complaint because I intend to seek public office in the future; therefore, I need to bring closure to the ongoing sabotage, false rumors, and threats of harm that are being inflicted against my candidacy and campaign.

I was affiliated with the Republican Party and then decided to become a candidate for public office. I was advised by friends and associates that the Republican Party was racist, reactionary, and hated the black community. But after becoming a part of the electoral process as a candidate in 2002 and 2003, I found that most of my difficulties as a candidate came primarily from local black Republican leaders. Unfortunately for the community of Harlem, many black Republicans in official leadership positions are engaged in activities other than party building and serving their community.

The mere fact that the black Democratic elected officials have no political competition from the Republican Party is an example of the lack of leadership by the black GOP. The problem has been institutionalized because many white and black Republican officials are implementing a strategic political agenda that protects certain Democratic incumbents from insurgent Republican Party electoral competition.

Based on my prior experience, I realize that should I run for public office in the future, I will have local Republican Party opposition, as well as from my Democratic Party opponent. Now, I have a first-hand understanding of why many African-Americans are fed up with the Democratic Party and disillusioned by the Republican

Party. Interestingly enough, it is the quality of black political leadership that is the problem in both instances.

"Damn, sis.," I said. "I'm glad that you didn't tell me about that before. That stuff is way below the belt; that's man-to-man stuff. That is not how a political leadership should deal with a new generational addition to the party. I don't know what to say."

Keisha continued, "There is nothing that can be said, B. What they do speaks for itself and needs no interpretation or embellishment."

I said, "I backed off because I wanted to give them the benefit of the doubt in terms of what they intended to do for your campaign if I was not involved, but they are way over the top. So how do you want to deal with this or will you fold your tent?"

She said, "Well, I don't intend to fold my tent. They have proven to me what they are really about: nothing. Actually the reason why I came to you is because I want to jump into the fight again by seeking the party nomination for congress in the 15th C.D. I want to do this for a few reasons, B. Number one, I want to show that I'm not afraid of them. I want to keep myself politically viable, and I would like to be the first registered Republican to receive the party's nomination for the Harlem seat. I think that the legacy of the Republican Party is to have a black Republican nominee for Harlem, the black American capital of the country. What do you think about that idea?"

"Well, stated," I said, "I'm inspired. Plus, we need to keep them busy with healthy and constructive exercises. I'm going to talk to the team, and we will come up with a strategy."

The following piece was published on the Internet web site: weholdthesetruths.com:

GOP Congressional Primary Election in Harlem?
By Vincent Burton

Harlem Woman Seeks to Uproot Democrat Stronghold in African American Community

While there is much political speculation and jockeying in the Harlem Democratic leadership and follow-ship relative to the inevitable, if not imminent retirement of Congressman Charges

Rangel, Harlem Republicans are generating their own colorful, political rivalries. Perhaps there is an emerging grassroots Republican leadership to challenge the black Republican County leadership status quo.

Keisha C. Morrissey announced her candidacy for the Republican Party nomination for the U.S. House of Representatives in the 15th C.D., following a meeting at the New York Republican County Committee headquarters on Monday June 7. 2004. Ms. Morrissey was the Republican Party nominee for the New York State Assembly and New York City Council in 2002 and 2003, respectively.

The campaigns of Keisha Morrissey generated much controversy at the district leadership level, particularly because Ms. Morrissey was interested in running a serious campaign to unseat incumbent Democrats, New York State Assemblyman Keith Wright and New York City Councilman William Perkins. The youthful Republican candidate was initially insulted when approached by some black Republican District leaders and admonished to run a "window-dressing" campaign because, they told her, "you can't win." Subsequently, Ms. Morrissey became irate when communication between her campaign and some district leaders deteriorated into political sabotage and threats of physical harm when she refused to go along with a cameo campaign.

Ultimately, Ms. Morrisey was advised to file a formal complaint with the District Attorney. Keisha Morrisey said, "I was reluctant to file the complaint, but because I am a single mother with a teenage son I had to think of his well being. Also, I was not going to let them intimidate me from seeking public office in the future. Therefore, I bit my lip, filed the complaint, and discussed with family and friends my interest in running for public office in November 2004. Following my decision to run for Congress, I presented myself at the county meeting because it was an appropriate step. But I was under no delusions of being the ultimate designee because my primary political opposition is internal in nature, as strange, as it may seem."

Sources present at the meeting said Ms. Morrissey gave a confident and brilliant presentation for the designation, as compared to her opponent Mr. Abdul Salaam, a.k.a. Kenneth P. Jefferson, a resident of Harlem. According to reports, the question of the political party affiliation of Mr. Jefferson was suppressed during the county meeting. However, according to designating petitions that the Democratic Party of New York County filed on behalf of Minister Conrad Muhammad in 2002 for the 15th Congressional District, Mr. Kenneth P. Jefferson was a member of the committee to file vacancies. A source close to the Harlem Republican Club said, "Mr. Jefferson is a political novice and was hastily chosen as a stop-Morrissey, maneuver." Nevertheless, Mr. Kenneth Jefferson was selected by the predominantly black Republican District leaders and others as the party's designee in the 15th C.D.

Longtime political leader in the Bronx, Alton Chase said, "It would have been unusual for the New York County Committee to give the Congressional Designation in the 15th C.D. to a real Republican because they never have. Until recently the New York Republican County Committee gave the 15th C.D. Designation to Congressman Charles Rangel. However, in 2002 the New York Republican County Committee gave the party designation to Dr. Jesse Fields, an official of the Independence Party. Unfortunately, for many years a real Republican Party electoral opposition has been thwarted by internal political machinations on the part of appointed district leader gatekeepers."

The fact remains that it is not a political accident that there are never viable Republican Party candidates supported by the local GOP to compete against black and Hispanic Democrats for elective office. As a practical political matter, the general public is deceived by a clandestine, esoteric political relationship between some local Democrat and Republican Party officials. The general public is hyped by the false notion of political friends and enemies, while the political elites operate a strange relationship of political bedfellows. Apparently, many in the emerging generations are able to pierce the false perception of an adversarial relationship between the Democrat and Republican Parties at the level of New York City's electoral politics.

Faro James, spokesman for the Grassroots Republican Taskforce said, "The taskforce has endorsed Keisha Morrissey's campaign for the Republican Party nomination in the 15th C.D. We have engaged the petitioning process and we are discussing with the candidate other areas where we may be helpful. The taskforce is also working with "Grassroots New Yorkers for Bush-Cheney 2004" and in this context we intend to explore the feasibility of Ms. Morrissey's campaign spearheading a grassroots Congressional initiative to provide local political legs for President Bush."

Vincent Burton, Political Coordinator for Grassroots New Yorker for Bush-Cheney said, "A GOP primary election battle for the Congressional nomination is a healthy political process. Those of us that understand the importance of maximum feasible political participation of the black community in the elective process welcome it. Generating a grassroots GOP groundswell will go a long way toward holding both political parties accountable." In 1984, Vincent Burton, Chairman of Voters Anonymous, was a statewide coordinator of the Reagan-Bush re-election effort and is credited with making a significant contribution to President Reagan's landslide New York victory.

Heretofore, local Republican County leadership reached out to black Democrats, as opposed to building a viable, organic black Republican leadership. This longstanding practice has undermined growth of the GOP on one hand, and marginalized the masses of black Democrats with a ruling political elite on the other. The new leadership in the New York Republican Party County Committee is an encouraging sign, along with others. But some are posing the question, "Where is the political beef?" The problem of poor and inept leadership at the district level has reached a critical mass, as the official black GOP leadership has nothing of substance at the community level that can speak for them.

Another press release was published on the same web site, "Morrisey Sues New York County GOP Officials and Others" by Vincent Burton.

Keisha C. Morrissey, the Republican Party candidate in 2002 and 2003 against incumbent Democrats Assemblyman Keith Wright and City Councilman Bill Perkins respectively, filed a law suit in New York State Supreme Court Friday August 27, 2004, for damages against some officials of the New York Republican County Committee and others.

The suit seeks $500,000.00 in damages based on allegations of sexual harassment, threats of physical harm, political sabotage, political coersion, and conspiracy to deny her the Republican Party designation for Congress in Harlem's 15th Congressional District.

The officials of the New York Republican County Committee are Marcus Cederqvist, Executive Director, and District Leaders Ronald Perry, Will Brown Jr. and Ruby Wright. Other named defendants are Claude Sharrieff, Thomas Kent, Anthony Kamose, Robert Hornack, Harold (Mawu) Straker. and Richard Scott, among others.

Vincent Burton, leader of the activist wing of the GOP, said, "The fact that all of these politically well placed, grown men would gang up on a young sister is an odious political machination. I am compelled to support her efforts to achieve legal and political justice despite the fact that plantation politics continues to manage the county GOP. They cannot hurt me because I have already been blacklisted by the leaders of the local political plantation system."

"White political masters and House Negroes have conspired to deny Keisha C. Morrissey the Republican Party designation to run for the House of Representatives in the 15th Congressional District. The political conspirators were not able to get a Republican candidate to be their political tool, therefore, they drafted Mr. Kenneth Jefferson, a.k.a. Abdul Salaam, a Democrat and political neophyte, to circumvent Ms. Morrissey."

He added, "The stop-Morrissey political conspiracy is the latest chapter in a book of political deceptions and dirty tricks that have served to compromise the local Republican Party infrastructure and that have seeded black electoral politics to the Democratic Party. As a consequence of the Republican and Democratic strange bed-fellow political relationship, the local Republican Party has melted down. It has no identity in New York City politics and does not present a viable alternative to the black Democrat elected leadership."

"As a practical and political matter of fact, should Ms. Morrissey have been successful in getting the party designation it would have been the first time that a Republican got the Republican Party's designation for the coveted 15th Congressional District in decades. Although black Republicans continue to campaign for the State legislature and City Council against incumbent Democrats, black Republican candidates that challenge Democrat incumbents are obliged not to run a serious campaign or run the risk of being blacklisted by the GOP political plantation system."

The Defendants in Ms. Morrissey's law suit have apparently accomplished their ultimate and longstanding political objectives.

That is to insure that there is no emerging electoral competition against local Democrat incumbents, to make sure that there is no Republican Party primary election, and to eliminate any opportunity for the emergence of organic local leadership, by any means necessary.

A source close to Jefferson, the Democrat that received the Republican Party designation in the 15th CD said, "Kenneth Jefferson may have his own baggage, as he was forced to resign from a lucrative Wall Street position under a cloud of SEC investigation. A Congressional race may shed light in sensitive areas that generate political heat," the source said.

Vincent Burton, a coordinator of Grassroots New Yorkers for Bush-Cheney said, "the way political business is done in New York City is an embarrassment to the Republican Party and is a detriment to achieving political empowerment in the black community. While black politics and activism has been relegated to the Democratic Party, all other political minorities are exercising strategic electoral politics and have effectively eclipsed the black community in terms of political influence and power.

Ironically, it is the black political leadership that continues to perpetuate the political plantation system on both sides of the aisle, Democrat and Republican.

"We have a short- and long-range political, legal, and public-relations strategy to break the chains of plantation politics and move the black community to political independence and hardball power politics. The House Negroes, white masters, and undercover political ventriloquists have exposed themselves and will be vanquished by the light of a new political day.

If the political truth be told and the black electorate is provided with the critical information necessary to achieve black political power, 30 percent of the black community will vote for President Bush and the Republican Party. A press conference in front of the New York Republican County Committee offices is being planned." Burton said.

Keisha Morrissey said, "A Democratic elected official approached me the other day and advised me that there is considerable support for me, should I switch to the Democratic Party and run for district leader in opposition to the current leader who is at political odds with the black Democratic leadership."

Darryl Brown was inspired at the Saturday session. He said, "Sister Keisha's got a lot of heart. Most dudes would put their tail between their legs and disappear. You never see them again unless you bump into them somewhere. But it escapes me as to why the party didn't support a primary election to decide the question of the nominee. An election primary is a healthy process for the party."

Alton Chase interjected, "Brother D., their bottom line is to avoid a party primary at all costs. Once there is a Republican Party primary in Harlem, the powers that be will begin to lose control because they will not be able to manipulate people and the process. The real political power is vested in an elected district leadership, so both parties play it close to the vest in all situations. But, I'm down with the sister all the way."

"Well," I said, "the young sister is strong, and I believe that we can generate a critical mass of strong young people to change the political paradigm; Keisha, Conrad, and others prove the point. We have to make sure that we have the political database accessible in order that they can be adequately informed and oriented to the electoral process. In addition to the data, we need to concentrate on a comprehensive media distribution system presented by digital and web-based technology.

Having said that, you will be pleased to know that I have completed a comprehensive historical political overview. It is entitled *Race Politics in Transition,* and I want your feedback after you review it. This piece goes a long way to complete the data base required to launch a third millennium black political power movement."

RACE POLITICS IN TRANSITION
Black, Tan, and Lily-White
By Vincent Burton

PREFACE

The path to freedom, justice, and equality for African Americans has had no single pattern or design. The political direction of the black community has taken many forms and shapes during the nineteenth and twentieth centuries. With the backdrop of history, one can say without contradiction that African inhabitants of America have explored virtually all possible avenues in pursuit of their freedom. These different approaches have advanced the black political struggle in America and have indeed advanced the idea of America. The call for freedom has been a constant refrain in the annals of African American history. The turf has been treacherous and the trek bloody and hazardous, but African Americans have persisted and kept their eye on the prize. The journey has been both rewarding and disappointing, exalting and disgusting, joyous and painful, as well as redemptive. Mostly it has been a journey of super human proportions. Yet, there is much work still to be done that presents challenges to us all as we enter the first decade of the twenty-first century.

The Democratic and Republican Parties have not been sufficiently analyzed and studied, in a comprehensive and systematic way relative to the African American political struggle for freedom in this country. Party politics in America, vis-à-vis the Democratic and Republican Parties, have facilitated the theater environment in which the political aspirations of African Americans are acted out since the Civil War. But the complexities and sophistication of the electoral process apparently continues to baffle the African American community at large.

Despite African American longevity in America, and the numerical advantage as compared to other ethnic community groupings, black Americans remain the weakest in terms of political power and leverage. This work represents a pioneering effort to shed some light on the history and development of party politics, in the context of the African American pursuit of freedom, justice and equality.

Race has been a principle driving force of American politics ever since African slavery was introduced to the fledgling British colony. Following the Civil War and Emancipation, racial prejudice against black Americans was the central thematic and philosophical construct of the new civil society concerning political, economic and social opportunities. The advent and nature of party politics crystallized and codified racial dichotomies (black and white) in the framework of Democrats and Republicans. At that time, the Democratic (white) Party and the Republican (black) Party fundamental racial divide was further complicated by the advent of "Black, Tan, and Lily White-ism," which persists in today's electoral strategy and politics.

It is common knowledge that African Americans are overwhelmingly affiliated with the Democratic Party, while the Republican Party is primarily composed of white folks and so-called "uncle" and "aunt" stereotype appellations are attributed to the few blacks who are affiliated with the Republican Party. Interestingly enough, the racial profile of the Democratic and Republican Parties during the years of federal Reconstruction (following the Civil War) was reversed. Originally blacks predominated the Republican Party while the Democratic Party was in fact "Lily-White."

The process that reversed the wholesale participation of African Americans from the Republican Party in the nineteenth century to the Democratic Party in the twentieth century was accompanied by unprecedented achievements in civil rights and individual accomplishment respectively. Yet, sustained political power and economic influence continues to elude the African American community at large. History records the political machinations and contrived ideas of racial superiority and inferiority as contributing factors to the pathological political and economic poverty that plagues black America. Sophisticated and malignant political concepts and ideas are skillfully woven into the general political discourse perpetuating a popular sense of entitlement and white political paternalism, at best. At worst, it is an under current of White Supremacy that continues to drive the racial and political paradigm.

On the other hand, black leadership may be the greatest impediment to improving the lot for the majority of black folk. Without question, the African American community must necessarily do politics in a more sophisticated and long-range way in order to improve the political power equation for moving forward. Ultimately, affirmative action for black Americans in the twenty-first century will be based on the actions of the first person singular, the black community itself. Nevertheless, there are still many external elements and factors that exacerbate this complex and comprehensive challenge including immigration, and the need to recast the notion of multi-racialism and the political juxtaposition of racial minorities. Politics in America is driven by a juxtaposition of racial minorities.

In this the third millennium of the modern era, we observe that the theological proposition of one human family of mankind is sustained by recent scientific discovery. Research has discovered a mitochondria DNA linking everyone currently on the planet to a woman born in east Africa. Ultimately this "new" scientific finding will trickle down and find its way into the political dialogue, and into institutions of learning as well as the public and private discourse. No, doubt this has already begun. Hence, the idea and propaganda that black folks in general are an inferior race as distinguished from the white race and others, is being exposed as a nefarious fraud that continues under its own inertia.

Indeed, the racial dichotomy and white supremacy lie was calculated to facilitate and enable slavery as well as economic, social, cultural and political exploitation. The racial paradigm is institutionalized, systematic, pervasive and divergent. According to the Kerner Commission Report on Civil Disorders of 1968, authorized by President Lyndon B. Johnson, "America was moving toward two separate societies, one black and the other white." It is worthy to note that the recommendations of the Kerner Commission Report were never implemented.

In addition, a cursory observation of immigration patterns indicates that African Americans are a diminishing element among black folks currently in America. The number of black people from continental Africa, South America and the Caribbean has nearly eclipsed black Americans born before 1980. The broad ethnic diversity among black folks currently in America will increasingly challenge the conventional political wisdom that has heretofore managed the political progress and dialogue of the African American community.

On one hand, emerging generations of African Americans are apparently unimpressed and uninspired by the civil rights leadership and disillusioned with politically correct voting and the electoral process as compared to previous generations. On the other hand, the new black immigrant citizens have little perspective and affinity for how the African American political leadership does its local politics. Moreover, the new immigrants have no connection to the civil rights leadership and movement.

Apart from the political factors and the dynamic demographic shifts associated with the high levels of immigration, the popularity of minority group politics further complicates the sophisticated Machiavellian nature of the current political paradigm. In order to accommodate political juxtapositions of so-called minority groups (blacks, Hispanics, other ethnic minorities), the concept of political correctness was advanced. It is currently politically correct to refer to minority groups such as African Americans, Asians, South Americans, Caribbean Americans, African Nationals and the respective Spanish speaking ethnic groups as people of color. The concept of people of color (majority of the minority) is vogue in terms of political rhetoric and hyperbole, but the practical political proposition is a merging of minority groups. As a practical political matter, the political combination of minority groups and the umbrella phrase, people of color both, in effect, minimize and marginalize the political significance of black Americans and their vote.

While people of color may be politically correct terminology, the respective minority groups that come under this umbrella category were not determining factors in the nature and development of America's politics and the electoral process, vis-à-vis, the black and white race dichotomy. As a functional application of the politically correct phrase, "people of color," obscures the essential challenge facing the American political construct: the idea of racial inferiority. In fact, minority group political mergers reinforce a multi-racial hoax with sophisticated political language that seems stylish, but is misleading at best. Although the discovery of modern science has sustained the single human race theory, apparently very few are listening.

African Americans were an appropriate description of the black population in America during the founding of America and the designing of its political and electoral system. However, the black population in America today cannot be accurately characterized by the term African American. The black population in America today can be more accurately described, segmented and organized in the context of first language, e.g., black Americans that speak English, Spanish, French and other languages. Skin color or phenotype and multi-racial terms are over used and outdated political distinctions. Perhaps a more accurate umbrella characterization of the diverse population of black folks currently in America is New World Africans.

The way in which black Americans are organized politically is a critical factor in achieving sustainable political power. In the nineteenth and twentieth centuries respectively, black Americans won their civil rights despite overwhelming odds. These unprecedented victories were not fully realized and sustained. Consequently, the black community at large remains in political bondage. Central to the reoccurring political dilemma plaguing black political and economic empowerment is how the black community applies the political and electoral process.

One salient point can be gleaned from an examination of the rich and colorful history of the black community's participation in the Democrat and Republican Parties. That is the fact that in both of the victorious civil rights movements, black participation was essentially organized and defined by white folks, and only a select few, self-serving blacks had limited access.

This work will examine, in a cursory way, the chain of events that brought about the transition of black American party politics from the Republican to Democratic Parties during the period following Reconstruction to the present time. The intent of this examination is to develop a context and frame of reference from which to assess and synthesize a constructive political course of action. The goal is to maximize the necessary participation of the black community in the political and elective process, and raise the level of voter sophistication in order to achieve sustainable political and economic advancement. To achieve this goal we will explore useful, relative facts and opinions in this chronology.

INTRODUCTION

The intensity and passion associated with contemporary history and the Democratic Party concerning the modern civil rights era has overshadowed the dynamic legacy of the Republican Party in the African American political history of the nineteenth century. Without question, the victorious modern civil rights movement (from 1950-1980) was the dominant political and social factor that impacted African American history in the twentieth century. Paradoxically, despite the cumulative advances in civil rights during the nineteenth and twentieth centuries, African Americans continue to remain challenged by virtually the same issues in this, the first decade of the twenty-first century. A critical and comparative analysis of nineteenth and twentieth Centuries political, social, and economic history must be the basis for a new strategy of achieving sustained development for moving forward.

The Democratic Party was the dominant political force in the black community during the modern civil rights era and continues to be. Hence, the contemporary political and social victories characterized as civil rights (integration, voting rights, affirmative action, equal employment opportunities, etc.) are ascribed to the Democratic Party and deservedly so. As a consequence of sixty odd years of successful civil rights and progressive politics, an emotional connection has apparently developed between African Americans and the Democratic Party in terms of political best friends. The extent of the political friendship is demonstrated in the voting pattern of the black American community for the Democratic Party irrespective of the quality or ethnicity of the candidate. In New York, for example, it is not uncommon for the Democratic candidate to receive more than ninety percent of the black vote. Consequently, in some quarters, it is argued that the relationship between black Americans and the Democratic Party is a political kinship. As such many black Americans register and vote the Democratic line by way of family tradition and group habit.

History informs us that politics is a competitive hardball power process that consists of permanent interests only and no permanent best friends or enemies.

As such, political parties are vehicles that animate the electoral process and facilitate progress from point A to point B. During the civil rights political movement of the nineteenth century, African Americans made unprecedented advancements by way of the Republican Party vehicle. History also records the white backlash that required a second civil rights movement in the twentieth century.

The second (modern) civil rights movement was successfully under taken in the framework of the Democratic Party political vehicle. African Americans were politically inspired and trained by the progressive and liberal wing of the Democratic Party to infiltrate the party en mass in order to wrestle control from the White Supremacist. The mass infiltration of the Democratic Party in the South by African Americans and progressive whites became popularly referred to as the integration and civil rights movement. African Americans and the progressive and liberal wing of the Democratic Party together achieved substantial success in the modern civil rights era. Concomitantly, the White Supremacist elements of the party made a strategic political migration to the Republican Party.

There are distinct signs of a repetition of history for black America, and the need for another political movement. This is notwithstanding the well documented statutory advances and legislative victories associated with civil rights gains in the nineteenth and twentieth centuries. Whether African Americans will finally overcome in the twentieth century remains to be seen, but the situation is obviously more complex and sophisticated than initially envisaged. Moreover, the role-players and stakeholders are more diverse and disassociated. For starters, the African American community is no longer able to boast about the numerical advantage (among minorities) that was touted in previous generations. The Hispanic community may have already surpassed African Americans in numerical strength. In addition, African Americans may very well be a minority among blacks in America.

In order to get a comprehensive understanding of the current political situation as it relates to the black American community, we must analyze the modern civil rights twentieth century movement in comparison to the former nineteenth century civil rights movement. In the historical back drop of a comparative education and analysis of the two great African American civil rights movements, a central question emerges as to who won the Civil War, the North or the South. The answer to this compelling question is not discernable in the annals of popular American history and mythology. As a practical matter, the touted victory of the Northern Union forces over the Southern Confederate forces may have veiled the victory of the South on the political ground.

National politics concerning both the Democratic and Republican Parties are currently based on a Southern Strategy. As a practical political matter the term Southern Strategy is a euphemism for targeting white voters. Whether referring to Reagan Republicans or Clinton Democrats, the code is white voters as the target group. Black voters, as a serious target group and political entity, remain unmentioned and invisible. In the context of the politically correct people of color or racial minority, black folk seem to fit just fine.

The ultimate eradication of the political, economic, and social poverty that continues to beset black Americans (new and old), is in the hands of black American citizens. Although, many black folk believe that undeserved suffering is redemptive and the ultimate victory of black Americans is inevitable. Much of this belief is based on the messianic expectation of a Savior, while minimizing the imperative of personal responsibility. This is unfortunate. The perspective history that follows will provide the basis for an informed, sophisticated, motivated and organized black American electorate to sustain the victories of the twenty-first century and for centuries to come. The intent of this work is to stimulate and inspire the process of inquiry, research, education and application to achieve sustained victory for the future.

CHAPTER ONE
SOUTHERN PARTY POLITICS

The foundation of the early Republican Party in the South was a political coalition of the following groups: scalawags or white southerners who became Republicans during Reconstruction, carpetbaggers or northern politicians and adventurers who went south after the war and sooner or later became active in politics as Republicans and newly freed African American men. This fragile political coalition was linked together by the Reconstruction Act of 1867. With this act, the Congressional Radicals took over the reconstruction of the South from President Andrew Johnson and reorganized the South into military districts, thereby giving impetus and political power to the Republican Party sympathizers and supporters.

Prior to the Military Reconstruction Act, the three components of the coalition existed as distinct and separate political entities. The blacks, with no political power, were organized into the Equal Rights Leagues and other similar abolitionist associations. The carpetbaggers remained separate and distinct prior to this Act because of their diverse interests and their personal reasons for adopting the South as their new home. Some carpetbaggers pursued their business endeavors and dreams, while others sought out opportunity and personal advancement. Still others followed their humanitarian impulses, such as equal civil and political rights for all.

The final element of the dubious coalition, the scalawags were also loosely organized and separate from other Republican groups in southern society. This disorganization was due in part to the fact that the scalawags were made up primarily of four separate and distinct elements in Southern society. One group was the Unionists, southerners who had supported the Union cause before the war and who suffered during the period that secessionists were in power. Unionists wanted to retaliate by participating in government. Another scalawag faction were the poor whites, primarily farmers who resided in the upland and hill country and harbored a natural animosity for the Delta farmer and planter class. "The cleavage between 'the planters of the Delta and the rednecks of the hill' as V. O. Key has stated, "has persisted for half a century, and even yet appears from time to time." A third source of scalawag strength came from those southerners engaged in business enterprises and those living in regions which were rich in natural resources and industrial potential.

The last group of scalawag supporters were the upper-class southerners who had supported the Whig Party before the Civil War. This group, being more affluent and socially secure individuals in southern society, saw the Republican Party as heir apparent to the Whig tradition.

It was questionable from the beginning how long such a convenient coalition could hold together. Therefore, from the outset, a major disruptive factor was present. Among two of the groups comprising the scalawags there were negative feelings about African Americans. "A very large proportion of the Unionist scalawag element had little enthusiasm for one aspect of the radical program: the granting of equal civil and political rights to the Negroes," says author Hanes Walton, Jr. Among the poor whites and yeoman farmers, race prejudice was very intense. "As men of low status and income they were keenly aware that the Negroes were potential social and economic competitors." Race prejudice was not the central focus of the carpetbaggers and the Whig scalawag element. "They too believed in white supremacy, but they seldom made a crusade to keep Negroes a subordinate caste the central purpose of their lives."

At the beginning, the anti-African American feelings and prejudices were submerged in order to further the Republican organization and its promise. But when competition and pressure arose and were applied, the fragile coalition very quickly came apart at the seams. The submerged and repressed race feelings immediately surfaced. As the Republican Party continued in the South, more and more stress was placed on it, and the three major factors of the coalition came apart. These factors were: inter-party factionalism, violence, fraud, and intimidation by Democrats, and Republican presidential policies toward the southern party after Reconstruction

Inter-Party Factionalism

"Every coalition," argues Professor William Riker, "has internal conflicts over the discussion of spoils." Almost from the inception, the Republican Party's coalition in the South began to be undermined by internal rivalry over the distribution of party favors and patronage. "When pressure from an opposing coalition is great, so great in fact that the opposition may win and thereby deprive the coalition of any spoils to distribute, these internal conflicts are minimized. But when pressure from the outside diminishes, there is less urging to settle the internal conflict amicably." This was definitely the case with the Republican coalition in the South. This is because there was little competition from the Democrats, who were scattered, divided, and disorganized. Moreover, the Military Reconstruction Act of 1867 enabled the new military government to disenfranchise most of the Democratic supporters.

Hence, with little outside competition, the carpetbaggers and scalawags battled each other for positions and other fruits of the Republican Party victories. In South Carolina, a feud broke out between the two groups when an honest, and conscientious carpetbagger replaced a corrupt scalawag governor. In Georgia, the scalawag governor, Joseph E. Brown, who used his office to become president of a steamship company, a railroad company, a coal company, and an iron company, antagonized both groups who tried to dislodge him and his supporters from the helm of the party in the state. In Mississippi, James Alcorn, a scalawag who became the first Republican governor of the state, collaborated with the Whigs and tried to give them control of the party. This action drew the wrath of other scalawags and carpetbaggers who combined to put a carpetbagger governor in office in 1873. In Alabama, upland or (hill) whites fought the Whigs and blacks for property in the rich delta planter region of the state, and still, in Louisiana the pro-Grants and anti-Grants fought each other.

In other states, rival Republican business groups fought each other for legislative favors, while rival Republican reform groups sought to destroy each other over desired polices and programs. Factionalism also arose because of rivalry between two prominent political leaders who sought to gain control of the party apparatus. Last but not least, factional discontent emerged as blacks began to assume more and more political offices. This increase in black politicians would cause party leaders to conspire to limit or fix the number of offices blacks could hold or the type that they could aspire to. When blacks didn't accept the quotas set by whites, further trouble accrued within the party apparatus.

Inter-party fights and divisions resulting from these factors greatly strained the southern Republican political coalition and dissipated much of the party's strength. But when the National Republican Party split during the 1872 election between the Stalwarts and Liberal Republicans and decreased the patronage which the party could disperse, the inter-party rivalry intensified over the meager spoils and diminishing fruits of victory. However, inter party competition was not the only factor that wrecked the party's fragile coalition. Another factor which wrecked the coalition was the resurgence of the Democratic Party.

Democratic Violence, Fraud and Intimidation

Southern Democrats began to regain their strength in 1870 when the Republicans lost 41 seats in the House of Representatives and 6 in the U.S. Senate thereby, losing partial control of Congress. In 1872, Congress, under pressure from the Liberal Republicans, passed a general Amnesty Act that finally removed the political restrictions upon most of the South's pre-war leadership and restored the right-of-office holding to the vast majority who had been disqualified under the provisions of the fourteenth amendment. Once these individuals began to assume power, they sought to overthrow the Republican coalition. In fact, they applied pressure to each segment of the coalition as well as upon the entire party.

Democratic Klansmen "broke up Republican meetings, threatened radical leaders, whipped Negro militia men, and drove Negroes away from the polls," says Hanes Walton, Jr. Democratic terrorism became the order of the day and was perpetuated on black and white Republicans alike. The pattern of violence that conservative Democrats developed became generally known as the Mississippi Plan or sometimes as the shotgun policy. The Mississippi state election of 1875, for example, readily shows how systematic force and terror were used to capture political office. On Election Day, blacks either hid in the swamps, stayed in their cabins or showed up at the polls only for Democratic ballots. Those who were brave enough to bring Republican ballots to polling places were fired upon, driven away, misled, or frequently manipulated so that their ballots didn't count.

Violence was not the only tool. Economic coercion was also employed against black and white Republicans. For instance, in Henry County, Alabama, landlords required black laborers to sign political contracts before they could acquire a job. This contract stated, that "said laborers shall not attach themselves, belong to, or in anyway perform any of the obligations required of what is known as the 'Loyal League of Society,' or attend elections or political meetings without the consent of their employer," according to author Hanes Walton Jr. In short, to vote meant the loss of a job, medical aid, credit, food, supplies, and materials.

Beyond violence and economic coercion loomed fraud and manipulation. According to social historian Lerone Bennett, "Ballot box manipulation

318

reached an artistic height. Polling places were located in bayous, on islands, in barns, and in fodder houses." This still wasn't all. The Mississippi Plan had some additional techniques for use against white Republicans. "White Republicans were ostracized. Their children were hounded in school. Their wives were cut to the quick at church," says Walton, Jr. The effect of these tactics was that the fragile political coalition within the Republican Party began to disintegrate and white Republican southerners started to switch back to the Democratic Party.

"Many of the parting scenes," states John Lynch, a black politician in Mississippi during reconstruction "that took place between the Colored men and the whites who decided to return to the fold of the Democrats were both affecting and pathetic in the extreme." Describing one such parting, Lynch says that the black president of the local Republican club, Sam Henry, was urging white ex-Confederate, Colonel James Lusk, to stay within the party ranks for the benefit of all. The following is an excerpt from John Lynch:

> "Oh! No, Colonel" Henry cried, "I beg of you do not leave us. If you leave us, hundreds of others will be sure to follow your lead. We will thus be left without solid and substantial friends. I admit that your party affiliation is optional. With me it is different. I must remain a Republican whether I want to or not. I plead with you, do not go."
>
> "The statement you made, Henry, that party affiliation with me is optional," the Colonel answered, "is presumed to be true but, in fact, it is not. No white man can live in the South in the future and act with any other than the Democratic Party unless he is willing and prepared to live a life of social isolation and remain in political oblivion. Besides, I have two grown sons. There is no doubt a bright, brilliant, and successful future is before them if they are Democrats; otherwise, not. If I remain in the Republican Party, which can hereafter exist in the South only in name, I will thereby retard, if not more, and possibly destroy their future prospects. Then, you must remember that a man's first duty is to his family. My daughters are the pride of my home. I cannot afford to have them suffer the humiliating emergencies of the social ostracism to which they may be subjected if I remain in the Republican Party."
>
> "The die is cast," Lusk insisted. "I must yield to the inevitable and surrender my convictions upon the altar of my family's good, the outgrowth of circumstances and conditions which I am powerless to prevent and cannot control. Henceforth, I must act with the Democratic Party or make myself a martyr; and I do not feel that there is enough at stake to justify me in making such a fearful sacrifice as that."

Thus, Lusk bade Henry and the Republicans farewell and switched to the Democrats. And whites all over the South, like Lusk, crossed over Jordan. In state after state the Democrats redeemed the state for and in the name of White Supremacy. Tennessee, Virginia, Georgia, and North Carolina were redeemed by 1871, and the remaining seven southern states fell to the systematic pattern of violence, fraud, intimidation, and social ostracism before 1876. Walton, Jr. wrote,

> *Black Republicans and their allies put up a good fight, but their resources were meager. White Democrats controlled the money, the land, and the credit facilities. The fragile Republican political coalition collapsed under systematic and sustained Democratic terrorism and soon the southern Republican Party became composed of only faithful, loyal and sincere Colored men who remained Republicans from necessity as well as from choice, and a few white men, who were Republicans from principle and conviction, and who were willing to incur the odium, run the risks, and pay the penalty that every white Republican who had the courage of his convictions must then pay.*

As the Republican coalition of carpetbaggers, scalawags, and freedmen deteriorated under the resurgence of the Democrats, a realignment took place. The new Republican coalition, which emerged in each state as Democratic redemption took place, became one primarily of black and white federal office holders and seekers. This new or second political coalition was well underway by 1877, after the disputed election had finally enabled the Democrats to redeem the last remaining states of South Carolina, Florida and Louisiana. Whites that remained in the party after the onset of the Democratic restoration tactic were those who had gained sufficient rewards or had been promised that rewards would be shortly forthcoming. Without rewards such as federal patronage (in terms of office and federal contracts, subsidies, loans, or appointments), whites had little reason to continue to associate with blacks in the face of nearly overwhelming opposition from the rest of the white community. However, even this second southern Republican coalition was short lived. It came under renewed attack by the Democrats and by various Republican Presidents from 1877 until three decades into the twentieth century.

The Republican political coalition in the South changed during Reconstruction because of resurgent Democratic power players. The coalition underwent even greater change after Reconstruction due to the southern Republican policies of Hayes, Garfield, Arthur, and Harrison. While each President had a different southern policy, the final effect of each was the subordination of blacks and an appeal to southern whites.

Hayes' policy was to woo southern Whites, while Garfield's policy was one of education and limited support to independence. Arthur's policy was of total support for the independents. Harrison's policy was to seek to organize a Southern Republican Party on the basis of protection. This tended to elevate the remaining whites in the Republican Party to positions of dominance and power. In so doing, Harrison's policy completely polarized the organization in the South. This trend toward polarization actually began with Hayes, and neared culmination under Harrison, who recognized several Lily-White Republican organizations in the South, notably in South Carolina, Alabama, and Louisiana.

In several other southern states (where independent movement was fairly effective and had achieved some small measure of success), Harrison gave the Lily-Whites the assent to head up his new Republicans. In all, Harrison's policy was a logical conclusion to those of Hayes, Garfield and Arthur. Together, their policies had built a new southern Republican Party that was not heavily dependent on blacks. To build such a party, top organizational and leadership positions had to be given to whites to attract them to the organization. These new white Republicans, having to compete effectively with the Democratic Party (known to be the white man's party), felt it necessary to purge their party of its black supporters and leaders. This move, however, was only one aspect of the larger trend that had been emerging in the South: the demand for white supremacy in all areas, and the insistence that politics was white men's business.

The ideology of white supremacy had permeated southern society and any organization that did not uphold this principle could not be effectively supported by local whites. The emergence of a Lily-White Republican Party in the South resulted, therefore, not just from Republican Presidential policies, but also due to the inherent demands and the customs of southern lifestyles. It was, in a word, inevitable.

Black and Tan Republicanism was born of two similar forces. First, were the white supremacy principles and policies, and the violent acts of terrorism from the Democratic Party. This precluded any significant shifts by blacks into the Democratic ranks. Blacks, even if they had accepted White Supremacy, could not switch in mass because the Democrats were determined to remove blacks from the political arena by whatever means available.

Secondly, the Republican Party, because of its actions from the Civil War to the end of Reconstruction, had tied both southern and northern blacks to itself. Their Civil Rights programs, the Emancipation Proclamation, and the Reconstruction Act, had drawn the black man deeper into the party ranks even the Republicans new shift in the South didn't, comparatively speaking, evoke as much black criticism from the black community. After Reconstruction, black criticism of the Republican Party was kept at a minimum through the judicious use of patronage and the appointing of black leaders.

Thus, for a variety of reasons, the southern Republican Party had begun to polarize itself on the basis of race, white and black. When McKinley came to power in 1896 the Republican Party had two clearly identifiable factions: the Lily-White, and the Black and Tan. The Black and Tan faction had a rapidly dwindling number of voters.

In 1890, Mississippi called a constitutional convention to rewrite the constitution that had been drawn up under the Reconstruction Acts and had given blacks the right to vote. The new constitution of 1890 stripped blacks of their right to vote with numerous legal devices ranging from grandfather clauses to reading and interpretation tests. Mississippi's new constitution, in effect, legally barred blacks from the polls. The only black delegate to the convention, Isaiah T. Montgomery, a wealthy and conservative businessman, greatly approved of the new constitution's elimination of black voters on the basis of lack of education and property ownership.

The most significant impact of the Mississippi Plan was that it became the American way in the South. State after state followed Mississippi's lead in disenfranchising blacks on one ground or another. During the ten years or more of this process, black voting in the South declined appreciably. In fact, each year after the 1890s the Black and Tan faction became a less and less viable vote getting organization. It became more of an assembly of cliques of office holders, and patronage seekers. The Black and Tans became small, self-seeking groups who looked to Washington, D.C. for support rather than to their own communities. The era of disenfranchisement effectively destroyed their local bases of community support.

President McKinley continued the Harrison policy of supporting the Lily-Whites and appointing a few blacks to federal office, but instituted a different policy at National Republican Conventions. This dualism in McKinley's southern policy was helped by two factors. One, Booker T. Washington's Atlanta Exposition speeches in 1895, in which he urged blacks to drop their interest in politics and seek to accommodate to the white man's politics helped to perpetuate segregation and limited demands from the black community for equal treatment. In addition, a Supreme Court decision in 1896 declared separate but equal to be constitutional thus legally sanctioning dualism in American life. This decision, coming prior to McKinley's nomination, provided obvious justification for his support of the separate Republican factions. These two factions came to play a major role in the making of the national convention strategy. McKinley's dual strategy would remain a policy at least until 1932.

President McKinley's new policy toward the southern Republican Party emerged during the 1892 Republican National Convention (RNC). At this time, he was running for the Republican Presidential nomination. At this convention, he didn't receive enough convention votes to win, but it became evident to him and his political manager, Mark Hanna, a millionaire industrialist, that the two Republican factions which had begun their seating challenges at the national convention could be useful in securing his nomination. Just prior to the 1896 RNC, Hanna made a tour of the South, seeking to commit one of the factions in each of the southern states to his candidate at the national convention. To get a faction committed, money and promises of patronage were offered. This tactic succeeded. McKinley was nominated on the first ballot in 1896.

At the convention were nine black delegates from six southern states. They were crucial in gaining McKinley the nomination. Recognizing the "crucial support of Negro delegates in the national nominating convention," McKinley adopted a policy of playing off one faction against the other in order to secure his next Presidential nomination. McKinley's southern Republican policy in this respect, maintained the two distinct factions, especially the Black and Tan, even when they had no vote value. This was continued by each Republican President that followed until Hoover's nomination in 1932. After 1932, Hoover capitulated entirely to the Lily-White faction and did all he could to destroy the federal basis of support from the Black and Tans. While Black and Tan-ism finally died shortly after Hoover's new policy change, one or two factions, like that of old tireless Joe Tolbert from South Carolina, continued until 1956.

President McKinley and subsequent Republican Presidents continued the policy of bi-factional, or dual Republican organizations, in the South because of the possible usefulness of one or the other, (Black and Tan or Lily-White), at the national nominating conventions. Either one faction or the other could be persuaded by money or patronage, to support a particular Presidential candidate for the nomination. This support became significant when there were numerous contenders for the party's nomination. Such prospective candidates (who could arrive with assurances that a certain number of delegates would back him) had half the game, if not all, won. The scramble for convention delegates became the primary reason that the Black and Tan faction remained a force, even when they had no possibilities of capturing state voters to the Republican organization. Southern Republicans became Presidential Republicans, useful primarily at the national conventions. For their cooperation, the rewards were indeed significant: numerous federal posts ranging from postmaster ships to consul posts, and ambassadorships with prestige and large salaries. For these rewards the two factions struggled with each other. They struggled for supremacy in their respective states, recognition by the national party and the president, and control of the patronage for the entire state.

CHAPTER TWO
STATE AND LOCAL ORGANIZATIONS

Following the passage of the Fifteenth Amendment in 1870, anti-slavery societies disbanded. Many of the old Radical Republicans and abolitionists had passed on, and efforts on behalf of the black man slackened as interest began to fade. The crusade was essentially over. "Regarding the ballot as a panacea," says Professor Gillette, "Whites could, in good conscience, leave blacks alone now because blacks could protect themselves with the ballot and without help of government." But the job was far from over because, while Radical Republicans and abolitionists were dismantling their battle equipment and demobilizing the political forces, the whites of the South were reorganizing, developing strategies and structuring a crusade to rid themselves of nigger domination. As one group of troops marched home feeling that the war had been won and victory secured, another group was marching to battle. "The plan reduced Negroes to political impotence. How? By the boldest and most ruthless political operations in American history. By stealth and murder, by economic intimidation and political assassination, by whippings and maiming, cuttings and shootings, by the knife, by the rope, by the whip. By the political use of terror. By fear," says author Hanes Walton Jr.

As these activities were carried on underground, above ground the Democratic Party attempted to control the votes of the former slaves. The plan and organization succeeded. "White rule was restored in Tennessee in 1869, in Virginia, North Carolina, and Georgia in 1870, in Alabama, Arkansas, and Texas in 1874, and in Mississippi in 1875. Thus, only South Carolina, Louisiana, and Florida remained to be redeemed by 1876," said Hanes Walton, Jr. Black Reconstruction was on its way to ending and black allegiance to the Republican Party was beginning to enter an era of profound reassessment as the Democrats continued their battle against the black voter. Since the National Republican Party had turned its attention to other issues in society, the task of furthering black rights fell to the state Republican Parties, which were not equipped to accept the mantle.

The term "Lily-White" Republican was coined in Texas by a black Republican leader, Norris Wright Cuney, after a riot occurred at the state Republican Convention on September 20, 1888. The riot grew out of a clash between black and white Republicans when the latter group attempted to wrest control of the party organization from a black Cuney. In addition to the fight for party control, there was also fighting between the colored and white factions over placing a ticket in the field.

The use and perpetuation of the phrase Black and Tan Republican can be linked to numerous southern newspapers. In Louisiana the term Black and Tan was applied to the regular state organizations after the Lily-White had withdrawn. "This name was applied to the group by newspapers and by general popular use and was never officially recognized by the regular organization itself," says author Hanes Walton Jr. Louisiana served as a model for other states. In state after state, whites withdrew from the regular party organization that was dominated by blacks and formed their own Lily-White clubs and groups. Once the Lily-White group had become a reality, the regular organization was then generally referred to by all the newspapers and public media as the Black and Tan group.

The term Lily-White referred not only to a political organization but also to its set of beliefs. This organization condemned and denounced the Negro in general and his participation in southern politics in particular. Lily-White Republicans upheld the idea of White Supremacy and the social system of segregation in the South.

Black and Tan-ism, on the other hand, endorsed black suffrage, black participation in politics, and black equality. As a newspaper euphemism, it also referred to the wide range of skin color and hues that exist within black groupings. Black and Tan Republicans not only didn't condone segregation, they protested it. The Black and Tans tried continuously to improve their lot and, from time to time, the poor conditions of the black community, too. However, their former role (improving their lot with better patronage, positions and larger salaries) became their chief concern as disenfranchisement removed more and more black voters from the political arena. In some localities, indeed, the Black and Tan organizations became merely self-seeking groups with no concern for the welfare of the black community. Because the Black and Tan leaders had no constituencies, like the Lily-Whites, they became primarily Presidential rather than local organized groupings. The local Republican electorate was not strong enough to enable them to win state offices. Although each group fused with either the Populists, Democrats, or Prohibitionists (in varying degree from state to state to win some election or other), neither group alone could attain enough votes for any significant state of local electoral victories.

In addition to the lack of a constituency, the self centered outlook of the Black and Tans was also fostered by the nature of politics itself. Politicians are generally more concerned with getting elected and re-elected than with the promotion of social, economical, and racial justice. The Black and Tans were politicians first and black second. The environmental and political circumstances of the South severely limited their social and racial consciousness. In a paradoxical way, however, racial and social consciousness did find expression at the state and national conventions.

In fighting each other for control of patronage and the right to be seated at the national conventions, both sides (Blacks and Tans and Lily-Whites) issued charges of racial discrimination and claimed that they had the backing of the entire black community. In these inter-party battles, racial discrimination and the needs of the black community were used by both groups to belittle or eliminate the positions of their opponents in the struggle for power. Out of these power struggles some small benefits would, with time accrue to the black community.

For instance, the Lily-White, in order to avoid the charges of racial discrimination from the national committee, solicited a small Negro membership but quite consistently with the avowed objectives of the Lily-Whites, the Colored members had no voice in the government of the organization," says, author Hanes Walton Jr.

The Black and Tan faction also had a mixed composition. Many whites were still remaining within it for reasons of ideology or ambition. In South Carolina, a white man, known as Tireless Joe Tolbert, led the Black and Tan faction for more than forty years. He and his black followers were either delegates or contestants for seats at every Republican National Convention from 1900 to 1956. In other states, black and white leadership alternated and there were some states where black leadership prevailed exclusively.

While some Black and Tan organizations had white leaders, the Lily-White organizations maintained a limited black membership. This was only to avoid charges of racial discrimination at the national convention, since such charges could hamper their efforts to get seated over the contesting Black and Tan delegation. Thus, they included blacks out of necessity. It must be noted though, that some blacks joined the Lily-White Republican organization, not out of fear but out of their basically conservative outlook: they accepted the tenets of white supremacy.

Despite their limited base and lack of constituency, despite their mixed racial composition, and despite their chances of achieving electoral victories within their respective states, blacks, Tans and Lily-Whites continually fought each other for recognition by the national committee. Each hoped to be recognized as the official party in their respective states as well as for control over state patronage. Each group employed a number of political techniques, ranging from electioneering and propaganda, legalism, and fists, to eliminate, suppress, or discredit its opponents.

CHAPTER THREE
GEORGIA

For nearly two years following the Civil War, "There was little discussion of party politics in Georgia." The impact of the war had been devastating and men and women were too "busy in the Herculean task of bringing order out of the chaos which surrounded them to spend very much time in discussing politics," according to Hanes Walton, Jr. President Johnson had appointed a provisional governor and numerous political leaders had not yet been pardoned. Thus, party lines did not develop immediately. During the last months of 1866 and all of 1867 however, political activity in the state was intense in anticipation of the emerging state Republican organization. Unionist elements of the state, anti-secessionists and Whigs, the Carpetbaggers, and the blacks began three separate paths towards political ascendancy, which culminated in the first Republican Party organization and state convention at Atlanta on July 4, 1867.

At first the southern element, i.e., the Unionists, Whigs, and anti-secessionists, began their own organization with the formation of a Union League. Blacks, on January 10, 1866, formed the Georgia Equal Rights Association. Carpetbaggers fused with one or the other of the two organizations depending upon their ideology and moral convictions. At first, each of these Republican Party- oriented groups in Georgia began going their own separate way.

The passage of the Military Reconstruction Act in February of 1867 brought these groups together into one political unit, the Republican Party. They united under a common banner because of the prospects of the upcoming election and constitutional conventions that were feasible as a result of the Reconstruction Acts. The promise of political rewards brought together this unwieldy and precarious coalition. The Republicans, during their first state convention in 1867, adopted platform planks that made it clear that the party would appeal to the Negroes and to the whites in North Georgia (hill whites) and in the Wire grass country (marshes) of South Georgia." With this "delicate alliance of

Negroes, yeomen, white farmers, and the few railroad and industrial promoters, the Republican Party was able to stay in power from 1867 until 1871 in Georgia.

During 1871, inter-party disputes badly divided and disorganized the party. There was antagonism between the carpetbaggers and the native whites, between native whites and blacks, as well as between office holders and office seekers. "The political activity of the Negro," claims Professor Olive Shadgett, "was a primary cause of splits and fractional fighting and of defection from the ranks." Many whites "who had aligned themselves with the Republican Party and acquiesced with the Reconstruction Acts, including the requirements of Negro suffrage, had never subscribed to the doctrine that this gave Negroes full political equality and the right to hold political office," he said. It was on this basis that white Republicans and Democrats came together in the Georgia House of Representatives, on September 3, 1868, to expel twenty-five of the twenty-nine black members. Later, they expelled two of the remaining four. However, all these black members were reinstated, with back pay, by the federal government in 1869.

Externally, the party was beset by charges of malfeasance and corruption in office, and the delicate coalition that was so vital to the party's success collapsed. The Democrats redeemed the state in 1872 and Democratic Governor, James M. Smith, was inaugurated on January 12 of that year. Ever since then, for a period of over one hundred and twenty-five years, Georgia has always had a Democratic governor. Although the Democrats installed a governor, the total redemption of the state didn't come in a single political campaign; it was a slow, torturous affair. Once the Democrats regained hegemony over the Republicans in the state, however, they didn't relinquish it. They made every effort, from 1872 on, to further suppress and weaken the Republicans.

With this white exodus, the Black and Tan faction became a reality. From 1872 until 1880, the party was like a pyramid with a few white leaders on the top in control and the masses of blacks at the base, furnishing the political muscle with small fragments of patronage being thrown their way. The arrangement was apparently so satisfying during this period that there was no clash between the two races within the party. This odd state of political affairs caused the leading Democratic newspaper in the state, the Atlanta Constitution, frequently to express surprise that blacks would submit to the control of the few whites that dominated the party. The paper took pains to point out in 1876 that there were many black men "of fine manner and more than ordinary education, mental powers of no mean merit," who deserved to lead the party organization. Under such Democratic chiding and prodding and with the emergence of new black leaders, blacks at the Republican state convention in 1880 took advantage of controversies among the few white leaders and seized control of the party machinery. This seizure caused a breach in party ranks and provoked proposals by several whites for a separate white Republican Party in Georgia.

The origin of the Black and Tan faction in Georgia can be dated from April 21, 1880, when the state party convention convened in Atlanta. J.E. Bryant, the white carpetbagger who was general Superintendent of the Freedman's Bureau and chief organizer of the black Georgia Equal Rights League in 1876 and its president thereafter, expected to be re-elected as state Chairman and sought to enhance this possibility by profusely stating his loyalty to his black friends. "Ordinarily Bryant was known as a shrewd and successful operator with the Negro element but on this occasion he made a blunder which was to cost him his leadership in the party," says Hanes Walton, Jr. Bryant, trying to stave off a discussion of the method of selecting a chairman and to conciliate the black delegates, offered a resolution on how patronage should be dispersed in the state. Bryant hoped that his resolution would capture the convention's attention. With all chance of state patronage gone and little hope of remaining in elective office, federal patronage was all that remained. Bryant suggested that the division of federal offices in Georgia should be on a 50-50 basis between the races. However, "others immediately suggested that three-fourths for blacks would be more in line with the racial composition of the organization."

Edwin Belcher, a black from Augusta, offered a substitute proposal to test the sincerity of Bryant and other whites. Designated as the last speaker in the state convention, Belcher moved that three-fourths of the delegates to the forthcoming national convention in Chicago should be black delegates. This motion drew great cheers from the black delegates and was passed since blacks were in a majority at the meeting. The white delegates, failing to get Belcher's motion tabled, tried to keep the committee on delegates from submitting a report in conformity with Belcher's resolution. They took this action primarily for one reason. To have a resolution about patronage adopted by a convention that they didn't control had little meaning, but to have another resolution slip by that instructed the convention on its choice of delegates was indeed significant. But even the white delegate's move to short circuit the committee on delegates went haywire. When the list that appeared was not in conformity with the Belcher motion, blacks asserted themselves and had the list revised to include fourteen black and eight white members. Of the four delegate-at-large positions, blacks got three. This latter triumph was particularly significant because the delegates-at-large were usually considered the leaders of the interstate delegation. J.E. Bryant, the white carpetbaggers who began the original resolution, failed to get a post as either delegate or delegate-at-large.

Even with the lion's share of representation on the state delegation, blacks still sought more control and advantage. They next turned their attention to the state chairmanship and the state central committee, electing William Pledger, the young black publisher of the *Athens Blade*, to serve as state chairman. This was a signal of honor for Pledger. He was the first black to serve in this capacity. Having elected a black state chairman, blacks then named twenty-four other blacks to a thirty-two member new states central committee. Once again, Bryant and most other white leaders of the party were omitted. When the convention adjourned, blacks were in full control of the Republican Party apparatus. Concomitant with this take-over by blacks was the emergence of several new younger black leaders like William Pledger. There was also Edwin Belcher, the sharp and articulate black orator from Augusta. Other new black party wheel horses included the following: T. M. Dent of Rome, Monroe "Pink" Morton of Athens, J. H. Deveaux and R. R. Wright of Savannah, and C. C. Wimbish, Jackson McHenry, and Henry A. Runker of Atlanta. These men replaced the old black party leaders and legislators such as Jefferson Long, H. M. Turner, Aaron Alpeoria Bradley, and Tunis Campbell.

Even with this new, young and better educated black leadership in control of the party apparatus, whites were not happy with the outcome. Immediately following the close of the convention, white Republicans set their plan in motion. They ran a call in all the Atlanta newspapers the day after the convention, urging whites to assemble at the city Hall on April 27, 1850 to make plans for a separate, Lily-White party organization. When the white Republicans convened on April 27, Jonathan Norcross, a wealthy leading citizen of Atlanta and former mayor of the city (elected 1850), gave a keynote address. He declared that this movement was not a bolt from the party, but a move to strengthen the party by attracting to it the thousands of whites who had not joined because that would have officially brought them in contact with blacks. Following Norcross' remarks, a committee was established to write to those whites who had withdrawn from the party because of its association with blacks, for two reasons: 1) to tell them the plan for a Lily-White organization, and urge them to become once again Republican members. Having made this decision to contact latent and potential white party members, the Lily-White meeting adjourned.

On May 15, 1880, this Lily-White committee issued a notice in the Atlanta Republican newspaper, asking white Republicans to attend a state meeting in Atlanta on June 22 of that year for further consultation on the action. The call also urged the regular Republicans organization, which blacks dominated, to hold simultaneously a similar but separate meeting, and suggested that the two groups could cooperate through conference committee. The notice registered that this movement was not intended to divide the party but to rebuild it. It also indicated that both chambers of the state house had been reserved; one side for blacks and the other for whites. The scheduled June 22 meeting didn't get underway until July 6. Only a small group of white Republicans attended. When it convened, Norcross was designated as chairman. W.L. Clark, editor of the Atlanta Republican, was named secretary. A number of committees were also named. Pledger, the black state chairman, came to the white meeting and told the Norcross group that the white movement was antagonistic to the interests of the state party. Sharp words were exchanged between Pledger and Norcross, and Pledger finally left the meeting.

After the meeting, the Norcross movement disappeared, unable to get the support of the white officeholders who composed the real power bloc in the party. The white officeholders refused to join the Norcross' Lily-White movement because they were busy making plans of their own to recapture control of the regular (black dominated) organization at the next state convention in 1882. The white office holders behind this strategy were clerk of the U.S.D.C., A.E. Buck, and a United States Marshall in Atlanta, General James Longstreet. Moreover, they organized a clique among the white office holders, dubbed by the newspaper as the "syndicate to dispose of the federal offices in the state, keeping the best ones for themselves." The syndicate members entertained the notion of a coalition with the independent movement, if necessary, to remove blacks from control of the party organization.

On July 31, the executive committee of the party (composed of blacks and a few white office holders) met to make plans for a state convention on August 2, 1882. Little was accomplished and the meeting was adjourned. On August 3, the Black and Tans held a caucus in the printing office of the Weekly Defiance in Atlanta. This meeting was headed up by William Pledger and T. H. Brown, the black editor of the Defiance. At the same time the Pledger-Brown meeting was going on, General Longstreet was holding a meeting of the white federal officeholders at the post office building. When the Defiance meeting adjourned, Pledger, Brown and several other Black and Tans went over to the post office and tried to gain entrance. Although the doorkeeper temporarily barred them, the Black and Tans forced their way in. A ruckus ensued and Pledger and Brown were arrested. Later, they posted bail and were released. The next morning the Longstreet faction held a caucus before the scheduled ten o'clock convening of the state convention and issued a call for a convention to take place at noon at the United States courtroom. To make this new convention appear to be authentic, the Longstreet faction issued and distributed circulars and dodgers containing the names of two blacks, John H. Deveaux and James Few, and two white names as well if for no other reason than endorsing the rescheduled meeting. Three of these men were also members of the regular state executive committee, which made the circulars appear all the more official.

The Pledger group convened at ten o'clock sharp and waited until eleven before they started party business, hoping party members would realize they had been duped and return to the fold. The Pledger group (composed primarily of blacks a few whites, and Black and Tans) would start at eleven, the Longstreet group (mostly white and a few blacks, Lily-Whites) began their separate convention at noon. The first order of business at each convention was the establishment of a conference committee to work out the differences between the factions and seek some means or grounds for reconciliation. But each attempt at reconciliation failed. With all hope of reconciliation cut off, each convention proceeded with its own business and drew up its own slate of candidates for state office. Both groups endorsed the candidacy of independent, General L.J. Gartrell, for Governor. Each faction evenly divided its slate so that it would appear to the public that it represented the real Republican organization in the state. After naming their respective tickets, each faction named its own state central committee and state party chairman.

After these developments, the Longstreet faction made an appeal to President Arthur McKinley (who had adopted a Southern Strategy of supporting the White Independent movement in the South as a way of building upon the Republican Party). The first appeal went unanswered, but a second appeal to the president and his political advisor on southern matters, William E. Chandler, resulted in a deal. The Pledger led Black and Tans were promised minor public offices in the state and national party positions if they would give up their control over party machinery, and let whites run the party and support of the Independent candidate for governor. The deal was accepted and A.E. Buck, a white man emerged just before the state election as the chairman of a united party. A coalition slate of candidates was offered to voters on Election Day, headed by the Independent General Gartrell, who was running for Governor. Prior to Election Day, black Gartrell Clubs began organizing the black committee in every county of Georgia.

After 1884, the Lily-White group remained dominant and the Black and Tan wing declined to a position of subservience in the party organization. That arrangement remained intact until 1920. In fact, racial matters subsided in the party and for the next decade inter-party clashes arose mainly over the question of fusion with the Agrarian and Populist movements that arose in Georgia in the 1890s until nearly 1900. Populism, being a movement on the part of farmers to gain a political hearing for some of their economic and agricultural problems, invariably involved blacks. When state elections came up, the Republican chairman Buck, urged his organization to fuse with the Populists and support them. This caused dissension in the ranks, and some Republicans, black and white, disagreed with Buck, and bolted the party. At the same time, the Populist movement had a strong appeal to black voters. In fact, during state elections from 1890 to 1900, some black Republicans voted with the Democrats, while others merged with the Populists and supported their organization. In the 1994 state election there was a great deal more fusion between the two parties (Republican and Populist) than there had been in 1892, and this trend continued until 1896 when the Populist movement collapsed on the national level. The movement steadily declined thereafter in most southern states, especially Georgia.

By 1896, the Republicans turned their attention to the presidential campaign, having lived for four years under a Democratic President, Grover Cleveland. Republicans were also interested in state elections and congressional races, and supported Populists for state offices while the Populists supported Republican congressional candidates. When the Republican meeting that year selected an all white ticket of presidential electors, the black wing of the party began to bolt. Led by new black leaders like C. C. Wimbish of Atlanta and Henry L. Johnson, an attorney and law partner of W. A. Pledger, blacks sought their share of possible national patronage. Knowing that the Populists wanted their votes but not their company, the majority of blacks at the state central committee meeting on April 17, 1895 refused to fuse again with the Populists. One black leader, H. L. Johnson, stated that, "The intelligent Negroes of Georgia know that there is far more hate and spleen against the Negroes in the Populists camp than in the Democrats." With this understood, black leaders who had conferred with Republican Presidential hopeful William McKinley in his tour of Georgia in 1895, began taking steps to be included among delegates to the National Convention.

McKinley's southern tours set the stage for another party division on racial lines. Here was the advent of a new tactic for Republican Presidential hopefuls. Since the Civil War, there had been numerous candidates at every Republican National Convention seeking the presidential nomination. These individuals would bargain and dicker with nearly every state delegation to attain their support. Generally, the bargaining and persuasion took place chiefly during the convention. However, in 1895, one year before the National Convention, McKinley's political advisor, Mark Hanna, (a wealthy industrialist), from Ohio decided to apply his business principles to politics. That is, he planned to secure the support of state delegations prior to the convention. As Hanna envisioned it, the best possible region in which to employ this pre-convention strategy was the South, since in most southern states there were two districts and competing factions. Each faction could be polled according to the candidate it planned to endorse. Also, at least one of the factions could be persuaded before hand to support a particular candidate.

With his business plan in mind, Hanna, in January 1895, rented a large house in Thomasville, Georgia, where he and McKinley met and entertained federal office holders, whites and Negroes, from the entire south. States Professor Shadgett, "All winter a steady stream of southern politicians flowed through the house on Dawson Avenue." His political strategy assured McKinley "of a large majority of delegates from the deep south." Although Hanna and McKinley saw both blacks and whites at their Thomasville retreat, McKinley held a special meeting with black Republican leaders in Georgia as well as the Black and Tan faction to insure their support for his candidacy in case the white McKinley clubs should change their minds at the convention. Before the meeting McKinley visited several local black churches and then proceeded to a meeting at the State Industrial College for blacks, presided over by the college president, a leader among Georgia Republicans.

At the meeting, Reverend E. K. Love gave the main address to some fifty colored preachers, teachers, lawyers, and politicians. After Love's address, McKinley spoke of the advancement that blacks were making in education and in agriculture, and of the pleasant reception given him. Then he advanced patronage promises on the group if they would support his Presidential bid, and quickly left for a tour of Florida, where again, the majority of Republican voters were blacks. His political advisor, Hanna, knew that it was wise not to antagonize the black community, at least before the Convention. McKinley wasn't the only candidate playing up to the two southern Republican factions. Others included Thomas B. Reed, Speaker of the House of Representatives, Senator W. B. Allison of Iowa, Senator Shelby M. Cullom of Illinois, Senator Mathew Quay of Pennsylvania, and Levi P. Morton, the New York Governor and former Vice President under Benjamin Harrison.

At the state convention on April 29, 1895 a tremendous fight took place. Each district had contesting delegations who issued charges of political deals. At first, the fight centered mainly on candidates, but later the division was along racial lines, since the majority of both whites and blacks were for McKinley. To add sparks to the fire, each presidential candidate opened a headquarters across from the state convention and openly and lavishly courted the prospective delegates. Shadgett says, "A special feature of the McKinley headquarters was a large room where only delegates were admitted, fitted with tables fairly groaning with eatables and drinkables, sandwiches and cakes, and a hogshead of lemonade. Cigars were passed out with a free hand; a bootblack dispensed free shines." The other Presidential hopefuls, not having the financial backing of McKinley, had a combined headquarters in the Imperial Opera House, next to McKinley's. "The headquarters of the combined presented a lively appearance along with the Atlanta Dixie Band as the star attraction." Both groups had people to meet the delegates coming to the state convention and take them to the reception rooms of their respective candidates.

This sharpened the competition between the two groups and no harmony could be ascertained. The A. E. Buck and Pledger led Lily-Whites named their delegates amidst the confusion and left the convention hall. Upon their departure, the Wright, Love (Rev. E. K. Love, President of the First African Baptist Church in Savannah, the oldest black church in America, founded in 1789) Black and Tans named their own delegates, a state central committee, and a platform endorsing McKinley. The two contesting delegations went to the National Convention and the dispute was settled by the convention committee. Twenty-two of Georgia's twenty-eight votes eventually went to McKinley, two to Quay, and two to Reed.

After the convention white Republican leaders made a bid to attract more white businessmen on the issue of protection and to drop black members. Black Party leaders were persuaded to go along with the move by offers of patronage favors in exchange for their agreeing to only whites being presidential electors and electors-at-large. Even after the November national elections, the all-white trend continued. Blacks acceded because of the many positions McKinley gave blacks in the state, ranging from paymaster to United States Marshall. Despite McKinley's wooing of white Republicans, writes Professor BaCote, blacks "regarded McKinley as the best friend they ever had, pointing out that he had appointed more Negroes to responsible positions in Georgia than all earlier presidents combined, including posts not held before by the race." For instance, on the state level he appointed blacks to the Internal Revenue Collectorship, Collectorship of the Port of Savanna, Postmaster ships at Athens and Hogansville, and the superintendence of the stamp division. On the national level, he appointed a black as Consul at Asuncion, Paraguay, and R. R. Wright as paymaster in the U.S. Army with a rank of major. When McKinley visited Georgia on December 18, 1898, he stopped off at the Industrial College for blacks (Savannah State College) and delivered an address to over one thousand people, urging blacks to "be patient, be progressive, be determined, be honest." Although he didn't during his tour, condemn race restrictions or lynching, which was on the rise, neither criticism nor independent action came from blacks so long as he continued his policy of giving them recognition as officeholders. Black Republicans were thus content to let whites run the party, and the Black and Tan revolt was once gain undermined by patronage.

Blacks again did little to stop the new move toward an all-white leadership of the Republican Party with black subordinates in the background, the Democrats, recognizing that such a party could break their hegemony over the state, took action. McKinley had polled more votes in Georgia in the 1896 election than any other Republican candidate since 1872. Thus, the Democratic state executive committee adopted a statewide primary system in 1898 and made it mandatory for all counties. This shifted the focus from the general election to the Democratic primary. In 1900, the primary was made a white primary. That is, it was limited to white voters only. Southern states had earlier disenfranchised blacks, the main supporters of the Republican Party in the South, and this new move decreased even further the limited powers of the Republican Party. It reduced the party a small closed corporation of a few blacks "and white men who kept up just enough organization to send themselves as delegates to Republican National Conventions and to keep themselves in office." In fact, the party was deliberately kept small because the "fewer there are to divide the pie, the more there is to go around." The party failed to put up candidates for state and local elections or to conduct all-out campaigns for new voters. The sole function of party members became that of controlling the state party machinery and nominating delegates to the National Convention every four years. The entire party became "Presidential Republicans," acting every four years, then falling back into oblivion until the next national convention.

From 1900 until 1932 when Hoover capitulated to Lily-White-ism, there was some dissension in the Georgia delegation. For example, when the few remaining blacks, (like newcomers A. T. Walden, a black attorney in Atlanta, John W. Dobbs, a black insurance executive, and Ben Davis of Atlanta), felt that they were not getting their fair share of patronage, they sent rival delegations to the national conventions in 1920, 1924, 1928 and even 1952. But while they gained seats based on the presidential hopefuls control of the Credentials

Committee, the Black and Tan's day had long since faded, as the party had faded in the southern states. The final blow to the limited Black and Tan-ism that existed after 1928 came after Hoover was elected in that same year. The president elect removed all black Republican officeholders and party officials and placed whites in their place. For instance, he used Ben Davis' delegation to secure his nomination and after the election removed Davis from his post of National Committeeman from Georgia. Democratic control of the Presidency from 1932 to 1952 and the attraction of the New Deal in Georgia gradually drew blacks into the Democratic fold. Black and Tan-ism in Georgia ended, essentially, in 1928, although, in any meaningful sense it had faded much earlier. Even its limited expression after 1900 ended with Herbert Hoover's election and the coming of the New Deal.

CHAPTER FOUR
TEXAS

On July 4, of 1867, Unionists, Radicals, and Freedmen converged in Houston and held the first state Republican Convention in Texas. This convention came about as a result of several mass meetings held throughout the state by the Union Loyal League during the first half of 1867. In Texas, as in the other southern states, the Loyal League aligned blacks and the black vote with the fledgling Republican Party. Professor Casdorph states that in Texas, the "Radicals through the League lost little time in enlisting the colored voters on their side." Consequently, when the convention met at Houston in July, it was "overwhelmingly African in composition; the white delegates did not exceed twenty in number while the colored numbered about one hundred and fifty." A state Republican organization was formally established and the outlook of the party was clearly delineated.

On July 19, of 1867 fifteen days after the convention, the second Reconstruction Act was passed by Congress and a call went out in Texas for a constitutional convention to be held in February of 1868. In that election, the Republicans were overwhelmingly victorious, receiving 44,689 votes for and 11,440 against the calling of a new convention. Nine of the ninety delegates elected to the constitutional convention were blacks. A new constitution, which took the convention more than a year to draw up, gave blacks full voting rights in Texas. Before adjourning, the convention set November 30 as the date for state election of officials to serve under the new document. However, the final document as drawn up caused a split in the Republican Party ranks. This split occurred over the so-called "ab initio" question, which asserted "that all laws passed in Texas during the Confederate regime were null and void from the very beginning." When the party members failed to write the "ab initio" doctrine into the state constitution and state party platform, a section of the Republican Party under the leadership of two whites, E. J. Davis and J. P. Newcomb, left the party. It was at this point that the Texas Republican Party became solidly divided into two different factions: the Radical wing led by Davis and Newcomb, the other being considered the conservative element in the party. Most blacks supported the Davis led wing.

Although the two wings sought reconciliation, even sending delegates to the Grant Administration to discuss the matter and ask for the president's help, no progress was made. Each group, therefore, prepared in its own fashion for the new upcoming election. The Radicals (or predominately black group) held their first pre-election convention in Galveston on May 10. A black, C.T. Ruby, who had been a delegate at the 1868 National Convention in Chicago, was made president of the convention. A tentative platform was adopted at a second meeting held in Houston on June 7, 1869, and naming a state ticket with E. J. Davis as their choice for Governor. The conservative wing of the Republican Party nominated a well known white unionist, A.J. Hamilton, and numerous Democrats promised to support his bid for election. In the election, the Radical Republicans captured control of both houses of the state legislature. Eleven black Republicans were elected in the party's landslide victory.

After taking power in 1870, the Republicans in Texas, already badly split and competing with each other, came under severe attack from the Democrats. The national split in the Republican ranks in 1872, (with the appearance of the Liberal Republican third-party movement), furthered the radical-conservative split within the state party. The conservative wing strongly supported the new Liberal Party movement. As a result, the Democrats captured both Houses of the state legislature in 1872. Since the governor was elected for four years, however, Davis didn't lose his seat to a Democratic candidate until 1874. That was the year when the Democrats supposedly restored home rule. In any event, the crushing defeat handed the Republicans in the 1874 gubernatorial election relegated the party to one of token opposition in Texas. Even after the defeat of E.J. Davis and his Reconstruction government, though, blacks continued to play a prominent part in Texas Republican politics. A sizable number of black delegates were sent to the national convention in 1876 and several blacks were in the state legislature during this period. For example, in the Twelfth State legislature (1871) there were eleven; in the Thirteenth (1873) eight in the Fourteenth (1874) seven, and in the Fifteenth (1876) four.

In January of 1876, at the party's state convention in Houston, blacks dominated the convention proceedings and even changed the method of electing delegates to the national convention from a vote by acclamation to a vote by counties. After the delegation returned home from the national convention, the Radical wing launched its state campaign. By 1876, the conservative wing had coalesced with the Democrats and what little support the Republicans did get on 1876 came from the area of high black concentration in east Texas. The Republican vote in 1876 was only 45,013. Having made such a poor showing, the Davis led predominately black party allied with the Greenback party in 1878 to support an Independent ticket for state offices. Other Republicans, who didn't go along with Davis, put up a separate Republican ticket with a black, Richard Allen, running for the Lieutenant Governor. Richard Allen later founded the African Methodist Episcopal Church. Both the Independent and the mixed Republican ticket lost.

By 1880, the Republican Party in Texas, which was rapidly losing its potency in the state, began to play primarily national convention politics and to support the proper individuals for the Presidency so that state patronage would be restored to them. Thus, at the Republican National Convention, the mixed Texas delegation switched to the winner, James A. Garfield, on the thirty-sixth and final ballot. Up to that point the Texas delegation had supported Grant on twelve ballots, John Sherman on one, Elihu Wasborne on one, Garfield on three and E.J. Davis on one. The other ballots were mixed. After the convention, the state Executive Committee named a state ticket headed by the perennial E.J. Davis. In the general election Davis polled 64,000 votes, while Garfield received 57,225 votes from the so-called black belt counties. In 1882 the Republicans held a state convention in Austin on August 23, with over 400 delegates from all over the state (one half of whom were black). At the convention, the delegates, at the suggestion of E.J. Davis, agreed not to put up a slate of candidates but to support the Greenbacker Independent ticket. This fusion move proved futile because the Independent ticket was well beaten by the Democrats, receiving only 102,501 votes to the Democrats 180,809. E. J. Davis lost his bid for Congress on the Independent ticket.

Governor E.J. Davis, (Texas) the perennial state Republican leader died on February 7, 1883. Norris Wright Cuney, a black, emerged as the new state party leader. The first test of Cuney's leadership came when the state convention convened on April 29, 1884 to select delegates for the 1884 National Convention. In-fighting developed over whom to support, President Arthur or James C. Blaine. Generally speaking, the blacks were led by Cuney supported Blaine, while the whites led by A.C. Malloy favored Chester A. Arthur. The conflict was not resolved at the state convention. "The old animosities of the officeholders versus the non-officeholders and the blacks versus whites were carried over to Chicago, and the Credentials Committee," which there fell heir to the task of resolving the internal conflict. After the National Convention,

Texas Republicans held another state convention on September 2, 1884 to nominate a slate of officers for the upcoming state elections. When the blacks in the convention voted to support a fusion ticket with Independents, the white Republicans bolted, held their own convention, and placed their own ticket in the field. The animosities and jealousies between the blacks and whites continued at the 1886 state nominating convention, the two groups resorting to fisticuffs.

Two years later, warfare broke out between white and black Republicans in Fort Bend and Wharton counties. In Fort Bend, the struggle between black and white Republicans for control of the government resulted in the jaybird-woodpecker war which lasted two years. Elsewhere in Texas, whites began early in 1888 to organize White Republican Clubs for the purpose of controlling the county conventions "so that they might elect their delegates for the state convention." At the state convention, another in-fight developed over party control. The members of the White Republican Clubs opposed Cuney's black leadership, for reasons of prejudice and ambition, and it was during this struggle that Cuney coined the phrase "Lily-White." Later the newspapers dubbed the Cuney-led faction the "of Black and Tans." From that point on, and on every election thereafter, a bitter rivalry ensued between the Lily-Whites and the Black and Tans. Beginning in 1892, each faction held its own convention. There were attempts at various times to reunite the two groups, but they all failed.

Cuney continued his leadership of the party until his death in 1897. Just prior to his death, however, his control had begun to wane. Early in 1896, for example, he supported William B. Alison for the presidency of the National Convention, while the Lily-Whites supported McKinley, as did another group. Both Cuney's Black and Tans and the Lily-Whites lost, and a white man, Dr. John Grant, was named Texas National Committeeman for the next four years. In the regular party convention of the Black and Tans, held after the National Convention, Cuney lost his state chairmanship, being defeated by another black, H.C. Ferguson, who assumed the temporary chairmanship of the convention. After Cuney's death, W. M. "Gooseneck" McDanald became leader of the Black and Tan Republican Party in the state and continued the struggle against the Lily-Whites from 1898 until 1912. In 1912, the Lily-White Republicans became the National Progressive Party, which excluded blacks and was sanctioned by Theodore Roosevelt. The Black and Tans continued to support the regular Republican candidate, Taft, and the rivalry between the Black and Tans and Lily-Whites parties went on into abeyance for a period. The rivalry was rekindled in the 1920 election and continued in varying degree until 1928 when the Lily-

White faction throughout the South had the support of Presidential candidate Herbert Hoover. The state of Texas was no exception. The Credentials Committee at the 1928 convention voted to seat the Lily-White group led by R.B. Creager, and there after Creager ruled unchallenged. The Black and Tan Republicanism came to an end in Texas in 1928.

The politics of the Black and Tans in Texas revolved around electioneering. Prior to every election after 1888, the Black and Tan group put up or endorsed a separate slate from the Lily-White, in hopes that the national convention would readily see which group controlled the majority of votes. Their desire was to gain seats at the convention, to have one of their members as state chairman for the next four years and passed on to them the right to disperse whatever appointed federal patronage was available. In almost every election the candidate backed by the Black and Tans received the most votes. One exception took place in 1920, however, the Lily-White delegation was seated because it backed the nomination of Warren G. Harding, while the Black and Tan group backed the nomination of Leonard Wood. After the national convention the Black and Tans held their own convention, nominated their own electors for president, and cast some 27,000 votes for them. This show of strength didn't help. The Black and Tan faction was again not seated in 1924.

During the period after disenfranchisement, the Texas legislature passed a law that declared, "Any political party desiring to elect delegates to a national convention shall hold a state convention at such place as shall be designated by the executive committee of said party on the fourth Tuesday in May, 1928, and every four years thereafter." This law greatly aided the Lily-White faction because, from 1920 onward, only the Lily-White faction received national recognition and state chairmanships. But the Black and Tans fought back, holding district conventions and electing delegates, both at-large and district-wide. In addition, they hoped that the Credentials Committee would agree with their view that no state law could be held binding upon the Republican National Convention. Arguments to the contrary prevailed and the Credentials Committee rejected the Black and Tans.

CHAPTER FIVE
LOUISIANA

In Louisiana, blacks had been associated with Republicanism from 1865. Although Republican rule came to an end in the state with the dispute of 1876, black Republican leaders continued their association with the party. Between 1877 and 1892 a full Republican ticket was presented for every state election. Numerous Republican state and parish officials of both races were elected during this period, and four Republicans were sent to congress. But each year the party's power declined, political offices became scarce and patronage grew in significance. It was over the control of patronage that an inter-party conflict developed within the Louisiana's Republican Party. In 1894, a group of white sugar planters and businessmen, who were sympathetic to the Republican tariff policy, bolted from the Democratic Party of Louisiana and formed the National Republican Party. They made an attempt to associate themselves with the regular Republicans. However, in 1896, the national Republicans joined forces with the white faction of the regular party and this union became known as the "Lily-White faction." At the Republican National Convention in 1896, though, McKinley recognized the black Republican group, he appointed a white man, A.T. Wimberly as National Committeeman. Walter L. Cohen, a black was appointed state chairman.

Two years later, Louisiana ratified a new constitution containing a literacy clause which reduced black registration by ninety-five percent. Although this weakened the Black and Tan faction, they still dominated the state convention which was held on March 5, 1900 in New Orleans. The Black and Tans nominated their own slate of offices for the state election; it polled only 3.18 percent of the vote. The Lily-White faction received 12.06 percent, but were victorious at the national convention in 1900 *(Black Republicans: The Politics of the Black and Tans)* The Black and Tans achieved some success in 1904, 1908 and 1916. From 1920 to 1928 the Black and Tans ruled the Louisiana Republican Party. Prior to this period the politics of the Black and Tans had been primarily a matter of electioneering and persuasion. But when the Black and Tans left the 1920 Republican National Convention (with blacks being appointed as secretary of the party's state and central committee and being in complete control of federal patronage), things began to change.

For instance, one of the black secretaries, Walter Cohen, was appointed by President Harding to the position of comptroller of customs in New Orleans. Congress refused to affirm the appointment but President Coolidge resubmitted his name for the same post. Approval was finally granted on March 17, 1924. During the entire period, the white politicians of Louisiana fought the appointment, but numerous national Republicans came to Cohen's aid. W.E.B. DuBois, then the director of publicity and research for the NAACP (National Association of Colored People), wrote letters to various newspaper editors supporting him. Finally, the Postmaster General used his power to pressure Republican Senators into voting for Cohen's confirmation. When this made the appointment almost certain, a white Washington, D.C. attorney, H. Edwin Bolte, filed suit against Cohen, challenging his right to hold a federal position on the ground that, "He is a person of African blood and descent, and therefore cannot be a citizen of the United States," says Hanes Walton Jr. In addition, Bolte claimed that the 14th Amendment, which gave blacks citizenship, had never been legally enacted. The case, was tried in the U. S. District Court in New Orleans, was dismissed on November 24, 1924. Bolte refused to give up: he charged Cohen with impersonating a federal officer on the grounds that no person of African blood can be a federal officeholder. This motion was also dismissed. Later, after Cohen assumed his post, he was arrested on August 17, 1925 and charged "with being a member of a gigantic rum ring" which was smuggling liquor into New Orleans from Havana Cuba, in violation of the Volstead Act. Another federal trial ensued, this being declared a mistrial due to lack of evidence.

Another suit was filed against Cohen in February of 1928 by a Lily-White faction because Black and Tans won eleven of thirteen positions on the state central committee in the primary election held on January 17, 1928. The Lily-Whites wanted control of the committee before the 1928 Republican National Convention and their suit asked the court to issue an injunction restraining the blacks from serving as members of the state central committee. The court issued a temporary restraining order. Later, a permanent injunction was issued but the decision was appealed. The final decision gave only two seats to the Black and Tans out of the contested eleven. Prior to the national convention the Lily-Whites, spurred on by their legal success, filed another suit against Cohen. This one asked for a restraining order to prevent him from calling a convention to select delegates to the national convention. The injunction did not halt the Black and Tan convention and two delegates from Louisiana went to the Republican National Convention. At the convention, however, Presidential candidate Hoover capitulated to Lily-White-ism and recognized it as a faction. After the convention the Black and Tan party was out of power and has been ever since.

CHAPTER SIX
ALABAMA

Republicanism emerged very slowly in Alabama. There was no major coalition of scalawags, carpetbaggers, and blacks immediately after the Civil War in this state as there were in other southern states. It was some time before limited Republican and Unionist sentiment in Alabama were welded into a formal political structure. The passage by Congress of the Reconstruction Act in March of 1867, and the establishment of military districts led to the emergence of several small Republican groups. For instance, blacks from twelve counties met in a convention at Mobile on May 5, 1867 and drew up a resolution proclaiming themselves a part of both the national and the emerging state Republican Party. But even with this declaration and all the political maneuvering prior to the election on October 1-5, 1867, no coalition or unification took place between numerous groups of blacks, scalawags and carpetbaggers, and disgruntled Democrats. At best, only a spiritual name or union held the diverse groups together (they competed with the conservative party) during the October selection of delegates to the constitutional convention.

Beyond these memorials, pleas and petitions, blacks of the Equal Rights Union also, set in motion a 6,000 man militia, to protect their property and person. Minor skirmishes took place at Huntsville, Eutaw, Eufauls, Belmont, Tuscaloosa, Mobile, and Lowndesboro. Despite their self-defense measures, blacks still were unable to retain their property, but this and political separation did not exhaust all of the black man's efforts in Alabama in 1874. A number of blacks joined the Democratic Party, despite its declared position as the party of White Supremacy. Some of these blacks joined the Democratic ranks to spite the Republicans and register a protest against their inaction and White Supremacist's practices. Others viewed politics as did the Democratic elite that is, as the only profession of gentlemen. Some black Democrats, viewing themselves as aristocrats of their race, felt that the masses of their race were "unprepared to assume the duties of citizenship and enfranchisement." Fearing that the franchise might be lost because of the unreliable support of the opportune party (the Republicans), which sought to use blacks for selfish motives, the aristocratic black became a turncoat. He became an opportunist himself.

Thus, black Democratic leaders like Caesar Shorter and Levi Ford, at the behest of white Democratic Party leaders, addressed the Democratic state convention as early as 1868 in an effort to attract more black votes to the party. During each election thereafter, the Democrats used black Democrats to help out blacks faced with lawsuits. The party from time to time even protected blacks who went to the polls with Democratic ballots, while at the same time visiting violence upon black Republicans. The Democrats courting of blacks came to an end in 1876. The Montgomery Democratic organization selected two black delegates, James A. Scott and John W. Allen, to attend the state convention on May 30, 1878. Some whites, however, objected to the black delegates and they were defeated by a vote of 260 to 229, according to Hanes Walton, Jr. Scott addressed the convention, then he and Allen retired from the convention. They were the last two blacks ever honored by a Democratic convention in Alabama. Thus, self-defense, political separation, joining of the Democratic Party, and withdrawal were among the options taken by the blacks of Alabama in that year. When the curtain fell in 1874, blacks found the Democrats in control of the state government.

Immediately upon coming to power, Democrats in 1875 sought to limit black suffrage. A constitutional convention was called on September 6 at Montgomery. Although the Republicans opposed the convention, four blacks were elected to the convention. Minor changes were made and black disenfranchisement did not become a major issue, largely because of the fear of federal intervention. Although a majority of blacks voted against the 1875 constitution, it was ratified by a vote of 85,662 to 29,217 *(Black Republicans: The Politics of the Black and Tans)* Democrats then moved quickly in the state legislature to curtail black voting, passing several laws from 1875 to 1882, which put curbs on black voting. The Democrats effectiveness was evident in 1876 when, for the first time since 1868, blacks were completely removed from the state legislature. Prior to the 1876 election, a majority of black leaders, along with a few whites, broke away from the white officeholders and literate black masses and formed the Smith-Rice wing or Black and Tan wing of the Republican Party. The portion of the party that was left, the Spencer wing or Lily-Whites, put their own candidate for the governorship, as did the Smith-Rice wing. But before the election, Alexander Curtis, a black Senator from Perry County, and others managed to heal the split and work out a compromise ticket. The independent ticket, which the Democrats called a trick "hatched in a den of thieves at a buzzard's fest," lost. In spite of intimidation by members of their own race led by whites, five hundred blacks in Sumner County alone voted the Democratic ticket.

This defection in 1876 was still not enough to convey to the Republican Party caucuses the depths of black dissatisfaction with their representation in the party's offices. In 1878, when blacks represented 1,400 of the 1,450 votes in Elmore County, the county convention chose only white candidates to attend the state convention. In Montgomery County, 7,000 blacks were allowed only ten votes in the county convention. Madison County gave all the patronage to whites, even though the party vote was 2,000 blacks to 300 whites *(Black Republicans: The Politics of the Black and Tans)* In 1878 the party once again broke into black and white factions, with the blacks holding their own convention and selecting a full black slate, headed by a prominent black businessman, James K. P. Lucas. In Selma, the blacks selected Jere Haralson to run for Congress again, while the Lily-White Republicans joined with the Greenbackers. During the campaign the Democrats made a tremendous appeal to the black electorate, also attracting the Greenbackers. The all-black Republican ticket did very badly, receiving only 105 votes in Montgomery County and even less in other counties in the state *(Black Republicans: The Politics of the Black and Tans)* In Jefferson County blacks voted solidly for the Greenbackers, while in the rest of Alabama the black voters went overwhelmingly for the Democratic ticket. Chief credit for the black switch went to black leader James Scott, who addressed the Democratic State convention that year and used his newspaper, *The Montgomery Advance*, to lure the black voter into the Democratic camp.

In 1880, blacks walked out of the Republican State and county conventions again and set up an all-black ticket as well as sending an anti-administration Republican delegation to the National Convention in Chicago. At the polls, however, black educator William H. Council, principal of the black state college at Normal, Alabama, led blacks into the Democratic column. The all-black Republican ticket was once again defeated. In 1882, Republican factionalism reemerged. The Lily-White Republicans held their own state convention, with one-third white officeholders and two-thirds black. They endorsed the Greenbackers platform of a free ballot and a fair count. The second Republican convention, composed of blacks only, declared their independence of the white party control and endorsed the Democratic ticket. Once again, blacks voted overwhelmingly for the Democratic ticket, but after the election the Democrats refused to give black supporters any of the spoils or to recognize them as jurors. Thus, blacks returned en masse to the Republican Party ranks, only to break away again in 1884.

That year, the two factions sent separate delegations to the National Republican Convention, but neither put up a state ticket or endorsed any party. In 1886 the two Republican factions united and put up their first joint state ticket in nearly ten years. The state election, which was held in August, proved to blacks that Republicans were still trying to use them for their own purposes, so the Black and Tan faction put up its own Congressional slate of candidates in the national election held in November. Although the slate lost, blacks maintained their independence. In 1888, they won several local offices in Tuscaloosa and Birmingham. The Black and Tan Republicans gubernatorial candidate, Frank H. Threat lost, but they received full black support.

Nationally, Benjamin Harrison was elected President and immediately adopted a Southern Strategy of supporting the Lily-Whites. In Alabama, he appointed ranking Lily-White high tariff men to offices throughout the state. Blacks retaliated by sending an ultimatum and a delegation to Washington to see the president on April 20, 1889. The president ignored their pleas and officially recognized the Lily-White Republican Party in June 1889. It was founded on April 10, 1889, when three hundred Republicans, Independents and Democrats from all parts of the state, met at Birmingham and organized a high tariff party from which colored men were excluded. When blacks protested, Charles Hendley, black editor of the Huntsville Gazette, received the post of Receiver of Public Monies of the state. A few other minor offices were granted to blacks but officially the Lily-White Republican Party was in control of the state. When the decade closed in 1890, blacks discovered that their twenty-five year fealty to the Republicans had left the blacks "still a hewer of wood, drawer of water, a ward of the party who was supposed to jump at the crack of the party whip, and a pilgrim on an eternal pilgrimage never reaching the shrine" (Hanes Walton Jr.).

In 1890, the Populist Party emerged in the state of Alabama and the Jeffersonian Democrats, the liberal wing of the Democratic Party led by Reuben Kolb, was ready for a new alliance. The Lily-White Republican leaders, lacking a following, were also looking for an alliance, with any political group except the Black and Tans. In 1890, the 1,600 member black Farmer Alliance merged with the black Knights of Labor. They also invited the Kolb led Jeffersonian Democrats to join, but Kolb held out. The Kolbites action not to join the new alliance in 1890 did appeal to blacks, so the State Democratic Executive

Committee, although it had selected as its campaign theme, "The white man's rule essential," sent black speakers into the black community. The National Afro-American Leagues and Colored Democratic clubs throughout the state in an effort to wrest the black vote from the Black and Tans Republicans. Said a white Democratic newspaper, the *Wedwee Randolph Toiler*, "Mr. Negro is all right whenever he votes the Democratic ticket."

In 1890, the Black and Tan held their own convention, with some whites in the audience. A platform was adopted which called Congress to regulate elections, grant equality of citizenship and free ballots, and insure fair courts. In the state and national elections, however, black Republican candidates lost by a large margin, mainly due to Democratic fraud and stealth in the black belt counties. The election resulted, though, in several Populists winning with the aid of black support.

Kolb officially left the Democratic ranks in 1891 and allied his group with the Populists. Kolb and his followers retained their independence by calling themselves the Caucusian Democrats of Alabama, but the Kolbites, nevertheless, appealed immediately to black voters for support. The Lily-Whites, led by Robert Mosely, tried deceptively to attract blacks by creating a black Republican League. Blacks were not fooled and held their own convention in 1892, choosing a black, Bill Stevens, to lead them. The convention decided not to offer a state ticket, and condemned the Mosely led Lily-Whites. They petitioned the Civil Service Commission to investigate their practices, and sent a delegation to the Republican National Convention. But the Lily-White delegation, which had one black, Jere Bleven, was seated. Thus, in the state national elections the Lily-Whites, the blacks and Tans, the Kolbites (Caucasian Democrats), Populists, as well as the Regular Democrats were all trying to attract the black vote. The Lily-Whites faction supported the Kolbites and Populists, while the Black and Tans maintained their independence. But the Kobites organized black clubs to offset the straight Republican ticket put forth by the Black and Tans, currently led by Bill Stevens. This action split the black vote and the Democrats, with the aid of fraudulent practices, won the day.

In 1894, the Kolbites tried to join the Democrats in the state election and set up a white primary that would bar blacks. When the suggestion was rejected to Democrats, who felt they didn't need the Kolbites, the latter merged with the Lily-Whites and the Populists once again. The Fusionists held their convention, elected Kolb to run once more and opposed any restrictions on the ballot. They discouraged black emigration, and favored "the setting aside of a special territory (in the state) for blacks exclusively, whereby they alone would be entitled to suffrage and citizenship." When Bill Stevens, leader of the Black and Tans, tried to attend the Fusionist Convention, he was threatened and hounded out of the convention. To retaliate, he tried once again to put a black ticket in the field, but failed. He then urged his Black and Tans to fuse with Democrats in the 1894 state election, which they did, (to the dismay of the colored Democratic clubs throughout the state), and had black ministers cajole their parishioner to support the Democrats. Moreover, black newspaper editors were paid to have their papers endorse the Democrats. Even with this urging, black voters failed to support the Democrats (nor any party) in large numbers. Nevertheless, Democrats won and Kolb promptly claimed fraud. In the controversy that followed, all the party leaders blamed blacks for setting the so-called harmony in the state. All year in 1895, cries of disenfranchisement were heard throughout the state.

In January of 1896, the Democratic Executive Committee declared that blacks should not participate in the Democratic primary. The same opinion, (plus the notion that a new constitution should be drawn up which would curtail black political participation), was voiced at the Democratic State Convention shortly after. Blacks immediately protested the Executive Committee's decision and the committee made a small concession by permitting each county to decide whether blacks should vote or not. Blacks also held their own Republican county and State conventions in 1896 and sent a black delegation to the National Republican Convention. At the convention, Bill Stevens was selected to serve on the state Republican executive committee. Stevens' appointment drew a number of both blacks and whites out of the Mosely led Lily-Whites into the Black and Tan movement. At the state convention of the Black and Tans, a platform was drawn up which condemned Democratic violence, fraud, perjury, and denial of civil rights. The Black and Tans went it alone in the state election, rejecting a proposed merger with the Populists. The Mosley-led Lily-Whites did join the Kolb faction of the Populist Party. All the Black and Tan state candidates lost. The Democrats were again victorious.

By 1898, the Democrats were more thoroughly united and aggressive than ever. Kolb and his Caucasian Democrats, after having taken such a strong beating, were now defunct. The Populist movement had also collapsed. Bill Stevens and the Black and Tans, however, once again placed an all black state ticket. Their platform called for fair elections, equal protection of the law and better schools. It also denounced the Democratic political machine. A black minister, A. J. Warner, was elected to head the Black and Tan ticket. The Populists put a limited ticket in the field themselves, but on the whole the 1888 electoral campaign was very mild. Warner received a total of only 422 votes, 150 *(Black Republicans: The Politics of the Black and Tans)* of them coming from one county, Etowah. The reason for the Warner (Black and Tan) ticket's poor showing was that blacks voted for all tickets rather than wholeheartedly supporting the black one. "This was the last important election," states Professor Brittain, "for the Negro, a kind of apex of Negro Independent political efforts for the decade." Although Rev. Warner along with A. N. Johnson, a black politician from Mobile, ran for Congress in November in the November during the national election they were both defeated.

By 1900, the Democrats were without meaningful opposition. The Populist Party collapsed after the 1898 elections. The Republicans in 1900, were split four ways: the Lily-White, Lily-Black, and two mixed Black and Tan factions. However, before April, 1900, the Lily-Whites merged with one of the other groups. During the county conventions, one faction of Black and Tans, led by Ad Wimbs, a black lawyer from North Alabama, went along with the merger after he had received satisfactory concessions in regard to the state organization. The two remaining factions, the all black one (by now infiltrated with whites) and the regular Black and Tans met in separate halls, adopted platforms which guaranteed a ballot free from fraud, and decided against a slate ticket. Out of his activity an all white Republican slate appeared just before the state election and was soundly defeated. Two black Republicans, E. H. Mathews and Jesse Ferguson, were elected justices of the peace on the local level. Since Booker T. Washington's influence, (which urged blacks to stay out of politics), was so strong, that only a few blacks took part in the 1900 election. Once again the Democrats were victorious, and after the election they set in motion plans to strip blacks of any remaining political power they had.

The Democratic state convention, meeting January 15, 1901, declared a constitutional convention that would disenfranchise black voters. Booker T. Washington agreed that some restriction should be placed on the ballot. H. V. Cashin disagreed with Washington and noted that, "the white vote was the menace, since the black vote had been controlled since 1874, and that a convention based on race prejudice would limit the franchise to white men and depress Negro voters" *(Black Republicans: The Politics of the Black and Tans)* The Republican Executive Committee vacillated on the issue, but the blacks and Tans were strongly opposed to it for several reasons: 1. because the Democratic move would deprive the illiterate black of the vote, 2. leave the Lily-Whites in control and void the Fifteenth Amendment. The Black and Tan press, the Huntsville Republican further contended that 20,000 educated blacks would also be disenfranchised. The black newspapers elsewhere in the state told blacks that the convention would have this result, and that this might be their last chance to vote in any election in Alabama. Blacks therefore went to the polls in droves on April 23 of 1901, in and effort to defeat the referendum for the constitutional convention, but to no avail. "The official statewide count was 70,305 to 45,505 in favor of the convention." Many counties recorded warped, deceptive returns. For instance, Lowndes County, with a voting population of 5,590 blacks and 1,000 whites in 1900, cast 3,226 votes for the convention and 338 against. Another county, Dallas, which had 8,285 white and 45,371 black voters in 1890, cast 5,608 votes for the convention and 200 against. States Professor Hackey, "The large majorities for the convention in the black Belt made it seem as if blacks were voting for their own disenfranchisement, but nothing could be further from the truth." White poll managers neutralized and circumvented the black electorate.

In 1910, a black editor in Alabama wrote, "It is goodbye with poor white folks and Niggers.... For the train of disenfranchisement is on the rail and comes thundering upon us like an avalanche: there is no use crying; we have got to shut the shoot." The editorial was prophetic for the convention gathering in Montgomery on May 21, 1910. (*Black Republican: The Politics of the Black and Tans*) The president of the convention, John B. Knox, let it be known in his keynote speech that black voters would be the prime issue. Blacks, as individuals and in groups petitioned the convention and its select committee on suffrage and elections. Three blacks, the Rev. A. F. Owens, a former slave Dr. Willie E. Stern, (who was also a leading North Alabama physician), and William H. T. Holtzolaw, a teacher and political leader, sent individual petitions to the convention. Owens told the convention that the interest of all intelligent law abiding citizens of both races are identical. Dr. Stern's petition warned the convention that "might is not all times right" and that it was unfair to judge the whole race by the criminals. Holtzolaw also accused the convention of placing a premium on ignorance for the young white man and barring the purposes of both races. Booker T. Washington and several other blacks petitioned the convention as well. They indicated that blacks did not seek to rule the white man; but "the Negro does ask," the petition continued, "that since he is taxed, works roads, is punished for crime, is called upon to defend his country, that he should have some humble share in choosing those who rule over him." (*Black Republican: The Politics of the Black and Tans*) The *Huntsville Journal*, a black newspaper, considered this petition a prayer of beggars that would prevail little on the convention doing its work against color.

The Journal was proven right. The petitions were tabled and forgotten about. The majority report of the Suffrage Committee required for the franchise that male voters be: twenty-one years of age, residents of the state for two years, the county for one year, and of the ward three months; pay all present poll taxes and those accumulating after 1901 they had to pay; be of good character, literate and able to write, gainfully employed and innocent of certain crimes (many of the crimes listed were commonly those committed by blacks). Prospective voters had also to pass a court registrar and swear to tell the truth. All veterans of all American wars since 1812 and their descendants and veterans of the American Revolution were to become voters for life, if they registered prior to January 1, 1803. The report was debated and then sent to the people for public ratification on November 11, 1901. Blacks took matters into their own hands and called a convention in Birmingham for the purpose of developing a strategy to defend their rights. H. B. Johnson, a black newspaperman from Mobile, headed the convention and urged blacks to raise money to carry a suit to the Supreme Court of the United States. The purpose of this action was to defeat the restrictive Amendment. Blacks at the convention accepted Johnson's view but generally stayed away from the polls. On November 11, the constitution was ratified by a vote of 108,613 to 81,734. Only in Lee County did the blacks dominate the vote, 1,214 blacks cast 827 votes against ratification *(Black Republicans: The Politics of the Black and Tans)*.

In the 1902 election only, twenty-five blacks showed up at the Republican state convention and they were turned away. The Lily-White faction drove blacks completely from the party and put guards on the door to keep them out. The Lily-Whites also put forth an all White ticket. The ousted blacks organized their own party, passed resolutions which condemned the Lily-Whites, and sent a telegram congratulating President Theodore Roosevelt for putting old time Republicans in federal offices in the state. The Black and Tans then sent A. Wimbs to Washington to confer with the president. Roosevelt's political manager, K.C. Clark, told Wimbs that the president would crush the Lily-White rebellion in the state and restore blacks to their rightful place in the party. Shortly after Wimbs got back to Alabama, several of the Lily-Whites were removed from office. Other whites, (that had quickly associated themselves with the Black and Tan organization), were elevated to power. The president made the Lily-White executive committee rescind their restrictive order and declared that the party would be opened in the future to all qualified voters. But this came too late.

Disenfranchisement had already taken its toll in all black communities. A few blacks did run in the November 1902 election. Dr. George H. Wilkerson of

Birmingham ran for Congress, H.C. Burford and Daniel Brandon for Alderman seats at Huntsville; A. Wimbs received write-in votes for Governor, and four blacks served on the election board. All the black candidates lost the election. This was no surprise because the size of the black electorate had dropped significantly with the onset of disenfranchisement. In 1890 there had been 140,000 black voters and in 1900, 100,000. Only 46 black were registered in the entire state in 1906 *(Black Republicans: The Politics of the Black and Tans)*

Understanding the limitations of the new disenfranchising constitution, and their dwindling electorate, (which was graphically revealed in the 1902 election), the Republicans, both black and white, met in 1903 to discuss what could be done about their plight. Of the 300 delegates to the convention, one hundred and seventy blacks were seated in a segregated section and a few of them were given an important appointment in the convention. Lily-Whites told blacks that they would allow qualified black voters to participate in their party affairs and that they had nothing against black office holding. Black delegates took exception but the Lily-Whites quietly ignored them and adjourned. At the 1904 state convention, however, Lily-Whites selected one black, Dr. E. Scrugg of Huntsville, to be one of the delegates to the National Convention. This was an attempt by the Lily-Whites to improve their relationship with the national party, but the gesture didn't help; a mixed Black and Tan delegation was seated at the Republican National Convention in Chicago. In the November 1904 election, Eugene Stewart, a black man, was elected Constable of Purtala. After the convention, President Theodore Roosevelt sent two referees J. O. Thompson and Charles G. Scott, to Alabama for the purpose of uniting the various factions of the party. However, the referees made matters worse by siding with one faction against the other. They supported the Black and Tans and denied the Lily-Whites the right to use the party's emblem in the 1906 and 1908 state elections. In each election, both the Black and Tans and the Lily-Whites lost.

In 1908, the two factions once again sent separate delegations to the national convention. The Julius Davis led Lily-Whites were rejected. The Black and Tans currently led by J.O. Thompson were seated because they favored the nomination of William Howard Taft. Booker T. Washington was perhaps the only black in the state, however, who was pleased with Taft's nomination. Other blacks were resentful of Taft's handling of the Brownsville, Texas, incident in which a number of black soldiers were dishonorably discharged for defending themselves. The majority of black registered voters, therefore, cast their ballot for the Democrats in the November election. Black leaders argued, "It was far better to vote an avowed enemy rather than a false friend." For the next four years after 1908, Taft gave a few black Republicans minor federal positions in the state.

This was viewed by most blacks as window dressing and the election of 1912 found blacks organizing the Bull Moose Progressive Party and sending a separate delegation to the Party's convention in Chicago. However, Theodore Roosevelt denied them seats and emphasized that, in the South his Progressive Party would be Lily-Whites.

By 1912, Black and Tan Republicanism in Alabama came to an end. The Lily-Whites were officially recognized from 1916 on, although they had no aid and little help from the national office. The Democrats were now in national power. From 1912 on, blacks dropped practical politics and tried other ways to re-enter the political arena. Black suffrage leagues were formed and several test cases were instituted, but little money could be raised to take these cases to appeals court. From 1912 to 1930 very small progress was made. In fact, the number of black voters declined from 3,742 in 1908 to 1,500 in 1930. Number campaigns for raising black registration were led by individuals like Mrs. Indiana Little. Civic Leagues such as the Tuskegee Civic Association and the Macon County Democratic club were established. Finally, in the early 1940s, blacks formed their own wing of the Democratic Party, the Alabama Progressive Association (APDA).

CHAPTER SEVEN
NORTH CAROLINA

In North Carolina, as in the other eleven states of the old Confederacy, emancipation in 1865 was not enfranchisement. Blacks needed to organize for political equality. In North Carolina a meeting took place in Raleigh in September of 1865. Heading the all black meeting was black minister, J. W. Hood from Connecticut, and James H. Harris, a native of the state who had received his education in Ohio. Two other prominent blacks in the assemblage were A.H. Calloway and Isham Sweat. Several resolutions were adopted. Among them was one calling for suffrage rights, but the meeting did little else. The demands for suffrage rights were met when the new Reconstruction Acts were passed. In November of 1867, some 73,000 blacks registered as voters in order to choose delegates for the state constitutional convention. They sent fifteen black delegates to a convention of one hundred and eleven people *(Black Republicans: The Politics of the Black and Tan)*. Among the fifteen black delegates were Harris, Hood and Calloway. After the convention in 1868, three blacks were elected to the state Senate and sixteen to the House of Representatives.

Blacks figured prominently into other political developments. According to Professor Mabry, "the launching of the Republican Party in North Carolina practically coincided in point of time with the enfranchisement of the Negro." When the first initial organization meeting of the party was held in Raleigh on March 23, 1867, black participated actively. "Proceedings were opened by a Colored minister, and the president was escorted to the chair by a white delegate and a colored delegate. Representatives of both races spoke, the white speakers joining with the Negroes in expressing satisfaction at the admission of the ex-slaves to the electorate." After the initial meeting, Republicans sought to perpetuate black support of their party by employing their secret societies in the state, (the Heroes of America and the Union League), to indoctrinate and propagandize almost exclusively among the black populace. The Union League, argues Professor Mabry, "instructed the Negroes in the principles of the

Republican Party and dictated the candidates for which they were to vote."
Despite the backing of their black allies, the Republicans lost control of both
houses of the legislature to the conservatives in 1870, only two years after they
had taken control. The Republicans remained strong enough, however, to elect
their gubernatorial candidate to office until 1876. Afterwards, the party, as in
other southern states, went downhill.

The Republican coalition in North Carolina came under increasing attack
from the Democrats immediately after the restoration of "home rule," States
Rights. The coalition began to break up under the pressure of the White-
Supremacist Democrats and the policies of various Republican Presidents.
Although the coalition rapidly deteriorated, the emergence of black, Tan and
Lily-White politics in North Carolina was decidedly uneven before 1900. "True
enough," said Professor Mabry, "the carpetbaggers, in the main had fled, the
scalawags were politically ostracized, and the Negroes commonly lacked able
leadership." But the Republicans "by no means ceased to be a factor in North
Carolina politics after the Democratic triumph," in spite of their internal
problems *(Black Republicans: The Politics of the Black and Tan)*.

Political impotency did not prevent racial flare-ups within the Republican
ranks. The first black, Tan and Lily-White separation came early. This was a
result of President Chester A. Arthur's policy of supporting White independent
movements in the South as a first step toward rejuvenating the Republican Party
in that region. white Republicans in North Carolina, (seeing Arthur's policies
take effect all around them in neighboring states such as Virginia, Georgia,
Mississippi, etc.), launched a movement of their own in late 1882. It included
numerous white Democrats and a majority of white Republicans. In its attempt
to gain adherents, the new movement lashed out at the Democrats slogan of
"Negro dominance," claiming it to be a "scarecrow to frighten whites" into
voting for the party. "Surely two million whites," the Liberal Republican
leadership argued, "with all the guns, can withstand one million poverty
stricken, defenseless Negroes, and if not, they deserve defeat." The Democrats
immediately retorted by connecting the new movement's party names with
blacks. The Democratic Executive Committee lampooned the new movement
in 1884, its campaign literature asserting that "North Carolinians will never
know the Radical Party, the party of carpetbaggers, the party of Negro equality.
Radical eggs hatch nothing but Radical chickens. Strip a Liberal and a naked
Radical stands before you every time" *(Black Republicans: The Politics of the Black
and Tan)*. Democratic newspapers ran cartoons showing liberal Republicans and
blacks riding together in the same carriage. Before long, the damage was done.

"The Liberal Republicans were handicapped by the party's name and by the inevitable connection with Negroes " *(Black Republicans: The Politics of the Black and Tan)*. In addition to being out maneuvered by the Democrats and acquiring a discredited public image, the Liberal Republicans lost their main backer and sponsor, President Arthur, when Democrat Grover Cleveland captured the Presidency in 1884. Shortly after the national election, the movement dissipated.

When this brief black, Tan and Lily-White clash died out, another, on a limited scale, occurred in the same year. Democrats not satisfied to discredit just the Liberal Republicans (Lily-Whites), tried to further weaken the regular Republican Party (Black and Tans) by creating dissension among blacks and the few whites who remained. In Granville County, in particular, the Democrats convinced blacks that they had not been allotted a fair share of places on the Republican County ticket, and urged them to put their own ticket in the field. Two influential blacks in the county, Tom Lewis and Banky Gee, called a Republican convention and nominated their own black candidates for office. Their candidates consisted of a black school-teacher, Walter Patillo, for Register of the Deeds, and W. K. "Spotted Bull" Jenkins, "a large powerful, freckled-face who raised cattle for the home market" and for the State Senate *(Black Republicans: The Politics of the Black and Tan)*. During the campaign, the black candidates proved very popular until the Democrats gave their support to the liberal Republican (Lily-Whites) in the final days of the campaign, even providing money to defeat the black candidates whom they had spurred on initially. The party usually returned to its old precarious unity after the election, at least for a while. The emergence of the Populist Party in 1891 as another political challenger in the state helped the black and white Republicans to put a momentary halt to their internal differences and present a united front in the 1892 election. The majority of the blacks voted the Republican ticket in the election but the Republicans and the Populists lost to the Democrats, who took strong measures in the legislature of 1893 to restrict the activities of the Populist Party.

This caused the Populist leadership to effect a fusion agreement with the Republicans for the up coming 1894 election. The agreement held that separate party organizations were to be maintained but only one ticket, partly Republican and partly Populist, was to be put in the field. Although expediency was the main binding force in the agreement, the arrangement proved victorious and the fusionists gained control of the state legislature. Some black Republicans questioned whether the Populists were worth supporting because of their seeming opposition to black office holding, but the actions of the Populists proved otherwise; the number of black officeholders more than tripled. It was under this fusion arrangement, in fact, that the last black Congressman from the South was able to obtain and hold office. That man was George White. Once in office, the Fusionist repealed the Democrats restrictive election law, re-gerrymandering the city and municipal governments in their favor, and urged blacks to vote.

The Populists and Republicans decided to try the same technique again in 1896. Just before the campaign got underway, however, a third breakaway of the Black and Tan Republicans occurred. Both parties (Populists and Republicans) had agreed to enter their own gubernatorial candidate in the field but to divide up the remaining elective offices. The Republicans named Judge Daniel L. Russell, as their gubernatorial candidate. During his earlier political career Russell had been disrespectful to blacks. In several campaigns prior to 1896, he was reported to have characterized blacks as "savages who stole all the week and prayed it off on Sunday," and who were "no more fit to govern or to have a share in governing than their brethren in the swamps of Africa" *(Black Republicans: The Politics of the Black and Tan)*. Although in his speech accepting the Republican nomination he made a concerted bid to capture black support, many black Republicans were unhappy about the nomination and withdrew from the regular Republican convention. These black Republicans held their own convention in Raleigh in July of 1896. They endorsed the Populist candidate for governor, William A. Guthrie, who appeared well disposed to black people, rather than nominating a candidate of their own. The bolt proved abortive; Russell won in September and the fusion victory of 1896 placed an estimated one thousand blacks in office.

Having lost twice, the Democrats began preparing immediately for the 1898 election with their one sure weapon, the call for white supremacy and the end of Negro domination. All during 1897, the Democratic Executive Committee used every method to play up the issue. Pro-Democratic editors, Democratic White Supremacy Clubs, and Democratic speakers kept the matter continually alive. The Democrats were so sure of themselves and the effects of their propaganda that when the Populist sought fusion with them on May 26, 1998, rather than join with the "Nigger Republican Party" they turned the offer down flat, indicating that they wanted nothing to do with supporters of Republican Negro-rule. The Democrats were shrewd enough, though, to appeal to individual Populists through the race issue and a platform that included many of the reforms the Populists desired. Some Populists and Republicans had joined forces solely for the sake of expediency, but many of the Populists held negative attitudes toward black participation in politics, and they moved over easily into the Democratic camp. Just a few days prior to the election the North Carolinian Democrats pulled out one additional technique to defeat the predominately black Republican organization. They imported the famed South Carolinian demagogue, Ben "Pitchfork" Tilman, who made several "Nigger-baiting" speeches throughout the state *(Black Republicans: The Politics of the Black and Tan)*. Tillman brought with him the "Red Shirts" a new version of the Ku Klux Klan who employed violence and intimidation to make sure that black stayed at home on Election Day. The Democratic technique worked. On November 8, 1888 the Democrats captured both houses. Only seven fusionists were returned to the State Senate and twenty-six to the House. Black representation likewise declined. The next year the legislature passed a new election law over the protest of several black lawmakers, completely disenfranchising blacks in the entire state. Since the law had a grandfather clause and didn't go into effect until 1902, the legislature in the interim appointed white members to local government boards to ensure white control at municipal and county levels.

The Democrats launched a tremendous White Supremacy campaign between 1900 and 1902, thereby arousing great racial feelings. The remaining whites in the Republican Party pulled out in 1904 and 1905 and formed a separate "Lily-White" organization that in 1906, as stated in the party Handbook, officially repudiated blacks and their participation in politics. By 1912, the Lily-Whites had become enough of a force that they put their own political ticket in the field, but it made a "miserable and disappointing showing in the state election." While Black and Tan competition before 1906 was sporadic and uneven, there was continuous strife after 1906 with both groups (the blacks and Tans and the Lily-Whites) having set up permanent operating organization. Fusionism in North Carolina during the 1890s had not only helped revive the Republican Party and increase the number of Republican political officials; it had also contributed to the revival of the specter of black domination and Negrophobia.

White supremacy Democrats were angered by the new emergence of black politicians and their repeated election losses to the fusion candidates. Their resulting emphasis of the notion of "Nigger domination" eventually won them many adherents and the fusion effort of the Republicans and Populists collapsed. By 1901, the collapse was final.

It should be remembered that while white "fusion was fairly sound under the surface, beneath were personalities and prejudices which constituted a problem," as Professor Helen Edmonds put it. "Historians who uphold the idea that blacks voted the Republican ticket with a slavish fanaticism must not overlook the fact that there was never complete harmony between white party leaders and Negro party followers during the fusion period." While fusionism did give the party more electoral success, it did not remove black and white antagonisms. The factional fighting continued during the fusion period and thereafter. The Lily-White Republicans did little to stop the disenfranchising amendment from being passed and the majority of blacks had lost their right to vote when the year 1900 ended. According to Professor Edmonds, "The Republicans Party proved its disloyalty to the Negro group after the election 1900. The Negro who could qualify to vote under the disenfranchisement amendment was forgotten and the party marched thereafter under banner of a Lily-White party."

However, the national Republican Administration's indifference to the disenfranchisement of the Negro Republicans in North Carolina did not pass unnoticed. A leading black paper, *The AME Zion Quarterly*, editorialized that, "Our friends, the national Republicans, are still in possession of the national government, but they have not done as much for our race as they had led us to hope." After disenfranchisement the Black and Tan Republicans did little challenging on the state level, concentrating more on the national conventions. Patronage became the key issue, not electoral or political power. The Black and Tan wing in North Carolina, although badly hampered by disenfranchisement, did lead several convention challenges against the Lily-Whites at the national convention.

CHAPTER EIGHT
VIRGINIA

Virginians sympathetic to the Republican Party and its goals met in Alexandra on June 12, 1865. The "Union Association of Alexandria," as this delegation called itself, adopted a resolution urging that the "constitution of Virginia should be amended so as to confer the right of suffrage upon and restrict it to, loyal male citizens without regard to color." The convention took additional steps to see that the Freedman's Bureau would be brought into the state. In fact, within three days after the convention, on June 15, 1865, the Freedman's Bureau was established in Virginia. The Bureau not only protected and cared for the Freedmen but, "also impressed upon their minds the debt which they owed the Republican Party." The next year, on May 17, 1886, the Union Association met again in Alexandria and this time adopted a resolution that declared, "No reorganized state government of Virginia should be recognized by the government of the United States which does not exclude from suffrage and holding office at least for a term of years, all persons who have voluntarily give moral or material support to rebellion against the United Sates and which does not, with such disenfranchisement, provide for the immediate enfranchisement of all Union men without distinction of color" *(Black Republicans: The Politics of the Black and Tan).*

The convention sent several delegates to a meeting in Philadelphia called by President Andrew Johnson to see how much support he had among the Republicans in the North and the Unionist in the South in his fight with Congressional Republican Radicals. After the September 2, 1865 convention in Philadelphia, several members of the fledgling Republican organization brought back with them the Union League organization to begin its work, late in 1866, in the black community. In its secret and mysterious meetings, the organization taught blacks that "their only friends were the Union Republicans, and their chief enemies were their former masters, who were not of the Republican Party." When the Reconstruction Acts were passed in March of 1867, (although

365

several white Democrats tried to induce blacks to join them rather than the Republicans). Registration of voters began in late March the Freedmen became more and more attached to the Republican Party.

Prior to the October elections in 1867, the Republicans held meetings in numerous black Churches to reinforce black allegiance to the regular Republican organization. At one mass convention of black and white radicals in the Capital Square in Richmond, there was a call for the confiscation of "rebel lands, cheers for Thaddeus Stevens, condemnation of President Johnson and of the rebel aristocracy" *(Black Republicans: The Politics of the Black and Tan).* Republicans, however, met some competition from the conservative Democrats in the state, who held several meetings with blacks and urged them to join with them instead of the Republicans. While the conservatives advocated black suffrage, however, they hoped to become the leaders of the newly freed blacks, and this hampered their appeal.

The election results revealed that blacks almost unanimously supported the Republicans mixed slate of candidates. In all, 91,869 of the 92,507 registered black voters voted for the Constitutional Convention, while only 14,835 of the 760,845 white registered voters did so. Of the 105 delegates elected, 35 were conservatives 65 were Radicals, and five could not be classified in either group. The black delegates made up 25 of the Radical delegation, and it was with their backing that the new constitution granted substantial rights, even the elective franchise, to black Virginians. When the convention came to a close on April 17, 1868, the vote for the adoption of the constitution was 51 to 36, with only one black and 11 conservatives among those voting against it *(Black Republicans: The Politics of the Black and Tan).* The constitution was debated back and forth for the rest of the year, and was finally approved by the Virginia House of Representatives on December 8, 1868.

Immediately after adoption, both conservative and Republicans began preparations for the forthcoming state election, each group propagandizing among blacks for their support. In one instance, "Conservative Negroes of Richmond, at the risk of personal violence from the colonial Radicals, arranged a barbecue for their men and invited a number of prominent white conservatives." The Republicans, playing upon the superstitious strain in the black community, declared that "The hand of God is to curse those who apostatize and to bless and guide those who go faithfully to the polls and vote the Republican ticket." Blacks voted for both parties, the Republicans and the conservatives, but the former received the majority of their support, and six black Republicans were elected to the General Assembly. Republicans' control of the state government did not last very long, however. The white conservative Democrats would recapture the state government in 1870.

With this resurgence of white conservatism, black representation in the House dropped from twenty-one to fourteen in the 1871 election, and from six to three in the state Senate. Each year thereafter, black representation declined steadily until 1879 when the conservatives lost power to the emerging Re-adjuster movement that held power in the state from 1879 to 1883. When the Re-adjusters began to come to power in Virginia in 1878, there were only seven blacks left in the state legislature. The Republican Party though in the period of conservative control, had become almost a black organization. In 1878, the Re-adjusters increased their numbers in the state legislature from six to twenty-three, a fact that attracted the attention of Republican President Hayes whose aim was to rebuild the Republican Party in the South. The Re-adjuster movement in Virginia grew out of the liability or the refusal of the conservatives to adopt a forthright economic policy that would enable payment of the state debt, while at the same time introduce new social legislation and reform programs. The conservatives took a hard-line approach and insisted that the debt be paid off before any new programs could be initiated. The Re-adjusters disagreed, and they put their ideas into political action.

First, they made strong appeals to the black community, particularly black Republicans, who had at this time tremendous electoral power. Since the white registered voters numbered approximately 150,000 and the blacks 121,000, the budding movement needed black voters if it were to wrest a substantial share of the power now held by the conservative whites. Blacks, who were suffering under the repression of the conservatives and continual losses at the polls because of black predominance in the Republican Party, saw the great possibilities of such a political alliance. Republican Presidents like Hayes and Garfield, looking for a way to revive the Republican Party, supported the Re-adjusters in varying degree during their tenure in office. Arthur gave the Re-adjusters full recognition and full support with Republican Party patronage. In fact, William Mahone, who headed the Re-adjuster movement, became chief dispenser of Republican patronage in the state. With such recognition and financial backing, the Re-adjusters drew many blacks into their ranks.

When the 1879 election was over, the Re-adjusters, with the aid of blacks, had won control of both Houses of the legislature. They elected fifty-six out of one hundred delegates and black representation rose from seven to eleven in the House and from zero in the Senate to two. Mahone, again with black support, later went to the U.S. Senate. But when the Republicans lost on the national level, the Re-adjusters in Virginia also lost control of the State government. While they were in power, however, they received so much black support that the Republican Party itself achieved very little. The first major accomplishment for the predominantly black Republican Party was the election of John Langston to Congress in 1889. In that year, moreover, five of the twenty-four Republicans within the general assembly were black, and one black Republican, N. M. Griggs, was elected to the State Senate.

In 1891, no black Republicans or Re-adjusters were elected to the state legislature. With only three Republicans holding office in the legislature that year, the party coalesced with the newly organized farmer party, the Populists Party in 1892. The fusion sent thirty-six Populists to the state legislature and set off a wave of concern in the Democratic ranks. When the Democrats regained sufficient power in the State Assembly, in 1897, they put in motion plans for a new state constitution, (as Mississippi had in 1890), which would disenfranchise the black voter. The call in 1897 for a constitutional convention was defeated in a referendum by a vote of 183,483 to 38,326. The Democratic-dominated general assembly tried again in 1900, calling for a vote for a constitutional convention on May 24, of that year. In the election, 77,362 votes were cast for a convention and 60,375 against. Professor Morton states, "Of the 35 counties in which there was a majority of blacks, 18 voted for the convention and 17 against it" *(Black Republicans: The Politics of the Black and Tan)*. Many blacks had apparently supported a convention that was bent on disenfranchising them. But the reality is that the conservative whites, who held the economic and political power, dominated and manipulated black voters and forced them to vote the conservative way. While the Republicans strongly opposed the convention and the proposed constitution, they were too weak, (with only twelve delegates out of one hundred and eighty-eight), to forestall the convention or its known purpose, to disenfranchise blacks.

Professor Morton, commenting on the convention and its purpose, said:

The black man had been a failure and a menace in politics. As long as he was in politics the color line was a line of friction and danger to both races. Therefore, he must be removed, not only because he was for the most part an ignorant and irresponsible voter who had usually stood solidly behind the worst elements in state politics, but also because he had been taught in the beginning to vote as a Negro and must therefore be disenfranchised because he was a Negro. While Republicans in the convention voted against the disenfranchisement of blacks, the convention decided to proclaim the document law of the state, rather than submit it to the electorate for their consideration.

On May 29, 1902, the new constitution was proclaimed to be in force. And in 1902 and 1903, when voters re-registered under the conditions of the new constitution, only 21,000 blacks became voters. Whereas, 147,000 black had been voters before the act, only this marginal number remained to give support to the collapsing Republican Party organization (Black Republicans: The Politics *of the Black and Tan).*

In retrospect there was no major schism in the Republican Party in Virginia before 1900 which produced well defined Black and Tan and Lily-White factional organizations. Although there had been friction within the party between the two races, the Re-adjusters and the Populists served as outlets for dissatisfied blacks and whites and an alternative to factionalizing the Republican Party. Black and Tan and Lily-White Republicanism, however, did start developing after 1902. When the disenfranchising constitution went into effect in 1902 many white Republicans saw it as an opportunity to revive the Republican Party in the state, and "restore two-party politics in Virginia as a process that enfranchised Negroes hampered." Therefore, when the state GOP chairman, Park Agnew, had the executive committee on June 17, 1902 issue a resolution condemning the proclamation of the constitution as illegal, black Republicans (being aware of past dubious white actions), viewed the matter as a façade. The black attitude toward the Republican announcement was justified in September of 1902 when blacks "in several areas of the state, found themselves excluded from Republican meetings and conventions" *(Black Republicans: The Politics of the Black and Tan).* Black participation in state Republican circles, in fact declined each year thereafter, as Lily-White-ism surged. Black participation was so stymied that black Republicans began offering their own candidates for local and state offices.

The first Black and Tan Republican candidate, J.B. Johnson of Manchester, was nominated for the third congressional House seat in Richmond on October 11, 1906. Johnson, a black man, was selected after the white nominee had indicated to blacks that they should take a back seat in party affairs. The Black and Tan Candidate received only 196 votes, and the Lily-White candidate received 639. The white Democrat who won the contest received 3,908 votes. Political exclusion of African Americans continued in the Republican Party State Convention at Lynchburg VA. on April 8, 1908, and blacks, therefore, held their own convention on May 14, in Richmond. The blacks selected a slate of delegates to contest the Lily-Whites at the Republican National Convention in Chicago. This Black and Tan delegation protested strongly to the Credentials Committee at the national convention that the Lily-White organization was illegal because it held closed city, county, and district conventions. The challenge failed, and the Lily-Whites were seated. Recognizing their weak electoral power, the Black and Tans forsook local and state politics, not reemerging again until 1912.

The Lily-Whites pledged themselves that year for Taft, while the Black and Tans supported Theodore Roosevelt for the presidential nomination. At the national convention the Taft forces prevailed and the Lily-Whites were again seated over the protests of the Black and Tans. The Black and Tans didn't reemerge this time until 1920, when a new "Lily-Black" Republican movement was begun to counteract the ever growing Lily-White movement. The new movement, started by the black editor of the Richmond Planet and some influential black leaders, nominated Joseph R. Pollard, a noted black attorney, for the U.S. Senate. The Lily-Whites didn't put up a candidate, so the race was a straight contest between a white Democrat and the black Republican. The Democrat, Carter Blass, received 184,646 votes to Pollard's 17,576 votes. In Richmond his home city, Pollard received 2,971 ballots; in Norfolk, 653; in Portsmouth, 469; in Lynchburg 446; and in Newport News 406 *(Black Republicans: The Politics of the Black and Tan)*.

Encouraged by Pollard's state-wide showing, black editor Mitchell called for a Lily-black Republican state convention in 1921 at the True Reformer Hall in Richmond. When the convention convened on July 8, of that year forty-five delegates were elected to attend the Lily-White state convention in order to urge the Lily-Whites to give blacks meaningful representation in the party organization. This request pointed to the number of votes, 17,576, the black Republicans had cast in the 1920 U.S. Senate elections and indicated to the Lily-Whites that if they hoped to win the 1921 state election, or any other, they would need these votes. The argument didn't prevail; the black delegation, except for three, was turned away. The attempt at reconciliation had failed. On September 6, in Richmond, therefore, the lily-black leadership nominated a full slate ticket as a protest against the Lily-Whites mistreatment. Editor John Mitchell Jr. was nominated for Governor, Theodore Nash for lieutenant Governor, J. Thomas Newsome for Attorney General, Thomas E. Jackson for Treasurer, J.Z. Baccus for Secretary of the Commonwealth, Mrs. Maggie L. Walker for Superintendent of Public Instruction and J.L. Less for Commissioner of Agriculture.

During the election campaign, dissension and personal jealousy developed among the black community. Opposing the Lily-black ticket was black editor, P. B. Young, of the influential *Norfolk Journal and Guide*, who had declined the nomination for Lieutenant Governor. Jealous over the success of Mitchell's paper, *The Planet*, Young strongly attacked the ticket and advised blacks not to vote for it because it was ill timed, unwise and it drew a color line by excluding whites from party plans. Young's opposition had an effect. In the election, the Democratic candidates for Governor polled 139,416 votes, the Lily-White Republican candidate, 65,933, and the Lily-black candidate, Mitchell, 5,046, nearly 12,000 votes less than a black candidate had polled a year earlier. In Norfolk, out of 1,600 registered black voters, Mitchell received only 90 votes. After such a dismal showing, the Lily-black organization gave up the ghost. A few black Republicans remained in the political arena after 1921, but organizationally, black Republicanism was defunct.

CHAPTER NINE
FLORIDA

Republicanism began in the black community in Florida soon after the war, before freedmen were permitted to vote. This activity was begun by the Union League, which began springing up all over Florida in 1865. It soon started to fade, because prospects for blacks getting suffrage rights in Florida at that time seemed bleak. The political organizing that the Union League started was continued by Thomas W. Osborn, an assistant to the head of the Freedmen's Bureau. Osborn had been the first head of the Bureau but was replaced in 1866, and stayed on in a subordinate capacity. Some time in 1866, he invited a few influential blacks to a meeting at the home of another black Freedman in Tallahassee. At this meeting, an organization, the Lincoln brotherhood, was formed with Osborn as president. The Tallahassee society became the parent lodge for the Lincoln Brotherhood organization, which had lodges throughout the state. The "combination of elaborate ceremony, secret signs and passwords, together with a promise of free land and civil rights bills" by this secret society was "such a strong attraction for the freedmen that by late summer of 1867, it claimed the fidelity of thousands of Negro voters." The oath of the Brotherhood read, in part: "I will not vote for any person, for any office who is not a brother of this league" *(Black Republicans: The Politics of the Black and Tan)*.

Osborn soon encountered competition in trying to organize the Freedmen politically. Liberty Billings of New Hampshire, (a former Unitarian minister and army Chaplin in a black regiment), spoke to an assembly of blacks on February 8, 1866 in a Baptist church at Fernandina. He condemned the conservative state legislature and the black codes, and had the meeting pass a resolution commending Republicans in Congress for trying to secure civil rights for all citizens. In the Spring, of 1867, Billings was aided in his attempt to organize Freedmen by Colonel William V. Saunders, a black barber from Maryland, and Daniel Richards, a white man from Sterling, Illinois "who claimed to be the representative of the National Republican Committee." Richard had been in

Florida since early 1866, served for a short period of time as a tax commissioner, and had been in constant contact with northern Republicans, insisting that black suffrage was imperative for the protection of the Freedmen.

Billings, Richards and Saunders combined and in the Spring of 1867, organized another secret society, the Loyal League of America, effectively competing among blacks with the Osborn led Lincoln Brotherhood. Saunders, who had been characterized as "one of the shrewdest, most influential and dangerous Negroes in Reconstruction politics," became president of the newly formed organization. The League made their rituals even more elaborate than in the Brotherhood's, using special handgrips, passwords and secret signs. Billings made numerous speeches throughout the states denouncing segregation and the black codes.

Kissing black babies and frequently lacing his speeches with shouts of, "Jesus Christ was a Republican." When asked by an inquiring reporter what participation in Loyal League meetings was like, one black described it this way: "Well, see, I'll tell you. See one man he takes a piece of paper and tears it in little pieces and gives us all a piece. Then another man, he comes round with a pencil and writes something on the paper, and gives it to us again, then the first man, he comes round with a hat and we put them all in; then he takes them up there and counts them all and says unanimous." The league was so successful that it replaced the Lincoln Brotherhood and in November, of 1867, Richard wrote, "Saunders, Billings, and myself have created the Republican Party and save not all cliques and factions before us."

At this point, however, the more than five percent of white Floridians who had been "Union sympathizers during the protection of federal soldiers," as well as small convention in May, of 1864 (attended by John Hay, President Lincoln's private secretary), were unhappy with both the Osborn led Lincoln Brotherhood and the Saunders led Loyal League. A meeting was held, therefore, on March 27, 1867 in a local attorney's office, Ossian B. Hart office in Jacksonville to form the Republican Club of Jacksonville. A later meeting was held on April 1, to adopt a constitution and by-laws, and a committee was formed to invite those who favored the organization to join. An invitation was sent to blacks and was answered: by two blacks: William Bradwell, a local minister, and Jonathan Gibbs, who later became the Secretary of State and then Superintendent of Public Institutions. These two blacks became officers in the new organization. Bradwell became one of the eight vice Presidents and Gibbs served on the Executive Committee.

Thus, shortly after the announcement of the Reconstruction Act, there were three factions, each calling themselves the Republican Party, in Florida. The three factions met together on July 18, 1867 in the first state-wide convention of the Republican Party in Florida, at Hart's request. Differences were resolved and the factions were united in a much more permanent organization. Seeing the emergence of the new Republican organization, and understanding the political muscle of the new freedmen, Democrats began preparing for the election to be held November14-16 by reversing themselves and appealing to blacks. They immediately won some black adherents. One black Democrat, William Martin, speaking in Lake City, counseled blacks to join the Democrats because, as he saw it, such a coalition was the only way to live happily in the South. To break with southern whites, he prophesied, would lead to racial strife. Black spokesmen and nice overtures didn't win any large numbers of black Democratic converts, however. On the election days, out of 28,000 registered voters (15,434, and the majority were blacks), only 14,503 ballots were cast. Thirteen thousand two hundred and eighty-three (13,283) blacks voted, and only 1,220 whites; 203 of the whites voted against the constitutional convention *(Black Republicans: The Politics of the Black and Tan)*.

In late December, General Pope announced the results of the election and designated January 20, 1868 as the date for the convention to assemble. "Of the forty-six delegates elected, eighteen were blacks, and they demonstrated in the proceedings of the convention a surprising ability." According to a reporter, Solon Robinson, who covered the convention for the *New York Tribune*, several blacks stood out. Charles H. Pearce and Jonathan C. Gibbs, both black ministers, delivered excellent speeches during the convention. Green Davidson, a barber turned politician, made speeches on social equality and political rights which many considered inflammatory. Robert Meachum, another black minister-politician who made talks during the convention, was considered by some whites to be a trouble maker and by others as an honest and respectable man. The most powerful speaker in the convention was William U. Saunders, who was described as an orator, who could "tear the wind and scatter thunderbolts."

Despite blacks and their ability, the new cemented Republican organization came apart in the heated convention debates. Osborn, who had lost most of his black support, opposed those Republicans like Billings, Richards, and Saunders who backed the proposed new constitution, and urged their ouster on the grounds that they were ineligible as delegates since they had not been residents in the state for one year. Osborn was joined by a group of conservative Republicans, and for two days these factions fought each other. Later, the conservative Republican factions withdrew, held their own convention, drafted their own constitution, then rejoined the original convention and reorganized it. At this point the Osborn led conservative faction was composed of white federal office holders, scalawags, and three blacks. The Saunders-Billings-Richards group had the support of all the other black delegates, including influential blacks like Pearce and Gibbs. When bickering continued after the conservative Republicans rejoined the convention, the military commander ordered a re-organization and a new selection of officers. The reformed convention ousted Billings, Saunders, Richards and Pearce, but drew up a constitution that granted universal male suffrage and remained in effect in the state until 1885. Whites apportioned the state in such a fashion, however, that legislative control would reside in white hands. One outstanding feature of the new constitution was that it granted one seat in each house to the Seminole Native Americans (American Indians).

Although whites objected to the suffrage rights granted to blacks, the new constitution was ratified in May of 1868 by a vote of 14,520 to 9,491. In addition to the ratification of the constitution, nineteen of the seventy-six delegates elected to the state legislature were blacks, and three of these nineteen sat in the State Senate. Five blacks sat in Florida's Senate in 1869-70, three in 1871-72, five in 1873-74 and six in 1875-76. In the House the number never rose above thirteen after 1868 *(Black Republicans: The Politics of the Black and Tan)*. In 1868, Governor Harrison Reed appointed Jonathan Gibbs as Secretary of State, a post he held until Reed was succeeded in January of 1873, by Ossian B. Hart. Hart, due to black pressure, appointed Gibbs as Superintendent of Public Instruction, a post that he held until his untimely death on August 14, 1874. In 1870, Josiah T. Walls was elected to the House of Representatives. However, the result was contested and a white man, Silas L. Niblack, was declared the winner by 137 votes. Walls was re-elected in 1872, serving in the 43rd Congress. He presented credentials to the 44th Congress and served from March 4, 1875 until April 19, 1876, at which time he was succeeded by Jesse T. Finley, a white man who successfully contested his election. Walls had the unhappy distinction of being three times elected and twice unseated. Numerous other blacks represented the Republican Party during Reconstruction, but Gibbs and Walls held the highest elective posts.

The split which occurred during the convention became a permanent factor in the Republican organization thereafter: the Black and Tan group, the Billings-Saunders-Richards faction, and the Lily-White conservatives, now led by Osborn. From the outset, the Black and Tan group dominated state politics and held state patronage, while the Osborn Lily-Whites held federal patronage. The latter had an advantage because federal posts carried cash salaries, while state salaries were paid in "depreciated scrip" because the state was bankrupt. This factor of lack of money, as well as the fact that Osborn was elected to the U.S. Senate in 1868 and had national connections, caused the Lily-White faction (which had been in the minority at first), to soon become a force equal in political power to the Black and Tans in 1875 and gaining in ascendancy each year thereafter.

The Black and Tan wing of the Republican Party received its major setback in the election of 1876 when the Democrats recaptured the state government of Florida and embarked upon a program of white supremacy which opposed black suffrage. Black suffrage was already being opposed by the Lily-White Republicans. Thus, when Reconstruction ended with the state redemption, the Black and Tans found themselves under violent attack by Democratic organizations such as the Ku Klux Klan and the Young Men's Democratic Clubs. The Republican cleavage was further aggravated by the Democrats of the state who made available to their Republican faction the opportunity to criticize the other. Newspapers offered full pages of such criticisms, paid for by Democrats. Black office holders dropped in numbers thereafter, while the shifty southern policy of Republican Presidents pushed the Black and Tan faction further and further back from view and real political power. Even minor appointments were given grudgingly.

Things became so hard for black Republicans after Democrats captured the state in 1876 that a few blacks "joined conservative clubs and worked openly for Democrats." During the 1876 election many black women "threatened to abandon their husbands if they voted Democratic." To help these black husbands, a Democratic paper, *The Monticello Constitution*, wrote that a prominent attorney had directed the legal fraternity in the state to grant divorces to black men so threatened. "Thus honest Democratic Negroes," the paper added, "can get rid of their old, ugly, and crazy hags, and be placed in a condition to marry young, sensible, and pretty mulatto girls." Democrats won the day and carried the election. Fraud was so prevalent in the election, by both Republican and Democrats that the result of the presidential election was thrown out. Later, a special commission awarded the election to Republican Rutherford B. Hayes, but the Democrats held power on the state level.

While a few black politicians held on thereafter, Democrats held a new constitutional convention in 1885 and instituted several devices, including the multiple ballot box law and a poll tax, to disenfranchise black voters. These moves proved successful because the number of black Republicans in 1888 had shrunk to 8,861 by 1892. Fusion with the Populists temporarily increased the number by 13,560, but violence, intimidation, Populist failures, and resurgence of the White Supremacy movement caused the number of black Republicans to drop to 6,869 in 1900. Black and Tan-ism was slowly fading into oblivion. After the white primary was established in the state in 1902, black voters were forced to register as Republicans because the Democratic Party would not accept them. But the Democratic Primary was in effect, the elections. "In practice, a few blacks of the right opinion were permitted to vote in Democratic primaries sometimes in states with a state-wide primary rule." The majority of blacks, who desired to register continued to do so as Republicans and fought the Lily-White Republican faction "who occasionally sought to impose Republican white primaries for the control of the state party organization and for possible feral patronage." The disenfranchised black voters fought back through determined black leaders and sundry black organizations, which led occasional registration drives. This raised the number of black Republicans in the state from 6,869 in 1900 to 15,877 in 1946 *(Black Republicans: The Politics of the Black and Tan)*.

Generally speaking, "between 1902 and 1937, a politically conscious black in Florida, found his way to effective participation in politics cut off by any on of the three legal barriers" set up during the era of disenfranchisement (1889-1902) in the state. These legal barriers, "the poll tax, the multiple ballot box, and the white primary, as well as the Australian Ballot, "contributed greatly to the destruction of the Republican Party (especially the Black and Tan supporters) as a significant force in state and local politics." As one student in Florida put it, "The party having become nullity, blacks lost what had been the traditional vehicle for the expression of their political demands, and general elections became ritualistic formalities" *(Black Republicans: The Politics of the Black and Tan)*.

Black and Tan Republicanism in Florida came to an end in state and local politics as in almost all other southern states, shortly after disenfranchisement was institutionalized. The politics of the Black and Tan Republicans in Florida assumed no clear-cut pattern; they had no characteristic political style. But Black and Tans, as in other states, became an occasional force to be reckoned with at the national convention.

CHAPTER TEN
SOUTH CAROLINA

Black Republicanism began in some areas of South Carolina before the Civil War ended, but not until after the war in certain sections. For instance, blacks living in the liberated Sea Islands of the coast of South Carolina began to express an interest in the politics of the Republican Party as early as 1862. They hailed their "Yankees" and "Massa Lincoln" as God sent and promised to be their loyal supporters and followers. For blacks on the mainland, Republicanism came only after the war. Before the war ended, free blacks in Charleston were calling for civil and political rights. In 1865 a "Colored Peoples" Convention of the state of South Carolina met in Charleston from November 20-25 and issued a document to the "White inhabitants of South Carolina" asking that black be granted their civil and political rights. This appeal supplied the Radical Republicans in Congress "with highly potent ammunition for their coming attack" upon the presidential policies for Reconstruction. Blacks continued their protest for suffrage rights intermittently and sent a delegate, William Beverly Nash, to the National Freedmen's Convention in Washington early in 1867. Nash "strove vigorously to have the convention endorse Negro suffrage without educational or property qualifications." After the convention, Nash visited the House of Representatives and sat in the gallery as that body overrode President Andrew Johnson's veto of the First Reconstruction Acts. Returning home, Nash called an assembly to thank God for having "seen fit to cause this great nation to release them from the disadvantages and deprivation that they labored under as a people" *(Black Republicans: The Politics of the Black and Tan).*

By March of 1867, the Republican Party held its first state convention in Charleston and endorsed the Reconstruction Act that enabled blacks and loyal whites to register and vote for delegates of a new constitution. The factions which coalesced into the Republican organization in South Carolina included blacks, scalawags, and carpetbaggers. The nominal preparatory work among the Freedmen had been done by the Freedmen's Bureau and the Union League. But in the case of South Carolina, blacks themselves had gained some political consciousness and strongly endorsed the Republican Party on their own. Following the structuring of a formal party organization in March of 1867 at the Charleston meeting, another meeting concerned with principles and platform was held in July of 1867 in Columbus. There, 45 of the 65 delegates were blacks and they helped to draw up a platform calling for universal suffrage and equal rights for blacks, including a broad program of economic reform. Specifically, the platform called for a system of free education, "internal improvement, public support for the poor and destitute, those aged and infirm people, houseless and homeless, the revision and reorganization of the judicial system, and the division and sale of unoccupied land among the poorer classes."

After the convention, the Republican Party began campaigning for its newly developed platform. In the meantime, registration of blacks had begun and continued through the summer. Black Republicans apprised the black masses of their new potential, and were aided by the Freedmen's Bureau and government agents. In the November election of 1867, "Nearly 69,000 of a possible 81,000 Negroes, roughly 85 percent, participated and voted for the convention" (*Black Republicans: The Politics of the Black and Tan*). When the delegates to the convention assembled at Charleston in January of 1868, there were 76 black Republican delegates and 48 whites. As in the other states, the convention of South Carolina debated the major issue of suffrage, the structure of the new government, and the proper role for black Americans within the new political structure. After meeting for fifty-three consecutive days, the convention adjourned, having drafted a new constitution, on March 17, 1868.

The document was submitted to the electorate for ratification on April 14-16 1868. In the period between the convention and submission of the document to the public, the Republicans and Democrats actively propagandized. White Democrats objected to the idea of black voters and black participation in the new government, and were so angered that they submitted a petition entitled, "Respectful Remonstrance on the Behalf of White People of South Carolina Against the Constitution of the Late Convention of South Carolina, Now Submitted to Congress for Ratification," to the House of Representatives. Later, another white appeal was sent to the United States Senate. Despite these protests, 67,000 of the eligible 81,000 blacks went to the polls, ratified the new constitution and returned Republicans to all major offices. The vote was 70,758 for ratification and 27,288 against it (*Black Republicans: The Politics of the Black and Tan*).

The first legislature of South Carolina under the new constitution assembled at Columbia in July of 1868. When the Senate convened in late July, it had 11 blacks among the 31 Senators; the House had 71 black representatives out of 124. The legislatures first action after organizing was the ratification of the Fourteenth Amendment *(Black Republicans: The Politics of the Black and Tan).*

With some opposition from the Democrats, the state legislature also ratified the Fifteenth Amendment before it adjourned. By 1870 the white Republicans so respected the strength of the black Republicans that they placed a black, A.J. Ransier, on their ticket for the post of Lieutenant Governor. The Republicans won with no trouble; Ransier received 85,071 votes. However, these continual Republican successes spurred Democratic hatred that culminated in the organization of Ku Klux Klan terrorism in 1871. Although several Klansmen were put on trial between 1871-72, this limited public exposure did not slow the organization's terrorist tactics against the black community. The Democrats used threats to intimidate blacks, though they also employed other tactics to attract them into the party. As early as spring of 1868, white Democrats had succeeded in several areas of the state in organizing black Democratic Clubs. "In Columbia, for instance, a Democratic association of Colored citizens was formed in mid April with about 40 charter members. By mid June it reportedly mustered one hundred blacks on the rolls." In 1870 the Democrats had two blacks of questionable background speaking for the party throughout the state. One, Jonas Byrd, described as, "a respectable Negro of Charleston," who declined the Democratic Party's nomination for the Lieutenant Governor's post that year, spoke in Edgefield, Lauren and many other counties, urging blacks to support their trusted friends, the Democrats. The other black, Richard Gayle, echoed these sentiments and said he was certain whites were going to win the struggle; white men "had conquered the Indians and the forest, had built cities, telegraphs, railroads and steamboats," and therefore would surely regain power in the South. These overtures failed because of vigorous Republican responses and black awareness of the Democrats past relationship to the slave-ocracy. Thus, shortly after 1871, the Democrats dropped or greatly slowed their efforts to attract black voters and began to rely more and more on political intimidation and terrorism in order to force blacks from the political arena.

By 1872, Democratic pressure on the blacks within the coalition was not the only force working against the Republican Party. From the outset, the party had some internal difficulties arising from its coalition of whites and blacks. According to Professor Williamson, "The most striking facet of the political behavior of Negroes in South Carolina during Reconstruction was their tendency to dissociate themselves from white persons." This was abundantly apparent, suggested Williamson, "within the Republican Party itself."

Williamson holds that, "The segregation of Negroes and Whites into Republican factions was the result of the prejudices each entertained toward the other." The white Republicans in the state consisted primarily of office holders and their immediate families. While the number of white Republican voters fluctuated in the state, (with whites entering and leaving the party from time to time for various reasons), it generally stayed between three and four thousand. The black wing or faction, the largest group, remained loyal and constantly tried to get more blacks to join or accept the party's ideas and platform. Although these two factions existed in the Republican Party ranks in South Carolina ideology had not at this point separated them; the basic separation or segregation was on the basis of color. But real factionalism came soon in 1872, spurred initially by the issue of party reform. Several conservative white Republicans began an attempt to rid the party of internal corruption, and of dishonest, incompetent and bad men in office. These conservatives also tried to commit the party to reducing the state's debt before it began any expensive program of social welfare.

At the state Republican convention in 1872, the allegedly corrupt wing or faction of the party, the Black and Tans, nominated a white man, F. J. Moses, for the governorship and four blacks for state office, including R. H. Gleaves for Lieutenant Governor. Other blacks were given the posts of Secretary of State, State Treasurer and Adjutant and Inspector General. The Black and Tans also drew up a platform endorsing the national Republican Party's suspension of interest payments on the legal debt, and pledging the party to place safeguards on the treasury. These assurances were not enough to satisfy the majority of white Republicans, and they and a few blacks bolted the convention and held their own. The defection was led by a leading Democrat now turned conservative Republican, James Orr, who had been Governor just prior to the establishment of the new government by the Reconstruction Act of 1867.

The newly formed group, calling themselves the Reform Republican Party (in reality the Lily-Whites or their forerunner), nominated a white man, Reuben Tomlinson, for Governor and James W. Hayes, a black, for Lieutenant Governor. Blacks were also nominated for the post of Secretary of State, Adjutant and Inspector General, and Superintendent of Education. These reform or "Lily-White" Republicans endorsed the national Republican Party platform, repudiated previous Republican administrations in the state. During the campaign, several key and leading black political figures in the state urged other blacks to vote for the Reform or Lily-White party. The Moses-Gleaves ticket i.e., the regular party (Black and Tans) won the election by more than a

33,000 vote, majority. During their tenure in office however, much corruption took place, and it wasn't long before criticism arose in all sections of the state and other leaders of the black community began calling for reforms. At the 1874 Republican State Convention, the Reform (Lily-White) Republicans failed to make any meaningful impact on the regular party (Black and Tan) nomination and platform. The regulars nominated another white man, D. H. Chamberlain, instead of Moses for Governor, and R.H. Gleaves, the Negro was nominated for Lieutenant Governor.

The reform (Lily-Whites), having failed to influence the convention, again bolted and held their own convention. Naming themselves the Independent Republican Party, the reformers nominated a white man, John T. Green, and a black man, Martin R. Delany, for Governor and Lieutenant Governor respectively. The party adopted a platform, which called for reform, retrenchment, and honest government. Before and after Green's nomination, supporters of the reform movement organized blacks into groups known as the Honest Government League of South Carolina, to work for securing Green's nomination and election in the black community. Further help came to the Independent Republicans from the Democrats who once again, (as they had in 1872), fused with the reformers. Despite this new support the Independents lost the election. Chamberlain received 80,403 popular votes and Green, 68,818. R.H. Gleaves defeated Martin Delany, the reform candidate who is considered the father of black Nationalism, by a majority of 86 votes for the Lieutenant-Governor post *(Black Republicans: The Politics of the Black and Tan)*.

In 1876, the Democrats spurned all fusion overtures from the reformed Republicans and launched their re-entry into state politics under the leadership of their folk hero, Wade Hampton. To facilitate their political resurgence the Democrats once again began a campaign to attract black voters. Hampton, (the Democrats gubernatorial nominee), devoted much energy to winning the confidence of black voters. He declared, states Professor Taylor, that the "rights of all would be respected and furthermore, to the colored man, he promised more work and better schools." In addition to Hampton's efforts, several Democratic Clubs throughout the state initiated good will campaigns in the black community. For instance, "The white Richland Democratic Club in Columbia brought Negro members into the club and held weekly meetings to convert others." The Democrats efforts were so strenuous that one black, Martin Delany, declared himself in favor of Hampton, "whom he considered a just, true, dependable man," and in October 1876, *the New York Times* indicated that between 1,500 and 2,000 blacks would vote for the Democratic ticket *(Black Republicans: The Politics of the Black and Tan)*.

Prior to Election Day, the Democrats held a Hampton Day Celebration and Negro Democratic Clubs rode in the parade. Meanwhile, the Hampton Red Shirts, (a para-military organization similar to the KKK), suppressed and intimidated those blacks who had not declared themselves in favor of the Democrats. Economic pressures were applied to black Republicans, but not black Democrats. To inducement and intimidation, the Democrats added fraud. Georgians and North Carolinians were brought over the South Carolina border to vote. Confusion and chaos abounded on election day, and the Republicans reacted timidly to the Democratic threat. Several black Republicans, also, could not support the Republican nominee, Clamberlain, for a second term and simply refrained from voting. At first both sides claimed victory and both men, Hampton and Chamberlain, went to Washington to discuss the matter with President elect Hayes. Hayes, removed federal troops from the state and supported Hampton. The future of Republicanism in the state was sealed.

Following the Democratic takeover in April of 1877, there was an increase in intimidation designed to destroy the Republican Party. At first, minor corruption which supposedly occurred during the Republican administration was exposed to justify the intimidation but later, intimidation became standard practice when it was realized that the Republican President Hayes would not interfere. Prior to the 1878 election, the Democrats passed a new election law aimed at further repressing the Republican Party. Ballot boxes were labeled for each office and any ticket in the wrong box would not be declared valid. At the Republican Party convention in 1878 a new split occurred along party lines. Some Republicans urged fusion with the new party, the Greenbacks; others urged party members to concentrate on only county and legislative offices; still others wanted a full state slate. The arguments were not resolved, but the majority of the Republicans did concentrate on county and legislative offices.

The divisions in the Republican ranks were reflected at the polls and permitted several black Democrats to get elected to state offices. Each year after 1876, indeed, policy matters split the Republicans into several factions. Almost every leading political personality had his own political clique. No one individual arose with enough charisma to unite the numerous factions behind a single program or candidate. One of the largest factions within the Republican Party, (a predominantly black group led by Robert Smalls, a leading black Republican office holder and wheel horse), electioneered on the local and legislative levels to maintain themselves in power. Other factions within the party were groups headed by Christopher C. Brown, Dr. A.C. Mackey, W.N. Taft, Ellery M. Brayton, E. A. Webster, and R. W. Memminger, among others. All these men were white, but some had black followers. The majority of blacks, however, stayed within the Smalls organization. In the 1878 election, six black Republicans were elected to the General Assembly (six black Democrats were also elected to the same body). Three blacks were elected to the State Senate but, Robert Smalls, the titular head of the group, was defeated for Congress.

In 1880, several of the white Republican factions fused with the Greenbacker Party, which nominated W.R. Blair for Governor. The Smalls led black Republican faction put up candidates for the General Assembly, county offices and Congress. The election of that year returned one hundred forty-two Democrats and six Republicans to the General Assembly. The latter included two black Senators from Beaufort and Georgetown, respectively, and four members of the House from Beaufort and Georgetown. One black Democrat was elected to the House from Charleston. In addition, Robert Smalls this time was seated in Congress.

Growing fearful of the alliance of the Greenbackers and the black Republicans, the Democrats enacted in 1881 the "Eight Ballot Box Laws" which confused the less intelligent voters. According to the Republican state convention in 1882, this law contemplated the disenfranchisement of four-fifths of the Republicans in the state. Fearful of the new election law and the Democrats repressive measures, the Republicans partly closed their ranks and a majority of the Republicans fused with the Greenbackers. As a result, "the Republicans sent twelve blacks to the General Assembly. Three of twelve were Senators, from Beaufort, Berkeley, and Georgetown, respectively." In the house, in addition to the nine black Republicans, there were also three black Democrats. Robert Smalls that year returned to Congress to serve out the term of white Republican E. W. Mackey.

By 1884, however, the new restriction law had led to a decline in black Republican political strength in the state. Republican factionalism was at a minimum but the Greenbackers were almost defunct due to continual election losses and anti-black prejudices, so no fusion took place. Only six blacks were elected to the General Assembly; one black Democrat was elected to the House. Virtually the same conditions prevailed in 1886, eight blacks being elected this time to the General Assembly. "Six of these were Republicans, two of whom sat in the Senate and four in the House." The other two blacks, Marshell Jones of Orangeburg and George M. Meas of Charleston, were Democrats. When the General Assembly convened in 1888, there were only three black Republicans and two black Democrats in the House. However, one black Republican, Thomas E. Miller, was elected to Congress. The basic reasons for the decline in black Republican power were the lack of any other political group with whom to coalesce and the impact of the Eight Ballot Box Law, which required the illiterate black voters to guess the right box or have his ballot thrown out. Democratic invasions into the black community and intimidation of black Republicans placed further burdens on the slowly collapsing Republican Party.

On February 4, 1889, a group of independents and old-line Union men held a convention in Pickens, South Carolina and officially formed the first Lily-White Republican Party in the state. After some years the party died, but it was revived again on October 28, 1930. *The Pickens County Sentinel* carried the following announcement:

> *Fourteen Republicans from Pickens County attended the organizational meeting of a new white Republican Party in South Carolina held in Columbia October 28. Total, attendance was 700 to 800 and every county in the state was represented except Dorchester. No Negroes were allowed. J. C. Hambright, businessman of Rock Hill was named state chairman of the new party.*

Although the black Republicans fought back and tried to revitalize themselves, they were only able to elect six black Republicans to the state house in 1890. This slight increase was due in part to the fact that the black Republicans fused with the Haskellite movement of independent Democrats. These Democrats had bolted in protest against the Democratic Party leader, Benjamin "Pitchfork" Tillman, who had deposed Wade Hampton, N.C. Butler, and A.C. Haskell, "respectable" white Democratic leaders. Tillmanites were poor white farmers i.e., Populists. Black Republicans and the Haskellites fused again in the 1892 election and three blacks were sent to the state House and one black, George W. Murray, was elected to Congress. By 1894, however, there were only two black Republicans in the House and Murray, although re-elected to Congress, was seated only after a dispute with the white Democratic opponent. The fraudulent character of the 1894 election, in part attested to by the difficulty the Tillman Democrats had in winning, the dislike that the Tillmanites half had for the aristocratic whites as well as the black prejudices Democrats harbored, all led the Democrats to call for the convening of a constitutional convention on September 10, 1895. The purpose of this convention was to "obviate the remote possibilities of a fusion of the white majority (Haskellites) and the black Republicans which might have brought such a ticket success in subsequent elections." In the general election of 1894, the state electorate had decided in favor of the proposed convention.

When the convention did convene, six black Republicans were in attendance but their presence didn't prevent the disenfranchisement of a considerable number of their race. Benjamin "Pitchfork" Tillman, the chairman of the Committee on suffrage, moved the suffrage article through the convention and got it approved by a decisive vote of seventy-seven to forty-one. Later in 1895, the new constitution went into effect. The new document embodied an "understanding clause," a Tillman device which he described as "the most charming piece of mechanism ever invented." He even explained on the floor of the U.S. Senate in 1900 (he was elected to it in 1895) how black voters were rejected through difficult questions and illiterate white accepted through easy ones. He further explained on the Senate floor how he had helped drive blacks in the state from political power: "We (the white South Carolinians) took the government away. We stuffed ballot boxes. We shot them (blacks). We are not ashamed of it. We have done our best. We have scratched our heads to find out how we could eliminate the last one of them" (*Black Republicans: The Politics of the Black and Tan*).

In such an atmosphere and with the aid of the new disenfranchising constitution, black Republicanism, at least on the state level, died in 1896. In that year, the last black Republican, R.B. Anderson of Georgetown, went to the state legislature. After 1896, the black Republicans had to abandon their party because disenfranchisement had removed their chief supporters, black voters, and they had no way to get new supporters. Moreover, with people like Ben "Pitchfolk" Tillman in control of the state government participation in politics was a dangerous undertaking for blacks. The black Republican leaders in the state either resign from politics, took federal positions elsewhere, or moved out of state. However, in 1900, a white man, Joseph W. Tolbert (nicknamed Tireless Joe or Fighting Joe, because he was a delegate or contestant for the seat at every Republican national convention from 1900 to 1944) rebuilt the Republican Party in the state, organizing it into a unit which "consisted of himself, a few other whites, and several hand-picked Negroes over the state." The purpose of the Tolbert organization was to choose delegates to the national convention and to distribute patronage to its members, particularly to Tolbert. Tolbert added several blacks to ensure his group a seat at the national Republican convention. Racial composition was a major argument at credentials hearings and a mixed delegation usually fared better than a Lily-White one. Tireless Joe's group of Republicans soon became known as the Black and Tans.

The group made only minor attempts to enter state or local politics but emerged every four years to go to the national convention, get seated and acquire patronage, (the latter being its chief objective). Tolbert's Black and Tan Republicans didn't go unchallenged, though. Another white South Carolinian, seeing the benefits that were accruing to Tolbert's Black and Tans and understanding that occasionally the national convention seated a Lily-White delegation, organized such a group for his own enrichment. This man, Joe Hambright of Rock Hill, in October, of 1930, organized his Republican group along lines similar to Tolbert's, with only one exception; Hambright excluded blacks. Hambright's Lily-Whites, like Tolbert's blacks and Tans, made no effort to attract supporters to participate in state politics. They only challenged the Black and Tans at the national conventions.

The efforts of tireless Joe and Hambright made the South Carolina Republican party a national joke in 1938. J. Bates Gerald, a wealthy lumberman, formed another Republican group to challenge the old Black and Tan and Lily-White groups. Gerald, understanding the importance of delegation composition, got three white, "approved" and well known blacks and two unknown blacks, all from the middle class, to dispose of Tolbert's main argument at the national convention, that of racial composition. Moreover, while Tolbert's blacks were handpicked and considered safe and loyal to him, the Gerald-led Republicans selected their blacks in a convention of executive convention fashion. This strengthened their case in 1940. The convention seated the Gerald-led Republicans in preference to old tireless Joe's group. By 1952, however, the Gerald-led Republicans, now feeling sure of being seated, formally ousted the three prominent black Republican leaders, from their ranks who had helped boost the faction from its inception, for alleged disciplinary reasons. Once in power, the Gerald group reverted back to Lily-White Republicanism.

Although no longer recognized as the Republican group in the state, the Tolbert group challenged the Gerald group at every national convention until 1956, intermittently, electioneering and putting up presidential electors to strengthen their arguments before the credentials committee, but with no success. When Tolbert died in the nineteen forties, another white man, lumberman B. L. Hendrix, assumed control and began organizing "Lincoln Emancipation Clubs" throughout the state in anticipation of a Republican victory in 1948 which never came. In the main, black Republicans in South Carolina from 1900 to 1944 never numbered more than 500; at the peak there were never more than 1,200 white members. Blacks established their own party, the South Carolina Progressive Democratic Party, in 1944, and supported it through three convention challenges until 1956. Other blacks simply remained outside the political arena. The mere 63 votes for the Black and Tans in 1944 reveals something of the disgust and contempt of the black community for a white-led black group. It was, in fact, chiefly the sinister tactic of Tolbert and Gerald that led to the emergence of the all black political party in 1944.

CHAPTER ELEVEN
TENNESSEE

In November 1864, a group of black Republican sympathizers conducted mock elections in the black community in Nashville, Tennessee Abraham Lincoln received 3,193 votes and McClellan, the Democratic candidate, only one vote. While this was indicative of political opinion in the black community, blacks in Tennessee had not yet acquired the right to vote and thus could not fully support their political friends. Assisted by visiting workers from the North and Freedmen Bureau agents, however, black leaders "sought voting privileges from the end of the fighting." Even before 1865, blacks, under the protection of the Freedmen's Bureau "were able to hold meetings and forward resolutions and petitions to the legislative and governor's office," asking for the right to vote. Finally, in 1865, blacks held a state-wide convention in Nashville that was addressed by the Tennessee chief officer who drew up a petition and sent it to congress, "paying for the exclusion of Tennessee Representatives unless the Tennessee Legislature acted on a petition for the suffrage before December, of 1865 assembly." Congress, however, gave the petition only minor consideration.

On the state level, black protests for suffrage rights also fell on deaf ears. One basic reason for this lack of attention to black protests was the manner in which Tennessee was reorganized after the Civil War. Unlike the other southern states Tennessee did not go through a period of Reconstruction, per se. "Attempts to restore civil government in Tennessee under federal authority began in the spring of 1862 when Confederate forces evacuated most of middle and west Tennessee" (Black Republicans: The Politics of the Black and Tan). President Lincoln sent Andrew Johnson back to his native state that year to become military governor and restore civil government. Continued strife and internal dissension slowed Johnson's efforts at first but he finally succeeded in creating a loyal government by the spring of 1865. Before the spring of 1865 had ended a new constitution had been adopted, a new state government restructured, and a new governor, William C. Brownlow, had been a Unionist Whig before secession and had strongly opposed the dis-unionist sentiment in the state. When the state finally succeeded, the Confederates had him imprisoned but he was later released. Upon his release he went north all the while denouncing the act of southern secession. In many eyes he became a of martyr symbol of Southern Unionism. After the federal forces captured Tennessee, he returned and was received as a hero by many in the state who held like Unionist sentiments. Assuming power on April 5, 1865, Brownlow supported Johnson's Reconstruction policy until a serious breach developed between the president and the Congressional Radical Republicans. At that point Brownlow formally broke with Johnson and supported the Congressional Radicals. Describing the situation, Professor Alexander states that "after Johnson and the Radicals were openly at war, and after Johnson's backers promoted the Philadelphia National Union Convention in August, of 1866 to seek coalescence around the president's Reconstruction policies, Brownlow, with all of his antebellum and war-time gusto, led a large Tennessee delegation to the Radical's counter attack at the Southern Loyalist Convention in Philadelphia in September of 1866" (*Black Republicans: The Politics of the Black and Tan*). Brownlow's bold action against Johnson, especially since he was from the same state as Johnson, and his call at the convention for the extension of suffrage to blacks brought him great admiration among the Congressional Radical ranks. Brownlow had personally forced the 14th Amendment through the Tennessee legislature, calling a special session and fraudulently obtaining a quorum to ratify it.

This had not been Brownlows's position on black suffrage at first. In January, 1856, Brownlow went along with the major position of the convention that was reorganizing the state. One delegate, Harvey M. Watterson, succinctly captured the convention's disposition in a major speech. He said to the delegates:

> This brings me to the everlasting Nigger, that dark fountain from which has flowed all our woes. I have always thought if the people of Tennessee, Kentucky, Maryland, Virginia and Missouri were paid fair price for their slaves property and the Colored population removed beyond their limits, it would be a good operation for the whites. Will the people of Tennessee permit the valueless Negro to stand between them and the establishment of civil government. I cannot, I do not believe it. I would not give one year of virtuous civil rule for all the darkies in America *(Black Republicans: The Politics of the Black and Tan)*.]

Brownlow made no criticism of this speech at the convention; he accepted it. Later in 1865 Brownlow, addressing the state assembly, urged them to entice immigrants rather than admit blacks to the ballot. He further advised them against enfranchising Negro men, offering the usual arguments concerning incompetence and adding mention of his fear that rural Negroes would be influenced by landowners, most of whom were former confederate sympathizers, in the counties where Negroes were most numerous. Brownlow's conversion to a positive position on the black suffrage question in 1866, stemmed, as he claimed, from two things: first, each new election indicated that the conservative Democrats in the state were about to regain power, and secondly, "the drift of national opinion on the subject of Negro voting" was in a positive direction, and there was a greater aptitude among blacks than he had earlier anticipated. Whether from motives of political self-preservation or because of outside pressure, Brownlow began prodding his legislature to pass the measure in 1866. Finally, on February 25, 1867, after much political maneuvering on Brownlow's part, the Tennessee House passed the measure, five days after Congress had passed the Reconstruction plan.

While the other ten southern states were about to embark on Reconstruction, however, Tennessee for the most part was concluding hers. Once blacks had been given the right to vote in 1867, the Union League stepped in and began the arduous task of marshaling the new black voters into the Republican Party. The league, which came to Tennessee in the early 1860s, had become a Radical controlled organization by 1867, and employed all the regalia and secrecy it could muster to channel black voters toward the Republican organization. Later, in 1867, Tennessee voters went to the polls to select a governor, legislature, and representatives to Congress. In the contest, black voters were also sought by the conservative (Democratic) party but the campaign failed for the Democrats had little to offer the newly enfranchised Freedmen. When the results were in, Republicans had made virtually a clean sweep of all positions and had completely routed the Democrats.

The Democrats retaliated for their overwhelming election defeat by renewing the Ku Klux Klan on a state-wide basis. "The Tennessee Klan," asserts Professor William Gillette:

> was first organized in middle Tennessee at Pulaski as a social club of ex-Confederates, in December 1865, during the first year of Radical rule, but it did not become a major political force until 1867, when Radical rule

became firmly entrenched, by enfranchising Negroes so as to align them with East Tennessee Republican whites. The first general test of the Radical Republican strength under duress from Ku Klux Klanism in Tennessee came in November, 1868, during the presidential election and the Congressional elections.

Although the state was carried for the Republican Presidential nominee, General Ulysses S. Grant, his total popular vote was barely one half of what was received previously by Brownlow. The effect of Klan intimidation in 1868 was clearly stated by Professor Gillette. "Many Negro voters were scared away from the polls during the federal elections of 1868. The Negro vote dropped off in West Tennessee and was cut in half in middle Tennessee." The following year, 1869, the Republicans, still under pressure from Democratic violence and intimidation, lost the state elections. The new Democratic government tightened their control and power in the state by disbanding the state militia (which protected black Republican voters), lifting martial law, re-enfranchising the conservative Confederates, and putting into effect a poll tax which further reduced the black vote. The new governor, himself once a Klan member, used the Klan to complete his Democratic restoration. Then, after 1879, Klan violence began to decline, but it did not disappear.

Another factor which figures prominently into the Republican electoral defeat was the low enthusiasm among blacks for the Republican Party. Under Brownlow's tutelage, "Office holding at the state level was totally denied Negroes," in practice, even after legal prohibition had been ungraciously abandoned. Rarely did county or town offices fall to Negroes, even where they were the majority among the voters. In short, blacks found little to motivate them toward participation in the party. For them, voting meant keeping white Republicans in power, with no visible rewards for their efforts. Many just abstained both from voting and from participation in party affairs. After losing the 1869 election, the Republican Party in Tennessee began to suffer from inter-party friction and factionalism arising out of personal ambitions and jealousies. During this internal upheaval, one group of white Republicans, in order to regain power in the organization began advocating nomination for blacks and declaring their right to seek offices. Such comments drew blacks into their camp. The alienated white Republican officers then formed a faction of their own.

The former group, the Black and Tan wing, now geared up for the 1872 election, heartened by the fact that the Democrat were embroiled in factional infighting themselves. The Lily-White faction, the white Republican office holders, supported Horace Greeley in the 1872 electoral canvas, as did many Democrats, and the result was a significant comeback for the Black and Tan Republicans. Although the Black and Tans were led by whites and six white Republicans were elected to Congress, the first black, Sampson Keeble from Memphis, was sent to the State House. The Republicans, having reassembled, joined with numerous independents in the State House and repealed the poll tax requirement for voting. This repeal gave the Republicans a potentially larger black vote for the 1874 state and federal elections and drew more blacks into the party. However, the contest for power in 1874 became the most heated and bloodiest one in Tennessee history after secession. The Democrats revived their Klan organization and resorted to mob rule. Many blacks were lynched, murdered, fired upon, intimidated or frightened away from the polls on Election Day. The result was disaster for Tennessee Republicans, only one Republican was returned to Washington and the state elections went just as badly. The Democrats had once again regained control.

The black vote in Memphis had been nurtured by the E.H. Crump machine ever since Crump became Mayor in 1911. He knew that the "Negro vote was an important element in winning elections and that successful candidates traditionally had Negro support, and he tried extremely hard to maintain and keep up the vote for his organization" *(Black Republicans: The Politics of the Black and Tan).* In the words of Professor, V.O. Key, "Crump sees that Memphis Negroes get a fairer break than usual in public services. His organization, of course, follows through and takes specific measures to hold Negro leaders in line." In one or another Crump ensured control over the black community. One means of control was to create a black politician with his own machine. One of Crump's black bosses was Robert Church, who although a Republican, worked for Crump and dispensed numerous favors for him in the black community. "He donated a public park in the midst of valuable urban property to blacks, and his people credited him with colored appointments to federal offices, with acts of charity, and with invincible political cleverness." Even Senator Heflin of Alabama paid tribute to Church by reading a poem into the hearing of a patronage investigation:

Offices up a simmon tree
Bob Church on de ground
Bob Church said to de pointing power:
Snake dem pointments down.
[*Black Republicans: The Politics of the Black and Tan*]

Professor Lewinson states: "Church could in short deliver the Negro vote of Memphis and influence it elsewhere." By 1928 Church's sub-machine, which had over 3,500 black voters, swung the majority election for the Democrats and later broke away from the Crump machine. Given this type of political power, the Credentials Committee was informed that, unless Church was seated, the black vote in Tennessee would be lost. The Lily-Whites contended that Tennessee would be lost to the Democrats no matter who was seated, but the convention finally seated Church. This clash was the last major Black and Tan factional fight at the national level.

Black and Tan Republicanism in Tennessee never really materialized to any meaningful degree, unlike in other southern states. Although there were two clashes in the 1920s, both arose from the same city and area, western Tennessee. Even if one goes back as far as Reconstruction, Black and Tan Republicans never had much of a chance. Although some factionalism along racial lines did occur, it was dealing primarily with whether blacks should hold offices or not. But even this limited schism eventually fizzled out.

Even on the eastside of Tennessee, with few blacks and white Republicans with a history going back before the War of intense anti-black prejudices, no such formation of Black and Tans and Lily-Whites took place. In Knoxville, the major city in East Tennessee, black Republicans were permitted to flourish and carry on their political maneuvering undisturbed. One black Colonel, Joseph M. Trigg, who served as the aldermen from the Negro ward in that city, wrote numerous editorials for the black owned pro-Republican newspaper, the East Tennessee News. In most of them he simply told how the national party neglected blacks, but there was never mention of any Lily-White organizations or efforts by local or regional groups to curtail black political action in the city. Black and Tan Republicanism, then, never materialized in Tennessee. Another reason for this was that the African American community itself was rife with factionalism. Blacks thus played only minor roles in state politics. Professor Key suggests also that the absence of black state-wide organizations for political action stemmed from the fact that there was no serious threat of a disenfranchising constitution nor a state-wide Democratic primary which would eliminate blacks as in other southern states. Devices like the poll tax were passed and felt to be effective enough, and harsher methods were never instituted.

CHAPTER TWELVE
ARKANSAS

Arkansas came under federal military control in 1863. That same year according to Hanes Walton Jr. "A group of Union sympathizers determined to reorganize the state sought Lincoln's cooperation. He cautiously gave it under this military power, but the group went ahead boldly, held a convention in January 1864, adopted a constitution and elected Isaac Murphy governor." When the two Senators elected by the new government reached Congress, they were denied their seats and sent back to Arkansas. Upon returning, the new government dominated by ex-Confederates, sent a commission in 1866 back to Washington D.C. to confer with federal authorities about the future of the state. The commission let it be known that the state's new constitution abolished slavery and prohibited black indentured servitude, but that this was as far as they were willing to go. Washington at this time was embroiled in a Presidential-Congressional fight and the Arkansas group was sent home with no definite commitment from federal authorities. Early the next year, Congressional Reconstruction began and registration for the right to vote for delegates to a new state convention was scheduled for May 1867. A few whites told blacks that "Registration was for the purpose of enrolling them for taxes but the Freedmen's Bureau sent out agents to instruct them in the purpose of voting" (*Black Republicans: The Politics of the Black and Tan*).

After registration was complete, voters in Arkansas went to the polls and cast 27,756 votes for and 13,558 against holding a constitutional convention (*Black Republicans: The Politics of the Black and Tan*). The military commander, General Alpert Pike, named the delegates who had been selected and set January 7, 1868 as the date for the convention in Little Rock. When the convention convened there were eight black delegates present: J. W. Mason, Richard Samuels, William Murphy, Monroe Hawkins, William Grey, James T. White and Pulaski. The counties, counties in the heavily populated black sections of the state covering middle and lower Arkansas. In the convention, conservatives strongly opposed black suffrage. General Alpert Pike remarked, just prior to the convention, that black suffrage would make "a hell on earth, a hideous, horrid pandemonium filled with all the devils of vice, crime, pauperism, corruption, violence, political butchery, and social anarchy." During the convention proceedings, a white conservative, Mr. Cypert, who had been a Freedmen's Bureau agent, claimed that "he knew the Negro in all his attitudes; that their people were now being misled." He then went on to say that he could never consent to see them (blacks) entrusted with elective franchise, and made the ruler of white men. The eight black delegates effectively challenged Mr. Cypert's remarks. For instance, Mr. Grey of Phillips County responding to the white conservative, said, He took no objection to the appellation; his race was closely allied to the race that built the pyramids of Egypt, where slept the remains of those whose learning had taught Solon and Lycurgus to frame the system of their laws, and to whom the present ages are indebted for the hints of art and knowledge. Numerous white Radical Republicans also took issue with Mr. Cypert. The leaders of the Radicals declared. We, the great Republican Party, hold that they (blacks) should have the ballot; and we intend that they should have it, and we will sustain the government based upon the principle of universal franchise and universal equity. Blacks and Radical Republicans carried the day. The vote on the suffrage amendment was 45 to 21 in favor of adoption.

The Arkansas delegates adjourned in February after a short session of 31 days, with fifteen whites refusing to sign the new document. Despite their objection, on April 1, it was announced that the constitution had been ratified by a vote of 30,380 to 41. In May 7, a bill for the read mission of Arkansas was presented in Congress by Thaddeus Stevens. It was finally passed in both Houses and over the president's veto on June 22, 1868. Before the bill was presented to Congress, however, the state legislature had met on April 2, of 1868 and adopted the Fourteenth Amendment which was one of the prerequisites to her admission. Following the ratification of the constitution, the date was set for the state-wide election in the fall. In the meantime, the Republican Party held a convention in April of 1867, at Little Rock and nominated a state ticket with Powell Clayton heading it for governor, he served on the Committee of Resolutions.

Although Governor Clayton ruled Arkansas with an iron hand from 1868 to 1873, the Ku Klux Klan practically carried on a civil war. The Klan, operating as the arm of the Democrats, sought in Arkansas, (as elsewhere in the South), to intimidate and suppress black voters and Republicans. Blacks nevertheless held a number of posts and continued to vote in varying degrees of strength.

396

Arkansas blacks held three state cabinet offices as well as positions in the state legislature. W.H. Grey became Commissioner of Immigration; J.C. Corbin, Superintendent of Education; and J.T. White, Commissioner of Public Works. In 1873, Mifflin W. Gibbs was elected city judge in Little Rock. Moreover, due to black political influence, "An anti-Ku Klux Klan law of great severity was passed which prevented all secret political organizations and declared their members public enemies. Even the possession of a Ku Klux Klan costume was a criminal offense. The law was sternly enforced and the Klan disbanded after a season of martial law." The bill was passed in 1869 *(Black Republicans: The Politics of the Black and Tan)*.

Four years later, in 1873, Arkansas passed a stringent civil rights law, "which compelled hotels and places of public amusement to admit Colored people and insured them equal school facilities in separate schools. Fines of $200 to $1,000 or imprisonment of 3 to 12 months was provided." Commenting on the toughness of the law, journalist and social historian Lerone Bennett states, "Arkansas passed a civil rights bill of such severity that it would not be possible to pass it today in either New York City or New York State." Democrats recaptured the state in 1874. In the spring of that year the predominately black militia of Arkansas fought "pitched battles in the streets of Little Rock and a naval engagement on the Arkansas River. The military struggle was a stand-off, but the Democrats triumphed by fraud and internal subversion and Washington refused to intervene." When President Grant and Congress refused to act, the Democrats finally secured complete control of the state by late fall. Another signal event of that year was a schism in the Republican Party ranks. One group of Republicans, calling themselves Reformers (composed mostly of white Conservatives, disgruntled Democrats and the supporters of the 1872 Liberal Republican movement) clashed with the regular Republicans (composed of carpetbaggers, scalawags, and blacks). At the other Republican convention neither group was able to force the other to bow out, and they went to the electorate with separate tickets. After the election both groups claimed to be the winner. The regular group gained control of the legislature, or at least was recognized by it, but the Reform group took possession of the state building by force. Later, the Reform group retreated and fused with the Democrats who toward the end of the year took the government by force.

Black Republicans were pivotal in the inter-party clash, mostly siding with the regular Republicans. Thus, a schism that began over policies ended up again involving racial division, and this proved the basis for a rudimentary emergence of Black, Tan and Lily-White factions, with several of the Reform Republicans returning to the regular party. Neither side, though, was able to exercise any meaningful advantage black Republicans continued occasionally to run for office and participated in state and local politics until the Democrats passed the poll tax measures in 1893 to curtail their activities. During the first decade of the twentieth century, Arkansas further curtailed black voters or disenfranchised them by adopting the white primary. In Arkansas the Lily-White opposition was extremely limited; it never got past district or county conventions.

There is hardly anything on record that reveals great clashes between Blacks, Tans, and Lily-White factions. There were numerous clashes between black Republicans and white Republicans but formally structured factions did not emerge in Arkansas after Reconstruction to any meaningful degree. Blacks appeared in the Arkansas to the national convention delegation from time to time, and there were several internal delegate disputes but no Black, Tan and Lily-White factional fight took place until 1920. The Republican state convention on April 28, 1920 seated the Lily-White delegation over the Black and Tan group for predominantly black Pulaski County (which sent two black representatives to the constitutional convention in 1868). When the convention voted to seat the Lily-White delegation from Pulaski County rather than the Black and Tans, the black delegates from Phillips County walked out of the convention. The Little Rock Arkansas Gazette, described it this way, "As the blacks from Phillips County swept majestically out of the hall, the group was followed by all the sons of Ham. About 50 in number, and all the Negro spectators in the galleries."

One white delegate urged the Republican state convention to seat the Lily-White delegates because blacks had failed to support his gubernatorial bid in 1911. He remarked, "When two races undertake to ride the elephant one must ride behind." The pro-Democratic *Gazette* endorse the White Supremacy action of the convention, opining that the Republican "Committee on Credentials performed a patriotic and congenial business by throwing out the Negro contestants from Pulaski and Hempstead counties and thus barred the black brethren from the possibility of holding federal offices under a Republican administration, unless they can get a helping hand at the national convention." After leaving the white convention black delegates from Pulaski, Hempstead and Phillips Counties held their own Black and Tan convention (some whites joining them) at the Mosaic Temple on the corner of Ninth Street and Broadway.

The Black and Tan convention chose delegates for the national convention, raised $6,000 for group expenses and nominated a complete state ticket headed up by a black, J. H. Blount, as their gubernatorial candidate. In the 1920 election Blount received 15,627, votes, the Democratic candidates 123,604, and the Republican candidate 46,339. Blount, who was principal of a black school in Helena, became the first of his race to seek the governor's post in the state. At the national convention in Chicago the Black and Tan delegates lost their fight with the Lily-Whites before the Credentials Committee. The Black and Tans carried their fight to the convention floor, but lost again, the entire convention voting against them.

Following that loss the Black and Tans disbanded. There is no record of their continued existence on the state or local levels, or of their again contesting the Lily-White leadership. It must be remembered that the dispute in Arkansas at first involved only one County, Pulaski. Other blacks retained their seats because they were unopposed. Had they been opposed also, they would probably have been denied seats at the convention, too.

In fact, Black and Tan-ism was so short lived in Arkansas, that it had virtually no meaningful impact on state politics. Part of the reason for this is that blacks made up a very small portion of the population in the state so black leadership in Arkansas was never really able to approximate the quality which prevailed in some other southern states. Thus, Black and Tan-ism in Arkansas died in its beginnings.

CHAPTER THIRTEEN
MISSISSIPPI

Black Republicanism began to emerge in Mississippi in June 1865, just prior to a convening of a state constitutional convention under the provisional governor, William L. Sharkey (former chief justice of the state). A few Freedmen with the aid of a white northern soldier held a mass meeting at Vicksburg and "drew up resolutions condemning the exclusion of loyal citizens from the convention and appealed to Congress to refuse readmission to Mississippi until she voluntarily enfranchised Freedman." President Johnson, responding to the resolutions, wrote Governor Sharkey "suggesting that Negroes of education and property be given the right to vote so as to forestall the Radicals in the North." Johnson indicated to the governor that such a grant i.e., a limited franchise, would completely disarm his adversaries, the Radicals Republicans in Congress. Neither Johnson's letter nor the black resolution received much attention from the convention. In fact, the convention denied the petition in short order by arguing that "This is a white man's government," and that "in the sight of God and the light of reason a Negro suffrage was impossible."

The convention drew up a new constitution and set the date of the election as October 2, 1865. A former confederate, B.G. Humphreys, was elected governor and his election was accepted by President Johnson in November, 1865. Once in office, Humphreys proceeded to disband the black federal troops and had the state legislature pass the infamous black codes. His actions precipitated the coming of Congressional Reconstruction in March 1867, General E.C. And was appointed the military commander in charge of the State. By April 15, he began to register the new electorate, colored and white, in preparation for the new state constitutional convention. The result of the registration was that 60,137 blacks and 46,636 whites signed the books. The election was set for the first Tuesday in November 1867. Seeing that black enfranchisement was imminent, white conservatives began, early in 1867, "an immediate and almost frantic campaign to bring the Negro voters under the control of the southern whites." White conservatives coalesced and mapped out and instituted their strategies. The result was a series of state-wide bi-racial meetings in which white and blacks participated on an equal basis; but at each meeting it was impressed upon blacks "that the whites were to furnish the supplies and the blacks were to prepare them." The entire movement was a "failure, utter and universal." The maneuvering clashed with the black man's new sense of freedom and his newly gained political rights. Even white, especially poor whites, in the cooperationists' camp revolted. They didn't like the idea of their top politicians "traversing the state, making Negro speeches, getting up Negro meetings and playing second fiddle to Sambo." Seeing that their strategy would not work, and hearing that the state of Ohio had rejected black suffrage, white conservative cooperationists decided to wait for a national Democratic victory in 1868.

In the meantime, blacks were enthusiastically entering political activity in the state. They gathered in Vicksburg in July to set up a black Republican organization. The regular Republican Party, seeing this move and noting its future potential, immediately absorbed the black group at its convention on September 10 and 11, over the cries and objections of the Lily-Whites. The regular Republican Party from its inception had failed to organize blacks, due to its racial prejudice; now, expediency drove the party to do so. On Election Day 70,016 voters cast ballots in favor of the convention while 6,277 voted against it. On January 8, 1868 the convention convened to write a new state constitution which would accord blacks equal justice in the state. To this convention, because of the color of the delegates, went seventeen black delegates out of the 100 selected. From the outset the convention delegates began to quarrel over proper rights for blacks and the question of suffrage. The debates were deliberately prolonged because the conservatives wanted to wait to see if a Democratic victory could be achieved in November on the national level. Thus, the convention continued for 115 days, not ending until June. Then the constitution was submitted to the people for adoption.

Since the new state elections would take place at the same time as the vote on the constitution, conservative Democrats went all out, not only to win the election but, to defeat the constitution. Organizing as the Democratic White Man's Party of Mississippi, the party openly and scornfully attacked black aspirations and those Republicans who were willing to support them, grant them franchise, and solicit their votes. Finally, the Democrats resorted to intimidation and violence to carry the day. Their tactics succeeded: 56,231 votes were cast for the proposed constitution and 63,860 against. And the Democratic candidate Humphrey was re-elected Governor. However, the elections were invalidated by the rejection of the constitution, thus ensuring a continuation of rule by the federal government. The whites were satisfied with this because they still hoped for a national Democratic victory in November. In November of 1868, however, the Republicans were overwhelmingly victorious and when President Grant was inaugurated, he placed a new military man in charge of Mississippi. The new military provisional governor, A. Ames, removed all Democrats, appointed blacks to office, and set the date for new elections. The Democrats prepared for the election by reorganizing their party and naming it the National Union Republican Party (NURP). President Grant's brother-in-law, Louis Dent, was selected to head it up. The NURP also placed one black on the ticket, Tom Sinclair, to run for Secretary of State.

The Republican regulars placed one black, James D. Lynch, on their ticket for the same post. Lynch's appointment proved to be a master stroke because Lynch was the best known in the state and a powerful orator who drew crowds of two or three thousand blacks at a time. The Regular Republican ticket, including Lynch, won and the constitution was ratified. It is not necessary to discuss the long list of black Republican office holders in Mississippi because they are dealt with in virtually every book on black history in the U.S. Suffice to say that Mississippi had perhaps the largest contingent of black office holders of any southern state. It is the only southern state, even up to the present day, to have had two black U.S. Senators, a black Lieutenant Governor, and a host of cabinet officers, legislators, mayors, etc. The results of this tremendous number of black Republican office holders were predictable: the regular Republican Party was branded as a black Party; white party members were stigmatized as "Nigger Lovers," and Democrats were determined to regain power at any price. And this, the Democrats did in 1875: "By blood, murder, intimidation, stealth, race war, feud, deceit, and repression, the Democrats regained political power in Mississippi."

For black Republicans, the Democratic revolution in 1875 had even greater implications. Professor Wharton illuminated this point well when he stated:

Once the general policy had been adopted the Negro and Republican control of the state government was to be broken at any cost. A number of methods were followed for this accomplishment. One of these involved intimidation of those whites that still worked for the Republican Party. Since the Democrats let it be widely known the Carpetbaggers would be first to be killed, the black Republicans, as time went by, found fewer and fewer white leaders at their meetings.

The party, still partly fractionalized, was now becoming completely black. The election of Hayes, Garfield and Arthur, and Democratic pressures led to a general white withdrawal to form their own Lily-White Republican Organization. Color factionalism was prevalent in the Mississippi Republican Party from the beginning, however. Blacks and whites had their own Republican organizations from the outset, and they only fused temporarily from about 1868 to 1879. A new factional upheaval began in Natchez about 1873 when John R. Lynch. B.K. Bruce and Jonas Hill seized control of the party in the six Congressional District. These black leaders were determined to advance men of their own race to public positions denied the black and white Republican leaders. The struggle between the black and white Republican factions in Natchez "threatened to disrupt the Republican Party throughout the river counties."

"The factions assumed the names of 'Warm Spring Indians' (blacks) and 'Modics' (whites) in their political battle with each other." The blacks won because Senator Ames "placed the influence of his patronage at the disposal of Congressman-elect Lynch." The rise of Lynch's faction was checked when the Democrats recaptured the state in 1875.

The next major black-white faction upheaval in Mississippi came shortly after 1880. The black wing of the party fused with the Greenbackers, then with the Democrats, while the Republicans, encouraged by President Arthur, set up their own independent or white Republican movement in 1882-1883. From the early 1880s on, the Mississippi Republican Party had two distinct factions. Although the Lily-White faction nearly collapsed after Arthur lost his election bid in 1884, they were rejuvenated by the Lily-White policies of President Harrison in 1889. The passage of the Mississippi disenfranchising constitution aided them even more because it removed most of the support of the party's black wing and made politics in the state a very risky business for blacks. The absence of black leadership and internal rifts were also factors in the eventual Lily-White take-over. Professor Harris says:

> During the mid 1890s a rift developed between Lynch's aide, James Hill, black Secretary of the state during Reconstruction, which resulted ultimately in the establishment of Lily-White control of the party. Lynch's miscalculation in influencing the party to fuse with Populist Party in 1892 and his lengthy absences from the state were important reasons for the development of this factionalism within the party.

403

In terms of chronology, Lynch left Mississippi in 1889 to serve a Fourth Auditor of the U.S. Treasury, an appointment given to him by President Benjamin Harrison as a reward for his long devotion to the party. He retired from the post in 1893 when the Democrats returned to power. Although Lynch opened a law firm and a bank in Washington, he occasionally returned to his Natchez home for periods of three to six months each year. Then in 1898, joined the army, received the rank of Major and stayed in until 1911. When he left he went to Los Angeles for a while and then permanently moved to Chicago in 1912.

Thus, from the mid-1890s the black Republicans in Mississippi were without one of their major leaders. The titular leadership position was assumed by James Hill, and upon his death, about 1904, control of the Republican Party passed into the hands of a white man, L.T. Mosley, who was elected national committeeman for the state. Although he was opposed by numerous black Republicans within party ranks, he held that position until 1915, when he moved to Chicago. Following his exit from the state there was a scramble for power between blacks and whites. Whites sought to replace Mosley with another white man. Blacks in the party, led by black attorney Perry Howard and black dentist S.D. Redmond, fought the move. The whites out maneuvered the blacks by holding a special meeting of the state committee and electing another white, M.J. Muldihill of Vicksburg, head of the state party and national committeeman. Ordinarily the selection was supposed to be made by the state delegation to the national convention. Since attorney Howard was a candidate for the national committeeman post, which would have made him state party leader, he contested Muldihill's election before the national committee when it convened in St. Louis in 1919. However, the national committee ruled in favor of Muldihill. The next year, 1920, at the national Republican convention in Chicago, and the contestants for President were General, Frank Lowden and General Leonard Wood. Mississippi sent two delegations: Perry Howard and Dr. S.D. Redmond leading the Black and Tans, and M.J. Muldihill the lily-whites. The Howard-Richmond group was supporting Wood's nomination, who had been actively promoted before the convention by Mr. Proctor, the P & G Soap man. The Muldihill group supported General Lowden. As the convention progressed, however, Dr. Redmond discovered that the Muldihill group was planning to switch and had even moved to the Wood Hotel where the Black and Tans were staying. Redmond obtained a certified copy of the hotel register to use at a later date as evidence against Muldihill's Lily-Whites. Both delegations were seated at the convention, each being given a half vote, but Muldihill was appointed as national committeeman by the convention.

The convention was stalemated for three days because neither Wood nor Lowden could get the nomination. On the fourth day Warren G. Harding won the nomination after the Lowden forces switched to his support. After Harding's inauguration on March 4, 1921, Dr. Redmond took his certified copy of the hotel register and his information on the Muldihill group's tactics to the Lowden people. Angered and seeking vengeance, the Lowden forces supported Dr. Redmond's efforts to get President Harding to give the Howard-Redmond faction:

> ...one-third of all Mississippi patronage, one, third of all municipal, county and state committee memberships, and the chairmanship of all committees. This agreement was quite unusual and unique in its provision for the handling of Republican patronage because as a rule the national committee and state chairman of the victorious faction is given full control of patronage dispensation for respective states.

One-third of the patronage may not seem very significant, but when Muldihill's two-thirds of the patronage was insufficient to go around, dissatisfaction and a scramble for patronage jobs occurred. In 1924 a meeting of the Muldihill state committee and the Howard-Redmond state committee took place. "At this meeting of the Mississippi Republican state central committee, six of the members of the Muldihill committee deserted and voted with the Howard-Redmond (Black and Tan) faction, giving them a majority."

Once this happened, the Muldihill faction, now a minority, called for a state convention. The Howard-Redmond faction at this point also issued a call for a state convention. Each group selected its own set of delegates to the national Republican convention in Cleveland in 1924. At that convention Calvin Coolidge was nominated for President, Perry W. Howard was elected national chairman over Muldihill, and Mrs. Mary Booze (a resident of the all-black community, Mound-Bayou) was elected national chairwoman. Dr. Redmond was elected state chairman. In short, the Black and Tans were given full control over state party matters in 1924, and the retained it through 1956. Although they were contested strongly and vigorously every four years, the Howard-led Black and Tans were seated each year through 1956. The task was not an easy one, however, and Howard came close to defeat in 1928 and 1956. In 1928 Presidential hopeful Herbert Hoover used Black and Tan factions in various southern states to secure his nomination. After obtaining the nomination, he then "created, under the chairmanship of a mysterious Colonel Horace A. Mann," a separate campaign committee "to drum up the white southern vote independently of the regular Black and Tan state organizations." After his inauguration, Hoover praised the existing Lily-White Republican organizations in the South and announced his full support of them. He removed such Black and Tan leaders as Ben Davis of Georgia, William (Goose Neck Bill) McDonald in Texas, and Walter L. Cohen in Louisiana, turning their top state party positions over to whites. He also launched an investigation of Perry Howard, the head of the Mississippi Black and Tans, and Howard "was subsequently removed from his position and shorn of party power while under charges of bribery and sale of federal offices."

Later in 1928:

> Howard, together with several other active Negro Republicans of Jackson, Mississippi, was indicted for sale of federal offices and for levying political contributions on federal employee in violation of the civil service code. He was given a jury trial in a federal court and the United States attorney in charge of the prosecution protested almost tearfully that the case against Howard was watertight and foolproof.

Following the Attorney General's announcement, the "Senatorial committee investigating the sale of federal offices in 1929-1930 condemned the Republican organization of Mississippi largely because of its opinion of Howard's activities." President Hoover, meanwhile, appointed a Lily-White patronage committee to take over Howard's duties in the interim period until trial. The major driving force behind President Hoover's actions and support of the Lily-Whites was a desire "to successfully invade the South against the Democratic candidate Al Smith in 1928 because Smith was remarkably vulnerable, as Democratic candidates go." He was Catholic, wet, and partial to blacks, and Hoover saw this as an opportunity to resurrect the Republican Party in the South, as past Presidents had, on a Lily-White basis. The strategy did not work. Howard, despite the massive evidence against him, was acquitted.

White Democrats in Mississippi came to Howard's aid and testified in his behalf. The chief justice and associate justice and the clerk of the state Supreme Court, some of the major newspapers in the state, and numerous Democratic politicians wrote glowing letters and editorials, and made speeches in his behalf. The basic reason for this support was that federal jobs obtained by Howard as patronage (or any other Black and Tan Leader) were often sold to white Democrats. Blacks could not hold positions like third and fourth-class post masterships in the South, so such positions and other jobs, which could only be held by whites, were sold to them. There were never enough "white Republicans to go around" for all available federal jobs in the South, "so they went to the Democrats." Hence, the gratitude and support for Howard. A second reason was that the new Lily-White Republican movement, which threatened to supplant Howard, refused to deal with the Democrats or with other Democrats than those already holding patronage positions. This threatened to upset the applecart, so whites that Howard had favored now spoke out in his behalf. After his acquittal, Howard returned to lead Mississippi's Black and Tan (or Regular Party). Although he lived and practiced law in Washington, he was seated as a Mississippi delegate at each subsequent national convention through 1956, despite serious challenges each year by a Lily-White group.

The year 1956 was another rough one for the Howard-led Black and Tans. That year the Republican National Committee's sub-committee on contests voted to seat both contending Mississippi delegations, i.e., the Black and Tans and the Lily-Whites, splitting the state's fifteen convention votes unevenly between them. The Howard delegation, consisting of nine blacks and six whites, received eight votes; E.O. Spencer's (a Jackson Mississippi hotel operator) Lily-Whites, comprised of all whites (nine) and six black alternates, received seven convention votes. E.O. Spencer's Lily-Whites waged a tough battle, bringing with them signed claims from several Mississippi courts recognizing them as the only party. A suit that the Lily-Whites had initiated against the Black and Tans was not accepted for review by the Supreme Court. After the 1956 election and Howard's death the reins of power changed and once again slipped back to the Lily-Whites.

In sum, Black and Tan Republican politics in Mississippi were heavily dominated by individual personalities; Lynch, and Hill, Howard and Redmond. The politics of the faction reflected the policies or whims of these leaders. Moreover, each of these personalities established friendly relationships with the Democrats. In Lynch's time, that relationship was with L.Q.C. Lamar; in Howard's day, from 1920 to 1956, it was with the small job-seeking Democrats. The Democrats supported their benefactors and were in turn supported with patronage favors. It is easy in this kind of atmosphere to conclude that the faction was characterized by greed, desire for personal gain and corruption. But it was condoned by the national party, which looked to the leader of the faction to keep the fences mended for the convention. The state leader, whether Lynch or Howard was expected to be, and the South could only be, a patronage referee. The black chairman of the Warren County Republican Committee stated reality succinctly:

> During then presidential campaigns, our committee performs its only cause for being. We proselytize these few score Negroes to vote for Hoover or whoever the Republicans standard bearer may be and, after pocketing the hand-outs from the party slush fund, and this is the only real purpose of our organization, we put our committee back in mothballs to await another Presidential election. Hell no. He got no local program. We are doctors and preachers and barbers. We make enough money to buy enough liquor to wash the inconveniences of being a Nigger out of your brains.

Essentially, Black and Tan Republicanism died in Mississippi when its personalities died.

CHAPTER FOURTEEN
OTHER STATES

The political history of the eleven states of the old confederacy has been reviewed in order to pinpoint and trace the rise, emergence, and decline of black politics. In some states Black and Tan organizations emerged long before 1900, in other states they didn't appear until the 1890s. Still in others the Black and Tan organizations emerged, declined and then re-emerged before their final demise. In Tennessee and Arkansas the Black and Tan movement hardly got underway at all. In other states such as South Carolina and Mississippi, Black and Tanism existed in one form or another from Reconstruction until 1960. No matter how different the factions may have been, nor how different the political maneuvering, they all shared one basic thing: they developed from and operated as a reversion from racism in the regular state parties. All of the Black and Tan groups developed as a result of deep-seated prejudices held and expressed by Lily-White Republican or Democratic organizations.

There were rumblings of Black and Tan movements in other states but for the most part they never came to be much. In Louisville Kentucky in 1929 blacks founded the Lincoln Independent Party, "as a reaction on the part of Negroe Republicans to the rule of the Lily-Whites who had assumed power in Louisville in 1917." During 1929 the Lincoln Independent Party (Black and Tans) put up a full black slate for the local election and waged a heated campaign. But it all came to nothing. Commenting on the situation, one member of the Lincoln Independent Party stated: "We were met with violence on the part of their Negro Republicans and at the hands of white police, tools of the Lily-White Republicans city administration. My printing press was smashed, and I was beaten up along with several others." The Lincoln Independent Party died the same year that it was born. So it was with other independent black Republican movements and efforts in the border and upper south states.

In the northern states, numerous studies indicate that a different situation prevailed. Professors L. Fishel, G. James Fleming, and J.E. Miller have indicated in their studies that blacks in the Republican Party in the North suffered the same kind of racism that generally faced blacks in the South, but that they reacted differently to it. In general, Northern blacks tried independent action only on the local levels. On the state and national levels they generally attempted unification with various third parties, and finally moved to the Democratic Party via machine politics on the national level in the mid 1930s. A more recent study by Professor, Joyce Gelb indicates that black dominated Republican organizations in certain districts of northern cities are now moribund, after years of neglect and unconcern by state and national leadership. Gelb found that they had received no recognition from the new Republican state and local leaders, much less any patronage to keep their organization going. Taking New York as a case in point, she found that Republican Governor Nelson Rockefeller and Mayor John Lindsay would appoint well-known black Republicans like baseball great Jackie Robinson or civil rights leaders like James Farmer, without consulting the local black Republican organizations. The governor and mayor, Gelb says, "paid little heed to the long-established black Republican leadership. Rockefeller and Lindsay's moves constitute an attempt to build a new black Republican leadership from the top down instead of from the grassroots up."

CHAPTER FIFTEEN
POLITICAL SYNTHESIS

Political, economic and social bondage continues to characterize the circumstance of the masses of African Americans, despite the advances associated with emancipation and civil rights victories of the nineteenth and twentieth centuries. Apparently there are other factors that perpetuate the conditions of political bondage and economic poverty in particular, beyond the imposition of legal and practical restraints.

American descendants from Africa continue to wage the battle to achieve freedom, justice and equality however illusive. In view of the history and pathology of American culture some suggest that freedom, justice and equality for black Americans is wishful thinking and illusory as a practical matter.

Racial distinctions continue to be the organizing context for political, economic and social relationships and activity in American society. As a consequence of the American racial dichotomy, extreme positions have served to polarize the "races." The Kerner Commission Report on civil disorders in the 1960s suggested that America was moving toward two separate and distinct societies one black and the other white.

The recommendations of the Kerner Commission Report were never implemented and the underlying causes of the civil disorders of the 1960s were never resolved. The distinct and separate societies have now multiplied and include not only the "white" and "black" "races" but also embody brown, red, yellow, and other "minorities" such as religions, women, gays, animals, etc.

The essential black/white racial dichotomy that was the foundation of the political, economic, social organization and development of America and her institutions has been eclipsed by the advent of the "rainbow." African American political leaders now represent the interests of the "rainbow" and "minorities" while giving rhetoric, sound bites and emotional hype to the best interests of the black American masses. At this point in American history African Americans are the sole managers of the political, economic and social bondage that continues to plague the community at large.

411

Racism remains a factor in the heart of some white and black people and is an institutional and systemic construct of American society. But racism does not account for the pervasive condition of political and economic poverty that characterizes the black community at this point in history. The black political elite maintains their dubious positions of leadership by the employment opportunities associated with managing the political, economic and social status quo. In this context the African American political leadership fosters political ignorance and thwarts emerging community leaders in order to maintain their front line position. The basic tactics of the political leadership are political machinations in the framework of the race card, fear, hate and emotional rhetoric that reinforce their precarious positions of leadership.

Self imposed political bondage as prescribed, articulated and enforced by the "legitimate civil rights leadership" is a prescription that will insure African Americans will be left in the wake of the advancement of other "minorities" as we enter the 3rd millennium of the modern era, popularly referred to as the twenty-first century. In the balance, the legitimate aspirations of the African American community at large have been compromised in order to perpetuate the leadership and legacy of the political "talented tenth." In fact, class distinctions among African Americans is an unspoken truth notwithstanding the perceived harmony among respective classes that embodied the civil rights movement. The black political leadership (talented tenth) have not engaged a trickle down opportunity and access process on behalf of the advancement of the under privileged masses. Apparently the leadership model is too self-serving to take responsibility in the tradition of "noblesse oblige."

The internal leadership dynamic in the black community between the ruling bulls and the emerging bucks has never been addressed since the rivalry of the 1960s. The analogy of the youthful "Black Power" movement of the mid 1960s and the "responsible black leadership" of the civil rights movement as compared to respective counter parts today draws interesting similarities. The youth of the 1960s eventually took matters into their own hands and formed organizations, movements and made various political alliances. In so doing black youth in particular and the community in general took enormous casualties in the face of conventional and unconventional warfare and reactionary forces coupled with the acquiescence of the "responsible black leadership."

The black youth and community of today are still left to their own devices and seem to be in a state of free fall. In the 1960s African American youth who were members of political and community organizations were profiled by the various law enforcement agencies and government intelligence apparatus. Now, black youth who are rap, hip-hop artists, and entertainers are being profiled. However, what may be lethal to emerging generations are the values, messages, and ideas emanating from particular quarters in the rap and hip-hop entertainment industry. The political leadership of today has no lines of communication with youth, no political leverage of their own, and no vision for the future political and economic empowerment of the African American community. African American youth continue to be expendable while the "legitimate civil rights leadership" attempts to extend their political rein.

While the general conditions between now as compared to then are similar as it relates to the vast majority of African Americans. Hopefully, the perspective of time and new information has given birth to a new level of political consciousness among the emerging generation of black leadership. Whether you subscribe to the idea of the dawning of the Age of Aquarius, where truth will abound and set us free, or ascribe to the notion that the end of the "cold war" ushered in freedom and a free flow of information, the fact remains that this 3rd millennium of the modern era offers a new world of ideas and, new political truths.

The end of the "cold war" and the East vs. West geo-political paradigm for example has rendered the conventional political organizing strategy; techniques and technology that embodied the civil rights era, essentially irrelevant. The role of protests, marches, demonstrations, rallies and civil disobedience has some impact, but generate no substantial short and long-term benefits of a few individuals. Beyond the "civil rights orthodoxy" there are few supporters for the direct action tactics that were so popular in recent history. Many in the emerging hip-hop generation are challenging the conventional political wisdom of African American political leadership and are raising legitimate grievances relative to moving beyond civil rights tactics as a political panacea.

Yet the black political leadership remains locked into the agenda of the progressive left wing of the Democratic Party. The Democratic Party leadership (neo-Lily-Whites) on the other hand has isolated and marginalized the left wing of the party, but the black leadership continues to hold down the front lines for the diminishing political fortunes of the classic progressive left wing. Perhaps the black political leadership is in clinical political denial relative to the state of political sophistication within the black community, or the black leadership is operating based on political half-truths. The clinical political denial on the part of the conventional black political leadership may require radical political surgery.

413

Examining the marriage of political convenience between the black community and the left wing of the Democratic Party raises more questions than answers. However, the marriage was a prolific union and gave birth to the civil rights movement, which merged the legitimate aspirations of the black community and the political objectives of the progressive left wing. Since the advent of the American slavery system African Americans fought relentlessly for freedom, justice and equality. In the framework of the history of African Americans struggle for freedom, well-meaning white folk made heroic contributions on behalf of black folk, at their own peril. During the period of slavery white "Radical Republicans" and abolitionists engaged the cause of freedom for African Americans and politically organized blacks to participate in the political and electoral process. Hence, the role of African Americans in the civil war and the Emancipation Proclamation process. The Republican Party was the political framework for the progressive left wing during the ninetieth century. In this context the Republican Party crusaded and achieved civil rights for African Americans and white women.

As African Americans resisted slavery, escape and fought for freedom, justice and equality, they where joined by white abolitionists who organized them to achieve their emancipation and civil right through the American political process. These early black Republicans made unprecedented advances during the period popularly known as "Reconstruction." During the ninetieth century black folks were more prominently affiliated with the Republican Party as compared to the twentieth century and present, as black Americans are now overwhelmingly associated with the Democratic Party. Unfortunately, when federal troops were withdrawn from protecting the civil rights of the African Americans, after emancipation the period of "Reconstruction" was over and white terror was unleashed against black folks as well as on their white supporters.

Fast-forward to the civil rights period following World War II, African Americans are becoming politically assertive, astute and resistant to the indignities associated with segregation and white supremacy. As black Americans began to pursue their legitimate rights and aspirations against white political operatives formulated relationships in support of the political, economic and social movement developing in the black community. In contrast to the nineteenth century, the black and white political coalition of the twentieth century was a political foray engineered by the progressive left wing of the Democratic Party. The objective of the political left was to organize the black community politically in order to advance anti-discriminatory statutes and legislation on behalf of the civil rights of African Americans, in the course of advancing the progressive and left wing local, national and geo-political agenda.

During the civil rights period the progressive left wing exercised increasing leverage within the party and was positioned to be a major factor resulting from the black/white civil rights coalition. Therefore the African American community's infiltration of the party presented the left wing with the opportunity to seize power from the southern belt of racists and segregationists that controlled the Democratic Party. Hence, the black/white progressive union helped African Americans gain civil rights, voting rights, legislative achievements and a plethora of elected officials. On the other side the progressive wing of the Democratic Party enjoyed significant leverage in local and national elections and was positioned to achieve their long-standing geo-political objectives.

The success of the progressive coalition in the context of African Americans, infiltrating the party under the direction and mentorship of the left wing, has essentially relegated the southern "Dixiecrats" to minority status in the Democratic Party. In the wake of the growing civil rights and progressive hegemony within the party power structure, many of the southern "Dixiecrats" changed their political affiliation to the Republican Party. The southern belt Republicans currently exercise considerable leverage on Republican Party domestic and international policy. The legacy of the white racist southern Democrat has been effectively transferred to the Republican Party leadership. However, following the end of the cold war the progressive agenda lost steam particularly in the realm of national and international politics.

During the 1992 Presidential election of Clinton/Gore, the political and electoral strategy of the progressive left wing was eclipsed and replaced with an increasingly conservative or right of center political trajectory. The new Democratic leadership in the framework of the Gore/Lieberman campaign adopted the same right of center national electoral strategy effectively locking out the progressives and left-wingers. Yet the black and progressive political leadership seem absolutely oblivious to the political truth.

Whether the African American leadership and the progressive wing of the Democratic Party are in clinical political denial or operating based on political half-truths, the effect is the same for the masses of African Americans. There is an emerging generation of leaders that are interested in helping to move the black community from point A to point B. There is a leadership vacuum in the African American community as the leadership is in a self-destruct mode.

Underlying the apparent success of the black/white progressive coalition was an unspoken internal contradiction in the context of a cultural dichotomy and paternalistic racism. As a practical political matter the issues associated with these internal political contradictions within the "movement" never surfaced through the political polemic and rhetoric. As a result of these internal contradictions the agenda of the progressive left wing never took hold and generated political legs within the African American community in general.

One of the most significant contradictions between the African American community and the progressive left wing is the fact that black folks overwhelmingly believe in God or a higher spiritual power. The general acknowledgment of a higher power on the part of black folk cannot be reconciled with atheistic ideology that is the basis of progressive politics. Therefore even in the hey-days of the progressive movement only particular African Americans were attracted to the progressive agenda. They include artist, intellectuals, entertainers and community political activists. The black community in general remained circumspect relative to the progressive agenda beyond the curious.

Racism from the left is just as virulent as racism from the right. But it is politically incorrect to suggest that racism is alive and doing well in the framework of progressive politics. Some in the black community argue that it is preferable to deal with blatant and overt racism typical of "right wingers" as compared to deceptive and covert racism from the progressive left wing. Also the racism typical of the left is paternalistic in nature consequently, blacks tend to be window dressing and front people and not policy makers, controllers or owners of the progressive political instruments. The black community has never constituted significant numbers among the rank and file of the progressive left wing, primarily as the result of the unspoken contradictions. Now that the Democratic Party leadership has locked the progressive wing out of the national election strategy yet they remain in denial of the political truth.

Nature abhors a vacuum therefore it is a foregone conclusion that a new generation of black political leadership will emerge from the maturing hip-hop community. The rate of attrition among the ranks of the inherited black political leadership coupled with the lack of a mentoring system has generated a leadership void. Moreover, the traditional emotional political rhetoric, deceptions, and the smoke and mirrors may have run its course. The light and perspective of political history and the level voter education and political sophistication may have preempted any significant political maneuvers in the foreseeable future.

As a result of an increasing level of political consciousness and voting sophistication due to contemporary history, education, application, experience and the benefit perspective and critical analysis it should be no surprise that black Americans have a predictable and utterly sophomoric voting pattern. African American voting rights have only been enforced since 1965 therefore black folks are comparatively new to the process. Moreover, the African American community was organized politically by white political operatives in the Republican and Democratic Parties respectively. As a matter of fact the African American community has not yet organized itself politically to compete as a power player in the American electoral process.

When the African American community was organized during the civil rights period, the progressive organizers were concerned that the black community remain loyal to the party therefore they formulated a mythology of the racist right wing enemy and the Republican boogieman. The political mythology has been very effective in terms of organizing the black community to infiltrate the ranks of the Democratic Party exclusively. In order to facilitate this process, political concepts such as integration, civil rights, affirmative action, minority rights etc. were deployed to mobilize and organize broad based support to achieve statutory and legislative victories. However, the paternal political organizers only taught and instructed on half of the political truth. Now that the progressive left wing has been marginalized within the "neo" Democratic Party leadership the African American community must now organize politically on their own terms.

CHAPTER 22

FOR IMMEDIATE RELEASE
July 5, 2006 Contact: www.voteranonymous.org
http://black-power-politics.blogspot.com

Black Mules and Rinos Cut Off
New Generation Leadership at Grassroots

Arguably one of the most significant hybrids in human history is the one between horses and donkeys, vis-à-vis, the mule. Breeding a male donkey with a female horse results in a mule; breeding a female horse with a male donkey produces a hinny (mule). Offspring from either cross, although fully developed as males or females are virtually sterile. Therefore a line of horses and a line of domestic asses must be maintained in order to perpetuate mule production.

The mule has greater endurance, is stronger and less excitable than a horse. Depending on the need, different horses are used to produce: fine riding mules, heavy draft animals or medium-sized pack mules, as the case may be. In Medieval Europe, when horses were bred largely to carry armored knights, mules were the preferred riding animal of gentlemen and clergy.

In 1495, Christopher Columbus brought four jacks and two horses to the "new world." They would produce mules for the Conquistadors' and facilitated expeditions onto the American mainland. Ten years after the conquest of the Aztecs, the first shipment of twelve horses and three jacks arrived from Cuba to begin breeding mules in Mexico.

Female mules were preferred as riding animals, while the males were used more as pack animals along trails that tied the Spanish Empire together. Mules were used in the silver mines. Along the frontier each Spanish outpost had to breed its own supply of mules, and each hacienda or mission maintained at least one stud jack.

On the Iberian Peninsular, Catalonia and Andalusia each developed a large breed of ass, putting Spain in the forefront of the mule-breeding industry. Exportation of Spanish jacks was prohibited until 1813. However, the King of Spain presented George Washington with a large black jack in 1785. This animal, called the "Royal Gift," is considered the father of the mule industry in the United States.

Mules were once used to pull fire-fighting equipment and were often employed by armies to pull artillery and to remove the wounded from the battlefield. The twenty-mule team that hauled borax from Death Valley has become part of American legend. Indeed, some western towns were originally laid out with extremely wide streets in order to allow the mule teams to turn around.

Popular mule-breeding centers in the United States developed in Tennessee, Kentucky and Missouri to provide work animals for the cotton fields of the "Old South." After the American Civil War and the development of tenant farming throughout the South, the mule continued as the major draft animal in American agriculture.

"Forty acres and a mule" was all one needed for self-sufficiency. The importance of the mule declined rapidly in the 1940s and 1950s, however, as gasoline-driven tractors became widespread, and mules all but disappeared from the American agricultural scene.

A curious political correlation between the creation and application of the utilitarian hybrid (mule) and the "orthodox" black civil rights leadership occurred to this writer.

Both the "Royal Gift" (black jack gift to President George Washington said to be responsible for the American mule industry) and black "orthodox" civil rights leadership have interesting parallels relative to the advancement and achievements of American culture, not to mention their hybrid nature.

The mule and nineteenth century black America enjoyed a most unique symbiosis and synergistic relationship. Just as the twentieth century witnessed the decline of the mule due to the advent of the internal combustion engine applied to the agricultural industry, the black civil rights orthodoxy has apparently outlived its practical application in relation to the political, economic and social needs of twenty-first century black America.

Beneath the surface however, there is an even more intriguing correlation between mule and the inherited leadership that constitutes *the black civil rights orthodoxy. Interestingly enough the "orthodox" black civil rights leadership is also apparently sterile and unable to produce political progeny, hence they may have gone the way of the dinosaurs. Consequently, the black political leadership may be phantom donkeys but are in fact political mules, with a similar pedigree.*

As a practical political matter Rev. Al Sharpton, former candidate for the Democratic Party's Presidential nomination in 2004, having been mentored by the "movement," may represent the last generation of "orthodox" black civil rights leadership. And there is no coherent civil rights agenda being advanced by the respective echelons of the traditional leadership to move the black American community at large from point A to point B.

Some in the black community argue that civil rights techniques, political tactics and rhetoric are not sufficient to enforce or sustain the legislative and statutory advancements achieved, during that era. Equally insufficient is their capacity to cover new political ground in the context of the emerging black American demographic. The political leadership bears considerable responsibility for the fact that African Americans are the weakest politically among virtually all political minorities despite the comparatively disproportional high number of black elected officials and longevity in America.

The voter turnout in the recent Connecticut Democratic primary pitting incumbent Senator Joe Lieberman against political neophyte Ned Lamont, is an example of illusionary politics. Party officials are absolutely ecstatic about the "overwhelming" and unprecedented voter turnout and attribute the hotly contested primary to the anti Iraq war sentiment within the Democratic Party. The fact that voter plurality in Connecticut was only 42 percent speaks volumes relative to the legitimacy of the state party leadership and the apathy among the states constituents.

Anti-war candidate Ned Lamont enjoyed support from the entire complement of black "orthodox" civil rights leaders and elected officials who were prominently displayed and deployed in his campaign offensive. There was not one traditional black political leader to support or endorse Joe Lieberman. The lone black politician to support Lieberman was the newly elected new-generation leader, the honorable Cory Booker, Mayor of Newark, New Jersey. Corey was, of course, derided by the civil rights orthodoxy for not walking in lock step. Nevertheless, the two U.S. Senatorial candidates virtually split the black vote.

If you follow the logic of "political correctness" relative to the delivery of the black vote in Connecticut, new generation political leader Mayor Cory Booker ran a dead heat with the combined efforts of Revs. Al Sharpton and Jesse Jackson, Congresswoman Maxine Waters, and the Congressional black Caucus. Despite diminishing electoral returns, pervasive voter apathy and overwhelming numbers of unregistered voters the black political establishment has yet to solidify its tenuous partisan advantage with aggressive voter education and registration efforts.

On the contrary, the national black political establishment defends its monolithic provincial approach to political ascendancy against all opposing points of view. The ferocity of the pack-dog-mentality political attacks against competing points of view to some extent takes the form of political fratricide. The recent attacks against professor, comedian, philanthropist, and neo-political activist Bill Cosby is but the latest example of the prevailing political-pack-dog mentality.

Perhaps the late author Harold Cruse described the black American dilemma best in his profound expose published in the late 1960s entitled, The Crisis of the Negro Intellectual. *You need only replace the word Negro with black or African American and the same crisis scenario remains here in the first decade of the twenty-first century. Too many black Professors and intellectuals in prominent positions simply profess. but know not. We need only take a cursory look at the recent literary works of professors Michael Erick Dyson and Ron Walters for confirmation.*

Professor Ron Walters, who came to public prominence as a political operative in the 1984 and 1988 presidential campaign of Rev. Jesse Jackson, is now one of the gurus of "progressive" black politics and member of the civil rights leadership establishment. In his most recent book, Freedom Is Not Enough, *Walters continues to promote the vagaries of social justice, racial entitlement, victimization, and partisan white paternalism.*

Alton Chase, a longtime community and political activist based in the Bronx and Harlem said, "Freedom is enough if we take full responsibility for ourselves, children, and community." Chase said, "Black folk need to be more sophisticated about how to maximize the power derived from the electoral process. Instead, we continue to buy into the political salvation rhetoric preached by the one-legged politician or political leader."

Chase continued, "But freedom is not enough if you are still pursuing 'forty-acres and a mule' and engaged in modern day victimization and reparations politics." When the famous Bill Cosby defied the protocol of "political correctness" by publicly admonishing black parents for the anti-social behavior, etc., of their children and decried the disproportionate number of out of wedlock births among black youth, he was roundly criticized by the gatekeepers of plantation politics.

The black civil rights orthodoxy lead the invidious political assault against Cosby followed by character assassination pop-shots by media opportunists with apparent personal motives. The flamboyant and popular black popular-culturist and rhetorician Professor and Rev. Michael Eric Dyson has monopolized the anti Bill Cosby political fallout by authoring a book entitled, Is Bill Cosby Right: or Has The Black Middle Class Lost Its Mind?

According to Rev. Dyson, "For most of his career Bill Cosby has avoided race with religious zeal." Well-known TV Journalist Juan Williams, who is currently working for National Public Radio (NPR), in a direct response to Rev. Dyson's book, has authored a book entitled, Enough, *that offers an eloquent and insightful argument that questions the premise of Dyson's political assault on Cosby. Williams' book has sparked a long-overdue, broad-based political, economic, and social discourse in the black community.*

The breath of the abounding discourse seems to focus on the transitional needs of black American politics to address the short and long-range crisis may be cathartic. Traditional civil rights leaders are currently hard pressed to justify staying the course of civil rights as a viable strategy to move black folk at large from point A to point B in the twenty-first century. Some call for a third civil rights movement in black America, while others say a third civil rights movement is a bad idea and wholly insufficient.

The political inertia of the black political establishment with the cooperation of their partisan paternal masters are making every effort to silence independent black political thinkers. The attack on Cosby, whose contribution to the advancement of black folk speaks for itself, is an example of how blacks that think outside of the political box are maligned and politically "black" listed.

But the attack on Cosby is an act of political desperation and in fact a rear guard action to forestall what is politically inevitable, vis-à-vis, a changing of the political leadership equation. The increasing shortcomings of the traditional black civil rights leadership continues to generate voter apathy that has resulted in a pervasive political denial and paranoia.

Prior to the Bill Cosby political controversy among black folk, public TV talk-show host and rising political star, Tavis Smiley, was being accused by some in the civil rights leadership of attempting to pull off a political coup when he published The Covenant With Black America, following his latest nationally televised annual forum on the state of black America. In the introduction to the book Smiley writes:

> Why a Covenant with Black America? In short, because. without organization, black folk will never be able to take, keep, or hold onto anything, much less the hard-fought gains that we have struggled to achieve. Our interest with this document was to create a national plan of action to address the primary concerns of African Americans today. Once we are organized and mobilized, we can create the world we want for generations to come. The Covenant is required reading for any person, party, or powerbroker who seeks to be supported politically, socially or economically by the masses of black people in the coming years.

On the local level in New York City the political fratricide continues, constricting if not imploding the black Democratic Party leadership leviathan. In Brooklyn's 10th CD incumbent Congressman Ed Towns is in a three-way race with two former political allies City Councilman Charles Barron and Assemblyman Roger Green. Tragically, of the 400, 000 registered voters in the district only 10 percent of the voters turn out in the general election. Hence, the three candidates are contesting over who will get the lion's share of 10,000 votes while the 390,000 voters are out of the electoral pool.

The political fratricide is so destructive in Brooklyn's 11ᵗʰ CD, a so-called black congressional seat as the result of the Voting Rights Act of 1965. The three black candidates (Mr. Chris Owens, Ms. Yvette Clarke, and Mr. Carl Andrews) will likely split the black vote enabling the white candidate David Yaski to win the so-called "minority" seat.

In Harlem, the political turf of the "old" guard, the term limited City Councilman Bill Perkins is facing a primary battle with a Latino Ruben Varges for the open State Senate seat vacated by Senator David Paterson as he runs for Lieutenant Governor on the State House coronation ticket of Attorney General Elliot Spitzer. There is great political speculation that should Mr. Varges prevail in his primary race there will a domino effect that could lead to a Latino successor to the Harlem Congressional seat of the honorable Charles Rangel.

Apparently the perceived political donkeys are in fact variations of the hybrid mule unable to produce offspring to carry the political agenda beyond the civil rights and racial paradigm of victimization and entitlement. But the black political crisis is compounded because the RINOs (Republicans In Name Only) have not practiced and abided by the rich legacy that brought them into being in 1854.

The anti-social RINOs have distinguished themselves by devouring new and young political sprouts at the grassroots. And in conjunction with the political imperative of the white RINOs the black RINOs are clandestinely allocated turf strong holds to help manage the "reservation" and the status-quo political scenario. By political design the black Republicans cannot be competitive in Brooklyn's 10ᵗʰ and 11ᵗʰ CD's and the GOP party leadership (white) will certainly negotiate short- and long-term power-relationship issues beneath the surface, as usual.

Likewise, the Grand Old Party in Harlem has no opportunity to be competitive in the short and long term. However, some note a major improvement in that for the first time in at least 30 plus years the New York Republican County Committee designated a registered Republican for the coveted Harlem Congressional seat in the 15ᵗʰ CD. Mr. Edward Daniels a political neophyte and local uptown party operative has set the unprecedented standard of being the first registered Republican to head the county ballot.

In 2004 the Republican Party candidate in Harlem's 15ᵗʰ CD was Mr. Kenneth Jefferson, a registered Democrat and political neophyte.

Mr. Jefferson's candidacy was supported by the uptown district leaders in order to stop Ms. Keisha Morrisey a hip-hop-generation, grassroots insurgent, who was the GOP nominee for New York State Assembly in the 70ᵗʰ AD and New York City Council in the 9ᵗʰ CD in 2002 and 2003 respectively. The resulting controversy between Ms. Morrisey and the uptown Harlem GOP leadership was the basis for a lawsuit initiated by Ms. Morrisey.

In 2002 the party gave the congressional designation in Harlem's 15ᵗʰ CD to Dr. Jesse Fields, an official of the Independence Party, reportedly controlled by Dr. Lenora Fulani. Many longtime local Republicans were irate because of the obvious snub and apparent compromise of GOP values in the political deal with the Independence Party. But the controversy began because Mr. Conrad Muhammad the former minister of the Nation of Islam's Mosque # 7 and his GOP supporters were lobbying for his (Conrad Muhammad) designation as the party's congressional standard bearer.

The popular and charismatic Conrad Muhammad had begun evaluating both political parties as well as the prospect of running for public office a couple of years earlier. The advent of Conrad Muhammad as a GOP Congressional candidate generated shockwaves within the leadership of both local political parties. The word on the street began to generate great curiosity, if not a ground swell, and much local and state political interest in the Grand Old Party was percolating.

Governor Pataki's re-election campaign quickly embraced Conrad's candidacy and reached out to the grassroots political activists associated with his (Conrad) campaign for cross endorsements. The high profile public re-election endorsement of black community leaders included Conrad Muhammad and chairman of the GOP Grassroots Political Taskforce among about twenty other prominent celebrities of varying genre and community and political activists from around the city.

Conspicuously missing from the statewide assembly of black leadership were the uptown black GOP district leaders and county operatives, who peppered the hundreds that constituted the audience.

On the contrary, the leadership of the New York Republican County registered in the strongest terms possible, that they had a problem with the notion of Conrad Muhammad as the party's congressional designee following a cursory interview. Consequently, the uptown GOP leadership who formally introduced Conrad to the county leadership as a prospective designee jumped ship and lined up behind the county chairman at the time former State Assemblyman John Ravitz. Somehow, Ravitz came to the conclusion that Independence Party official Dr. Jesse Fields was the best designee for the party.

Not only had Conrad upset the County Republican Party leadership, but the energy associated with his (Conrad) proposed campaign smoked Congressman Rangel's people out, who made direct inquiries to the campaign organization. And the writer was advised that the esteemed congressman has considerable leverage with GOP county officials and may have had some influence on the decision of county chairman Assemblyman John Ravitz.

Excitement was resonating in the media as well as the community concerning Conrad's planned entry into the congressional race. The New York Press *published a comprehensive interview July 17-23, Volume 15, Number 29 with Conrad Muhammad, that also included Congressman Rangel and GOP County chairman John Ravitz. The extensive piece was, "A Great Race In Harlem—Will 'Hip-hop Minister' Conrad Muhammad Go From N.O.I. to G.O.P?' by Adam Heimlich.*

Ravitz was hard pressed by Heimlich to justify resorting to an officer of the Independence Party in general and Dr. Jesse Fields in particular while ignoring local registered Republicans to head up the county ballot. Dr. Fields, and her associate Dr. Fulani have been mired in controversy in the context of alleged anti-Semitic statements and the lesbian, gay, transgender and bisexual agenda which is in direct contradiction with the values and standards of the Republican Party. Ravitz without question compromised the GOP by insisting that the county endorsed Fields for the designation.

Ravitz was totally against a GOP primary to let the voters make the decision, between the candidates and sited Conrad's alleged anti-Semitic statement when he was the minister of Mosque number 7. Ravitz maintained that a primary was not a healthy process for the local party.

According to Heimlich's piece, "Ravitz said there are reasons why the G.O.P. is wary of Muhammad, and none of them are secret.

427

Directing me (Heimlich) to the Anti-Defamation League's website for specifics, he says, "Conrad knows about the problems with some of the things that he's said in the past. I believe he's going to have to address and deal with them. I think that all of us who are in public life have to be held accountable for our words, and there are a lot of things that Conrad still needs to work with—people who are still feeling very hurt about some of those comments." Ravitz said.

Some astute political analyst suggest that Ravitz made a serious miscalculation with the Fields and Muhammad scenario and may be held accountable for compromising the values and growth of the party should he seek public office in the future in New York City.

Meanwhile, embattled new generation grassroots GOP activist Ms. Keisha Morrisey said, "I will continue undaunted with my efforts to help grow the party at the grassroots level. And I remain encouraged by our forward movement."

FOR IMMEDIATE RELEASE
August 5, 2006 Contact: www.votersanonymous.org
http://black-power-politics.blogspot.com

African American Vote Hijacked by Jackasses and Rogue Elephants

Among the mosaic that constitutes "minority" politics in the United States, the African American vote is increasingly less influential despite its historical numerical advantage. Recent polling and census data indicate that the Latino American community has eclipsed the longstanding African American numerical edge as the result of recent immigration patterns from the Dominican Republic, South and Central America and Mexico, in the past generation.

Some in the African American community dispute the data and argue that a good number of Latino Americans are in fact black Americans until they speak their indigenous language. Some suggest that there is political motive behind the black-Latino juxtaposition and is a convenient if not classic divide-and-conquer scenario. And to compare a person's phenotype with language as a distinguishing characteristic is an odious political machination. However, such arguments are superfluous and it avoids the political reality on the

428

ground that Latino Americans have totally eclipsed African Americans in terms of raw political power whether or not they currently enjoy a numerical advantage.

Moreover, all other "minority" communities such as Asians, gays, Jews and women for example have more political leverage than African Americans despite their comparatively small numbers. Paradoxically, African American elected officials outnumber all other "minority" communities combined, but the proliferation of African American elected officials has not translated into political power for black Americans comparatively.

The political odyssey of African Americans in the "new world" is perplexing when viewed through the lens of advancements made by African Americans following emancipation in the nineteenth century and the modern civil rights movement of the twentieth century, juxtaposed to the current state of black political power here in the first decade of the twenty-first century. The state of African America political power is without question a complex and perplexing situation and merits strategic observation, critical study and a practical sustainable resolution.

Interestingly enough, the celebrated social, political, and economic victories and advancement of African Americans during the modern civil rights movement of the twentieth century are dwarfed by the achievements of blacks in the nineteenth century following emancipation from slavery and the imposition of martial law characterized as the period of "Reconstruction." Comparatively speaking the African American leadership of the nineteenth century were apparently light years ahead of their contemporary counterparts of the twentieth century in terms of imagination, character, principles and elective achievements.

Concomitantly, the Democratic and Republican political Parties have effectively morphed to their current political rhetoric and applications from their respective polar opposite and both have virtually exchanged their politics as they relate the African American community. The modern civil rights movement of the 1950s, 60s and 70s was a cornerstone of the Democratic Party's prominence during that dynamic period. Likewise it was the Republican Party of the nineteenth century that crusaded civil rights of the time in the framework on the abolitionist movement that facilitated an unprecedented number of African American elected officials and accumulation of wealth.

History is witness to the Republican and Democratic Parties' political ambivalence when it comes to the bottom line interests of the African American community and the enforcement of laws and statutes that safeguard their civil rights. Unfortunately, the level and quality of the current African American political and elected leadership continue to exacerbate the political crisis in the African American community and position the community at large as political pawns in the context of the generic "black vote" and power-sharing process.

African American donkeys (Democrats) and elephants (Republicans) of the twentieth century have demonstrated political similitude and essentially function as gatekeepers for the ruling white political elites and have advanced no coherent agenda since the civil rights era, for moving black Americans beyond subservient partisan politics. On the national as well as the local level both Democrat and Republican African American leadership have demonstrated no imagination or initiative for political and economic improvement beyond continuing the civil rights agenda items and self indulgence.

On the national political scene, the esteemed Congressional black Democratic Caucus in the decades following its auspicious founding and the cumulative legislation enacted by all of its members cannot compete with the singular legislative achievements of the late Harlem congressman, Adam Clayton Powell Jr. On the contrary the Congressional black Democratic Caucus is renown more than anything for its weekend parties and social gatherings as opposed to power politics. In fact the caucus is informally referred to by many as the black Congressional ruckus.

For their part, "black conservatives" (Republicans) are apparently politically delusional in their attempt to intellectually justify and market the politics of "White Republican social conservatism" as a practical partisan political alternative to liberal Democratic paternalism. Unfortunately both national black Democratic and Republican Party leaders apparently lack the political imagination and independence to think and organize outside of the conservative vs. liberal political paradigm to argue and organize in the context of bi-partisan leverage power politics and the organic issues required to move the community from point A to point B.

In New York City the crisis in black politics is most acute and has caused substantial political disillusionment and apathy among black voters over the decades. In 1969 the election plurality was 80 plus percent as compared to half that (40%) these days. And the percentage of registered voters as compared to eligible voters among black Americans calls into question the legitimacy of the inherited civil rights leadership. Internal rivalries among black Democrat and Republican leaders have further neutralized the potential of the black vote in addition to the lack of strategic deployment.

The longstanding political rivalry between the black political leadership in Brooklyn (vanguard) and Harlem (old guard) that began in the 1970s (when the Brooklyn contingent achieved elective office) has accounted for a traditional split of the black vote and has facilitated the current divide-and-conquer political scenario that plagues the black community, particularly in city and state-wide elections. The Latino American political leadership was played out of political position by the political machinations of the "vanguard" vs. "old guard" when then mayoral candidate Herman Badeo was undermined by the black Democratic political leadership rivalry. As a consequence the potential of a "black and Latino" electoral coalition for city-wide office was seriously undermined for the future, not withstanding the one term of Mayor David Dinkins.

While the Harlem "old guard" political leadership has maintained hegemony over the Brooklyn "vanguard" to date, political cleavages are emerging within each respective political camp. As the prospect of the eventual retirement of the Congressman after 30 plus years in Congress looms large on the Harlem horizon. In Brooklyn Democratic leadership is imploding with the retirement of Congressman Major Owens and the internal challenge to unseat Congressman Ed Towns. As there is no apparent African American successor to the veteran Congressman within the Harlem "old guard" ranks or community at large, speculation abounds that Congressman Rangel may be the last black Democratic Congressman to represent Harlem.

Be that as it may, it is highly unlikely that a black, white, or Latino Republican candidate would be competitive in the eventual sweepstakes to succeed Congressman Rangel. As a practical political matter there is no Republican Party in New York City in general and Manhattan in particular capable of competing. And the black GOP district leaders in Harlem have been effectively compromised by the Democratic Party operatives therefore they have no party infrastructure, political troops or leadership capable of fielding viable Republican Party candidates. Black GOP district leaders and candidates for political office are appointed by a haphazard and vest pocket arrangement and have no credibility or visibility in the districts that they represent.

This year's gubernatorial election in New York State will likely mark a watershed for both local Democrat and Republican Parties relative to black electoral politics. Brooklyn's 11th Congressional District, established in 1965 by way of the Voting Rights Act as a "black" Congressional District, is currently an open seat due to the retirement of 24-year-incumbent Congressman, Major Owens. It may get its first white Congressman. In typical political fashion the black political leadership has demonstrated how fragmented it is as three would be black Congress persons Chris Owens Jr., Yvette Clarke and Carl Anthony are competing in the party primary election. The likely result is that the three black hopefuls will cancel each other out thereby enabling the election of David Yasky. There is a three-way primary contest in the 10th CD wherein incumbent Congressman Adolphus Towns is being challenged by Charles Barron and Roger Green, all three were former allies.

Despite the fragmented black political leadership, ultimately, a Democratic Congressional candidate will prevail as there will be no viable Republican Party infrastructure or candidate in Brooklyn or Harlem to be competitive. But it is a foregone conclusion that black Democrats are a diminishing political force in party power relationship yet the leadership continues to advocate a dead end partisan civil rights movement political agenda.

The black political fragmentation in Harlem is a particularly interesting studying in view of its historic hegemony over the Brooklyn "vanguard" leadership. Under the veteran political of Congressman Charles Rangel, the political operative of an esteemed triumvirate that includes the honorable Percy Sutton and the honorable Basil Paterson, Harlem electoral politics has over the years enjoyed a reputation of being the hallmark of African American politics around the country. With luminaries like the late Congressman Rev. Dr. Adam Clayton Powell Jr. and J. Raymond Jones referred to as the "Harlem Fox," Harlem became world renown as the foremost African American community world wide.

For most of his Congressional career, the honorable Congressman Rangel enjoyed running on the top of both the Democrat and Republican Parties' ballots, yet he has been a Republican Party basher throughout is career on Capital Hill. The longstanding political deal between the Harlem black Democratic leader and respective Republican County bosses was a benefit to white Republican Party county leadership who doubled as elected officials and had political assurances that their seat would be exempt from competition from black Democrats in particular. On the other hand, black Democratic elected officials received political assurances that the GOP would thwart the emergence of viable black Republican electoral opposition and leadership.

In the balance, the Republican Party district leadership infrastructure was rendered none existent and potential organic community based political leaders both Democrat and Republican continue to be cut off at their political knees. The process of marginalizing "unsanctioned" organic black political leadership is reinforced on the Republican aisle black political geldings who function as "House Negroes." Alternatively, insurgent black Democrats have to navigate invidious technical and legal tactics by incumbents to gain ballot status.

Former Bronx GOP district leader and titular head of the infamous and defunct National black Republican Council (NBRC) and the New York State Council of black Republicans for 25 plus years has help to perpetuate the black GOP political power illusion by slight of hand and smoke and mirrors. Reported to be in charge of 44 states nation wide Brown has skillfully neutered the black GOP presence in New York City and in Washington. In Harlem, Brown was the central figure in positioning district leadership of Mr. Leroy Owens, Mr. Ronald Perry, and Mr. Will Brown (no familial relation), for county leader anointment. The pervasive political deception has effectively thwarted the emergence of organic, community-based black Republican leadership in Harlem.

But the Republican Party has its own unique style of plantation politics that mitigates against the emergence of organic grassroots African American leaders. Lack of a party primary election facilitates the selection and anointing of district leaders and candidates for elective office. And the GOP political plantation operates on two basic principles. The first is to keep the "official" black Republican district leaders and leadership ignorant of the "how to" as it relates to the petitioning and ballot access process, hence no need for a primary. The second principle is to select candidates for elective office that are simply happy to run as window dressing but not interested in changing the local political status quo. Alternatively, some get to do cameos in conjunction with state-wide or national candidates.

It remains to be seen if this years slate of GOP candidates and "official" black leaders in Harlem will be helpful to the gubernatorial ticket and the growth of the party. Local Republican candidates in Harlem usually receive a single digit plurality in the general election and this year there are two perennial candidates and one no show candidate, which speaks volumes. Perennial candidates Al Mosley is running for New York State Senate in the 30th SD and Edward Daniels is running for Congress against the incumbent Congressman Charles Rangel. Will Brown district leader in central Harlem's 70th AD officially declined to run for the New York State Assembly in the 70th AD on July 17, 2006.

Speculation abounds as to why Mr. Will Brown decided to pull out of the race at the eleventh hour and there is an interesting controversy as to why a replacement candidate was not selected. While Brown has been a district leader for several years, he first ran for public office in 2005 for New York City Council against incumbent Will Perkins. However, Brown's campaign was the subject of a devastating controversy when in the December of 2005 edition of the Amsterdam News under the by line of Talise D. Moorer published a story with the headline: "Bronx Students Get Lesson in Political Scam by GOP Candidate." According to the story a teacher, June Smith Bryant, of the Bronx High School for Law, Government, and Justice alleged that the students were owed at least $1000 based on a contractual agreement they had with the Will Brown campaign. The political fallout and potential future fallout from this reckless and irresponsible act seriously put Brown off limits for another electoral *run in the immediate future. Hence, he was wise enough to assess that he should step down as a candidate for the New York State Assembly in the 70th AD, in the interest of the party.*

On the other hand, the issues associated with the fact that there has been no replacement candidate named for the Republican Party line are a bit more complex and requires exploration in order to appreciate. Ms. Keisha Morrisey former GOP Assembly candidate in the 70th AD during 2000 and 2002 was ready, willing and able to be a replacement candidate and there are others that may have been available such as Ms. Denise Johns (GOP aspirant in 2005 for New York City Council), but the state of the personal animus and political ineptitude carried the replacement process to its most illogical conclusion. Unfortunately, both Morrisey and Johns had challenged the political status quo in the Harlem black leadership and were therefore ruled out by the black Republican leadership as replacement candidates.

Keisha Morrisey sent the following e-mail to the Honorable James Ortinzeo chairman of the New York County Republican Committee, Mr. Marcus Cederqvist, Executive Director of the county committee and Mr. Will Brown, district leader in the 70th AD as a potential replacement.

I am writing in regard to the agenda that I discussed with Mr. Alphonso Mosley the candidate for the New York State Senate in the 30th SD in an attempt to unite the many factions of the Uptown Republicans, while working on his campaign. On Monday May 17, Mr. Mosley suggested to our district leader (Will Brown) that I replace the withdrawn candidate, Mr. Brown, and run for State Assembly along with him (Mr. Mosley State Senate) and Ed Daniels for Congress as a way to help accomplish the goal of unity in this years election.

Although I may not be the Assembly candidate to at this time, I still believe that the unity agenda can be accomplished after talking with Ms. Denise Johns, Ed Daniels, and Leroy Owens, among others. I will continue to help grow the party by inviting young people into politics and to promote Republican candidates in general. I am in the process of developing a grassroots organization as well as my own political club. I want to share this information with you so that you can know what my agenda is from my mouth and in my own words.

I intend to keep lines of communication open, and I am available if you need to reach out to me. I understand that some wounds may not have healed due to various controversies in the past; therefore I want to be careful and cautious to make sure I communicate directly, so no one can speak for me. Thanking you for your consideration and time in advance.

Keisha Morrisey.

But the plot thickens. Keisha was working with the grassroots GOP reform movement that drafted Al Mosley for New York State Senate because he (Al) was falsely accused of aiding Morrisey in her law suit against the Uptown leadership in 2004. Because of the accusations against Mr. Mosley he was passed over for consideration as the GOP designee for the New York State Senate in the 30th SD, although he (Al) had been the party's Harlem electoral standard bearer and crusader for many previous campaigns. In the wake of the exclusion of Al Mosley as the party's standard bearer for State Senate and his rejection by the uptown Republicans for the designation a petition campaign was organized by the grassroots GOP reform movement to draft Mosley as a GOP reform candidate and petitions were filed on July 13, on behalf of Al Mosley.

Following the filing of Mr. Mosley's petitions he (Mr. Mosley) received a phone call early on the following week from district leader Will Brown Jr. who invited Mr. Mosley to be the official party designated candidate for New York State Senate in the 30th SD, as the original candidate of record district leader JoLinda Ruth Cogen reportedly had no intentions to run. Mr. Brown told Mr. Mosley that he (Brown) was the candidate of record for Assembly in the 70th AD but had officially declined his candidacy. According to the taped conversation Mosley then touted Ms. Morrisey as a replacement candidate and Mr. Brown indicated that it was a good idea and asked Mosley to have Ms. Morrisey call him for that purpose.

Apparently the conversation between Ms. Morrisey and Mr. Brown was not productive, as Ms. Morrisey is not the designated candidate, and therefore there is no GOP candidate to compete against incumbent New York Assemblyman Keith Wright. Interestingly enough Assemblyman Wright successfully knocked his Democratic Party primary election competition off of the ballot and will face no opposition from either Democrat or Republican. Arguably the most vulnerable Harlem Democrat, the incumbent Assemblyman will get a free pass without even an illusion of GOP competition.

Alton Chase, a longtime community leader and Republican Party activist, and one of the architects of the GOP reform movement that drafted Al for Senate campaign said, "Apart from the personality and sophomoric political intrigues that typify Harlem GOP politics the bottom line is that the "official" uptown leadership have successfully picked off Al Mosley from the GOP reform movement to embrace him once again. Now that Mosley is apparently back in good graces with the uptown leadership fold it is clear that his agenda is divergent from the objectives of the GOP reform movement," Chase said. "Mosley will face the winner of the Democratic primary battle between Bill Perkins and Ruben Vargez for the open Senate seat.

"The GOP reform movement deserves kudos from Mr. Mosley because the draft Mosley petition campaign secured his nomination and acceptance back into the 'official' party fold. Also, the absence of a Harlem-based State Senate and Assembly would constitute a major embarrassment and defect in the state wide gubernatorial campaign. At this point with only one candidate lacking on the uptown ticket it may be only a minor embarrassment."

FOR IMMEDIATE RELEASE
SEPTEMBER 5, 2006 CONTACT: www.votersanonymous.org
http://black-power-politics.blogspot.com

Will There Be a Paradigm Shift in Black Politics?

The 2006 mid-term elections are being touted by many political analysts as a referendum of the "Presidential" war on Iraq. Respective polls are unanimous in their calculations relative to the anti-war sentiment growing among the American public and the dismal approval ratings of President Bush. Without question, the president is now a lame duck and his agenda will suffer the consequences as Senate and House Republicans keep the president at arms length as they fight to retain their seats and the GOP majority.

Democrats smell blood but are tempered from gloating at the prospect of their ascendancy to Senate and Congressional majorities following the November election. Although there is great optimism among the party leadership and the rank and file concerning the final outcomes of the mid-term elections, discretion as the greater part of valor appears to be the approach to their possible elevation to congressional majority status.

While the Democratic Party has the momentum going into the mid-term elections, there is a noteworthy dichotomy among the party leadership as well as in the fragile coalition that constitutes Democratic constituency. The result of the Connecticut Democratic Senatorial primary election in which incumbent Senator Joseph Lieberman was narrowly defeated by political neophyte and anti-war candidate, Ned Lamont, is a snapshot of the fissure separating critical elements of the party, vis-à-vis the war in Iraq.

The Connecticut general election promises to be a titanic battle as the defeated incumbent Senator Lieberman will be on the ballot as the Independent Party candidate. The controversy associated with this senatorial race may invigorate the electorate to an unprecedented high voter turnout according to some party leaders. However, notwithstanding the rate of election turn out, the polarization between the vociferous "anti-war" elements of the party and centrist Democrats will likely cut both ways in the November election and in 2008.

Should Lieberman prevail and retain his seat the party centrists with the help of their friends would have defeated the anti-war elements in the Democratic Party which is comprised of a general amalgamation of "leftists," "radicals," "progressives," the "black" vote and some liberals. On the other hand, if anti-war candidate Ned Lamont wins the general election the respective left of center Democrats would have wrested control of the state party. In both instances there is a potential negative political fallout for the Democratic Party in November as well as during the 2008 Presidential election.

As the anti-war contingent and liberal-centrist square off in the Connecticut race, the bi-polar political rhetoric within the

Democratic Party may spill over and infect other elections. Extremist rhetoric from the left will likely polarize competing party contingents and negatively impact their hopes to gain control of the House and Senate this year. But the Democratic Party coalition is showing internal tensions beyond the Lamont vs. Lieberman political juxtaposition.

Perhaps the most graphic example of the ideological split among Democrats generated by the Lamont vs. Lieberman juxtaposition can be gleaned by the results of the "black vote." A virtual split of the black vote between both candidates speaks volumes relative to the internal dynamic of the party. The only black American political leader to line up behind Lieberman was the newly elected Mayor of Newark, New Jersey Corey Booker. On the other hand, the entire black civil rights leadership, including Revs. Jackson and Sharpton and elected officials, were very visible in their support for the anti-war candidate, while chiding Booker for stepping out of line.

Apparently, Mayor Corey Booker's endorsement is competitive in Connecticut, with the entire black leadership contingent, and/or the black American electorate has demonstrated an unprecedented level of political independence from the conventional civil rights and elected black leadership. In any case, the chilling of the black electorate towards the traditional black Democratic leadership coupled with the radical political antics of the party's anti-war radicals, and leftist ideologues threatens to truncate the party's positioning and political momentum in the November elections and prospects for 2008.

Needless to say, the November general elections will forecast the political climate for the next two years and beyond. The multiple blunders of President George Bush and his administration, and the lack of congressional oversight by the Republican House and Senate majority has put the future of the GOP Congressional leadership at risk. But, poor leadership on the part of both the Democrat and Republican Parties (black and white) has alienated the electorate and has fostered apathy and isolation of would be voters.

Hence, the outcome of the mid-term elections is anybody's guess, as both parties and the Bush administration increase the level of political hyperbole. But there are a few certainties, such as the fact that the black vote is not as predictable as it once was, and the anti-war "movement" embraced by the "left," "radical" and "progressive" elements of the Democratic coalition are destined to exacerbate an already-fragmented party leadership and rank and file. Whatever political party prevails in November 2006, the results will likely mark a watershed relative to the future of the proverbial "black vote."

Recent voting patterns among black Americans indicate an increasing disposition to vote independent of the Democratic Party machine particularly in urban municipal elections. This increasing independent voting trend was crystallized in the 2005 re-election campaign of New York City's Mayor Michael Bloomberg who got 30 plus percent of the black vote running as a Republican and on the Independence Party's ballot. Mayor Bloomberg achieved this plurality milestone, despite his lack of support from prominent black civil rights and elected leaders who endorsed his Democratic opposition.

All indications suggest a growing level of voter sophistication among black Americans, and an aversion to club-house politics by both Democrat and Republican Parties. Should this increasing trend toward unpredictable voting by black folk continue in the mid-term elections, there may very well be a paradigm shift of the black vote in the 2008 presidential election. As a practical political matter the black leadership in both major parties may have played themselves out of position as possible stewards of the paradigm shift and will likely be eclipsed politically, by new generation leadership.

The black Democratic civil rights and elected leadership have no effective lines of communication to the disillusioned, apathetic and disaffected constituent or the tons of unregistered voters. This fragmentation of the leadership coupled with the need for a coherent and lucid agenda for the future beyond civil rights has apparently confounded the leadership. Moreover, the "liberal," "progressive," white Democratic paternalism that co-opted if not help to politically organize black Americans for the goal of "social justice" was unable to produce measurable results beyond bequeathing to black Americans at large their inherited political leadership.

Regrettably, the black Republican Party leadership on the national as well as the local level has also failed miserably in terms of making black Americans and the party relevant to the local and national black political power process. Apart from the symbiosis between black Americans and the Republican Party at its very founding in 1854, the elective and civil rights achievements of black Americans during the nineteenth century remains unprecedented in comparison to the achievements of the modern civil rights movement.

Interestingly enough, the modern Republican Party and black America had an auspicious beginning in 1972 when the National black Republican Council (NBRC) was established by an amendment to the party rules of the Republican National Committee. NBRC was founded by people like Gerald Ford, Robert Dole, Henry Lucas, Art Fletcher, and Ed Bivens, for the purpose of providing a mechanism for black participation in the Republican National Party (RNC). Following its timely beginnings, NBRC in the early 1980s became mired in financial controversy and scandal and lost its official credentials with RNC and its offices at party headquarters was closed in the 1990s. Nevertheless, the titular head of the phantom NBRC from its days of infamy to the present is a former GOP district leader in the Bronx, Mr. Fred Brown.

Alton D. Chase, former NBRC Vice President and Bronx district leader and longtime political activist said, "The new generation grassroots leadership can see beyond the political smoke and mirrors of the bygone leadership generation and seem to understand their responsibility associated with building leverage, Black Power politics."

Ms. Keisha C. Morrisey, entertainment and boxing industry entrepreneur and former GOP nominee for the New York State Assembly and the New York City Council from Harlem said, "I have started a political club with some associates directed to the 'hip-hop' generation focused on teaching electoral politics and how to run for elective office. Based on my personal experience I have chosen not to link our Republican Party activism and organizing with NBRC."

Fortunately, the increasing level of voter sophistication among the black community at large and the emerging grassroots leadership has a more practical and utilitarian understanding of politics as a tool, as opposed to a group of like minded political friends. Is there a political paradigm shift underway in the black American community? Stay tuned.